Closing Circles

Also by R.B. Scott:

Mitt Romney: An Inside Look at the Man and His Politics
(Lyons Press, 2011)

and the forthcoming second book in the Pratt Pentalogy:
The Mending: A life too well remembered

Closing Circles

TRAPPED IN THE EVERLASTING MORMON MOMENT

6/15/2012
Best wishes

R.B. Scott

GRAY DOG PRESS
SPOKANE, WA

Gray Dog Press
Spokane, WA
www.graydogpress.com
facebook.com/graydogpress
@gdpeditor on twitter

Closing Circles: Trapped in the Everlasting Mormon Moment

Cover design: Michael Dixon
Interior design: Andrew Marcus Corder

ISBN: 978-1-936178-49-0

Printed in the United States of America

For Diana

The Closing Circle

Mountain shadows
melt the sun away
as starlit heavens
spread cross the land
masking imperfections
seen by day
well known to God,
if not to man

Eternal clarity fogs
sleeping heads
of unfinished chores,
thoughts left unsaid
of half lives and loves,
elusive still
from misdirection,
for wont of will

Time fast lapses
to mind the store
to husband goods,
to order more
to savor each truth
knowing life is fickle
and oft entraps
in its closing circle

Closing Circles

Sarah and Me

Even by the demanding standards of Canyon Mills, the Russells of East Cumorah Road were thought to be profoundly, if oddly, spiritual. Blame it on the lady of the household—that would be my mother—who routinely set an extra place at our already crowded dinner table on Easter, Christmas and April 6—the day Mormons believe Christ was born. It was her way of taking on the role of the biblical wise virgin (she was neither), standing vigil, anxiously awaiting his Second Coming.

In her mind, at any moment the immortal Jesus was likely to drop by our house in Canyon Mills, a suburban alpine village arranged in and around the scrub oak, sage brush and sandy foothills that rise to greet the Rocky Mountains barricading Salt Lake City from the real world. He would personally lift the curse from the overcooked beef and mashed potatoes she had prepared for the meal, and magically purify the tap water we consumed in copious amounts to wash it all down.

Mother insisted if we were really good, the Savior might stick around for hot fudge sundaes, even join us for a word of family prayer. Life would be good! I imagined He would kneel with the rest of us around the dining table that for special occasions like this one would be centered in the living room between the sprawling Hammond C3 electric organ—coveted by churches, cathedrals, synagogues and juke joints alike—Dad had purchased second-hand from the Norman-Dee Roller Rink and the ridiculously ornate—some would say gaudy and gawky—G. Schwechten upright piano inherited from my grandmother.

Had Jesus actually responded to my mother's heartfelt pleas, I would have no need to tell you my story for I would be fully converted. Like Paul, I would have had my very own Road to Damascus awakening.

Mother's unflinching faith was not successful in attracting a heavenly visitor to our dinner time nor did it prevent my own faith from wavering as I became aware and increasingly wary of mind-changers—psychologists and therapists and preachers and other posers who claim they can facilitate personal reconciliations with what God deemed irreconcilable in this life. That is, life itself.

My strict upbringing saddled me with more than a few contradictory philosophies and conundrums, most of them having everything to do with the meaning of life and my particular role in God's eternal scheme. Clear thinking and probing questions were tolerated, even praised so long as they were deemed likely to validate the fundamental tenets of the gospel. Otherwise, they were dismissed self-righteously, if kindly.

"Certain mysteries must be taken on faith," reproving elders always said when I asked a question like: "How did God come to be God anyway?" They routinely implied that if I studied and prayed hard, sooner or later, but perhaps not in this life, I would reach an accord with the Great Unknown, even if for now He rejected my entreaties as routinely as His Son did my mother's invitations to dinner.

She claimed if prayer and study failed to unravel the mysteries of the universe that a couple of hours pounding the G. Schwechten would. Later a battered Underwood 5 seemed to work too, never mind that it foreshadowed the real problem: strike the *s* and *e* keys simultaneously, more or less, and they would entangle themselves with the *x* key. Mother would have preferred a long heart to heart talk with the bishop. His rates, I have to admit, were considerably more affordable than those charged by the local professionals.

My contempt for mind-changers intensified during the 1960s when I was a pre-medical-cum-English and journalism student at the University of Utah. It was a time when campus radicalism abounded, even in tranquil places like Salt Lake City. People were, to use the vernacular, "getting in touch" with themselves, doing whatever felt good, expecting just-in-time absolution from the feel-good high priests of the day: the hordes of psychiatrists and psychologists and posers like sex therapists and psychics and palm readers and wayward preachers who descended on the scene so suddenly that it seemed they must have been hiding out in a closet somewhere waiting to ambush.

Now that I think of it, it also seemed that students who succumbed to the rigorous disciplines of chemistry, physics, philosophy and religion, mathematics, and economics swarmed like locusts to the ripening fields of sociology and psychology. Instead of steeping themselves in the time-tested maxims and formulas that lend order to the world, they bought into the conflicted (if popular) sophistry that the quick fix for chaos was, well, more chaos.

This is not to suggest I have no interest in the study of the human brain and in the way it processes thoughts and reacts to the stimuli presented by the everyday world. Had I pursued my dream, I would have become a physician who specialized in either neurology or urology, both of which, I think, have everything to do with the way men—at least men—process and apply information.

I made my deeply seeded contempt for mind-changers clear to Dr. Irving Rosenbaum of Westport, Connecticut, whose client I became rather grudgingly and with profound prejudice when my thirteen-year marriage to Sarah Brooke Thompson Russell, erstwhile psychology student at the University of Utah and now resident of Westport, was collapsing around me.

On the phone, I assumed "Quack Quack," as I came to call Dr. Rosenbaum, was a small man. As I briefed him on my needs, he said things like "I see" and "I understand how you feel" and "Why do you think that"—each a parrying phrase any little boy would say to a bigger one to avoid a playground fistfight. Instead of the dulcet tones I expected from one who soothes troubled souls, Quack Quack's pitch neared breathless hysteria—a voice squawky and agitated, as an adolescent boy's, cracking between second soprano and first tenor with each change of syllable.

"So, we should see each other," he croaked. So we saw each other the following Tuesday.

I was surprised that his tall, lanky body rose at least a few inches above my six-foot-two frame. I couldn't be sure. He appeared at least a foot taller than I had imagined him: hand-knotted bow tie, blue polka dots on yellow; heavily starched and tailored dress shirt with pale-blue pinstripes and French cuffs secured snugly by double-knotted, yellow and blue elastic cord cufflinks; yellow suspenders slackened, allowing crisp-pleated charcoal flannel trousers to hang loosely about his hips. A man buttoned-up, well turned out, precise, confident. Intimidating.

Rosenbaum's office was equally meticulous and well coordinated. On an end table beside his chair was a rack of pipes, each a different shape and color, each fully packed with pungent sweet cherry tobacco that permeated the office and adjoining waiting room. As we talked, he inserted one pipe beneath the neat but bushy mustache that obscured his entire upper lip. As he mumbled through clenched teeth, the pipe bobbed up and down as if it were having sex with his mouth; I imagined it was his way of dealing with whatever carnal hang-ups he'd acquired as an adolescent.

"So," he said, sucking hard enough on the pipe stem to evoke a faint rattle from the dried tobacco particles, a sound similar to the early-warning raspy wheeze of a lung beginning its slow collapse from emphysema, "if you don't trust shrinks, why are you here?" I heard him exhale, but did not see smoke spurt from the corners of his mouth nor sense any sweet telltale odor of smoldering cherry-soaked leaves.

"It's Sarah, my wife," I stammered. "She insists that I see you."

"I see," he said, scratching a note on his yellow legal pad. He inhaled and exhaled several times as if waiting for the pipe to finish its business with his mouth. "And, what do we think?"

"I can't speak for you," I said, annoyed that Rosenbaum and his pipe were transforming me into an unwitting voyeur, "but I think I need something to hold my marriage together."

"Will this do that?" he asked. The pipe twitched and shuddered, then collapsed, spent, into a corner of his mouth. Still no smoke. I realized the tobacco had not been lit, yet the exercise alone—just Rosenbaum with his lips clamped on the pipe—seemed to produce great pleasure and satisfaction.

"Maybe. I hope. Sarah thinks it may help me come to grips with the reality of our need to divorce," I said. I shifted uncomfortably, wondering if he had deferred lighting up as a courtesy to my religion, which regards tobacco usage as a sure witness of general moral depravity.

"What is this reality?" he asked, studying me intently as if trying to assess whether I were in the room but not of it, lost in space and time and place. That would match Sarah's characterization of me: present and accounted for physically, but detached emotionally.

"If I knew, I wouldn't be here," I snapped. Hey, I'm the patient here, you're the professional brain expert. Divorce? Reality? Nothing realistic about it, if you ask me.

"I thought you came because of Sarah?" he said, startled by my curtness.

"Right, I did."

"I see." He leaned forward in his chair like a cat about to pounce on some significant piece of data he'd spied racing across the gray tweed carpet. "That's all?"

"It's the damned book," I fairly shouted. "Sarah hated the Goddamned book. That's why she wants out."

"What damned book?" Quack Quack quacked, his pipe shivering convulsively. "What GD book?"

For about ten years or so, I had been working on a sequel to *Catcher In The Rye, Portnoy's Complaint,* or *The 158-Pound Marriage.*

No Salinger nor Roth nor Irving, me, I dabbled at fiction while I earned a real living writing everything from worshipful magazine stories on over-publicized celebrities to high-flown speeches for the captains of industry. "It's what you do if you want to be a serious writer," I sheepishly told train companions on the daily hundred-mile roundtrip commute between Westport, Connecticut and Manhattan.

Early in our marriage, Sarah had recognized my frustration. She thought writing for hire a waste of time, a convenient excuse to delay some nobler calling. "If you want to really write, why don't you write?" she'd say smugly, as if to imply one could will such things. "Why spend your life writing stuff you detest?"

One night, six years into the marriage, I announced: "I'm writing a book."

"About time, and it'll probably be a bestseller," she said solicitously, not taking her eyes off Eliot (Elli), our second child, who was lying on the changing table, his wand waving wildly like an elephant's trunk in search of peanuts. "What's it about?" she asked, deftly smothering Elli's appendage with a fresh Pamper.

Edgy and uncertain about what I would say next, I stuck a cigarette in the corner of my mouth and fumbled for the lighter in my trousers. "Don't even think of lighting that damned thing here," she growled. I quickly retreated to the cramped extra bedroom, which served as my study—the only room in the house where I could smoke unmolested, more or less.

An hour or so later, it was well past the children's bedtime, although I thought I could hear five-year-old Janie playing in her room. Elli had long since quit fussing, so I assumed he'd either fallen asleep or had choked to death in his crib (a regular worry of mine). I was about to go check on him when Sarah came through the door, waving her arms wildly. Such histrionics were *de rigueur* for her, and usually accompanied by a loud, harsh cough, which she thought was a clever way to remind me that I was smoking way too much for my own good. If she were feeling especially theatrical, she'd collapse on the floor, writhing and gasping for air.

"So what's it about?" she asked brightly.

"What's what about? My smoking?" I asked, mentally preparing how I would offer yet another weak and contrived defense of puffing just under a half pack of cigarettes each day.

"Not what I had in mind, however if you'd like to discuss it, I'd be happy to schedule an appointment at your convenience," she goaded.

"Well, what then?"

"Your book…you did mention a book to me a few hours ago, didn't you? I would guess it would be the one right there," she said, pointing to a stack of papers on the desk.

"Oh that book," I responded awkwardly. "You want to know what *that* book is all about. Right?"

"Right," she sighed incredulously.

"Why do you want to know?" Don't ask why I was suspicious of her motives. I just was.

"Why? Because I am interested," she said, irritated. "You said you wanted to tell me all about it. That's why. Have you changed your mind already?"

"No, of course not—just distracted when I couldn't hear Elli. Did you check on him?"

"That's where I've been—fell asleep on the floor," she said. "You worry a lot about him. Way too much. You should talk to someone about it."

"About the book?"

"About your obsessions, your compulsiveness. Judas Priest, Jeddy, come to." The corners of her mouth stretched in a grimace.

"I thought you wanted to talk about the book," I said.

"I do, it's just…forget it. Tell me about the book before you wander off on another tangent."

It irritated me that Sarah thought I was unfocused, detached—"lost in space"—a trait more characteristic of a slacker, not someone who had worked full-time as a reporter to support his family while taking a full load at the university. Not one who hovered over his children. "You'd think you were the mother here," Sarah often chided defensively. I didn't feel that way, although it was true I taught her how to diaper Janie and tended to all of the children's wounds because she recoiled at the sight of blood.

"It's sorta autobiographical," I said sheepishly.

"Oh boy—a Mormon version of *Portnoy's Complaint*," she hooted, her eyes rolled backward in their sockets. "Good therapy for you, but who in their right mind will buy it?"

Perhaps that's why I stashed that original manuscript in a drawer, where it remains to this day, and refocused my energies on turning literary tricks for anyone who offered ready cash to support our growing little family in the lifestyle to which they were becoming accustomed. Too accustomed, as it turned out.

Sarah also deserves credit, however backhanded, for the resurrection of my serious writing career a decade later. In the interim, literary prostitution had paid off handsomely enough for us to purchase our small farmhouse in Connecticut. Forsaking psychology, thankfully, she had returned to college and graduated summa cum laude in fine art. Both children were doing well in private school, and now, at last, her professional career as a graphic designer was taking off like a shot.

We'd weathered ("endured," Sarah often said) the normal storms of marriage and some abnormal ones too, which were somewhat provoked and compounded by the fact that we'd only known each other for eight weeks when we married—she was 18, I was 22—and by the shrill rhetoric of the emerging women's liberation movement that seemed to label all white Anglo-Saxon men like me as "oppressors," an irritating concept that she voiced whenever she needed to get my attention.

Although she never accused me directly, I think she held me fully responsible for pushing her into marriage. It's true, I was sick of the dating scene, with the limits on what respectable Mormon boys and girls can do together before marriage. And for eventually trapping her in the suburbs of New York City. It didn't seem to matter that I was the one who encouraged her to resume college (although I feared it would lead her away from me) or who found her a part-time job as a designer during her last year in school.

Despite my commitment to marriage and its behavioral restrictions (sure, there were a few lapses when I was traveling: "They were but dalliances, nothing serious or lasting to them," I confessed one night, hoping to clearly demonstrate to Sarah that I was finally ready for an open and honest relationship) she had a festering, vengeful rage that boiled over most inopportunely. At my thirtieth birthday party she drunkenly and defiantly began to unlace the bodice of her peasant dress, egged on by the grinding beat of "The Stripper" and cheers from equally besotted friends. Knowing full well that my determined wife, not born to tease, was naked beneath her linen dress, I rushed to her side and persuaded her to stop.

Later in bed, she groused that I had revealed my true colors. "It wasn't about me, per se," she said angrily. "It was all about you and your ego. There you were, protecting your chattel. If you could, you'd strap a chastity belt on me. If my teasing bothers you so, sprinkle some saltpeter on your Wheaties."

I should have recognized the warning strains then, but I was oblivious. I found solace and truth in the fact that our friends presumed our marriage was ideal, rock solid, if routinely feisty. Looking back on that turbulent time, it is obvious to me now that stretch marks girdled the belly of our marriage long before it burst. Yet on the surface I supposed it appeared firm, resilient and alive.

"You could have written this ending years ago," Sarah chided after the marriage began to disintegrate.

She was right, of course. Had I been paying attention, I could have conjured practically every bizarre twist and turn. No imagination required. Issues involving the children pulled us together, as did our bed, where we remained remarkably and erotically compatible right up to the last bitter night before I departed for good.

Beyond that, our lives were increasingly peripheral and disconnected. As her career gathered momentum, she seemed to presume that I would willingly subordinate my professional ambitions to hers. At the time, I thought such notions trite. Surely they were fleeting byproducts of the turbulent times and the wacky, overwrought side of the fervent feminist movement, a movement whose aims I supported and accommodated, by and large.

In public settings, at parties, and in our professional lives she seemed to say, "It's my turn now. This family has room for but one rising star. You've been at it for twelve years. Now it's my turn; you owe me this for the babies I bore you and raised." She did not find ironies in such assertions and God forbid I should be foolish enough to point them out.

To be fair, I also saw her career and the additional compensation as a potential security blanket, a liberator that could free me from the drudgery of writing no-brainer magazine stories and the like. It would allow me, at long last, to focus on writing novels and significant, thought-provoking stories.

Such was the collision course we were on, although neither of us likely saw the train wreck ahead. Neither of us really understood the other's objectives. For instance, Sarah gleefully endorsed my plan to build a new three-car garage with a studio above it. Terrific, she could make money by freelancing and finally have a space of her own to do it in.

This did not necessarily obstruct my plans. "I could carve out a study in one corner there where I could work on books," I added.

"Use the extra bedroom in the house," she said. "A writer doesn't need as much space as a designer."

"Too much noise. Too many distractions. I couldn't concentrate, and I wouldn't be near you," I answered, certain that she would understand, would be moved by my offer of increased closeness, of daily professional interaction.

"Whatever. Let's get it built and then we can figure out how to use it—besides, you've got an office in the city," she added. Although the warning signals were pretty plain, I did not recognize them.

When the garage and studio were finished, she moved her drawing table into one corner of the room under the north-facing skylights. I installed a desk and sturdy typing table into the opposite corner, under the south-facing skylights. We separated the work areas with freestanding wall units.

Because I was working in the city, I made very little use of the studio at first. No doubt that suited Sarah just fine. In my absence, Janie anointed my desk as the perfect place for her homework. Elli deemed the studio ideal for watching Sesame Street and camping out. I often found Elli on the floor, curled up in his sleeping bag when I arrived home late in the evening. Janie would be at my desk or sleeping alongside her brother, with Sarah at the large drawing table.

It was a pleasant sight, unsettling only because I was not part of the happy little picture. Not to worry. The children staked a "family claim" to the studio. I assumed that would temper any of Sarah's objections when I finally encroached permanently. This space—like the house, our family, our marriage—was ours: Sarah's, Janie's, Elli's. And mine!

The money to build it had come from two lucrative ghostwriting assignments. "Filthy lucre," my mother snapped when she learned that I was writing for the International Tobacco Institute. For the Nuclear Energy Association, I wrote a very persuasive white paper that asserted it was perfectly safe to position concrete storage vats of nuclear waste above aquifers that supplied drinking water to arid regions of the United States.

I absolutely did not endorse these organizations or their positions. I was simply turning writing tricks. Provide the subject, info and cash, and presto, my typewriter would crank out a tight, well-crafted bit of friendly persuasion.

Sure, some assignments pricked my conscience and caused my ears to itch. But they were lesser-of-two-evils choices. If I declined, someone else would do the job. The greater good was earning the extra cash to pay for the studio, provide space for Sarah to spread her wings and build a business of her own, thereby absolving me of the guilt I suffered from errant dalliances and from buying into her arguments that I stymied her intellectual and professional development by marrying her and getting her pregnant. God would forgive me my minor immoral accommodations, compromises and lapses, even if my mother wouldn't.

Like a magic wand, the studio would banish forever the acrimony in our marriage. Sarah could work and remain close to the children. I could be around, too, if I finally got serious about becoming a novelist. Sarah would be delighted to have me home full-time, a burden-sharer. Perhaps we would recapture and enhance the intensity of our lovemaking in our side-by-side working relationship. She was my best and most demanding critic. I was her most loyal supporter. It was the perfect setup.

As the train rolled much too slowly from Manhattan to Westport, I wondered if I'd miss the daily commute, the forced opportunity to read, the camaraderie of my train friends, the half-penny-a-point bridge games and the good-natured (though sometimes petty) bickering that always accompanied them, and the bustle, bump, grind and heady inspiration of New York City. Would I long for the security of the Time Inc. "corporate tit," a characterization applied by veteran insiders and former staffers? Should the adventure not turn out well, would Time provide emergency succor, like she had for hundreds of other adventurers before me who sought fortune and fame on their own, turning tit-ward whenever bank accounts ran thin?

No matter. The personal risk and sacrifice would be well worth it. Sarah and I would finally share in the exhilaration of working separately, but together. I would have time to again get involved with our children. Janie was bearing down on 14, Elli on 11. They needed me around. Sarah too. And I needed them like I never had before. My decision would result in a temporary modest reduction of income, but that was of no real consequence when stacked against considerable benefits, not the least of which was the long-awaited opportunity to write seriously. And, if I faltered, surely there would always be father *Time* and mother *Life*.

Pinch in Time

Sarah didn't raise her eyes from the drawing board when I slunk into *her* studio three hours later than promised. The railroad drawbridge in Norwalk—just three miles from home—got stuck open just in time to block passage of the 5:02 train from Manhattan and everything behind it.

Like rotting sardines in sweltering tins, for three hours, cut off from the outside world by double power doors and sealed double-paned safety glass windows. No phone. No way to disembark and hike home. Worse yet, the bar had quickly run dry, as it always did on such occasions.

A decade of dealing with the vagaries of the New Haven line had not steeled Sarah to such exigencies, nor had she become any more forgiving of me or the railroad. At first she was charmed, actually, to be living our little version of *The Man In The Gray Flannel Suit*—dropping me at the quaint red clapboard station for the 8:32 in the morning, and rescuing me off one train or another each evening, usually the 6:05 or 7:05. But one year of attentive door-to-station service was enough: "It's either that or I'll name the New Haven as a co-respondent to our divorce. I know it's irrational, but I can't help blaming you."

Long ago, Sarah had come to suspect—not always incorrectly—that the railroad provided a ready, credible cover for dallying too long in any number of watering spots that lined the route from Rockefeller Center to Grand Central Station. She even reacted suspiciously to media-heralded disasters—fires in the tunnel, derailments and power failures—as if I had wangled them into being for my own delicious purposes. Furthermore, she assumed I took full advantage of every legitimate opportunity to be late. Her paranoia was not entirely without foundation. I regularly indulged in the spontaneous, self-centered activities that normal twenty-something young men do, but nothing that could have diverted me away from her.

If memory serves me well, the only time the train delivered an excuse Sarah deemed believable was the night a particularly attractive young woman, wearing not a stitch under a knee-length mink coat, scooted behind the counter in the bar car and jerked open her coat as she politely asked a weary commuter: "Care for a double, sir?"

No one claims to have heard his startled response, but Rueben, the gnarly munchkin of a bartender who worked the 6:05 for the decade and a half I frequented the train, fled to safety on the platform and refused to re-board until the transit police arrived. While we waited, the conductor gave us up-to-the-minute reports, as if he were doing the play-by-play for the Yankees over the public address system. At 6:00 he intoned in his most dispassionate train voice: "Attention, attention all commuters on the 6:05 to New Haven, making all stops from East Norwalk to New Haven. This train will be delayed indefinitely in Grand Central due to the fact that we have had us a stripper in a brown mink coat in the café car serving cocktails and highballs for your pleasure." And so it went for nearly forty-five minutes until decorum was finally restored and the train declared a stripper-free zone.

There was no extraordinary alibi this night as I slunk in. Just the pedestrian excuse of the chronically malfunctioning bridge in Norwalk. Before I could even utter the words, Sarah snapped: "Jeezuz blanking Christmas. You're three, count 'em, three hours late."

"Sorry, the bridge stuck open again," I said as though I had been solely responsible for the running of the railroad, or at the least was its chief maintenance engineer.

"Should've gotten off and walked…or called…or hitchhiked…or jumped in." She was in her "take no prisoners, accept no excuses" mode. I should have retreated to the house and the kids.

"They wouldn't open the damn doors," I said, stepping within nose length of the drawing board.

She sniffed the air theatrically. "Catch any stripper action in the bar car tonight? Plenty of time for *whatever* tonight?"

"Actually, I was alone. Had a lot of thinking to do. Big decisions to make," I said.

Sarah looked up from the table. Her eyes studied me intently, even apprehensively.

"Big decisions?" she said slowly. "Big decisions about what?"

"I'm going to write the novel," I said nervously. I knew full well this was not exactly the proper time to be breaking the news. I was three hours late. But I needed to tell someone. Who better than the wife?

"Oh, the novel fantasy. Let me know when it's finished," she snapped sarcastically.

"Want to talk about it?" I said.

"Can't you see I'm busy? And the kids are in the house, probably killing each other for all I know. I've got to get this board done…it's due first thing in the morning. You were supposed to bail me out three frigging hours ago—I'm trying to build a business, you know."

"Got to keep your priorities straight." It slipped from my lips before I could lock my jaw shut.

She rose, furiously slicing the heavy air with the X-Acto knife she wielded like a fencer's epée. "Listen buster, that may be very easy for you to say. You who go off to a nice quiet office every day to be coddled by pretty researchers ever ready to split their infinitives for your dangling participle. You don't contend with carpools, music lessons, doctors and demanding clients all at the same time. You wanna talk priorities? You ought to get a few…because right now yours are singular. You!"

"I plan to," I said, angry at her cheap-shot broadsides, ones she knew would drive me right up the wall. I loved being a father. I worked hard at it. It wasn't just *my* fault that we lived an hour from Manhattan, that I had a job that offered plenty of perks but required a fair amount of travel and long hours in the office. Wasn't she the one who often strutted (to my embarrassment) the fact that her husband worked for the great and glorious *Time* magazine?

"Hell freezes over soon," she snarled.

"Sooner than that. Actually I wanted to talk about it."

"About staying home?" she asked, looking up at me, curiously.

"About the book."

"What book."

"I want to do a book, finally…that's what I was trying…"

"Great. Just flipping great. Now you can hang around your office till midnight. Maybe you can arrange direct deposit for your paychecks. You'd never have to come home. Janie and Elli will grow up to think you're a frigging byline, an ordered, hah, aggregation of roman characters."

"I'd write at home," I almost whispered.

"At home? When? The few nights you're home by a decent hour, you're asleep before the seven o'clock news ends. You're barely conscious on weekends, except when you're coaching basketball or soccer and—"

"I'd write during the day…at home," I said firmly.

"What? At home? Did Time give you a sabbatical or what? Or have you been bad...banished to limbo land, offended one fascist editor or another, but not seriously enough to get canned outright?"

"Not banished. In fact, I was offered a position as senior national correspondent today."

"Whoooey. Aren't we the big banana now? More excuses to absent yourself. Just when does this charming and delightful new assignment begin?"

"Never," I said.

"Whaddyamean never?"

"I turned it down..."

"Good," she shot back, knowing full well that to turn down a promotion was tantamount to corporate suicide.

"Then I quit," I said.

"Good...quit? You did what? Quit?"

I had gotten her attention.

"Quit, finitio, quit," I said, my hand chopping through the air like the falling blade of a well-maintained guillotine.

"You joke?" she said. My beheading hand severed the air again. "Just up and quit? Just like that. No discussion. No planning. Just quit. Never mind the orthodontist's bill for Janie's braces or basic shit like food and clothing. No, not you. Just quit. The Lord, He will provide."

"You're working now..."

"Just barely, and I make twelve thousand something and this is 1980 and we live in Westport, Connecticut where the damned median family income is sixty thousand and something and you up and quit. Are you crazy? Am I crazy? Is this a frigging nightmare or what?"

"And, I'll take on freelance assignments for the magazines...and then there's the book. I'm sure it can make us a buck or two," I said.

"What book?" she said again.

"The one I'm going to write now that I have time."

"The book! Sheesh, I can just hear it now," she said disgustedly. "'Pleeeze welcome Jedediah Pratt Russell, the author of the book that has the whole world abuzzing: *Mormon Masturbation Myths*.' Somewhere in your bestseller, be sure to work in the scene...you know the one, where your father breaks down the bathroom door and finds you, how shall I say this delicately: *in flagrante delicto solo*. No wait! Embellish the story a bit. As he crashes in you should be spilling your sanctified seed into the American Standard. Rich irony...holy allegory."

Typical Sarah, I thought. Chronically short of patience and with a mouth that responded accordingly, she could always be counted on to rattle out some old skeletons from the closet—the more embarrassing the better. And Sarah never let the facts get in the way of spinning a good story. Scenes from my stormy adolescence were prime targets for resurrection. This one had been revealed in the strictest of confidence, hoping that the telling would put this ghost behind me, once and for all. But Sarah was neither a particularly sympathetic nor exactly a discreet Sister Confessor.

"It must have been humiliating?" Quack Quack said.

"Sarah is the mother of humiliation," I answered.

"Your father breaking in…"

"The mother lode of exaggeration."

I am the firstborn of nine children *sent* to exceedingly proper Mormon parents, who never referred to themselves as Mormons. We were Latter-day Saints to outsiders, LDS to insiders, and Mormons to practically no one we cared to associate with. Like other fellow travelers, we gathered each and every Monday night—"unless the second coming comes first," my father often said—in the living room for Family Night. It was a time for sharing personal talents, exploring gospel topics, and discussing and resolving various thorny family issues.

On this particular occasion, my sister was at the G. Schwecten upright struggling her way though *Melody In F* while the rest of us listened dutifully. It had nothing to do with her torturous playing, but as she thumped away, raging testosterone took control of my body and began inflicting its particularly exquisite form of torture. I tried to rearrange myself on the sofa, hoping the change would quell the ache, but it only became more disquieting. Enough. Hunkered over, like I was suffering from terminal back spasms or intense stomach cramps, I excused myself and sprinted to the bathroom.

A few minutes later—just as I was about to get some relief—my father started banging on the door.

"Open the door," he yelled. Bang, bang, bang.

"Can't. I'm going to the bathroom," I hollered back. I should explain that banging on the bathroom door is an accepted practice in practically all families of eleven that I know of, especially those, like ours, with only a bathroom and a half to service all. On any given school morning, it was not at all unusual for one Russell boy to be in the shower, another taking a leak, and a third brushing his teeth—all in one steamy four-by-ten-foot room. It's no wonder that, later in my life, I had no trouble whatsoever adjusting to open Army latrines. Well, honestly, the lineup of exposed toilets was a bit hard to take, but other than that…

"Open up the door, I've seen you urinate before," yelled my father, ever careful to avoid slang. "English is a very descriptive and precise language," was a favorite chide of his. "There's a proper word for practically everything. There's no need to use mindless juvenile euphemisms to describe natural biological functions."

"Can't, I'm sitting," I said. *Sitting* was the only suitable reason for a locked door. He backed off, but tossed out a warning advisory: "Well, hurry up."

Coming as it did at the onset of my life-long wrestle with testosterone, I have often wondered if his ill-timed demand gave rise to my early-marriage tendency to rush, a practice Sarah found extremely annoying and altogether selfish.

"Did it?" Rosenbaum asked.

"That's what Sarah claimed," I answered. "Should I go on?"

"Whatever suits you," Rosenbaum said.

"So when I finished, I washed my hands…"

"Washed your hands?" Rosenbaum asked. He looked up from his notepad, studied my face intently.

"Yes, then let him in."

He stalked in sniffing the air like a suspicious old bloodhound. "Constipation," I said, sensing a certain dubious snort to his sniffs. His glower made his doubts clear, but he didn't press the issue directly, perhaps recognizing a guilty face when he saw one. "Don't try to fool me, young man," he often warned, "I can see the lies in your eyes." He closed the door softly and sat down on the edge of the bathtub.

As was his custom, he was blunt and to the point. "You know God didn't intend your penis to be a plaything. You're a teenager now. You'll be getting erections all the time. If you think wholesome thoughts, they'll go away. Masturbation can lead to very severe mental and physical problems."

Quack Quack laughed. "Such problems!"

It was the first time in weeks and weeks of regular meetings he'd been something more human than a very absorbent corporeal tape recorder.

My yearning to manipulate my phallus (father would love the language if not the practice) only intensified, even though I really tried to think wholesome thoughts and get plenty of exercise. I could only assume this tool of the devil dangling between my thighs would lead me to no worthy end. And, it did, more or less.

Worse, although I had never seen erections other than my own, I had seen enough flaccid danglers to suppose that mine was larger than most my age. It made me self-conscious, annoyed actually: God really had it in for me. Why else would He give one of his anointed sons such a prominent and persistent distraction? A less intrusive one would be just as functional and not half the problem. Levi's would fit more comfortably. No one would notice if I happened to be called to the blackboard at the precise moment trouble was stirring in my trousers.

Quack Quack laughed loudly. "You said self-conscious. How so?"

"Well, take Sarah…she brought it up, shortly after we were married. She said I was rather large. So I asked how large. And she says: 'larger than any I've known.'"

"Longer or thicker?" I asked.

"Both," she said. "Lance was the biggest before you. You're bigger. But his was more than adequate, I'm sure, although I never did let him go all the way."

"Is that why you let me…because I was bigger?" I asked. It was an equally curious and cynical question.

"*Naturally* curious," added Rosenbaum.

"I let you for two reasons: We were married; I loved you and wanted to have your babies. Period. Size is no big deal. It's what you do with it."

What we did with it was create Janie, who arrived precisely nine months after our wedding, waiting just long enough to dispel any notion that our decision to move up the wedding date was provoked by the proverbial shotgun to the back.

"Was there one…did you have to get married?" Rosenbaum asked cautiously.

"Absolutely not…we were madly in love. We'd only known each other two months. Even if we'd been doing it, there's no way we'd have known she was pregnant. No way," I said, indignant at the question. QQ sounded as suspicious as our family and friends in Salt Lake City.

"Easy, easy, I'm not a judge or your father," Rosenbaum said, soothingly. "Why the rush?"

"Love…lust more than a little bit. And the Church…Mormons marry young, you know. Frankly, we were both afraid if we waited any longer that we'd have to invite the shotgun to the wedding."

"A baby nine months in must have caused some strain..."

"No. Not at first. We both believed that the purpose of marriage was to have children. So we were delighted. In fact Janie's arrival seemed to ease some of our newlywed troubles. It also created a few logistical issues, the least of which were pails of dirty diapers and piles of medical bills."

Janie's birth also put the final nail in Lance's coffin. He'd been away in the Marine Corps and had written Sarah right up to our wedding day. He was stunned by the marriage, in disbelief, I suppose. When he came home on leave a few months later to find Sarah more than a little pregnant, he begged her to leave me, pregnant and all. She was flattered, perhaps even tempted given our somewhat rocky first months.

Then Janie arrived. A year later—precisely a year later—Lance returned home from Vietnam, body and penis intact apparently, pled fruitlessly with Sarah one last time, and then blew his brains out with a .45 caliber pistol in the middle of University Street during the homecoming parade. I guessed he figured he just hadn't measured up. Thereafter, Sarah told me that while we were making love, she often fantasized about doing it with Lance. Just as he was about to *arrive*, a gun would fire and she would see him lying face up at her feet, his gray matter gushing out on the pavement, while the "Incomparable University of Utah Marching Band" strutted by playing "Utah Man."

I am a Utah man, sir and I live across the green.
Our gang it is the jolliest that you have ever seen.
We drink our stein of lager and smoke our big cigars
Our yell, you hear it ringing through the mountains near and far.

Who am I, sir, a Utah man am I:
A Utah man, sir, and will be till I die
We're up to snuff: we never bluff.
We're game for any fuss.
No other gang of college men dare meet us in the muss.
So fill your lungs and sing it out shout it to the sky.
We'll fight for dear old crimson for a Utah Man Am I

We may not live forever on this jolly good old sphere,
But while we do we'll live a life of merriment and cheer.
And when our college days are o'er and night is drawing nigh,
With parting breath we'll sing that song: A Utah Man Am I.

The band reached the refrain, the flutes and xylophones were in full trill, the bass drums were thumping and the tenors and basses of the trailing men's glee club in full voice were thundering proudly: "*Who—am—I—sir? / A Utah man am I / A U—tah—man—sir, and will be till I die,*" when, on cue, ka-blam, Lance flopped onto the pavement face toward the heavens, which afforded him a perfect opportunity to crack open his bloody eyes and squint longingly up Sarah Brooke Thompson Russell's miniskirt one last time.

"He did what?" gasped Quack Quack.

"Actually, Sarah was in front, obscuring my view…Lance was lying at her feet, so I couldn't really see that much…"

"Good God!"

Frankly, I was relieved that Sarah had acquired a few hang-ups of her own. Mine was the nightmare of my father at the door, which Sarah said explained my inability to last long enough for her to fully experience the joy of making love.

From Masters and Johnson came the precise diagnosis of my condition—"premature ejaculation"—and the prescribed treatment regimen: the woman takes the superior position. "Prompted by her partner, using her thumb and index finger, the woman should squeeze the tip tightly moments before ejaculation is to occur."

Sarah, imagining me a sexist like all the other adult white Anglo-Saxon Protestant males in America circa 1975—a plank in the inflammatory platform promoted by radical feminists—presumed I hated her in the superior position, was pained by the squeezing. In fact, just the opposite was the case. After a month or so of hard training (forgive the double entendre), I was ready.

"Now remember, take it slowly. Your father's not going to break down the door and catch us in the act," Sarah said smugly. "And if he does, so what?"

Dad never again hammered on our bedroom door.

Old George and Friends

Please understand: I was relieved that my little problem was cured by the now world-famous Masters and Johnson Pinch Technique. After three weeks of intensive training I was whole. Thereafter, I am happy to report, Sarah and I attained simultaneous Nirvana consistently and often.

That the procedures only focused more attention on Old George was ironic. Had he not been given far more than his rightful due over the course of my young life? Certainly he had won more attention than, say, my nose or ears.

Old George is the name Sarah bestowed on my dangling participle, which, if you asked me, was more like a run-on sentence that ends in a preposition. Sarah was not at all supportive of father's fixation for proper language. "Penis, penis," she exclaimed one evening when I intoned my version of my father's high-flown lecture on language. "Penis sounds like something that squirms around on the dissecting table in biology lab."

Her imagery made me wince, though her point was well taken. Why she proposed "Old George" as an alternative remains a mystery. It certainly wasn't familiar street argot. And, so far as I know, there was no Old George in Sarah's past. Or Young George, for that matter.

"Would it have mattered if there had been?" Rosenbaum asked.

"Never thought about it," I replied.

Rosenbaum quickly withdrew the unsmoking pipe from his mouth and vigorously tamped down the tobacco. He looked up. "Really? Are you so sure?"

"How's Old George?" Sarah casually asked one Sunday afternoon while we were eating dinner at her parents' home. It was code signaling she was bored out of her mind and craved some action. Knowing that the mere mention of his name would make me painfully uncomfortable, she often sent out these secret messages in unusual settings.

"What time is Old George coming this afternoon?" Sarah teased, smirking.

"What's the deal with this Old George, anyway?" Sarah's mother asked, as if she knew him well herself.

"A life-long friend of Jed's…and now mine," Sarah said.

"Brutal tennis game yesterday. He's stiff as a board today," I said, playing along but cognizant of the stirrings in my trousers.

"Sounds like what he needs is a good massage and rest," her mother said.

"Precisely," I said.

"He's coming soon, right Jed?" Sarah cooed.

"Yup. Unless he gets pinched for speeding," I said, trying to make the most of an increasingly uncomfortable predicament.

Sarah hurriedly excused herself from the table and headed for the door. "Guess it's time to run. Shouldn't keep Old George waiting—he's an impatient fellow."

"Someday, I'd like to actually meet this Old George of yours. You both talk so fondly of him," Mrs. Thompson said.

"Actually my father doesn't like him one little bit," I said. I excused myself from the table and tossed apologies over my shoulder for Sarah's abrupt departure as I untucked my shirttails.

Father encouraged me to be especially diligent when cleaning the private areas of my body. "They are particularly susceptible to disease," he warned. As a teenager, I was intrigued that a bar of soap provided useful lubrication as well as prophylaxis against degenerative disorders that result from self-abuse and over-indulgence. How tidy. How closed this circle.

The summer I spent as a surgical assistant in urology convinced me all the more that my father was right: *chiromania* can lead to permanent, if not fatal, consequences. Most of the men who underwent transurethral resections were older. Testosterone had driven them to youthful excesses which now were exacting their painful tolls. It was bad enough that most suffered excruciatingly from severe blockages of their urinary systems. It was profoundly depressing to learn that most emerged from surgery incapable of sustaining anything more satisfying than a lurid conversation.

As my own stream diminished from a powerful laser beam to a sloppy dribble akin to what one expects from a calcified faucet, I blamed my condition on the filth and depravity I was exposed to daily in Manhattan. Or the sins of my youth, although at twenty-four I hardly qualified chronologically as a degenerate dotard. When it sealed up altogether, I thought God was prematurely vindictive.

"Sounds like the clap to me," Dr. Taylor Young pronounced bluntly, boldly, without so much as cursory inspection of the afflicted area. Dr. Young was the corporate physician at Time Inc. Because I was a recent arrival in Manhattan, I took my little problem to him knowing it was his job to refer corporate medical problems to appropriate private physicians.

Clap: The symptoms in males include a yellowish discharge, which causes painful, frequent urination. Symptoms can develop from two to thirty days after infection. A few percent of infected men have no symptoms. The infection may move into the prostate, seminal vesicles, and epididymis, causing pain and fever. Untreated, gonorrhea can lead to sterility.

"The best doc in Manhattan for problems like yours is Dr. Holden Hartung down on Twelfth Street. He's treated more than a handful of Time Incers, heh, heh," Young said, laughing cynically at his intended double entendre.

I was grateful for the referral but incensed that Dr. Young, without any hard evidence to support a diagnosis, had assumed the worst of me. I was also furious that he betrayed the privacy of legions of coworkers who apparently had been similarly afflicted, gonorrhea being the corporate medical condition it was. However, I had to concede that if Dr. Hartung was the most famous clap specialist in all of Manhattan, he surely had to be the best, most experienced clap doctor in the entire world.

From the day I first set foot in New York City, I figured it was the easiest place on earth to catch all manner of dreaded plagues, clap especially. The island seemed to ooze contagions. The handrails on the escalator between Grand Central and the Pan Am building, the banisters on stairs to the concourse under Rockefeller Center, not to mention every subway station anywhere in the five boroughs, were all suspect creeping crud carriers. Touch one and two weeks later you'd be pissing blood and pus. That's when I acquired the habit of always washing *before* I relieved myself. When that was impossible, I'd grab my boxer shorts and shake them until things took care of themselves.

Dr. Hartung laughed scornfully at my confession over the phone. "An escalator's a hell of a place to be doing it." Without pausing for breath, he added almost as smugly and assuredly as Young had: "Sounds like the clap to me."

"Gonorrhea! I've got to see you soon," I sniffed, wondering if there was any connection between my runny nose and my other little problem. Was it another closed circle kind of thing? Bodily fluids had to get out somehow. When one orifice could not provide relief, another would. Or, you'd die!

"How long you been stopped up?" Hartung asked.

"About five days," I said, thinking he meant my nose.

Hartung gasped. "Five days. Five days? Jeeeezuz—you haven't passed water for—"

"Oh that stopped up," I said, considerably embarrassed. "Actually, I passed water—if you can call it that—this morning." How long could a man survive sealed shut, extruding himself every couple of hours or so through an ever-narrowing bore hole, anyway?

"You haven't just returned from Vietnam or been with any strange women lately, have you?" he asked, expecting easy verification of his knee-jerk diagnosis.

The offer to join *Time* had arrived just in time to prevent United Press International from shipping me off to the rice paddies of Vietnam. "Managed to avoid the evil Ho," I said. "Make that plural." While it occurred to me that Sarah could be quite strange at times, to equivocate would only provoke more probing, if lame, questions, ones that I was ill prepared to answer. "No strange women that I can remember," I said. I'm not sure why he assumed wives could not be "strange" and have the clap too.

Hartung asked what I meant, but before I could lecture him on the precise use of English, he put me on hold. A minute or two later a nurse picked up and asked if she could help.

"Just get me in to see Dr. Hardon ASAP," I said, annoyed that I was no longer dealing with the legendary savant of creeping crud himself.

"How does four thirty sound?" she asked pleasantly.

"Sound? Fine. I'll be there and for crying out loud don't keep me waiting," I moaned.

"We'll try not to and, by the way, his name is Har-*tongue*. Your little play on words was neither funny nor very original, especially for a clever *Time* writer, Mr. Russell. Cheery bye." The phone clicked in my ear.

Hartung's phone diagnosis was way, way off base (Mother, Dad, are you reading?). I wish it had been as simple as The Clap. A week later they wheeled me out of the urology surgical suite in St. Joseph's, a clear plastic tube running from the ailing body part to a drainage bag strapped to the bed frame. It was the beginning of the end, I thought. God had really gotten even. Soon I would die.

The plainly startled reaction of the young nurse—Nurse Donahue—assigned to my care and feeding wasn't exactly reassuring. I had seen similar pitiful looks before, visual gasps. Even though I was way, way too young to be worthy of a transurethral resection, all the earmarks were there. The Foley catheter. The bloody, pussy drainage. The alternative diagnosis was even more depressing to contemplate: cancer.

Hartung strode into the room, smiling a smile, beaming a beam. It was a very good day for him, even if it wasn't turning out so well for me. Perhaps noticing our stricken looks he inquired brightly: "So why the forlorn faces? It was nothing more than a congenital stricture—and one hell of a stricture it was, too. The good news is you're now as wide open as a New York City viaduct. You'll be able to douse a candle flame at 15 feet in no time."

I was relieved, so to speak.

"The bad news is you'll have to be dilated about every year or so for the rest of your life. A minor inconvenience I know, but you'll live," he said condescendingly.

It was clear Hartung had never suffered from a congenital stricture himself. Of course not! While annual recalibration of the male aqueduct would be of little personal concern or consequence to the *reamer*, it would be precisely the opposite to the *reamee*. "Meantime, no sex until I see you in two weeks. After that, be sure your partner takes it easy."

"Trust me, the thought of sex never crossed my mind," I said.

"It will," he said knowingly.

Young Nurse Donahue nodded in agreement, making it unabashedly clear that it may have crossed hers. "Probably would be advisable to test the effects of dilation under the strict supervision of trained medical personnel," she grinned.

"Might be, might not," Hartung advised, eyeing Nurse Donahue suspiciously.

Each day for two weeks following my release from the hospital, Nurse Donahue phoned my office. "And how are *you all* doing today?" she would ask brightly. After a fortnight of recuperation, she invited me to lunch. I credit Nurse Donahue's concern and attentive care for the fact that I never needed to return to St. Joseph's Hospital, Dr. Hartung, or to her, for that matter.

A Mormon Goy

"Write about what you know," my favorite English teacher always said. Easier for Mrs. Margaret Mulder to do, garden variety *shikse* that she was, than for this Mormon goy. Her selection of religion was more connected to temporal matters than doctrinal correctness: the thoughtfulness of the minister, his oratorical skills and personal charm, the architecture and ambiance of the sanctuary, whether the organist had mastered Bach's *Prelude and Fugue in D,* and if tenors in the choir sang in tune. Doctrinal correctness for her was incidental. She saw truths as malleable and relative, not hard and fast edicts etched in granite by God Himself, or divine decrees rolling off the tongue of His prophet, seer, and revelator on earth today, the President of the Mormon Church—The Church of Jesus Christ of Latter-day Saints.

What I knew best were my life and times—topics so inextricably linked to the Church that writing about them would be complex, troublesome. Mormonism—the religion and the culture—were so deeply embedded in me that it is hard to tell where one leaves off and the other begins. Therefore, it would be practically impossible to conjure up anything original or fresh, however benign, without running considerable risk in offending or unsettling my ancestors living and dead (there are scores of each). Worse, writing about what I knew best could put me crosswise with church leaders, from the bishop of my ward upwards to the Apostles themselves (or figuratively in their crosshairs, if they saw my acts as ethnically treasonous and heretical).

I had my share of doubts about the church too, but I was no turncoat. I was born to unflinchingly stand my ground. Though my head be bloodied, it would remain unbowed; I was the captain of my fate, the lord and master of my soul. No Gentile blood coursed through the veins of Jedediah Pratt Russell, the fruit from the loins of those roaring Lions of

Zion: Joseph Smith and Brigham Young, the resilient Apostle brothers Pratt, Parley and Orson. And, all of them descended from the womb of the stalwart founding mother of feminism and unshrinking head witch, Anne Marbury Hutchinson of Massachusetts, Rhode Island, Connecticut and New York. As well as through the Lathrops and Howlands and Tillies, and the *Mayflower* itself. Scratch any vein on the family corpus and it would spurt Yankee royal blue. Moreover, in my mind and heart I was a bona fide member of the house of Israel, an anointed son of Joseph and his colorful coat, and his begotten Ephraim and Manassas, a kissing cousin of Judah and his tribe. I was called. I was chosen. What I once sang in guileless plangent soprano (a year before testosterone-engorged testicles knocked my voice down an octave—and, eventually, perhaps even my faith and works, too) was a simple fact of life: *I might be envied by a king for I am a Mormon boy.*

"Ethnicity?" Rosenbaum asked. His eyebrows arched. "I thought Mormonism was an American Christian religion. What's this ethnicity and gentile stuff all about, and from a Mormon *sheygets*?"

"Mormon what?"

"*Sheygets* as in *shikse*; a boy goy, a girl goy—you'd think an alleged kissing cousin in a *shtetl* like Westport, Connecticut and *Jew* York City would be familiar with such pejoratives."

It is true that many old-line Mormon families like mine—ones that converted when the headquarters of the fledgling Church were still in Ohio—descended from Puritans who disembarked at Plimoth.

In my own pilgrim heritage, one, the founder of Hartford, was rewarded for his diligent service to King George with title to practically all that is now Essex County, Connecticut; another founded Pratt & Whitney Aircraft. The remarkable progress of these forbearers was quite enough to make me resentful that God consigned me to the perpetually, religiously zealous wing of the family: those Pratts and Russells who never forgot they came to America to worship how, when and what they may, which Mormons do often.

By the time I arrived on the scene—mid-point between Adolf's and Eva's suicide in a bunker beneath the Reichstag in Berlin and the flight of the Enola Gay to Hiroshima—Mormonism was firmly ensconced and thriving in regions surrounding the semi-arid Great Basin. There, the Wasatch Range of the Rocky Mountains presented a formidable barrier that sequestered Mormonism from the world around it. In its nearly hundred years of isolation, Mormonism unfolded as a religion—arguably the most successful one founded in America—and became a distinctive and somewhat idiosyncratic culture.

Mormon ethnicity is not just a birthright one is born into; Mormonness can be acquired, as well. Being Born In the Covenant (BIC) ensures a lifetime of conflicts, the severity of which has everything to do with how much *of* the world one becomes. It always astonishes me when some converts assimilate so rapidly and thoroughly that it becomes nigh unto impossible to distinguish them from BICs.

Given its New England roots and sociological parallels with Puritanism, it amuses me that other Americans find Mormon culture and religion weird, even threatening. I always assumed it had more to do with Lion Brigham's marital trove than basic doctrines and practices. No matter what Sarah thought, Mormonism's links to Puritan New England and Judaism—its success, its increasing power, wealth and influence, and, yes, Brigham's multiple brides and bedrooms—made it all the more likely that people beyond the reach of the shadow of the everlasting hills would become interested readers of my book.

The deft trick would be to fashion a compelling, revealing and non-apologetic novel that would neither offend my parents nor invoke the stealthy and subtle wrath of The Brethren, whose numbers are legion and whose memories are tenacious. *As a man thinketh, so is he.* If fiction mirrors the soul, I had reason to worry. I found comfort in the fact that hypersensitive parents and Judaism had not exactly constrained writers like Roth or Salinger (I guess technically he doesn't qualify because his mama only *pretended* to be Jewish) or even Chaim Potok, the rabbi's son. Should I be inhibited? If Judah un-tethers its authors, why not the same release for cousins from Joseph's tribe (we are both of Israel's house, though Mormons probably more by belief and patriarchal blessing than by DNA)? Especially so for a son of Lion Parley's and spiritual-giant Orson's lines; this sturdy offshoot whose strict and strident grandmother learned Hebrew and Yiddish directly from her Uncle Orson and Grandfather Parley.

"Your Mormon ancestors spoke Hebrew?" Dr. Rosenbaum asked.

"Amazing, but true. Both learned from the then-prominent Hebrew teacher and lexicographer Joshua Seixas, who taught Hebrew to the Mormon prophet Joseph Smith and members of the original Quorum of Twelve Apostles that included both Orson and Parley."

The training enabled them to read the scriptures in the original text. They could grasp important subtleties that had been washed out when the Bible was translated. Orson, star of the Hebrew class at the School of the Prophets in Kirtland, Ohio, not only passed on a facility for languages to his children and grandchildren, but taught them Hebrew and Yiddish as well. That's how Grandmother Russell acquired it, along with various Jewish dietary practices. When presented with concoctions of pork she'd invariably express her righteous indignation rather colorfully: "*Chozzer drek macht goyisher kopf* (pig shit makes gentile brains)!" It is important to note that she would never indulge in or abide such expressions in English. Perhaps it was her way of passing on her love of vibrant Yiddish words and phrases to my generation.

The big difference between Judah and Joseph is humor. Jews poke fun at themselves and their culture. Mormons don't have a comparable six millennia on their side. We are a hell-bent, hypersensitive lot indeed, too desirous of superficial acceptance from mainstream Christian sects to mock our own cultural idiosyncrasies. Like groveling *shmatte*, we go to great lengths explaining, justifying, appeasing, and turning the other cheek. We search for common ground, even when none need be found, when no compromise is required. It comes, quite frankly, from being overwrought about our peculiar history and culture.

That too is changing. But not fast enough to suit me. I should have known better when a Mormon friend in New York persuaded me to submit rough drafts of the opening chapters to an "open-minded intellectual in Salt Lake City, a critic of books dealing with things Mormon, a man who could open a few doors for you with publishers." I reluctantly caved in. I'll say one thing: the critic didn't waste any time getting back to me. Within a few weeks this rambling diatribe arrived in the mail:

> *You are no Chaim Potok, although I do enjoy your writing. Too many reprobate LDS writers like you lack the courage—you would likely say "balls"—to either withdraw from the church or conform and measure up.*
>
> *By the way, in case you don't know it, Judaism is a culture to the Jews. Judaism as a religion is spiritually dead. It is bound up in its own traditions and rituals. Procreation is the only way it will grow and goodness knows the Jews, like everyone else, are doing precious little of that these days.*
>
> *Mormonism is afflicted with too many people like you—Born In the Covenant heirs of historic Mormon names that continue to resonate—who sadly have begun to regard*

themselves 'ethnic' Mormons, not necessarily members of Christ's true church. Yet, these ungrateful legatees demand their place at the table, and, like over-indulged trust-fund brats, take umbrage whenever the church considers disowning them.

The father of Reuven Mather [sic] *in The Chosen is striving to preserve Judaism. Mormonism is in no danger of dying out; there's no ambiguity anywhere about the blessings of believing and practicing God's word. Mormonism certainly does not need a Rabbi Mathers* [sic] *to pump life into an archaic religion, a tottering relic from a fulfilled dispensation.*

We have a vibrant community of evangelizing, literal believers. Wannabe LDS Potoks have no reason to suck the blood out of Mormonism so it too can be embalmed and consigned to a museum filled with dusty antiquities and myths from eras bygone.

Put bluntly, you and people like you are weak intellectually if you continue to cling to the church while defying its teachings, grasping vainly to position yourself as the Mormon equivalent of Asher Lev. Apostates like you should either shape up or ship out.

You and others persist hoping the church will eventually toss you out so you can worm your ways onto all the anti-Mormon-oriented symposia where birds-of-a-feather gather to have their delicate egos massaged. All of you should repent or find unfertilized pastures on which to spread your scat.

Trouble is, Jed Russell, real or imagined, is quite amazing. I sympathize, empathize at times with him; his storytelling is riveting; his brutal candor honest and convincing (though as hilarious as I find his discussion of Old George, I could get by with a little less). He has great, original language: "mind changers" is a term I have entered into my personal lexicon. And, I want to read the next chapters. The writing is just too good!

It is easy to see why outsiders may think Mormons—from respected intellectuals to street-smart businessmen—take themselves way, way, way too seriously. We're really not like that, honest. Like the "intellectual critic," Mormons may quickly turn indignant and humorless when they encounter attacks. We simmer down eventually, like he did. Didn't he? Well, I guess I didn't help matters much by sending him a copy of *The Chosen* with all the references to Reuven Malter highlighted in fluorescent pink and a handwritten cover note that read: *If it mathers, the name of the good rabbi is Malter.*

The fact is, Mormons are just as plagued by temptations of the flesh and bank book (especially the bank book) as any tribe that ever lived on earth. If there's a significant difference, it's the otherworldly sense of guilt we suffer for simple shortcomings, like just *thinking* carnal thoughts. Action earns unique and unthinkable consequences: *There once was a good Mormon boy / who enacted a dastardly ploy / with the bishop's fair daughter / he'd done what he oughtnotter / and swiftly was rendered a goy.* Which is why Mormons are quick to repent. And forgive. One humorously outspoken General Authority (a super ordinate that applies only to Apostles, Seventies, and members of the Presiding Bishopric of the church), adored for his plain speaking if oft criticized for his use of mild epithets, apologized from the pulpit for his indiscretions: "Hell, Heber [Heber J. Grant, then The Prophet and President of the Church], you can't excommunicate me because I repent too damned fast!"

Wholly unrepentant over the backsliding New Haven Railroad, I hovered around Sarah's drawing table, *nudzing.* I needed to talk. Tonight, while ideas and needs were fresh. I needed her approval not only to write but her agreement to participate—to share her personal insights and family history, which, over the course of our marriage, had become closer to me than my own. In my case, the old Jewish saying was quite appropriate: "When a son gets married, he divorces his mother!" Given that, I wondered why women customarily take their husband's surnames. It should be the other way around, I thought. Sarah would like that.

I knew a little *utzing* would eventually provoke the reaction I desired. I'd apologize, we'd talk—finally talk. Maybe heart to heart. It took a good thirty minutes before she caved in. "So, what's this latest grand book of yours about?" she sighed. "Get on with it; I've got real work to do, even if you don't." As if to underscore the demand, she sliced open a sheet of foam core poster board with the X-Acto knife.

"It's about us," I stammered.

"Oy, us," she sighed.

"I hope you'll help. It has possibilities," I said timidly.

"I don't type well, remember? This is me you're talking to. And, the subject matter is just a tad thin, if you get my drift," she said sarcastically.

"To the contrary," I argued. "You may think us not interesting, but that's our advantage. We're Everyman!"

"Everyman has trouble with, er, reconciling…?" she sneered, glancing in the general direction of my trousers.

"Not Everyman, and please…" I winced. "There are plenty of similarities. They'll read it because they see themselves. There's cultural commonality between Mormons and Jews and Catholics and Episcopalians. At their cores, people are the same."

"Immaculate connections. Mormons are like everyone else—only more so?"

"Please? The whole *megillah* I don't need…"

"The underlined parts will suffice?"

"Just a few insights—sure, a little craziness would be nice too," I said cautiously. "As much as you'd care to reveal: perceptions of life, marriage, me, the kids…"

"*Craziness*? Like, Old George?" she asked. A bemused sneer turned the corners of her mouth. "Your readers should know that *pekl putz* of yours reliably performs like a well-conditioned seal. Like the metaphor? Or is it analogy? Simile, perhaps?"

"Really, Sarah! Just spend a few hours writing down your thoughts. Just think about it. I'd like the same from your sisters if they're willing. It would mean a great deal to me." It was a sincere request.

Sarah shrugged. "Some *schlimazel*, you, but if a book will help, I may contribute. Later. Now, if you don't mind, get the hell out of my studio."

"'My' studio? Since when did it become yours?"

"Slip of the tongue," she answered, embarrassed.

"Freudian," I said.

"Freud, you know?"

"Freud was Jewish."

"Freud, Jewish? No!" she sneered.

"Okay, a *cultural* Jew."

The subject never came up again. A peace unlike any I had witnessed before filled our home. For once, everything seemed to work right. It was as if the prospect of my returning to home and hearth settled everyone. I was not so anxious to beat it for the train in the mornings. I dallied over breakfast and conversations with the children until it was time to drive them to school.

Although she was unusually busy with work, Sarah found time during the day to straighten the house and prepare dinner. Because I was working a relaxed, phase-out schedule at Time, for the first time in our lives together I regularly arrived home in time for a real family repast. This was life as it should be, giving the mundane its proper due, focusing on the important things: wife, children and the book, not always in that order.

Gone, forgotten—perhaps healed, finally—were the schizophrenic hallmarks of our thirteen-year marriage, with its routine if unpredictable nasty bursts of turbulence that got becalmed between the bed linens. The more heated, stunning and humiliating the attack, the more dazzlingly lickerish the rapprochement.

More than once Sarah accused me of maliciously instigating and intensifying petty arguments simply because, predictably, they would end libidinously.

"Did you…was there forethought to your malice?" Rosenbaum asked.

"She thought so," I said.

"What do you think?" he asked, annoyed.

"I never thought about it… Ulterior motives?" I said.

"Perhaps it was unconscious…?"

"Not likely. I was always conscious, aware, grasping for any reassurance that we had an unconditional bond."

"Unconditional? Pretty heavy stuff, wouldn't you say?"

"Umm, yeah, the sex was pretty intensive. Reassuring."

We'd had more than a few moments of intense serenity and calm. But none had been as durable as this one. A fortnight of tranquility passed. Our bedroom liaisons—normally regular and intense—became daily erotic tarantellas. Just when I was certain we could go no further, we'd whirl off into uncharted territory. One peek through our bedroom window would provide prurient evidence aplenty that our marriage was rock solid. Picture perfect.

I was getting ready to leave the office for home when the telephone rang in my office. Sarah was on the line. Breathless. "Oh, I'm glad I caught you. Are you about to leave?"

"Just walking out the door," I said.

"So you'll make the 5:02. Good," she said, displaying more knowledge of the New Haven schedule than I ever thought she had. "I'll be there to pick you up. Hope you're finally ready..."

"Sure, but you do remember my car's at the station." I hadn't heard her this excited for years. "What's cooking?"

"Right, I wasn't thinking. Just catch the damn train and pray God it's on time," she said, a little flustered. "I'll wait for you in the parking lot at Longshore..."

Sarah's Volvo was hard to miss. As promised, it was parked, motor running, lights blazing, in a remote area of the lot a few feet above where the Saugatuck River met Long Island Sound. It was a nippy April evening, but as we walked toward each other she deliberately let the trench coat fall open, revealing a slinky black cocktail dress slit from hemline to mid-thigh. Coat wide open, she threw her arms around me and kissed me squarely on the mouth. Her tongue probed as her pelvis pressed into me just enough to get my attention.

"Whew," I said, pushing her gently away. "I could do with that every night. What's the occasion?"

"Let's just say, tonight we can really talk—the kids are sleeping over at friends'. So we have the whole night...we can talk over dinner. I've reserved a table...away from the band...and I have a room reserved at the Westporter...just in case we need to *talk* more," she said, blushing a bit, like she was ashamed to admit she needed to *talk* as much as I did.

"Could we skip the preliminaries and cut straight to the *talk*?" I teased.

"Real talk, important talk first," she said, pressing against me instinctively. "And, we could dance...if you feel up to it...and have more *talk* if you need it, for enders..."

"Enders? Are you giving me up for lent or what?" I grinned.

"Call this my Good Friday sacrifice," she said, way too seriously.

"Always struck me as sacrilege—celebrating the death."

"Whatever. For us it's enough to be alone, at last, to cover important ground, to understand each other better."

The wine flowed. We were working on our second bottle while the band beckoned. Although I could tell Sarah had something important weighing her down—something that she needed to unload—it could wait: I persuaded her to join me on the floor where we whirled as though I were a soldier about to depart for the killing fields and this was our last chance until we linked up in the great eternity.

When she was ready to go home, I reminded her of the "just in case" reservation at the Westporter. She protested. "It would be better if we continued at home…it's closer, quieter, more conducive…"

"The phone will ring early. We don't get this chance often…just let me lead you there, for old times' sake," I cajoled.

And so she followed, reluctantly acquiescing, it seemed…and whatever she had on her mind she pushed to the side on her drive to the Westporter, for once we were there, the flirtation we'd begun at the club became intense, consuming, ravenous. Sweaty and fully spent, we fell asleep, dead to the world around us, entwined in a sticky tangle of flesh. The finale to our mortality had been a desperately erotic, fully consummating, yet ultimately fatal act of love.

Sarah was sitting on the side of the bed shaking me. The black dress had been replaced by blue jeans and a Yale sweatshirt. "Jed, it's almost checkout time. You've got to get showered and dressed."

When I emerged from the bathroom twenty minutes later, a fresh shirt, sport jacket and gray flannel slacks were laid out on the bed. Beside them was a neatly wrapped gift and card she had personally designed. In perfect calligraphy she had written:

Dearest Jeddy:
Whatever comes,
remember everything.
Yours First, Sarah

Her present was a finely patterned, one of a kind Italian silk necktie. It was exquisite. I was snugging it into place when Sarah entered the room, a bulging manila folder under her arm. "Like the tie?" she asked brightly.

"Beautiful," I said. "Must have cost a fortune?"

"It was worth it," she said, studying my face intently, as if trying to ascertain whether I really loved the gift or was just being polite. Patting the folder under her arm, she said, "I had wanted to go over all this with you last night, but you know…"

"The old silver-tongued devil, me, strikes again." I grinned.

"This too is true…again and again, unfortunately. This is not the way I would have preferred to handle this. I wanted you to better understand…what was on my mind—why now, what now," she said quietly, staring at my shoes. She pushed the manila folder toward me.

"What's this?" I asked, noticing that her hand was trembling. ("I was deeply pained, frightened half to death, feeling cheap, manipulative, and terribly disloyal," she told me months later.)

"Legal papers," she said, "...what I wanted to talk about last night."

"More house stuff?" I said dismissively. "What a pain."

"Sort of. They'll be filed on Monday. You can go down to Ned Nichols' office today and be served or, if you prefer, he can get a sheriff to pay you a visit. I told Ned you'd prefer the office." Her voice cracked.

"What the hell have we done?" I moaned as I pulled papers out of the folder and began reading:

> *Plaintiff: Sarah Brooke Thompson Russell*
> *vs.*
> *Defendant: Jedediah Pratt Russell*

"Ned Nichols said you may choose to leave voluntarily," she said, avoiding eye contact at all costs. "He said this would avert having you evicted from the house."

"Evicted? Evicted from my house?"

"From our house," she said evenly. "You'll get your due, if anything, when the divorce is final."

"Divorce? You're divorcing me? Why? Why didn't you say something?" I wailed, the reality settling into my mind and stomach.

"I have tried, for months—even last night—but you weren't listening, you are always so tuned into your own agenda," Sarah said softly, almost comfortingly, like she was a psychologist or a mother.

"It's the book, isn't it?" I said.

"What book?"

"The book I'm writing."

Sarah cleared her throat. "As I was saying, if your choice is to leave voluntarily it makes things much simpler. I've packed several bags for you. They're outside in my car. Your call."

"Just like that?"

"Not exactly, although it may seem that way to you. You've left me no other choices. Believe me, I'd have opted for any other choice, but none was provided," she said. Her voice trembled.

"Choices I've left you? Hah! What choices have you left me?" I snorted angrily. "I feel conned, abused."

"Ditto," she said. "Long ago I begged, pleaded with you to get help, to get to the bottom of your...issues. Have you done it?"

"I've been thinking about it..."

"You've been thinking about it since you were twenty-five—that was over ten years ago," she said. "Just who was conning whom?"

"I've made some phone calls," I said weakly.

"Good," Sarah said. "You still need help. With or without me."

"It'd be better with you," I said, searching desperately for any opening to get a foot into this slamming door.

"It may be better for you—but it definitely is not better for me and the children," she said firmly. "You had that opportunity and didn't take it. A last-minute heroic effort won't save this one...not this time..."

"Since when are you running my life?" I snapped. This was absurd. Completely absurd. Hadn't we just soared beyond the cosmos? Were we not flushed and clear-eyed from a night of delicious intimacy? And from a fortnight of one-a-day pick-me-ups? Surely this was Sarah's idea of a perverse put-on.

"Since you abdicated," she said. "Great sex isn't all there is to a relationship...although there was a time..."

"It's the book...it's my quitting *Time*, isn't it?" I challenged.

"Perhaps, the *coup de grâce* but only that," she said, turning for the door. She returned a few minutes later toting two large suitcases. "You can get the rest of your stuff tomorrow...or whenever you find a place to live. And you should call the children. They know about this. They do love you. They've been told it's a mutual decision."

"Mutual, my ass! If it was mutual, why didn't we tell the children together?" I hissed, fearing that she had bared every intimate and painful detail of our marriage.

"Don't be paranoid. I simply told them that we had problems and had decided that divorce was the only solution; that we both still loved them and that you would still be their father, but would live in a different place; that they would see you regularly on weekends," she said as though she had been rehearsing the lines for weeks.

"That assumes you can stay in the house and get custody of the children," I said defiantly. "What makes you so sure I won't contest—"

"Do you want the children to move?" she said, tears welling in the corners of her eyes. "Believe me Jed, I don't want this. But it has to be. The least you owe me is...Ned tells me there are grounds..."

"Does he now?" I said sarcastically. "Well let the snively little sunnuvabitch prove them. I'm ashamed at your behavior."

"Ashamed? You gave me no choice." She wiped her eyes on the sleeve of her sweatshirt.

"Never in a million years will I believe that. Your deception and manipulation has been phenomenal. There we were: tangled, rolling around. Sweaty. Breathless. You said you loved me. And now this? What deception!"

"I did…I do love you. My God, how could I not love you—I've been with you for what… Last night, I felt absolutely everything."

"You faked it," I snapped, recalling early times when she had pretended to have orgasm so she wouldn't make me feel inept, or her frigid.

"No fraud last night…or any other night for a long, long time… Our marriage is pretty…very over, but we can always talk." She opened the door abruptly. I walked onto the porch. She strode toward the car, never once looking back. She glanced sideways as she put the car in gear and caught my plaintive stare. I shrugged mournfully. She shrugged and blew a kiss, mouthed "I love you" as the green Volvo station wagon drove off, then disappeared around the corner of the Westporter, with Sarah and our thirteen-year marriage rattling around inside.

SINGLES NIGHTS

The desk clerk assured me that my accommodations for the night had been arranged a week earlier by "Attorney Nichols."

"Ned Nichols?" I asked.

"The same. He always uses us," the clerk said knowingly.

"For what?" I asked, annoyed.

"For all of his, uh, clients," the clerk stammered.

"A volume business he does these days I'd bet," I snapped.

"What?"

"Never mind. What am I paying for this dump anyway?"

"Seventy-five a night…normally it's ninety-five. We give special rates to *friends* of Attorney Nichols," she said sweetly.

"He's no friend of mine. Charge me full rate."

"You're kidding?"

"Not," I said, hanging up the phone.

I called home. Janie answered and burst into tears when she heard my voice. I assured her I loved her and promised this nightmare would go away once her mother and I had a chance to sort things out. Elli was cheerier. His first question was whether he could live with me, which he asked at the precise moment I heard the back door of the house open. Before I could answer, Sarah came on the line: "You start putting funny ideas in the kids' heads, buster, and I promise, you'll never see them again." The phone clicked off.

Stunned is what I was. Stunned and lonely: lonelier than I'd ever been in my life. It was bad enough to be without Sarah. She was sleeping there in the house that was ours, a wreck of a place we had rebuilt together with my money, added a studio where we both could work side by side. She was sleeping in our bed alone. Our kids were down the hall. *Our* kids. What the hell was I doing in this two-bit motel with its special introductory rates for forlorn victims of Dimes & Nichols & d-i-v-o-r-c-e? I should have gone along with her suggestion to return home for what turned out to be our last night. After she dealt her blow, I might have persuaded her to make love once more and insisted that she let me remain in my home until I could secure suitable quarters. That would have given me sufficient time to talk her out of this craziness. What right did she have to throw me out? The house was in my name too. She hadn't given me any legal writ. I should go straight home, demand my rights, and bunk in the studio if necessary. I called home again and was greeted by my voice: "Hello this is the Russell home. We can't come to the phone right now so please leave a message at the tone and we'll call you as soon as possible. Wait for the beep and be sure to leave your phone number."

"Hi, it's me. You misunderstood. Please pick up. I miss all of you terribly. Please pick up, I know you're there," I pleaded. No answer came.

Room service for breakfast, an afternoon Red Sox game on television flew by, unregistered. Still no call. It was dark out. I called home again and this time was greeted by Sarah's recorded voice: "This is the Thompson-Russell residence. At the tone please leave a message for Sarah, Janie or Elli. You may reach Jed at the Westporter Inn in room 26."

My intent was to go home. Just walk in. It was my place too. But as my car passed slowly in front of our house I thought better of it. Sarah would call the police or create a big scene. And, through the windows, I could see that the house was packed with people—people that I knew, people I had counted among my closest friends. They seemed to be celebrating. Cheering my demise. Toasting Sarah's new freedom. Some friends.

I shut off the headlights and coasted in behind one of the many cars parked along the street. For five minutes or so, my view partially obscured by leafless bushes, I surveyed the happy scene inside. There were Megan and Pete: Pete had been my first boss at *Time*, one of my dearest friends. This did not prevent Megan from coming on to me whenever she got a drink or two in her belly. I wondered how long Pete had been in on this. Had he looked me in the eye each day at the office, knowing full well the divorce axe was about to fall? No wife, and no corporate tit either.

Another car drove by—a gray Mercedes sedan—and pulled onto the roadside strip of grass about a hundred feet away. A tall, reedy man extracted himself from the driver's seat, looked cautiously up and down the street as though he were expecting a hit man to show up any second. He strode quickly across the grass into the spotlight of the front porch. It was an illuminating moment: there, on my front porch, stood Vincent Adams, professor of art at Southport University whom I'd met at Sarah's graduation. "Vinny to you," he had said, heartily pumping my arm. "That's some wife you have." Vinny was married to a journalist too, a woman who was good friends with another *Time* editor, another *friend*. But this night Vinny was alone. Sarah answered the door, stepped out onto the porch and kissed him more than perfunctorily. After he entered the house, she lingered on the porch surveying the cars parked along the street, squinting through the brush to get a better look at those that weren't in plain view.

Mine—an indistinct chocolate brown Peugeot—blended into darkness, obscured by the Mercedes, BMWs, Volvos, Saabs and Audis parked along the wide strip of scrub grass between the road and a Revolutionary War-era stone wall that separated the Thompson-Russell property from the town's right-of-way.

A few minutes later I caught another car in the rearview mirror coasting slowly down the street, sliding into the grassy space just behind my car. Knowing that the driver could not get to the front door of the house without walking past my car, I slunk low in the seat. A scruffy sort of man climbed out. He was alone and not dressed to party—Yankees cap and windbreaker, rumpled chinos. He reached back into the car and retrieved a package, then walked up the street toward my car. The idiot had not seen the well-lit opening in the stone wall adjacent to his car.

Slouching lower into the seat, I heard the gravel crunch with each step. He reached the rear door of my car, retreated to the trunk area. Flashlight rays danced in the rearview mirror as he examined the back of the car. His footsteps approached the driver's side window and a broad beam of light spread over my chest and legs. The scruffy man tapped his flashlight against the window. "You okay in there mister?" he asked in a raspy, officious voice.

Slowly I sat up, pretending to rub sleep from my eyes. I turned my head his way and was blinded by the full force of the flashlight. I shielded my eyes and rolled down the window.

"What are you doing?" the man demanded. His coat was unzipped to mid-chest, revealing the red flannel of a hunting shirt.

"Listening to the radio," I said sheepishly. He ignored the lie.

"You okay?" he asked once again.

"Fine, just fine," I said.

"What are you doing here?"

"I was just about to go inside…to the party. I live here," I said confidently.

"You wouldn't happen to have some identification to prove it, would you?" the man demanded, bending down to watch my every move. He trained the flashlight so it would illuminate the entire inside of the car.

"Who wants to know?" Within seconds, without turning his head or altering the focus of the flashlight, a gnarly hand extended a wallet through the window. He jerked his hand and the wallet unfolded, revealing a five-point star centered in a silver shield, similar to the badge Marshal Dillon wore on *Gunsmoke*. I obediently produced a driver's license.

The man examined it intently, flashed the light in my face one more time to make sure I indeed resembled the photograph on the Connecticut license.

"I believe this package is also for you," he said, handing me a large, bulging envelope.

"What's this?"

"I don't read the shit, I just dump it wherever it belongs," the scruffy sheriff said. "But it came from the offices of Dimes & Nichols LLP, from Ned Nichols himself. He said you forgot to drop by this afternoon."

"You got that straight. Shit is what it is," I said, realizing I was being served official notice of Sarah's misguided intentions. "How'd you know I was here?"

"Education," he said simply. "You weren't at the Westporter. So I swung by here on my way to Dameon's." He grinned. "Don't fault me for doing my homework—and that cute little wife of yours seems to know you pretty well. I wouldn't advise going inside. She'd likely call the police, and they wouldn't be very hospitable."

"I really wasn't intending to," I said. "In fact I was headed for Dameon's."

"Good plan. It's usually jumping on Saturday night," he said, grinning. "Almost makes a married man like me want to be single once again."

The sheriff trailed my Peugeot for a good two miles—far enough, I thought, to convince him that I was indeed headed toward the railroad station and Dameon's, a cozy little watering hole frequented by weary commuters during the work week and on Saturday nights by the lonely Westport divorced (or wannabes) in need of conversation.

It was packed, but through the crowd I could see Bob Fenster, married but a notorious philanderer and commuting pal, chatting up an attractive woman at the bar. As I ordered a drink, he spied me through the haze and bellowed, "Hey, Jed. What's the Mormon doing in a place like this alone on a Saturday night? Sarah must be out of town."

"At home, I guess," I said.

"You guess," he said, surprised at my vague response.

"That's where she went after she dropped me at the Westporter," I said, dodging the painful fact that she was celebrating being rid of me for good.

"Aha, the Westporter. I see Nichols and Dimes has been up to no good again," he teased. "And another family falls into the clutches of the notorious Doctors of Divorce."

"Fantastic luck," said a woman who knew me about as well as she didn't know the ticketing agent in Grand Central station. She edged through the crowd toward me. "So your old lady threw you out?" Her voice was jaunty, almost abrasive.

"Figuratively, yes, but she's young," I said coolly.

"Whatever. My gain. This place needs younger blood. Too many seem to have emerged from a prehistoric swamp," she said, nodding toward the fossils at the bar. "You'd do much better if you offed your glasses."

"Offed? What? My glasses?" I gasped. "I've worn these since I was twelve. I'd be quite blind without them."

"Remove them," she ordered. I obliged. "Yes, quite attractive. Great eyes. Gas permeables are the answer for you," she snorted, launching into a two-hour lecture on the comfort and cosmetic benefits of contact lenses, ones that just happened to be available at the optical shop where she was the owner and resident optometrist.

I returned alone to the Westporter, fully informed about the latest breakthroughs in contact lenses. Great eyes my ass. In boring staff meetings, my squinty, droopy eyelids led some people to suspect I'd nodded off. Sometimes I had.

Bob Fenster called early the next morning to tell me of a furnished house available immediately. "The owner has been through a divorce himself, so he understands your situation. By the way, did you get to…beyond the eyes with the gas permeable gal?"

"Yeah, she got to me, but not in the way you mean," I said.

"That *beubele* has some tush on her, Jeddy boy," he said. "No need to be so damn particular, especially in a time of dire need."

"We'll see," I said. "And thanks for the house referral."

Just like that, a few hours later I was the new tenant of a small house on Bermuda Lagoon, a well-protected inlet off Long Island Sound. The house had no phone or television to distract me, so I spent the balance of

Sunday typing out a prospectus for the book, which I copied and mailed to each of Sarah's siblings along with personal notes detailing my side of the story that was unfolding before their very eyes.

As planned, I returned to the marital home late in the afternoon to remove my belongings. No one was there to witness the sad event, but a note Sarah had taped to the door directed me to the studio, where the rest of my personal wardrobe, half of the books, typewriter and files, records, a few useless pieces of furniture and kitchen equipment had been stacked. Another note was taped on top of the heap:

> *Dear Jed,*
>
> *I hope you're finding your first weekend of freedom agreeable. I realize you're due more than what's here, but all this should get you through the next few weeks while you look for a place to live in the city.*
>
> *Love, Sarah*

It took three trips to move all the stuff to my new digs on Bermuda Lagoon. On the last trip I left her a note of my own:

> *Dear Sarah,*
>
> *Actually the first weekend of freedom was pretty decent. Taking advice from a very persuasive optometrist, I'll soon be investing in gas permeable contact lenses. And, my new address is 10 Bermuda Road, Westport. Give Vinny Adams my best.*
>
> *Love, Jed*

The following Saturday, I endured a Fenster-arranged surprise party at my new digs and another lecture from the gas permeable lady. The following week—officially my last as a regular employee of Time—brought on nonstop farewell lunches and cocktail parties deflecting more erudite come-hithers from several single female coworkers. "Thanks, but not yet," I responded politely.

A fortnight of singlehood came and went without any word from Sarah or her siblings. I became a regular at Dameon's. The results were always the same: too many drinks and far too many vacuous conversations. In hopes of attracting less than the empty-heads to my side, I had started writing doggerel poetry on the backs of paper napkins, which Tom Joyce the bartender saved in a binder he labeled "Perverses of Dameon's," a collection of maudlin poetry penned by one forlorn customer or another. In a sober moment, I copied one and sent it off to Sarah:

Singles Nights

Stilted, vapid conversations
tiptoe games of twenty questions.
How much? How long?
Name drop Ping Pong
Barstool foreplay, better Mahjongg.

Leering glances
programmed prances
feigned entrances.
Guarded replay
hollow parlay:
pardon me please
have you met Herpes?

Who could miss
such ersatz trysts,
flatulent adulation
sans sensation?
Ergo ego masturbation

A few days later I returned home after another futile night at Dameon's to find a large manila envelope lying on the kitchen table. Inside were a tape cassette and a note from Sarah:

Dear Jeddy:

You need to start locking your doors. Your house was wide open, so I just assumed you were home. Here are some of my thoughts—enough to get you started. Anyway, I called Penny and Polly. They'll contact you directly. I have it on good authority that Dameon's becomes you. Figures.

Loves and kisses,
Sarah

I was surprised but very, very pleased and excited. Despite the lateness of the hour I loaded the tape in the recorder and put on headphones so I could hear more clearly. I could hear the sounds of paper rustling (Sarah must have really done her homework, I thought). I heard her clear her throat, then: "With or without my help, your novel should be a best-seller: you always were a rather convincing liar..."

Midway through the ten o'clock news the phone rang.

"Hi Jeddy, it's me, Polly, your sister-in-law, I guess I should say your ex-sister-in-law." She was the chipper one, second of the three Thompson sisters. Penny, the oldest, routinely claimed God had been unusually kind to Polly in blessing her with a face, body and manner that would open doors wherever she went, compensating—overcompensating—for her lack of gray matter.

It was a bum rap. Polly got away with playing dumb because, in addition to giving her unusual door-opening good looks, God had also made her friendly, warmly engaging. Had she also been equally bright, she could have ruled the world and upstaged her older sister, which is why Penny perpetuated the myth that Polly was several logs shy of a cord.

"Thanks for calling," I said weakly, but truly thankful that someone from the family was talking.

"Welcome. John says to say hi. So, hi from John and he wants to know what it's like being single again at thirty-five. So, how is it Jeddy?"

"Tell him plain lousy," I said sincerely. "Tell him if they ever develop a vaccine against divorce to be sure and take an overdose. You do the same too, Polly. The alternative is worse."

"That bad, huh?" she said, and without waiting for me to respond she rattled on. "I thought it'd be a gas with all those single horny women around and you with your ways with women..."

"Could have fooled me," I said.

"Read your poem," Polly said.

"What poem?"

"The one you sent to Sarah. About the singles scene, herpes and farting—still using those big words, huh? I had to look up flatulence," she admitted.

I was stunned. Polly was about the last person on earth with whom Sarah would share anything of a confidential nature. "Tell Polly and you've told the whole of Salt Lake City," Sarah often griped. So what the hell was Sarah doing, sharing my poetry, private pleadings I hoped would help her understand how much I missed her, how I longed to work things out.

"So you're pretty bad off, depressed," Polly said.

"It comes and goes, mostly the latter," I said, Sarah's rejection still fresh in my mind. "Sometimes I feel like the kids are choking to death on our disasters. And, Sarah, well..."

"Miss 'er, huh?" Polly's voice turned more serious.

"Good old Sarah."

"Humm," Polly said. "So I called about your book. You wanted advice from me, right? Imagine that, me giving advice to the writer Jeddy Russell. From me you want advice so I'll give advice, I guess."

"Absolutely. Let it fly," I said, thinking she ought to take a crash course in building self-confidence.

"Actually I don't have any advice. But Sarah says your problem is with Old George and that if you fixed your relationship with him you probably wouldn't need to write this book at all."

"What problem? I don't have a problem, and what do you know from Old George?" I snapped.

"I don't know him...but Sarah says that's the problem. That you'd understand if I said it that way. I was confused, myself. Did the divorce make you hate women, switch sides? Are you gone gay, Jed? You must understand, don't you, Jeddy?"

"Not very," I said. "But it's getting clearer."

"Was it something that happened to you while you were in the hospital, something they couldn't fix exactly? Anyways, I'm better face-to-face"—this was too true—"there are some things you ought to understand," she said, almost pleading. "Perhaps when you're next in Utah?"

"Sure, sure," I said, furious that Sarah had just laid me out on the family's dining room table to be punched, poked and dissected. It was quite enough that I had willingly begun opening up to Quack Quack. I didn't need or want to spill my guts to the Thompsons—especially Polly.

In the next day's mail, Penny weighed in with her own response to my plea for help.

> *Dear Jeddyboy,*
> *Regards your request: Piss off, buster...if you still can.*
> *Penny*

WHAT GOD HATH ROT?

The sessions with Dr. Rosenbaum often degenerated into nothing more than one-upping verbal jousts. Still, they were thought-provoking in their own rights. He consistently avoided dispensing advice on what to do about Sarah, though there were exceptions.

Sarah insisted I filter all contact with her through *Attorney* Nichols, as he introduced himself whenever he called: "Hello, this is Attorney Nichols," he would say. "Oh is that you, Ned," I would say, just to annoy him. Or, if I was feeling especially hostile, I'd blurt out, "Did you say Attorney Ned, esquire from the worldwide headquarters of Nichols and Dimes LLP?"

It took nearly five months for Dimes & Nichols to take me at my word: Sarah would get full title to the house (she was required to split the profit with the children when and if she sold the house) and alimony and child support expected of someone earning sixty thousand a year, although, technically, I was unemployed at the time. It obligated both of us to equally support such things as education and medical care. My offer was contingent on just two demands: we must jointly seek marriage counseling before finalizing the divorce; and, should the counseling fail to salve our wounds, we would have equal custody of the children.

Acting on Quack Quack's wise advise I dropped the demand for marriage counseling. "What marriage? You are a divorced man. Why prolong the agony? You can't coerce her back."

Joint custody was the big bone of contention. Ned maintained that the Connecticut courts circa 1980 would never order such a thing. "There is no precedent in law," he droned each time the subject came up. I reminded him, over and over again, that neither would a Connecticut court give Sarah full title to the house. Exasperated by frequent, time-consuming parry-and-thrust exchanges, I finally turned blunt: "And don't forget,

I'm the one that's agreed to pay your bloody fee, which I have been told no Connecticut court would foist on a defendant in a *contested* divorce unless fault had been convincingly established."

Dimes & Nichols reminded me to call him Attorney Nichols. I encouraged him to beat his fist on the packed sand at Burying Hill Beach, warned that if the matter was not straightened out quickly he would see me in a court contesting the divorce, and named the famous New York lawyer who would be at my side should such a confrontation take place.

Rosenbaum bore the brunt of my frustration. He worried out loud that I was letting my contempt for attorneys, generally, get in the way of reasonable negotiations.

"If Dimes & Nichols convinces Sarah to agree to joint custody, this whole feud will dry up overnight," I insisted.

"You'd just find something else to beef about, to delay the inevitable, to remain engaged," Rosenbaum said.

"Wrong. It's over. The only thing worth fighting for at this point are the children," I said. Quack Quack studied my face like my father had years before, searching for the lies in my eyes. Then he did what he had never done before: he acted. He picked up the phone and scheduled an appointment with Ned Nichols. He had gotten to know Ned quite well over the years, a fact he hadn't revealed until I was well into therapy. Within days, the matter was wrapped up. The no-fault divorce pleading and out-of-court settlement, giving me joint custody of the children, was ready for filing with the First Circuit Court of the State of Connecticut.

Another month passed before we had our half-hour before the bar in Stamford. In the interim, we actually began talking, kindly for a change. She was plainly disturbed to learn I could not be in court for the final hearing. "Interviews in Chicago for a new job—they can't be postponed or changed," I responded, noting that I was selling out, taking a full-time job in public relations so I could afford to support her and the children in the manner to which they had become accustomed. "Once again, I'll have to put the book on the back burner."

"Just as well, you need more time with Dr. Rosenbaum before you can write with clarity," she said. "But Chicago? What's with that?"

"New York office of a Chicago firm. What's Rosenbaum got to do with clarity?"

"Quite a lot, I'd say. He did get us to agree on joint custody," she said.

The evening after the divorce was final, Sarah tracked me down in Chicago. The court hearing had gone off without a hitch. She marveled that the judge had asked so few questions, was quite mechanical in granting the divorce decree. There were no words of moral approbation or paternal chiding, not a peep about the economic and social costs of divorce that were dramatically altering the fabric of family life in Fairfield County, Connecticut and all of America.

"You'd think the government, acting in its own selfish economic interest, would be more grudging about divorces," I said.

"Would you want the government meddling in marriages too, say fining you every time you provoked an argument with your spouse?" Sarah said.

"Obviously not. It just seems that divorce has become too easy, an acceptable alternative to thrashing through problems."

"We tried...besides, it was no fault. The alternative would have been worse."

"No fault. What an interesting, outrageously absurd description," I said. One could rightly ask: if no one is at fault, why is the divorce necessary? Perhaps if the plaintiff was required to establish fault, the process might produce evidence that the faults weren't serious enough to grant a divorce. Do your garden-variety whoopsies rationalize splitting a family apart? Is it in society's best long-term interests to make it easy for couples to prematurely, impetuously, and for no good reason abandon hope? To protect the interests of minor children, should not the plaintiff be required to establish cause, to at least make a sincere effort to reconcile differences?"

"But that's the way it is," Sarah said quietly.

"How are you doing?" I asked.

"Under the circumstances, okay."

"Now that it's over, perhaps the air will clear enough so we can objectively reexamine what we've given up."

"In time, perhaps. I need to think and be on my own for a while," she said, her voice cracking.

"There's a route out of this...the love isn't going to fade away overnight. As long as it lasts, there will always be hope. But absence does not always make the heart grow fonder."

Despite the new job in public relations—or perhaps because of it—my desire to finish the manuscript intensified. Quack Quack took this as a healing sign provided it did not distract from the job that was paying the bills. His especially, no doubt.

"I would be less obsessed if Sarah and family cooperated," I said.

"You're the writer. Why do you insist on involving them? The marriage is over. Still, her family is yours?" he said.

"So what do you think of divorce?" I asked him.

"It makes no difference what I think when it's you who should be doing the thinking."

"What? Thinking? For gawdsakes, man, all I've been doing is thinking about love and marriage and divorce. I can't think about anything else."

He leaned back in his lounge chair, sucked deeply on his pipe and asked, "So that's resolved, now today begins where?"

I fidgeted, building up courage to ask him the question that had been lurking in my mind since the first visit. I had dreamt about it; wondered if it was an indication of a dangerously degenerative fixation. No question Quack Quack's penchant for bowties belied a certain anal compulsiveness. How could I trust a man who had trouble with both ends of his body?

"Your pipe, it is not worth being lighted?" I blurted.

"Detest smoke," he said, drawing deeply on the pipe. "It's brutal on the teeth and lungs too. And, besides, I'm training to run *the Marathon*."

"The Boston Marathon? At your age? For what?" I said, amazed that someone bearing down on retirement would willingly endure the rigorous training required to cover twenty-six miles, three hundred and eighty-five yards in under four hours.

"My life, is it not enough?" he said as though he was offering up a statement laced with hidden meanings. He studied my face for a reaction.

"Hmmm," I hummed, wondering what deep messages, double meanings he'd intended to convey in his simple question. I had interviewed many celebrities—business and political leaders, actors and actresses, assorted jocks—who claimed to have subdued all manner of complex physical and psychological torments by running. One dazzling starlet claimed she experienced multiple orgasms whenever she ran more than five miles. (As she covered seven miles daily, I assumed she had absolutely no use for a man, even ones who had been treated and cured by the celebrated Masters and Johnson Pinch Technique.) Others said it had healed chronic heart and circulation problems, resolved serious neuroses and provided numerous spiritual experiences as well.

It made me wonder if Old Quack Quack's own Old Quack Quack was a weather-beaten pair of Nikes and a long stretch of country road.

Thereafter, I imagined from time to time, he may have pulled even with running-orgasm-obsessed-starlet at the five-mile marker and well…

"Tell me about your book," he said, perhaps sensing that I was drifting again. "I think it's about time you started closing some circles."

"Closing what?" I asked, startled from my semi-conscious reverie.

"Closing circles. You know: making half circles whole, putting tails on your small *q's* and *g's*," he said.

Some teachers complained they occasionally had trouble distinguishing my 4s from my 9s, but none of them ever griped about my circles or *g's* or *q's*. "Which means what?" I asked, puzzled.

"Here you are, a middle-aged man…"

"Barely thirty-five," I corrected.

"Whatever…no spring chicken. You still have lots of open circles—big open circles. Your career or new career. Sarah. Her family. Your family. The Mormon thing. The novel. All are pretty wide open at the moment. The novel is the circle you can close the quickest. God knows where it could lead." Quack Quack was right: God only knows. And Sarah.

"He's right," Sarah said when I told her of Dr. Rosenbaum's advice. It was just the response I wanted to hear when I called again to ask her and the other Thompsons to cooperate. I hoped Rosenbaum's observation would inspire her to be more compassionate toward people who don't put tails on their *q's* and *g's*.

"You can help by helping me close this circle," I pleaded.

"Finish the tails on someone else, not me," she snapped. "If my father were alive he'd break every single one of your metatarsals. Slowly. One at a time."

"He would not. Old ROT would understand, he would empathize," I insisted. The phone clicked and I was listening to the dial tone. Middle C.

Ralph Orson Thompson—Old ROT to me and practically no one else living—would be very displeased to learn that, since his passing, I had been reduced to *former* son-in-law. He would be humored, however, to learn that I intended to use the family's story in my first novel. "You could write the whole truth and nothing but the truth about this family and it would read like fiction," he had often said. He did not exaggerate.

For nearly three decades he dealt daily with his own *impending* death with considerable frankness and wry self-deprecation. He had laughed loudly when I inadvertently called him "Old ROT."

"Pretty goddamn good description if you asked me," he said as I stammered out a lame apology, pleading guilty to acronymic obsessiveness but innocent of ridicule and malice. "Whatever, no matter," he laughed. "Rotting away much too slowly to suit me, just sitting here in this GD stinking wheelchair."

He wasn't exactly irreligious in his applications of God's name. Nor was he religious about slowing his rendezvous with his maker. I cannot recall a moment when there wasn't a king-sized, recessed-filter Parliament dangling from his graying lips. I suppose the milder Parliaments did less damage than the two packs of unfiltered Lucky Strikes he had inhaled each day of his adult life, from about 1925 until January of 1958 when he discovered Parliaments.

Despite chain-smoking and progressive debilitation from a mysterious crippling disease he contracted while serving as an Office of Strategic Services (OSS) operative behind enemy lines in France, Germany, Italy and God knows where else, Old ROT didn't fully rot away until he was nearly eighty. When he finally got some relief (his description, not mine) Sarah was understandably distraught. By any measure, he was a mythological creature: talented, bright, loving, attentive, and secretive. However, to most of the Thompson children he was also a bit of a tyrant. Sarah, the youngest, was the notable exception, partly because he was wheelchair-bound from the time she was born until he died.

The fact that he was a withered image of his former self when I met him only made what little I learned of his story all the more remarkable. As it unfolded, I became something of a devotee myself, only somewhat less worshipful than his own flesh and blood. The bullet points on his vitae read like this:

- rebellious son of a prominent General Authority of the church and historian
- highly-skilled graphic artist and painter
- fled the security of the everlasting hills for San Francisco, where he opened a small ad agency
- hung with, as he put it, "Fascists, Commies, weirdoes, Russians, pansies, and *artistes*"
- fluent in five languages
- four marriages, three divorces ("serial polygamy," I called it)
- *drafted* at age 42 to serve in the OSS because of his language, artistic (forgery) skills, and plenty of guile and cunning

- maintained ties with OSS and its successor, the Central Intelligence Agency, until his death in 1974, when he was officially discharged from the "US Armed Forces." A thick, oversized manila envelope from the White House arrived five days after his funeral. Inside were the discharge certificate and a personal letter to the family from President of the United States, Richard M. Nixon.

A year after his death Sarah, who had dropped out of college after Elli was born, returned to school and switched majors from psychology to fine arts/graphic design. With only the ghosts of Old ROT to contend with, she graduated summa cum laude and went on to become reasonably well known in New York graphic design circles. Her work is light years beyond Old ROT's, who doubtlessly would be thrilled, if in his current condition he is capable of emotion. If he is, well the Mormons are right after all—there is life after death, an oxymoron if there ever was one: it should be "life after life."

Anyway, Sarah was in tears after she took the call from her mother in Salt Lake City. She buried her face in my chest, thoroughly soaking the thick green chamois shirt I was wearing. I wondered what I could say that would be soothing, something fondly reminiscent of her skeptical, cynical, satirical father, a man who had powerfully influenced both of us. I pulled her hair back, kissed her ear and whispered, "What God hath ROT?"

"Not funny, you bastard," she cried, swinging in the general direction of my nose. Old ROT wouldn't have agreed. He would have found my crack amusing if, perhaps, thoughtlessly timed. ROT was not one to throw stones anyway, legend that he was for ill-timed and inappropriate stunts that usually gently mocked what practically everyone in Salt Lake City—himself included—considered sacred.

He too was the fruit of devout Mormon stock. His connections to church leaders (his father was a member of the First Presidency of the Church), not to mention his potential, won him admission to LDS High, a semiprivate institution reserved for the children of substantial church leaders and well-connected members. In the early part of the century—before it was branded "elitist" and disbanded by the increasingly egalitarian hierarchy of the Church—LDS High was where the "called" proved they were also "chosen;" it was a veritable vetting ground for general church leadership callings later in life.

Artistic skill and renitence—traits that served him quite well in the

OSS and later the CIA—nipped in the bud any ecclesiastical callings that may have awaited him. He defaced each and every portrait of the Twelve Apostles, the First Presidency (including that of his own father), and the President, Prophet Seer and Revelator of the Church that were hung in the foyer of LDS High. It was bad enough that he added very realistic unkempt beards and randy moustaches to each portrait. The *coup de grâs* were the smoldering pipes or cigars he inserted in the mouths of these called and chosen messengers of God. Coming, as it did, at the precise moment in history when the Church was demanding strict adherence to the Word of Wisdom, the gospel principle forbidding the recreational use of tobacco and alcohol, the artistic prank assured Old ROT's summary expulsion from the school of the prophets.

Predictably, he went on to lead a life that was, from all appearances, distinctively *goyische*. As a young man he fled Zion to depression-, dust-bowl- and prohibition-riven San Francisco, where he acquainted himself with the aforementioned anarchists and revolutionaries, neo-Messiahs and doomsayers, Mafiosi and petty thugs, pansies, pimps and prostitutes and their fellow travelers, not to mention their worldly ways. Whether he participated avidly in the perversions or was merely a conscientious observer remains a matter of some controversy within the family. I suspect he may have indulged occasionally simply to pass muster with the low-life subjects of his reports.

Whatever he did or did not do, it was not conducive to marriage. By the time he was forty, he was on his fourth. It is not known how he acquired a certain facility in French, German, Italian and Russian, although members of the family assume he learned from the expatriate denizens of various North Beach warrens of iniquity, or from the thousands of foreign nationals, Mormon converts who emigrated to Zion-by-the-Wasatch in the early years of the twentieth century.

Throughout his descent into the ways of the world, he never turned his back on the Church. "No matter how far afield you drift," he once cautioned, "never, ever reject the Church. Mormons are your people. They will always be there for you and you should always be there for them."

When he took sick after the war, he fled to his Zion home, where he spent the remainder of his life poking fun at local culture one minute and reprimanding its critics the next.

Perhaps his sojourn on the "other side" made a closet true believer out of Old ROT. He was particularly unsettled that birth control pills and free sex advocates had brought to the streets and youth of Zion what once had seemed safely quarantined a world away in San Francisco and New York. That Sarah, his youngest, came of age as the *Summer of Love* bacchanal unfolded, made him all the more apprehensive.

Although he never said it, I sensed ROT was quite relieved that he lived long enough to see his youngest daughter preemptively rescued from harm's way, attached at least for this life to a prospective young lion of Zion.

Old ROT was late for the wedding. Ridiculously late for the host; inexplicably late as the ceremony was scheduled for his very own living room, which we selected for several reasons. We had no money to speak of and neither did our parents. It would allow ROT, who was wheelchair-bound by then, to participate fully, which provided a reasonably suitable explanation as to why we had eschewed a ceremony in the majestic and historic Temple on Temple Square, the preferred location for worthy heirs of Israel.

Given his penchant for punctuality, I assumed his tardiness was deliberate. I could hear him rumbling around his bedroom and adjoining workroom, where he kept a shortwave radio broadcasting unit and tape recorder that he used to correspond with *friends* around the world. After a delay of fifteen minutes or so, the bedroom door opened, the hardwood floor in the hallway creaked as his wheelchair rolled toward us. A freshly lit Parliament dangled from his lips. He stopped suddenly. He eyed the guests suspiciously as if they were visiting teachers who had dropped in unexpectedly and caught him with his trousers agape. "Well, let's get on with it," he snorted, "a lot of GD trouble to go to, to get them into bed legally." He winked at me. My own father laughed uproariously.

Happily, mercifully, the bishop glossed over the *de rigueur* lecture on why we should plan to eventually have our marriage sealed in the Temple. However, his somewhat oblique references to the subject brought tears to the eyes of Mary Martha Woods Thompson, Sarah's mother, who truly believed that Sarah was the only one of her four children in the "virginal" pre-marital condition required for admittance to the Temple. Seeing how I was an ordained elder who had fulfilled his duty to God by serving a two-plus-year proselytizing mission for the Church, she assumed that I was well qualified too. It was quite apparent that Old ROT and my own father suspected otherwise. To this day I'm not sure what to make of their outrageous votes of no confidence.

⊙ ⊙ ⊙

Marriage ceremonies were not big deals to the Thompson clan. ROT and Mary Martha Woods Thompson had eloped to Nevada shortly before he shipped out for "the war": he was forty-two, she was barely eighteen. Polly, the second-born in this Thompson clan, followed in their footsteps, albeit briefly. The day after graduation from high school, she eloped to Wendover, Nevada (a quick annulment followed). Two years later, when Polly wed my school chum, John Liddy, Mary Martha recommended a small ceremony. "Nothing white, nothing big, nothing virginal," she said bluntly. Polly and John insisted on a large affair, after which the entire wedding entourage went camping at Deer Creek Reservoir, where they smoked marijuana, skinny-dipped and so on and so on. The next morning Polly woke up in a sleeping bag with her maid of honor—no one gave it a second thought. It was 1966 for crying out loud.

Reese and Penny had a small wedding, like ours. Reese was a real catch: a resident in obstetrics and gynecology at Immaculate Conception Hospital where Penny was a graduate nurse. When their eight-pound daughter was born five months after the wedding, Reese and Penny were banished from the Thompson house for months. I was never sure whether their temporary ouster stemmed from their profound carelessness or from their willful disregard for Mary Martha and Old ROT, who expected only the worst for a child born four months early. "You'd think a doctor and a nurse would have ample access to birth control measures and the smarts to use them," ROT grumped.

Reese's errors were compounded by ROT's increasing distrust for physicians. "GD doctors are useless—always shoving a tube in you like you are some kind of blithering guinea pig," he often said. By this time in his life, ROT had more than a casual relationship with a number of doctors at the Veterans Administration Hospital, which he frequented as his rotting accelerated. At the time I wondered exactly where the doctors were shoving the tubes. Now I know that ROT had his own Dr. Hartung and those tubes were substituting for his own, now corroded and calcified by a lifetime of abuse. After one particularly long stay at the VA, which saved him in the nick of time from another bout of acute uremic poisoning, I dropped in for a conversation and a game of chess. We played in silence for about a half an hour. Although the foul-smelling bag strapped to his wheelchair provided both a visual and olfactory report on his condition, I lamely inquired: "How ya doing?"

"Great, just great," he growled. "GD doctors never know when to take it out."

"Take what out?" I asked.

"Whatever. Spigots. Tubes. Needles. Whatever," he snapped.

I looked up from the chessboard. Pain was etched in his face; he strained a grin as I studied his gray eyes.

"Whatever? What's whatever?" I asked.

"Whatever you like. Fingers, toes. Whatever!"

"Fingers, toes, whatever?"

"Yeah—whatever they can stick in you or up you they do: docs rarely know when not to put it in and never when to take it out. Have you gone deef or are you taking notes?" he snarled.

"Notes," I laughed. "Someday I'm gonna write about people who don't know when to take it out."

"Lots of good material in this family," he said. "When you write it, do me a favor and fix my plumbing—GD doctors can't seem to get it right. Maybe a smart-ass writer like you can. Before they started poking around twenty-eight years ago the Old Boy worked just fine-r-ee."

I didn't know as much then as I do now, but I knew enough to know that Old ROT had gotten around quite well indeed through 1948, although, in truth and fairness, he had no more variable an experience with marriage and women than, say, his or my polygamous ancestors. His DNA was spread from Rhode Island (where Penny and Reese lived at the time) to California, the home of his oldest daughter: Mary Martha Thompson. This Mary Martha is not the Mary Martha who was introduced earlier as Sarah's mother. However, both Mary Marthas were the same age. In fact they were members of the same graduating class at East High School in Salt Lake City. Eventually, one classmate became the other's stepmother and the other became the other's stepdaughter. This is the last you'll hear of the daughter Mary Martha because the Thompson clan of my acquaintance lost track of her. Perhaps it was the other way around. Whatever. Old ROT was not a person who believed in looking back, or so he said.

"Death is a whole lot easier than divorce," he told me one day. "If your wife dies, she's gone for good. Zappo. But divorce—she hangs around to bug the bejeezuz out of you. So I figured when *I gave them* the old heave-ho, it was better to be like dead." True to his word, he cut off all contact with his former wives and children. He signed papers permitting a change of surnames should the first Mary Martha Thompson's mother find a new husband (she never did).

There was one exception to the "never look back" and that came after his marriage to Penelope Cannon Woods, who bore him his first and only son: Ralph Orson Thompson, who went by the ironically incongruent name Randy. By a previous marriage, she also bore him his last wife, Mary Martha Woods nee Thompson, mother of Penny, Polly, and Sarah.

I will not attempt to diagram the improbable Thompson family tree here, but if I did it would look like an ancient interwoven banyan with about as many bracing trunks and tap roots as branches. It would position Sarah as her own aunt; her mother as her mother and half-sister and stepsister; her grandmother as her stepmother; and Randy as her uncle and three-quarters brother.

A few years after ROT and Mary Martha eloped, Penelope wrote a novel about the affair—*Devils or Angels*, which eventually became a best-seller. This led Old ROT and Mary Martha to sue for custody of Randy; the Thompsons of my acquaintance lost. Yet, despite ROT's rococo lifestyle, he and Mary Martha may have been the better choice. Rumor had it that Young ROT bounced from one mental institution to another before being committed to a maximum security hospital for the criminally insane: apparently he tried unsuccessfully to suffocate his overbearing mother with a plastic pillowcase.

These are facts neither Sarah nor I knew when we married. So, at the time, I thought ROT's prescription for divorce made perfect sense. I certainly had no intention of ever ending my relationship with his daughter.

"Had you known, would you have married her in the first place?" Quack Quack asked.

"Never gave it much thought…but now that you mention it, I'd guess it should have been a cause for concern. But I adored ROT so…"

"Sarah seems to have taken her father's advice," Rosenbaum ventured.

"Superficially, yes. She wanted me to be like dead and said so."

"Be like dead and we'd all be better off," Sarah had said.

"That's what your father did and look what happened to Randy," I argued. "Better that I be really dead than just pretend."

"Just like you to threaten suicide. Cheap-shot way to get my attention, to get out of paying alimony," she said. "He was saying 'butt out, start your life over.' That's what he did and with some success—his marriage to my mother lasted a long time."

This was indisputable. However, in my opinion Old ROT's fealty to Mary Martha had more to do with his tenuous physical condition than his natural druthers. He was drafted shortly after they'd eloped and he spent the next several years secreted behind enemy lines. He saw Mary

Martha twice during the war—both quickly arranged, almost clandestine trysts at the Warwick Hotel in New York City, which produced Penny (1944) and then Polly (1946). He came home from the war hobbled, but still vital enough to produce Sarah in 1949.

His health deteriorated rapidly thereafter. More than once Penny and Mary Martha rescued him from the police who presumed incorrectly that he was intoxicated, a charge that is frequently leveled against people in the early stages of multiple sclerosis, whose onset and symptoms seemed to describe his general affliction, mysterious war-induced elements notwithstanding. To be fair, Old ROT didn't help matters much because, as the disease progressed, he frequently sought solace from the bottle, giving rise to speculation that his most serious illness was booze.

Military medical personnel added fuel to the confounding dilemma by taking nearly a decade to come up with a medical diagnosis that finally gave the family access to appropriate veterans benefits. Although the army's final diagnosis was a hedge—"possible multiple sclerosis"—the government began making payments anyway. Grudgingly.

Oddly, what he did and where he served during the war remained classified until long after his youngest daughter discarded me. Whenever surgery was required, ROT was not allowed to be anesthetized until a CIA man was present. In the last months of his life, while surgeons made the best of his diseased colon, the CIA minder passed out. I'm told the doctors cleared the room of all nonessential personnel, then debated whether they could continue with the surgery. Happily the man was quickly revived.

Afterward, one of the doctors explained the quandary to the agent. "The remedy should have been obvious," the spooky CIA man snapped, still annoyed and embarrassed at his reaction to the disemboweling. "Black capsule the sunnuvabitch!"

ROT would have appreciated the pragmatism.

Night Lights

Golden lights from your windows blaze
refracted through the summer haze.
Silhouettes of visions past,
vivid memories made to last
flicker across the luteus glass

of wet lawns,
birds' songs,
children's chatter,
mornings after.

Would that I could cross your door
but what was once, is no more:
love's flown,
no one's home,
vacant rooms from wall to floor.

Standing there in full moon's gleam
my racing mind is wont to stream
thoughts of lives in flight
through endless night,
of empty houses and broken dreams

JP Russell, March, 1982

Freedom felt downright odd, numbing, confusing and unsteadying. It occurred to me that though I'd been on this earth thirty-something years, I'd never, ever experienced "real freedom" for an extended period.

I had always been tethered to something profound: my parents and siblings; then for two years the church and my missionary companions; then, almost immediately thereafter Sarah, then Janie and Elli. I had done it exactly the way *they* planned it. Now I was free. I had become a tetherball without a rope, or tetherball and rope without a pole. Whatever metaphor works, apply it. The exceptions were my cautious—obsessive, Rosenbaum argued—efforts to reestablish something with Sarah. I would invite her to dinner. She would refuse. I would call to talk about the children and whatever. She limited conversation to the kids. I purchased an elegant cookware set and sent it to her for Christmas, flowers and a Cuisinart on our anniversary, flowers and a juicer on Mother's Day. (She finally sent a terse thank-you note: "Shall I expect a new apron soon? Your sexist metaphors are not lost on me!") Poetry, practically every week.

"Distractions," Rosenbaum said. "You're stalling," he snapped one afternoon, his voice gyrating between falsetto and second tenor.

"She doesn't want me to do the book, so she's not helping," I said.

"So? You have your memories. Convert them to paper," he said.

"I have," I lied. "But I hit roadblocks, limits to my knowledge. Knowledge that only she and her sisters can provide."

"Your life is theirs?" he said.

"It would seem so," I said. "It's more like I was a brother than an in-law; it's like divorcing a whole family...the family that encouraged me to write a novel, ROT, especially."

"I see," said Quack Quack. "And your family expected what?"

"Not much, really. Don't know, really. They were interested, vaguely, but I think they were more concerned that my writing might lead to trouble. Like analysis. Thinking could turn a person into something they were never intended to be," I said.

"Analysis can only provide understanding."

"That's it. That's what troubled them. Writing could make a person comfortable with himself as he is; unwilling to become who he *should* be," I said. "If I wrote about someone who wasn't exactly a moral exemplar, it was as though I had become him, myself, or endorsed his behavior."

"Wouldn't they want you to discover who you really are?" he asked a little too eagerly, as though he was about to perform a startling psychological reveal.

"Of course they would. They would like me to come to terms with everything, to get comfortable being the good Mormon lad I was called and chosen to be, quit my pointless rebelling."

"Pointless?"

"Their opinion, but it was more than that to them. They knew. They were certain they had it right," I said.

"So they had a box for you?"

"Vaguely. I guess."

"So?" He calmed himself, adjusted the controls of the recorder and took out a notepad.

"So? So? So I wasn't fitting in their *box* for whatever reason. It bugged me that I didn't, but I didn't. On some levels I did, I suppose."

"How?"

"Well, I was also intensely loyal, empathetic…to the Church."

"Like your father-in-law?"

"Right. Loyal but arms-length," I said. "ROT understood the combination. He sensed where my writing would, should take me. He thought it was good—for me, the Church. But he died."

"And, Sarah took his place? Became the listening, empathetic ear?" Rosenbaum said, writing furiously on the notepad.

"No. Absolutely not. She didn't understand that part at all. She thought it regressive, stupid." Quack Quack stopped writing. "She never saw the shades of gray in him. Hated it when she saw shades in me—like they were compelling, crippling hang-ups, fallout from early brainwashing."

"Were they?"

"Aren't they always, leastwise at first?"

"Until you come to terms with them."

"Exactly. Then all you have to do is convince others that the issue has been resolved," I said.

"If issues like that ever are," he said.

"Never are, I suppose. But at least understood, sorted through. No one, Sarah included, ever believed that I had done the sorting. To her, it was all dither, second thoughts, remnants of brainwashing," I said.

"Were they?" he said.

"In the final analysis, no," I said.

"What was there…in the final analysis?"

"That I was intensely loyal, intensely interested, but intensely independent. I'd modified Mormonism—the religion, the culture—to suit me," I said.

"Okay, good, good."

"Bad," I said. "It's a hard thing to modify without coming off as a heretic, or worse, a hypocrite."

"Appearing to whom?"

"Other Mormons, the world, Sarah."

"Are they important?" he asked, writing rapidly.

"No one likes to be thought *meshumed.*"

"Whah...Meshumed? Oy, stop with the Yiddish, please."

"Apostate...I don't know," I said.

"So it's not resolved?"

"Is it ever?"

"Is it?" he asked.

"It was for ROT—it was for Sarah."

"Write the book," he said.

"Sarah could help," I sighed, exasperated.

Quack Quack sat straight up in the chair. His face reddened. His voice squeaked. "Why do you need the approval of the woman who abandoned you?" he said. "You send her poetry, you write a book about her family. To what end? To win her approval? To win her back? To convince yourself that you really were in love? There is no marriage here, it ended at least a year ago."

"Nevertheless, it is worth saving," I said.

"There's nothing to save. Whatever was there is gone. It's flown, as you put it in your poignant little poem. 'No one is home.' You wrote it yourself."

"That's the point, I want someone home—no vacant rooms," I said.

"Deal with what *is*," he said. "What is, is emptiness, nothingness. You've both outgrown the relationship."

"You're begging the point, word games," I said. "The point is the marriage—the family—*is* worth saving. Period. It wasn't that bad."

"The marriage to Sarah or her family?" he asked, annoyed.

"There you go again—the marriage, our family life and our relationship are indistinguishable."

"Maybe that was the problem."

"What?"

"Think about this," he said. "Is it possible for two people to be married, have a wonderful family, make love passionately and do all the things that married people are supposed to do and still not understand each other?"

"Sure, I've seen lots of marriages like that—my parents' generation," I said.

"And what happened?"

"They hung in there—sometimes they grew closer or more distant, depending on the circumstances. But they went the distance."

"Would you say it was because divorce was not fashionable—not socially acceptable?"

"Possibly," I said.

"The difference now is divorce is more acceptable, right?"

"Worse than that. It's become a solution of first resort."

"So is it possible that Sarah and you focused all of your efforts on the trappings of marriage—in-laws, house, kids, schools, Little League teams—and inadvertently neglected putting at least an equal amount of effort into your relationship with each other, wholly separate and distinct from everything else? One that would survive on its own, without need for the trappings that bind?"

"But they're intertwined," I said.

"But separate. The trappings are like the body of a Mercedes. It looks good so long as it's cleaned occasionally. The engine is another matter. It needs constant attention. Neglect lubes and regular oil changes and it will continue to sputter along. But, eventually, even though the body and interior are looking fine, it will burn out prematurely."

"Interesting analogy. So let's get Sarah in here and we'll work on the relationship," I said eagerly.

"Would she come?"

"Maybe, if you asked her," I said.

"What did she think of your poem?"

"She bought new drapes and blinds—accused me of being a voyeur," I said.

"I doubt she'd come," he said. "Even if she did, it would be futile. Your estimation of yourself needs to become stronger. Then you can hope to share yourself with another person."

"Isn't that why I'm here?"

"Is it?" he said. "You'd never know it from our sessions. I know more about Sarah than you."

"You want true confessions?" I said.

"Confessions are best left to God. Write the book, maybe it will help you…help us find the you in you."

I wrote cautiously at first, but within three weeks three more chapters were done, a couple more roughed out. As promised, the process was producing clearer insights into the past. However, I wanted this novel to be more than another thinly veiled comic-true confessional, the kind that made Nora Ephron famous and wealthy.

Perhaps these were matters left well enough alone. In the end, I hoped it would prevent Janie and Elli from making similar mistakes and stand as witness that they were borne of love and remained love. Of course, I also worried that the book could have just the opposite effect.

Saturday morning first thing, I called to check up on the children. Sarah was pleasant enough on the telephone. Almost chatty. She caught me up on our friend Jennie Childs' campaign for First Selectman (sic). Another friend's battle with the bottle and so on. Had there been eavesdroppers, they would never have guessed that the parties on the line were often blood combatants, quite capable of ripping each other to emotional shreds at a moment's notice.

Should the conversation degenerate into vicious epithets and high-voltage baiting, the eavesdroppers would conclude we were likely candidates for lengthy sojourns in some fashionable retreat for the emotionally troubled, prospective ax murderers.

No one would suspect she figured I was afflicted with a serious if ill-defined mental disorder, one that, if left untreated, would surely degenerate into unfathomable psychoses. She seemed pleased, surprised and curious that I was continuing to see Dr. Rosenbaum, pleased that I was, to use her words, "finally getting help," surprised that I was sticking with it, curious to learn what Rosenbaum was making of me, no doubt hoping that he would endorse her pop diagnosis of me, one she'd cocked up with Penny's assistance. She became irritated when I told her that slapping labels on routine problems was not Rosenbaum's style. She acted cheated, like I was deliberately, maliciously withholding critical information. She desperately needed a smoking gun to validate her decision to end the marriage, absolve her of any wrongdoing.

"So, how's it going with Dr. Rosenbaum?" she asked cautiously.

"Fine, fine, I suppose. But I really don't know where it's headed. Whether it's worth the cost. I think I could put the money toward more useful purposes."

"Your insurance pays. It takes time. And you've got to work hard at it," she said.

"I am. He wants me to start closing some of the circles of my life..."

"Good, good. That'd be good. You've got to find the you in you," she said encouragingly.

"That's exactly what he said. But it's complicated. I'm not sure I can."

"Can or *want* to?"

"Both. What good comes from regurgitating scenes from my childhood, school, old girlfriends, the marriage and so on?"

"The past shapes your present and future, and unless you understand it, you'll continue to repeat it, be screwed up," she said firmly.

"Screwed up? Rosenbaum hasn't drawn that conclusion, so you shouldn't. It's counterproductive."

"So do it," she snapped.

"Well I am. Rosenbaum thinks it's good that I'm putting it down on paper. It helps me close two circles—putting my past in perspective and finishing the book."

"So do it," she said again, slowly, precisely, enunciating each word like she would for someone hard of hearing.

"I am—of course, I'd be thrilled if you read…"

"Already have and they're pretty good, although I hope you've changed the title. *Mormon Masturbation Myths* is a tad *outré,* don't you think?"

As I had long suspected, she had read the book—the one I started well over a decade earlier and had, indeed, titled *Mormon Masturbation Myths*. "Not that one; I gave up on that one. The new one."

"Oh, right, the new one about us. Scintillating material. I think I know way too much about the subject already," she said.

"Just take a quick look at it—check it for accuracy."

"Thank you, no. Give it to Rosenbaum."

"I will, but he doesn't have your perspective."

"How are my perspectives going to help you get your act together?"

"They're so intertwined," I said.

"Not since last August, and not much before, if you asked me."

"Give it a read. It just might surprise. You never know. You may learn something about yourself, about me, about the kids, about your father. But, if you don't want, you don't want."

In no uncertain terms, she didn't want.

I returned to the typewriter, hoping that the conversation with Sarah had loosened memories. All I could think about was the way we were now: locked in combat, inflicting wounds that would not heal in this life or the next one, assuming there is a next one. Those nights when we held each other and talked of our dreams and fears, the problems of our children, the elements of our pasts that had shaped us were still fresh, but dimming by the moment.

Once, I told old Quack Quack that the intensity was still there. The sexual and emotional intimacies that once drew us together had become razor-sharp weapons we used on each other.

Quack Quack observed that neither of us was much good at letting go.

"You both want to control the other's life, but are afraid to let the other one back in. You both seem terrified that you will never find another person with whom to recreate those intimate ties. You can, of course," he said. "It's been almost a year now and you both—you especially—are holding on for dear life, like you can't move forward."

"A year next week," I said.

"How are you feeling?"

"Sad. Like she's slipped over the edge of a cliff: I'm holding on to her for dear life, but her hand is slipping…"

"You talk to her about your feelings?"

"Sorta."

"Either you did or didn't," Quack Quack said.

"Sorta," I said. "Poetry."

"Again? You sent her poetry? Your own, I suppose. Did it say what you wanted to say?" he asked sarcastically.

"Better than I could have talked it."

"Do you have a copy?" he asked, knowing full well that I copied practically everything. He'd asked me to share with him anything I wrote about the divorce and former marriage.

"Yes, it's not much. Maybe I shouldn't have given it to her," I said.

Year's Eternity

Dearest, and you will always be,
whatever the future.
Today my love for you
is more intense
than I ever supposed possible,
or admitted it was. How blinded then.
Despite a year at bay
the intensities, emotions
seem fresh as though they thrived

this morning, or yesterday. Did they?
The sleep images of my mind
are endless, never repetitive.
Upon awakening
the wrenching in my gut's pit
evidences the night spent with you,
the wretched agony of existing solo,
craving the strength of your resilience,
wanting for ballast from your mind. Foundering
visions of what must be your todays
send me reeling.
These too are lessons deserved. Learned.
Once we believed our intimate ecstasy
witnessed of compatibility.
Anomalistic, you muse now. I wonder.
Was it more the manifestation
of our union's promise,
unperceived then, but real,
focused now by a year's eternity? Living.
We parted so impersonally:
you in a dreary hall before the bar,
me in a cloned hotel room somewhere. Faraway.
Sealed and signed legal edicts
shed little truth on our yesterdays
nor on tomorrow's hope.
Nor need they bind forever. I long.

JP Russell, August, 1982

"Not bad, but what's the point?" he said, glancing up from the page. "How'd Sarah react?"

"Pleased. She kept a copy, but told me to get on with my life."

"I see," he said, which is what he always said when he didn't see. "Why is it that you blame yourself for what happened?"

"I was only trying to say I now understand what it's like to live alone."

"Is that something you told Sarah you wanted to do?"

"No, it's something she thought I wanted to do, something I was revealing by my actions—like missing trains home at night, working on weekends, getting a little carried away at parties and so forth," I said.

"At one point in your marriage, did you want to live alone—be single again?"

"Thought about it from time to time, but never seriously. I mean, when I traveled, I would run up huge long-distance telephone bills. We'd talk for hours, almost like we were making love over the telephone," I said.

"Were you?"

"That's what she said. Yes. Or that I called just to convince her I wasn't out making love to someone else. Sometimes she said it was a cover, so I could go out after I'd called. Or, if it was late, it was because I'd already been to bed with someone."

"What made her think that?"

"God, I don't know. I mean I thought about it. And I certainly had the opportunity and so on."

"But did you ever have a love affair?" he asked.

"Love affair? No, never had one—except with Sarah that is. I never met anyone who came close to Sarah. Just like after the divorce, no one measured up. Nice women. Affectionate. Good listeners. Intelligent. All the while I'm comparing them to Sarah—their words, their kisses, everything. I'd see Sarah's face in theirs. They'd see anxiety in mine. I'd say, 'Wine's gone to my head tonight. I dunno what's wrong.'"

"That always happened?" he asked.

"Just about every time. One woman, terrific person, right after the divorce. Bright. Attractive. Nice body. Opinionated. Fantastic lover. Some of my friends who knew Sarah thought Ellen was her double. They even sounded alike."

"So what happened with you?" he asked.

"It was too soon after the divorce."

"Really? You cut it off because it was too soon?"

"More or less those reasons," I said.

"More? Or less?"

"She was getting serious…too serious. Like Sarah, she was convinced that I had flipped out; thought she could help me work my way back."

"Did you need that?" Rosenbaum said.

"Seemed so at the time, but I just couldn't do it. Too weird. We'd be on the verge of making love, she'd ask me if I was fantasizing about Sarah, seeing Sarah's face in hers, or if her breasts were the same shape, so on."

"And so on…"

"Well they were a lot alike, so I told her they were," I said.

"That must have upset her?"

"She just told me to go right on pretending, but to talk about it. I really cared for her; in fact I thought I loved her."

"Did you tell her?"

"Once, at the end. Sort of. We'd had a lot to drink. We were feeling good, happy, close…we started to fool around…I carried her into the bedroom, kissing her breasts. 'I love you, Sarah,' I whispered."

"You're kidding…the ghost of Sarah saves you," Rosenbaum said.

"To prevent me from making love to a surrogate, hoping it would lead to the real deal," I said honestly.

I was lazing in the bathtub Sunday afternoon when the doorbell rang. Sunday? The Jehovah's Witnesses must have returned. "I'm Mormon," I had told them last time they dropped by, realizing it was the kind of lame, passive turndown I got when I was a missionary in New England. "I've got my religion," they would say to us as we stood freezing to death on some snow-buried doorstep in New Hampshire.

"Does that mean that if John the Baptist were standing here telling you he had an important message for you, one that you had never heard before, you'd tell him 'I have my religion?'" I would argue, praying we'd be invited inside to sit a spell in the warmth.

"Are you John the Baptist?" some would ask.

"No, but the message I have is of equal importance," I would say. At this point they would invite us in, or politely—sometimes not—encourage us to move on.

It was often said that Jehovah's Witnesses were a more persistent breed, more obnoxious. They always conned me into buying one of their tracts that ended up in the trash.

I continued soaking. Anyway, there was no hope for me: I was the consummate anti-Christ—a Mormon, the great whore of the earth to begin with, and a tool-of-the-devil journalist to boot. It mattered little to them that I easily defeated their wacky assertions, confounded them with my better-than-average command of the scriptures and knowledge of basic tenets of their religion.

Still, they kept coming like the Mongolian hordes. Each month brought a fresh assault team to my doorstep. It was tiring and pointless, I thought, for them to hound someone who believed that there were only two, perhaps three possibilities: Mormonism or atheism, possibly Judaism, a point I frequently argued with Catholics, Protestants, the home teachers from my own church and practically anyone who would listen. JWs didn't listen very well.

Because I was keener on resolving my own religious conundrums than jousting with people who believed that only 144,000 people would be "saved," I didn't answer the door on the second or third ring. Nor did I respond to the knocking that followed. But, when the knocking resumed—this time on the sliding glass door that led from the deck overlooking Bermuda Lagoon to my bedroom—I wrapped myself in a beach towel, thinking I would drop it if the Jehovah's Witnesses were women (that'd keep them away for a while, I thought) and opened the door.

Sarah barged into the room, eyeing the unmade bed suspiciously. "Sorry, did I interrupt something?"

"Just my bath."

"You always showered before, except when you got in the tub with me. Someone's in there…I mean, if there is, I'll just come back later," she said matter-of-factly.

"No one's here," I said, flinging open the door to the bathroom. "But wouldn't you be embarrassed if there was? You and Janie—she did that to me once in the middle of the night, when I had a friend here. Poor woman crawled all the way to the bottom of the bed under the sheets."

"Janie saw you making love? God."

"Had all my clothes on."

"You do it with your clothes on?"

"Not lately. Not ever, except with you in the car," I said, recalling the numerous times passion had overtaken us on long drives, necessitating relief stops along the way.

"So your book. You want me to read it?" she asked.

"Yes. If you would," I said, startled, pleased.

"I will, if you'll listen."

"That's why I wanted you to read it—it's downstairs in the den." I motioned toward the door.

Sarah started reading while I fixed her a cup of peppermint tea. She was deeply engrossed when I returned. From across the room, I studied her face as she read, occasionally shifting my gaze to her slender, tanned legs that were bare all the way up to her white tennis shorts, which I suspected covered a bathing suit.

"Why is it I always feel like I'm being undressed when I'm around you," she said without looking up.

"Old habits die hard." She did look rather inviting.

"It's always sex first—just like your novel," she said. "I don't know what to make of it, although it puzzles me that you're focusing on my family like we are the ones responsible for the way things are now. Why the vendetta?"

"Vendetta? Quite the opposite. Sometimes I feel more a part of your family than I do my own."

"You think it's going to do the kids good, to read about their grandfather? Or to know that their friends and their friends' parents are reading too? They'll think we're nuts, if they don't think that already."

"It's true isn't it? And don't forget this is fiction. I'm not sitting in judgment. In fact I rather respect and admire your father. I make it clear."

"Bizarrely, yes. But, God, you're just so wrong about him—about them—and about us, about my sisters," she said.

"How?"

"Wrong, wrong, that's all. I don't know what else to say. But tell you what, if you'll give me a copy I'll read it again. I want to think on it for a while, maybe call Penny and get her thoughts too," she said.

"I won't hold my breath on that one. I don't seem to be high on her list."

Sarah stood to leave. "I do hope analysis does you some good," she said. "But it won't—until you start opening up more."

"I'll tell Quack Quack you said that," I said. "He's going to read the book too."

"Rosenbaum and how many other thousands in Westport?"

"Just one or two—no one you know."

Sarah's response was prompt. It arrived in the next day's mail. The appraisal was pointed:

> *Dear Jeddy,*
> *I've thought about it, long and hard. I can't see that any good will come of this unless, should it get published, you agree to share half the proceeds with me. Consider it a licensing fee.*
> *Sarah Brooke Thompson Russell*

By the end of that week I had received written responses from each sister. From Cincinnati, Penny wrote:

> *Dear Old George,*
> *I disliked you intensely when I first met you. I always told*

Sarah you were a jerk—you continue to prove me right. By the way, Reese and I made love only once before we married and actually he tried to withdraw, although neither of us was sure it was in. Actually, daddy didn't hate doctors, he loved them. May your memory give out soon.
Penny

P. S. There's a terrific new urologist here at the hospital who will be thrilled to read that you've treated him so kindly.

From Salt Lake City came two letters: one from Sarah's mother and the other from Polly. Sarah's mother wrote:

Dear Jeddy,
It pains me deeply to read your filth. I hope your children will forgive you because I won't. I thought Sarah was making a mistake when she divorced you, now I wonder what took her so long.
Mary Martha Woods Thompson

Polly's letter was longer, surprise, and more restrained, no surprise:

Dear Jed,
I sent this letter in an unmarked envelope 'cause I was afraid you'd throw it away without reading it if you knew where it came from. Sorry 'bout hanging up on you, I was just awfully nervous. I've heard the first three chapters and I must say you have a great imagination and write so vividly—I mean it seems so real to me what you say. This is also very frightening to me. Please, please go easy when you get to me—to us. We have our problems now and things from the past aren't going to do us much good. I didn't know you called him Old ROT—how appropriate. Please destroy this letter. Penny told me you're not making progress, that's why you write the way you do. Get well Jed. For your own sake. Please.
Love, Polly

The last of the Thompsons—Polly's husband John Liddy, a friend since childhood—telephoned late the following Friday.

"That you, Jed Russell?" he said. "John...John Liddy here."

"What a surprise," I said, truly astonished. John had become practically invisible since joining the CIA two years after his parents, both CIA operatives in Asia, were assassinated in the waning days of the Vietnam War.

"Sarah read your novel to us."

"The first three chapters."

"Right. It's funny as all hell." Is Hell funny? I wondered. "I didn't know you had pecker problems too. Where'd you catch it, in the Army?"

"As a matter of fact, I was in the Army when I first noticed the problem, but it went away. It wasn't until much later that it came back in spades; just reached up and surprised me."

"Jeez," he said catching his breath. "I didn't think the Old Gombu could do that."

"What Old Gombu?"

"You know, the crud, the clap. God, you had it for Chrissakes."

"No I didn't. Never had it," I said indignantly.

"So why Hartung, the clap doc who works with Reese, who says you gave it to a girlfriend who gave it to him or something like that?"

"Old Hardon? He's in Cincinnati? Says what? What girlfriend?"

"Do I have to go through it again?"

"Not really, I think I understand."

"Understand what?"

"When to pull out."

Quack Quack Isn't In

Had I ever caught the clap, I certainly would not have passed it on to Doctor Holden Hartung, Manhattan's most famous clap doctor, if the corporate physician at Time Inc. knew what he was talking about. It was therefore distressing that the Thompsons had become so convinced. Worse, so far as I could ascertain, the errant information seemed to be coming directly from Hartung himself, who was now laboring at a hospital in Cincinnati, alongside my former brother-in-law.

"You get what I mean, I'm sure?" I fumed.

"What am I supposed to get?" asked Rosenbaum.

"I am straight. Straight as an arrow. Where do they get off leaping to such outrageous conclusions? This is getting downright vindictive. And, it's all because I'm writing about the family."

I planned no family exposé. Initially, I figured if I reported their story just the way it happened that it would read like fiction. I feared some skeptical critic would write: "Jed Russell's fiction doesn't work because it steers way too wide of reality."

"So I take it you have changed your mind, then. Now what?" Rosenbaum wanted to know.

"I was getting to that. I was more concerned about the children. Would they be ridiculed by their friends? Would they disown me? Would they become like me? Would the twists and turns of the family's ornate history—if partially exposed by my book—unloosen their bolts? Those were things I worried about. They are sufficient reasons to kill the project even though, out of necessity, I have become an indentured servant to my publisher."

Rosenbaum's eyes rolled backward in their sockets, registering his disapproval.

◎ ◎ ◎

A decade earlier, a regular no-shuffle bridge on the 8:30 express train out of Westport to Manhattan—the so-called "Son-in-law Express" because of the lateness of the hour and the number of young garment industry heirs, copywriters, graphic artists, models, dilettantes and other creatively employed types—put me face to face and knee to knee balancing the lap table with Lawrence Hargrave. (Wren to those who knew him well, Lawrence to those who didn't, especially those who made the mistake of calling him Larry.) I was just as surprised to learn that he was one of the city's better known literary agents as he was to discover I was a magazine journalist. "Most journalists I know keep to themselves or associate only with other journalists. In fact, what's a young guy like you doing living in Westport, Connecticut, anyway?"

"Spending more than I make. But, two kids, almost ready for school. The perils of being Mormon, a child bride," I kidded.

Though he was easily twice my age, we quickly became good friends. In fact he became something of a fan of mine, a critic and, eventually, an *agent provocateur* of my decision to exchange the succor and comfort of *Time* for the freedom and insecurity of writing novels, longer freelance pieces and indirectly the divorce (it made him downright uncomfortable whenever I teased: "Count your blessings Sarah didn't name you as a co-respondent").

Sensing that my bank account was running dry, without my encouragement or sinecure, he sent several lucrative freelance assignments my way—including one to ghostwrite part of an instructional book for a professional golfer of considerable reputation. Wren said he hoped the assignment would move me closer to writing something serious, memorable, a novel. "How do you know I want to write a novel?" I asked him at the time.

"All *real* writers have at least one good book in them," he said confidently. "Usually a couple of bad ones too. True, I assume you are a real writer. A good one." It was a statement of fact. He wanted no argument, least of all from me.

"True...but all you really know of me is that I'm incompetent at bridge, half-decent at conversation, and an utter failure at marriage."

"There's a book in that," he teased.

Turned out he'd compiled a complete collection of my stories, dating back to my student days.

"How'd you ever get those...and why?" I asked.

"Called the editor. You're pretty well known out there...sort of a hero.

He did the rest. Why'd I do it? Well let's just say, I wanted absolute proof that there was at least one good book in you."

I was flattered. What writer wouldn't be? It more than compensated for his all-too-frequent patronizing references to me as his "special case." He wanted everyone to know that he had rescued me. To hear Wren tell it, until he intervened, Jedediah Pratt Russell was "just another tortured, backwards-rolling prose writer at *Time*."

As the house on Bermuda Lagoon was directly on the route from Wren's house on the Neck to the train station, he'd occasionally drop by for a drink at the end of the day.

"Pour me a double," he demanded the moment I opened the door one evening. He hurtled into the kitchen, huffing and puffing as if he was very, very proud of himself. "And pour yourself one," he ordered.

"Can't, I'm still working," I said.

"Forget it!" he barked. "There is cause for a little celebration. I reeled in a big fish today."

"Congratulations," I said. "What big fish?"

"Net, net. McWorter agreed to drop bundle on my say-so, on a novelist they don't know from the paint, who hasn't even completed an outline or rough, rough draft or any Goddamned thing on which they could base a decision other than my say-so and a few random writing samples." He grinned proudly.

"Fiction? Good Lord. I am impressed indeed. Here's to you," I said, raising my glass.

"To us."

"Right-o. Here's to Larry's Literary Luminaries Limited," I mocked, clinking glasses and taking another swallow.

"The *us* is you and me, asshole. I get a measly fifteen percent for hanging out my *tokhes* so far I can feel it being drawn and halved again. You can save it by finally uncorking the Goddamned novel that's bottled up inside you, just begging to be let loose on the world. When can you get started? An outline and sample chapter would do for now...anything... just buy time enough for me to get to Argentina."

"You serious? It's for me," I said, astonished.

"As serious as your bill collectors are...which the contents of this little envelope should keep at bay for the time being," he said. "Now when can I expect something besides booze from you?"

"I'm still working on some stuff..."

"Any good?"

"Dunno, have a look yourself."

When I returned with a copy of my labors I could tell he was impressed, at least by its heft. He scanned the first couple of pages. "This'll do for now. Mind if I take it with me?"

I shrugged. (Of course I didn't mind!)

As he headed for the door, Wren added a postscript: "The kicker is they are primed for your second book."

"What next book?"

"You tell me, you're the writer," he said. "I just make the deals that keep you out of jail."

Within a week I'd squandered most of the contents of the envelope settling divorce debts, including Ned Nichols' whopping retainer. If I failed to produce a manuscript now, I'd let Wren down too. Which is why I called Quack Quack.

"How's the treatise coming?" he asked brightly when he came on the line.

"That's why I'm calling. I need to see you pronto."

"Let's see," he said. I could hear him turning the pages of his appointment book. "I mean is this a life and death thing?"

"Important. But not life or death."

"Today's Wednesday, booked solid tomorrow, I'm out of town Friday and Saturday. How about Tuesday at three?"

"If that's the best you can do."

"Normally, I could squeeze you in on Saturday, but I'm doing the Boston on Monday. I'm going up early."

"Doing the Boston? What the hell's the Boston, a new dance?"

"The Marathon, *the* Marathon. Where've you been?" he said.

"Depends on who you've been talking to."

"How's that?"

"It'd take too long to explain. But if you'll have time to read over the weekend, I'll drop off drafts—they'll get you started. I can fill in the rest on Tuesday."

"Bring 'em on—never read a great American novel in the making," he said. "How can you be certain I won't run off and fence it for a million bucks?"

"It's already been sold. The publisher would sue your skinny little runner's ass off," I said. "Besides, if you can't trust your shrink, then who?"

"Praises be. A breakthrough at last. Nurse, note this on Jedediah Pratt

Russell's chart: 'after twelve months in analysis, JPR finally connects with headshrinker.'"

I arrived at Rosenbaum's office around noon, hoping to engage him in a brief conversation. But the only one around to engage with was his way-way-too-young receptionist, Rebe Ben-Adams: attractive, funny, sarcastic, but early twenties too young. "You just missed him—emergency at the hospital. I'd be gone too, except I promised to wait for you and your *top secret* manuscript."

"It's a book," I said, handing her the manuscript. "Would you see he gets it before he goes to Boston?"

"A book?" she asked. "What's it about?"

"Fiction," I said. "Just the first chapters."

"I do like fantasies," she said.

"Slight difference, but I won't quibble."

"The perfect job, fantasizing all day," she teased.

"As a matter of fact it is."

"And what do you fantasize about?"

"You charging?"

"For fantasy, I charge by the minute," she said.

"Mine would take hours."

"So I've read…I have the whole afternoon," she said matter-of-factly.

Early twenties too young. Safely too young. Never mind that for the year I'd been visiting Rosenbaum once or twice each week, Rebe's pre- and post-visit stream of one-liners, double entendres and engaging, provocative banter hadn't slowed. I would have made something of it were she not safely too young. Not much older than Janie.

She was a truly handsome young woman. Handsome is a word often employed to describe large, intimidating women, or as a courteous way to dismiss rather prominent, distracting physical flaws in an otherwise attractive woman. Some say *handsome* Barbra Streisand would be a raving beauty were it not for a nose that spites her face. I say *au contraire mon ami*: Streisand is go-to-heaven gorgeous *because* of her nose…and mouth…and voice. Rebe was Streisand-handsome, distinctive features, a young woman who would grow more stunning as she aged. Although she worked long hours, including some weekends, her face, neck and willowy arms and legs always appeared tanned, an illusion created by her natural creamy olive skin tones and her jet-black hair. The pale pink cast to her lips was the only evidence of artifice about her. If she hadn't once revealed to me that her genealogy, like mine, trickled back to the Mayflower, I would have assumed she was the product of a handsome, rawboned Anglo-Saxon Navy captain and an unusually tall and stunning geisha. Her prurient sense of humor seemed to confirm that she had sprung from a relationship that was made up of equal parts steam, tenderness and intellect.

"May I read it before I give it to him?" she asked.

"I'd rather you didn't."

"Is it that lurid?"

"It's bad luck to let people read it before it's accepted for publication," I said, though I had already asked Wren for his comments, tried to get Sarah and her sisters to read it, and now old Quack Quack too.

"What's it about?"

"What's what about?" I said, staring directly at her breasts, which seemed to be rising toward me under her white cotton dress as we talked.

"Your book. What's it about? Are you okay, Mr. Russell?"

"Jed, please! I'm just fine."

"Just fine, huh? Funny, you look panicked, drained, like you're about to f-ing puke," she said, grasping my arm. "Look, I was just going for a lunch, then home," she said. "If you're buying, I wouldn't mind having lunch with you. You look like you could use some food. And, maybe if you got to know me better, you'd let me read your book."

"What, what?" I said, dazed and confused a little. "I mean, sure," although I was not exactly sure. Or what I was saying sure to, exactly. I was trying to come up with an obscure restaurant where none of my friends or, god forbid, Sarah would see me with *safely too young*. Not Oscar's, right smack dab in the middle of everything… "Something different than Oscar's," I insisted.

Rebe responded quickly, as if she'd anticipated my concerns. "Something outta-the-way. Well…your place is down by the water, isn't it. It'd be quiet enough to talk, throw some burgers on the grill, a salad. If your cupboard's bare we could stop for fixings along the way. I'll drive."

As she drove, I laid my head back on the seat and stared at the ceiling. Fantasies of Rebe and Sarah intermittently wafted through my mind. Sarah scolded: "Dazzling, smart, but way too young, Jed. Having an early mid-life crisis?" There was Rebe hanging on my arm, whispering in my ear: "Don't listen to her Jed…how could you have ever been in love with such a shallow shrew. You weren't really, you know. I've read the charts."

"The mother ship has landed, space cadet," Rebe said as she pulled the key from the ignition. We had been riding about ten minutes, and I'd barely said a word. "Looks like the view out back is pretty spectacular."

"Glory be," I said.

"Freud would make something of this place," Rebe muttered as I gave her the cook's tour of the house. "I've never seen such immaculate bachelor's digs." I wondered just how many she'd seen at her tender age. "But then, I've only been inside my father's house and he's a consummate slob—you know *artistes*."

"Your mother is dead?" I asked, voicing my assumption that divorce was unique to we of the un-tethered (Liberated? I think not!) '60s generation.

"Divorced, now," she said. "He's a professor, and true to form he fell in love with a student."

"Oh. Big ouch," I said.

"Big ouch. She wasn't just any student. A married one. After she divorced, dad started seeing her—in fact they sort of lived together, off and on." Rebe seemed sad, embarrassed, tentative.

"So you met her?"

"Never. It was supposed to be a big deal secret. But I saw them together twice while the woman was still his student, still married."

"So did they marry?" I asked.

"Nope. After mom threw him out, his lover blew him off too. She told him her ex was a crazy bastard who would probably blow their brains out if they continued seeing each other. Sound familiar? I mean, I didn't believe that excuse then, and I certainly don't now. Few are that crazy and God, I should know."

"So what's happened to him since?" My curiosity was pricked.

"That's the tragic part. He had been going blind for some time. Diabetes. In fact that's what attracted his lover in the first place. She had some overwhelming need to nurse a sick person—maybe it was as basic as giving a dazzling last orgasm or something like that, I dunno. Who knows what goes on inside needy, twisted minds?" She smiled, shrugged.

"They thought they had this wonderful professional simpatico—he the learned professor, she the bright, young student, his fresh eyes. So when she backed out of his life with that phony excuse everything came unglued. His sight continued to deteriorate, then it was prostate cancer that had metastasized, and well, you can figure the rest."

I sighed empathetically, recalling my earlier work in the hospital, not to mention my personal close encounter with Dr. Hartung and his dilatators, catheters, drainage bags and excruciating pain. "I'm sorry, I really am. Will he make it?" I had asked before realizing it was terribly insensitive of me.

"Will any of us? He'll last for a while, thanks to the marvels of medical science, but his days are definitely numbered," she said.

"I'm really sorry. I would like to have met him. What's his name?"

Rebe was incredulous. "Adams. You do remember my name?"

"Right, Ben-Adams. His first name."

"Ben, Benjamin is my mother's maiden name. I sort of adopted. Not legally or anything. You know Abou Ben Adams, child of Adams," she said, haltingly, nervously I thought. "Vincent Wheeler Adams..."

"Vincent. How appropriate for an artist...you say he taught..." I said as warning lights flashed through my mind. Vincent Wheeler Adams, artist, Professor Adams. The memory lights were flickering: "Vinny to you" Adams, Yale, PhD; now Southport University, Department of Fine Arts. Ah hah! Like Old Lance, he hadn't measured up to Sarah Brooke Thompson's standards either. Instead of blowing out his brains, Old Vinny was letting them ooze out through a plastic tube attached to his shriveled pecker. Served the sunnuvabitch right. He had no business fooling around with any student, let alone one married to me when they met.

Encouraging her to return to school, finish her degree, to take off where ROT ended, was not intended to lead me into cuckoldry by unknowingly funding her rendezvous with other men. However, Sarah was incredibly bright and beautiful. She was also unusually headstrong, impetuous and, ironically, very unsure of herself. Read it: vulnerable to flattery and easily led. And, I was the only man she'd ever known in the way God ordained it.

Sarah and I met midway through her first quarter at the University of Utah. Although I first spied her walking through the cafeteria (I mistook her for her sister Polly), official introductions were handled by John and Polly, both of whom had ulterior motives (as they admitted months later). John's was to distract me from his wife (a brief entanglement with her at a party left me, if not Polly, hungering). Polly thought an introduction to Sarah would eventually cut me down to size. Sarah was known for trashing her way through young men, tossing each one on the rubbish pile to figuratively blow their brains out over her, as Old Lance eventually did, literally. Polly thought I was in sore need of a humbling. Recompense for coming on to her, I suppose, or was it the other way around? I forget. Why can't these things ever be mutual?

Within a month Sarah and I were engaged and another month later, married. As could be expected, our first year together had its many stormy moments. Janie's birth settled us into steadying routine. Sarah returned to school the next quarter part-time, continuing her pursuit of a degree in Child Psychology and Home Economics. The move to New York City—more precisely, to its Connecticut suburbs—two years later and the impending birth of Elli propelled her into full-time motherhood: "Just rotting away in the suburbs, while you were off in the city having a wonderful life as a magazine writer," she kvetched years later as our marriage unraveled.

All along, I encouraged her to resume her education. I knew it wouldn't be easy. Like most Mormon women, even lapsed ones like Sarah, she believed that motherhood was a full-time calling, the most important responsibility she would ever have. (Ironically, fatherhood is a man's primary responsibility too, although it hardly relegates him to hearth and home. Just the opposite.) She knew education was highly valued. Church teachers had persuaded her that education would help her be a better mother and give her the foundation to earn a living should her future husband die prematurely or be unable to work (divorce was never mentioned as a possible outcome—*as a woman thinketh, so is she*—although it certainly was not that uncommon then, even in Mormon communities).

So, I was pleased when she applied, albeit grudgingly, to continue her education at Southport University, just a few miles from our home. An excellent grade from Introduction to Graphic Design—not to mention superb rapport with its teacher, Vince Wheeler Adams, PhD, Yale '62—coincided, more or less, with ROT's passing. A few months later, with the doting professor's blessing and oversight, she became a Graphic Design major.

Inadvertent cuckold that I became makes me want to minimize or forget entirely the influential, possibly pivotal role I played in her decision to switch majors and rush headlong into the arms (figuratively and literally) of Dr. Adams. "You're so talented, it would be a waste for you not to switch into design," I reasoned after she earned an A+ in the introductory course. "I think you're hesitating because you're afraid you won't measure up to your father."

"Good point—I mean there's no way I could. Daddy was so progressive for his time. If he hadn't gotten sick in the prime of his life, he'd have been recognized for his genius," she said.

"You make him out to be larger than life. Who knows what he would have done if he hadn't gotten sick. Maybe he would have married ten other women and screwed his brains out until he dropped dead from exhaustion? The point is, who knows? It's so obvious that you're ten times more talented, and you've got your whole life to prove it, if proof is necessary."

"You're just a little prejudiced, aren't you? You never have had much respect for my father anyway," she said.

"More than I think you know. Anyway, a husband is supposed to be a cheerleader. Remember when you told me I was good enough to write for *Time*? Well I didn't believe it then—but you did. Now it's reversed. History proved you right as it will prove me right."

"That was different. You were good, even then. You wrote like a *Time* writer. It was so obvious."

"Nevertheless, you were blinded by prejudice. But I wanted to believe you in the worst way because there was nothing I wanted to do more than become a *Time* writer. Your expectation raised my sights a little and look what's happened. That's all I'm saying: listen to someone who may see a little more in you than you see in yourself. You won't find out if he's right if you continue to be intimidated by the half career of your father."

"Harsh, Jeddy. He was good, damn good, and you know it," she snapped.

"Good? Yes. He may have been great if he hadn't gotten so sick. In fact he may have become a well known fine artist instead of a designer if he hadn't let himself become so hemmed in by what he imagined the church deemed unacceptable."

"He thought it was a joke—he was an atheist," she said.

"And I'm a Holy Roller. If he was an atheist, why then did he keep his paintings—the good ones, the sharp, cynical, controversial ones—under lock and key in his bedroom? Because he thought they would offend the Mormon community because all his paintings dealt with man's eternal wrestle with God and temptation. He could have dealt with the backlash, but he knew his kids couldn't. It was his very best stuff, yet he kept it locked in a closet because he was afraid the wrath of the Church would be visited upon his children. Most of all, he wanted you to fit in, probably because he thought he hadn't. What did he tell us over and over again?"

"What? What are you getting at?" she said. She banged a cast iron pot on the butcher-block countertop.

"He always said never, ever turn your back on the Church. It will always be there for you. Mormons are your people."

"He never said any such thing. You're trying to rationalize your own hang-ups, the ones that prevent you from becoming a novelist," she said.

"Well he did. Very distinctly and very repetitively. And, yes, I have similar views. We both came from the same place spiritually. You're sort of a half step removed, so maybe his advice didn't register with you the way it did with me, but he said it just the same. Look at his life. When things turned sour in the early '40s, he bailed out of San Francisco and a promising career, fled straight to the womb of Zion where he couldn't possibly earn what he did on the coast, but where he and his children were out of harm's way. After the war, when he got really sick, and the government balked, he accepted welfare in exchange for hand lettering the scripture cards for the Sunday School. He bitched and moaned about how the Church wasn't paying him enough, which kept his pride intact. Sure the Church was getting a good deal, never mind the fact it could make out quite adequately without professionally lettered scripture cards."

"Your imagination is outrageous," Sarah seethed.

"Is that what happened or not?"

"The facts are correct, but wildly distorted. You talk like you know my family better than I do."

"Perhaps I do…know your father better. At least, I'm a hell of a lot more objective about him. For instance, when he evaluated your high school art like he was a *New York Times* critic, his intent wasn't to intimidate or discourage; he wanted you to push yourself, to be good, better than he was. He would say that he pushed because he wanted you to understand that, despite your inborn talent, you would have to work very, very hard to be really good. If he was concerned about anything, it was about your willingness to make the necessary sacrifices to achieve your potential. He'd be thoroughly disgusted to hear that you turned your back on art because it was hard. Anything worthwhile is hard. He didn't just wake up one day and discover that he'd become a skilled designer, did he?"

"No, but you don't need to get so worked up about it."

"It bugs the bejeezuz out of me when you quit before trying and blame it on your father."

"It's more than that. If I major in psychology, I can always get a job as a teacher, but art? It's just an unstable field."

"That's what your father was driving at. He was concerned that you didn't have the stomach for sacrifice," I said. "Maybe, in retrospect, he wished he had become a high-powered businessman so he could have been a steadier provider. He did have a security streak in him—remember when he reamed me out for switching from pre-medicine to English. He always said he liked my writing, but when I made the switch, he damn near died. He told me that there was better money in the sciences and so forth."

"I remember that, but I also remember he was pleased to death when you landed the job at *Time*."

"By then he knew I was committed. And the job at *Time* was no harbinger of abject poverty. It was one of those one-in-a-million writing jobs, a definable success, with a stable, big company that rewarded its employees well. He also worried the profession—the long hours, the weeks away from home et cetera—would spoil relationships with people I loved most, something he was very familiar with. He had tons of firsthand experience and all that."

"What? He did rather well financially," Sarah said.

"After your mother married him he did. He was forty-two then. What about when he was twenty-five and thirty? What about the lost marriages and children? If the divorces weren't his fault—which we really don't know, do we?—he couldn't have been very pleased about how things turned out, even if your family remained intact, miraculously."

"Easy, boy. What do you mean miraculously?" she asked.

"Miraculously because any psychologist would tell you that your parents' marriage was a disaster waiting to happen, a disaster that was averted because he got sick. Your mother stayed the course. And, they wisely kept the family secrets from you until you were old enough to handle them."

"What secrets and what do they have to do with this?"

"Do you think he really wanted you to know that your mother was once his stepdaughter? Or that he had a son, by your mother's mother, a son who has since, apparently, been committed to an insane asylum? Why do you think your mother makes such a big deal out of how financially secure they were until he got sick? I'll tell you why. Because he was suffering, suffering hard. Just as he gets a lid on his life, he gets sick and loses his source of income. You and your siblings were his only bona fide, lasting successes. He probably feared that if you saw his failure it would destroy your respect for him, perhaps mess you up for the rest of your lives. Isn't it obvious to you that the man you grew up with was remarkably different from the man he had been twenty or thirty years earlier? Doesn't the fact that he chose a woman twenty-four years younger—his stepdaughter to boot—as his last wife suggest to you that he craved recognition and adulation from someone who had not lived through his ups and downs? Your mother freely admits he was the only loving male—both father and husband—she ever knew."

"Good book material, but distorted," she said sarcastically.

"Accurate. Good book material, but no one would believe it. Besides, your crazy grandmother or stepmother, whatever you're calling her these days, already turned it into a bestseller. The point is, your father didn't want you burdened down with his failures or intimidated by his successes. He wanted you to be better than him in every way possible."

As I said, I'd just as soon forget about the provocative role I played in launching her art career and torrid, albeit brief, fling with Vincent Wheeler Adams, Yale '62. Boola boola.

"I can't believe you're going into art," Penny said when Sarah told her. "You of all people. I was the one in the family with all the art talent."

"She's just trying to put you into a box, just like she did Polly," I told Sarah. "She doesn't want you to surpass her in anything." It amused me that Penny would have moved heaven and earth for her sisters, yet obsessively one-upped them whenever she got the chance.

Later, at Sarah's graduation, Penny was the first one to notice how close Sarah and Vinny had become. Sarah was hanging on his arm, posing for pictures, when Penny nodded toward them and cooed: "Nice that Sarah's developed such a *warm* relationship with Professor Adams. He seems to be a very *kind* and *caring* mentor." She gave me one of those "I know something you don't know" snickers. At the party that followed, my anxiety increased when I sensed Vinny was almost as pleased about Sarah's graduation as I was.

"Go ahead. Read while I fix the hamburgers," I said, pouring safely too young, fruit of Vinny's loins a glass of pinot noir. What did it matter if Nurse *Ben*-Adams became part of my ever-extending, somewhat incestuous family, made up of obsessed fools who seemed to never know when to say when? If Rebe had her own bizarre reasons for wanting in, why should I care? Had she added Ben to her surname in a deliberate attempt to deceive me? So what? If she needed me to avenge the betrayal of her mother, perhaps it would turn out that I needed her for my own purposes too.

"I'm really sorry about your father. I really am," I insisted, trying to convince myself that I was truly sorry and, being a well-indoctrinated Mormon boy, was willing to turn the other cheek, as it were.

Not in a million years.

Rebe Stays

Some of the learning I acquired as the founding, if interim, editor of the cooking magazine *As You Like It* sunk in. I paid scant attention to instructions for time-wasting tasks like carving apple birds, baking brioche or preparing worthy béchamel sauce. However, I listened up to advice on preparing food from scratch. This day I opted to keep it simple.

I quickly tossed a fresh green salad and grilled a couple of hamburgers while Rebe read. When the meal was ready, I carried it into the living room. "Lunch is served," I announced grandly.

"Honestly, I'd rather keep reading," she pleaded as I placed the tray on the coffee table. "I could do with another glass of wine." So while I ate, Rebe read. When she had finished, she thumbed through the entire manuscript, such as it was at the time. She picked up the cold hamburger, stared at me absently, took a bite and, with her mouth full, mumbled something like: "Why are you still in love?"

"Love with whom?" I said, surprised.

"Sarah, who else?"

"Am I? How would you know anything about that," I said, relieved that I hadn't somehow betrayed the contents of my daydreams whenever I encountered "safely too young."

"I can read. I can think," Rebe said, waving about the half-eaten hamburger for emphasis.

"Why shouldn't I still be in love?" I asked. "Isn't it quite logical that it would take just about as long to fall out of love as it did to fall in love? Fourteen years!"

"Possibly. If you will it so. If you asked me, which you didn't, your life returns to square one, because you will it. You seem to find self-pity satisfying in some twisted way. You're no different than Old Lance or whatever his name was. You didn't measure up, in your own mind. Instead of sticking a loaded gun in your mouth and pulling the trigger, you kill yourself slowly, wallowing and drowning in the shit."

"You sound like Rosenbaum," I said.

"I do have some training in the area, although you wouldn't need much expertise to divine what's going on here." She sounded like my high school counselor had when I failed the first semester of junior English.

"Philosophically opposed to handguns," I teased, hoping to cut the tension of the moment. "Black capsule would do the trick and be a lot prettier."

"If suicide continues to be your conscious choice, why drag it out?" She paused, deep furrows spread across her youthful brow. "*Conscious* is the key word. I don't think you're consciously choosing suicide. Consciously, I think you want to pull it out, as you put it. You have every reason to live and thrive. But, at least subconsciously, you have your finger on the trigger. Actually, it seems your finger was on the trigger *before* the divorce. Sarah saw it, so did her clone. Whatshername? You can't blame them for not wanting to be a co-respondent to a suicide."

"Following your analogy, Sarah could prevent it—that should be obvious too."

"Obvious to whom? To you, perhaps. That may be the problem. How can anyone *prevent* you from killing yourself? No one can, so no one will. You have to take action first, voluntarily, one way or the other. Then someone may be able to help you stay on track. Neither Rosenbaum nor Sarah nor Whatshername nor I can prevent you from pulling the trigger."

"Not you?" I said apprehensively, curiously.

"Example only. I'm not yet involved with you the way Sarah was," she said.

"Not yet? Curious choice of words."

Rebe shifted uncomfortably in the chair and began shuffling the pages of the manuscript. She stared at the ceiling, then at me. "I guess I really shouldn't be butting in here. It's not my job and I'm not that qualified. Dr. Rosenbaum would be furious."

"Anything else?" I said somewhat sarcastically, a defensive tactic I use when people make assumptions about me that have elements of truth in them, even if they are pop-psych stabs in the dark.

"Probably, but I don't know what exactly," she said as though she saw clearly the trap I was setting. "I need to think more, I need more time. Besides, we're letting a perfectly summery April afternoon go to waste when we could be drinking up the sun on the deck. Would you mind?"

"If you stay around, I may be able to give you one more chapter for Rosenbaum."

I led Rebe to the deck and wiped the dust off a lounge chair. "There's more wine in the cabinet under the sink in the kitchen. Help yourself. I'll be downstairs in the study if you need anything." I stepped toward the house, then stopped and turned around. Rebe was peeling off her white pantyhose, revealing most of her thighs. "I hope you stay long enough to read the next chapter. You may find it interesting."

Rebe looked up, but matter-of-factly continued to remove her stockings. "More than the others?"

"Different than the others," I said.

It was quite dark, around nine, when I emerged from the study, spied the staircase thanks to the flickering light from the television in the living room up the stairs, where, no doubt, safely-too-young Rebe Ben-Adams nee Adams would be sitting reading or thinking while nursing a second or third glass of wine. But the room was dark; the chaise lounge had been folded and stacked against the deck railing. Despite her promise to wait, she had fled to the safety of her own apartment. Just as well for now, I thought. Then it dawned on me: I was stranded. My Peugeot was still sitting in Rosenbaum's parking lot, exposed to anyone, including Sarah, driving down Westport's main street.

A quick call to Teddy's Taxi wasn't much help: a cab wouldn't be available for at least an hour. I wasn't about to walk the four miles to Rosenbaum's office at this hour. I'd sleep now, fetch the car in the morning, and deal with the inquiring minds as they inquired. Dreams were dreams; reality was reality. No need for nimble explanations—accurate on their faces but abstruse, pliable, and inclusive when parsed. If safely-too-young had her own daring delusions, they had been quelled by a couple hours of reading. She had done the right thing: she'd fled temptation. I was relieved and grateful she had taken me off the hook.

I was not at all relieved to see a woman lying face down on my bed, skirt hiked high, revealing more than what my eyes were prepared for. It was such a lovely sight that I let Rebe sleep on while I brushed my teeth, changed into sweats, alternately edited the new portion of the manuscript and gazed longingly at her bare tan legs. Midnight was nearing when she stirred, rolled onto her side.

"What time is it?" she asked, rubbing her eyes and stretching. She buttoned her one-piece nurse's uniform, which had previously been undone to the waist—probably to expose more of her body to the sun.

"Midnight or so. Have a good nap?" I said.

"How long have you been sitting there?" she asked.

"Not long."

"Why didn't you wake me?"

"I didn't think to. You were sleeping so peacefully. Obviously you needed the rest after the sun."

"It was glorious—you should have been with me."

"I really should have," I said, thinking as much about her unbuttoned dress as the warm sun.

"So'd you finish?" she said.

I nodded. "Maybe you should read them in the morning, when you're fresh."

"Morning? Aha, is that a come-on or what?" she said with mock indignation, folding her arms protectively across her breasts.

"No, no," I protested. "I mean, you should take them with you and read them when you're fresh."

"Thou doth protest too much. Hast thou a guilty conscience?"

"Always. I meant morning. Nothing more. Tonight, you've got to drive me back to Rosenbaum's. Remember my car?" I said very seriously, guiltily.

"Morning," she said. "Not tonight."

"So pick me up on the way to the office," I said.

"Settled. You have a place for me to sleep?"

"Here?"

"Where else would you have a place to sleep?"

"True…well, okay…if you don't mind a messy room, there are beds in either Janie's or Elli's room," I said.

"If you insist."

"I don't insist on anything. I'll drive you home if you're too tired and pick you up in the morning or whatever."

"Whatever is fine." She gave me one of those coy, semi-sincere stares, which, frankly, only served to confuse me more.

"Whatever what?" I said.

"Whatever the other options are…" She hesitated, as though discomfited by what she had been thinking. "Which I suppose would include right here."

"My room, my bed?"

"And why not? You've seen practically everything of me there is to see, so what's the harm. It'd be nice to have someone next to me for a change." She said it so evenly that it didn't seem like an overt invitation to make love.

"It's habit forming, hard to kick," I said.

"I know, I read the book. So?"

"So okay. Okay, I'll behave myself. Okay?"

"Whatever," she said as she got up and headed for the bathroom, leaving me to figure this one out on my own.

"Have an extra toothbrush?" she called out.

"I don't, sorry."

"Mind if I use yours?"

"Sarah would…not if you don't," I mumbled.

"What?"

"Not if you don't."

"Any extra bath towels around?"

"In the closet near the door."

Now the shower was running. How would I structure this explanation? I'd never gotten a woman into bed so easily. We'd not done anything, but absolutely no one, Sarah especially, would believe that we hadn't. Be careful what you wish for.

The water stopped; she would be toweling off, wrapping it around her. The door opened, the light from the bathroom backlit a young body, responding instantly to the blast of cool air: goose bumps spread across her inner thighs, her breasts tightened, nipples engorged and erect.

"Have an extra T-shirt?" She stretched, flicking wetness from her stringy jet-black hair.

"Does it matter now?" I pointed toward a fresh stack, doing my level best to appear cool, in complete control, casual, like this sort of thing happened to me every day.

"Which side?" she asked.

"Left, facing the headboard. But I'm a very restless sleeper," I warned, knowing that I was instinctively prone to hug tightly anything that happened to be next to me—Sarah, pillows, the blankets, perhaps even safely-too-young Rebe.

"Ditto," she said, smiling invitingly, kindly, like she was taking pity on me knowing that just the sight of her goose-bumped skin might sate the hunger she knew was there, waiting, longing for someone like her to come along. She'd read the blasted charts!

When I returned to the bedroom after showering and shaving, Rebe was sound asleep, gently snoring (more of a breathy gurgle than a snore). I climbed into bed, edging as close to her as I dared—near enough to realize that she was no longer *safely* too young.

Rebe's left arm was draped around my body when I awakened the next morning, breasts pressed into my back, legs intertwined with mine.

"Sleep safe and sound?" she whispered in my ear.

"I think so."

"You could have had your way with me, like in the book."

"What book?"

"Your book," she said. She gently kissed my neck. "While you slept, I read the new chapter."

Rosenbaum Makes Time

The phone on the bedside table rang at not much past seven. One person, and one person only, would call at this hour. As I was indisposed momentarily, Rebe answered.

"It's for you," Rebe said, hesitating. "Sounds like a wife—but she wouldn't give me a name."

"Former wife," I corrected as I raced to the phone in the kitchen.

"Fresh prey?" Sarah snipped when I came on the line.

"A friend," I groveled before I realized I was groveling; damn it, she had long ago given up rights to such information. Rebe, who positioned herself in the kitchen doorway, mimicked the worried expression that must have been on my face, lip-synched: "a friend," rolled her eyes, pursed her lips and began kissing the refrigerator as though she was begging its forgiveness for some egregious transgression.

"She sounds sweet…young," Sarah was saying.

"Does she?" I said. "Why are you calling at this hour?"

"Sorry, didn't mean to break in on you."

"You didn't. What's up?"

"I have a business appointment in the city today. Would you mind picking up the kids after school if you're not making it an all-dayer with Her Firmness?"

"Actually I was planning to work on the book. But I can pick the kids up at three thirty."

"I could be late…quite late."

"They can stay the night," I said.

"Will *she* be there?" Sarah said snidely, especially snide for someone asking a favor. On a Friday, no less.

"Would it change your plans?"

"Can't."

"Then my answer would be irrelevant," I said.

"I don't want you doing it in front the children."

"The living room has never been one of my favorite trysting spots."

"Sleeping with her. If you are, I don't want the children there." She sounded more possessive and self-righteous than she had in at least a year.

"So call me when you get home, I'll bring them over."

"I could be very late."

"I thought it was business?"

"There's a party afterward, I could miss the last train."

"Ah, new opportunities. You should drive. Take my Peugeot. Better yet, throw a mattress in back, save a hotel bill."

"Forget it, I'm sure they can sleep over with friends." Click.

On the drive to Rosenbaum's office, I gave Rebe a large manila envelope containing the manuscript.

"Promise on your typewriter that I can return to read the ones that follow," Rebe commanded.

"Promise—whenever you want, you can…you may," I said, wondering who should be reassuring whom.

I was relieved to see that my car was the only one in the parking lot. Rebe pulled her car into the space next to it and cut the ignition.

"When will I see you again?" I asked.

"Soon," she said as she opened the door.

I climbed into my car and started it up, allowed it to warm for a few minutes while I contemplated Rebe's shifting hips in the aptly named, for this occasion, rearview mirror. She had been straightforward. No reason to doubt her word. Yet, in my gut I feared I'd missed a golden opportunity. She would not likely cross my threshold again. As if she sensed my eyes on her backside (if not my innermost fears), she turned around, waved and blew a parting kiss before disappearing inside the building.

As I waited for traffic to clear on the main road, a black Saab pulled alongside and out popped a curved briar pipe, its bowl packed with unlit tobacco.

"Mighty early for the Great American Novelist to be out and about," he said, eyeing me a little suspiciously.

"Dropped off the manuscript…ran into Miss Whatshername in the parking lot," I said, trying my best to control the lies in my eyes.

"Rebe Adams!" he said.

"Right, Miss Ben-Adams," I said.

"Hope it's a good read."

"Interesting, I think."

"See you Tuesday—I've booked some extra time," he said.

"Tuesday. Have a good Boston," I said, finally spying a gap in the traffic.

"What?"

"Have a good Boston—a good run."

Rebe returned to the Russell house later that afternoon and didn't leave until early Tuesday morning, by which time I had come to feel like she had always been a part of me. She seemed out of place behind the reception desk in Rosenbaum's office when I arrived for my appointment, twenty minutes ahead of schedule.

"You're early again," Rosenbaum said as he emerged from his office. "Rebe and I were just going to consult on a couple of patients. But let's do you instead."

"Both of you?" I said, wondering if she'd already confessed her weekend consultation and we were headed for some kind of kinky psychiatric ménage a trois.

"Just me, Rebe's got other work to do. Let's get at it. It's not often that I get to shrink up a Great American Novelist-in-the-making."

"I'm the only writer you have as a patient?"

"At present. I had one a few years ago—but he suffered a fatal heart attack freebasing cocaine. Great writer, John Barton. Perhaps you knew him?"

"Knew of, not personally," I said, wondering whether it was the nature of all writers to kill themselves, one way or another. My end wouldn't come suddenly from pipes, powder or booze or anything remotely dramatic. Such storybook exits were reserved for the truly great. My death would be prolonged and pedestrian, agonizing and messy. Old George would freeze up for good. Uremic poisons would back up through my system, corroding my organs inside out. I'd swell up and explode like a fermenting bottle of last autumn's apple cider.

"What's crossing your mind?" Rosenbaum asked.

"Nothing really... So Old John Barton did drugs? Huh. And a heart attack too. I mean forget cocaine, the guy was a ferocious runner, wasn't he?"

"Sure could write too."

"Sure could," I said thinking perhaps Rosenbaum could transform me into a literary giant by prescribing a line or two. "Just sniff it four times a day and, bang, in practically no time you'll be writing like Old John Barton," he would say. Perhaps he would add: "At the worst, you'll die like a real writer. Stylish and graceful. Milestones obit in *Time*, perhaps even a mention in *People*."

Rosenbaum waved me into his inner office: the Head Sanctuary to me, named for the activity that took place therein and its basic colors—variations of pastel grays and dusky pinks, which I imagined roughly matched the tones of the cerebral cortex. A leather chair in the corner had been tucked and stitched so its arms, back and seat resembled the ridges of a brain.

"And over there is the chair upholstered with John Barton's superficial lamina," I imagined some tour guide would say years later. "That tuck down the middle of the cushion is his interhemispheric fissure. Perch on its forward edge and your cheeks will be scrunching down on his superior frontal gyrus. Can't you feel John Barton's creativity oozing up through your bottom? Notice the texture and definition of the ridges, which are indicative of creative genius. Like other thinkers before him and since, Mr. Barton succumbed prematurely to a total body orgasm produced by that powerful aphrodisiac cocaine. At least he died with dignity and style. No blood stains on his boxer shorts, or tubes dangling from his pecker like Old Jeddy Russell, a lesser American writer who slowly rotted away right here in this office, dripping blood and pus on the carpet. That stain on the wool rug over there is his."

"Jed, Jed, let's get started," Rosenbaum was saying, as he waved his hands in front of my face. He plopped onto John Barton's brain near a rack of fully packed pipes, fumbled for the controls to the tape recorder. The actual machine was encased in a white wall unit that lined the one windowless wall of the room. On my first visit, Rosenbaum told me he'd be taping our sessions. "It's really rather painless, you won't even know the tape is running. Several highly sensitive microphones are implanted in the ceiling. They can pick up conversation from any spot in the room," he had told me proudly.

"Just like the frigging Oval Office," I had said.

Since that first meeting, I read a few books on psychology—they're filled mostly with supercilious rot—so I knew that what seat I chose for each session revealed something of my mood, attitude and personality. So as I sat down on a large floor pillow and braced my back against an extraordinarily plain gray sofa (probably covered with the cerebral cortex of some urologist), I wondered what Freudian messages I was transmitting. "So where do you want to begin?"

Rosenbaum shrugged his shoulders and fiddled with the buttons on the control panel. "Suit yourself. It's your nickel."

"My eighty-five bucks you mean. Am I speaking loud enough so this session can be taped for future generations of literature students?"

"Will this be worthy of that?"

"Sure," I said, thinking that some eleventh-grade English student—perhaps Rosenbaum's grandson—could have great fun with this recording. His class would be assigned to read *Closing Circles*. Having given the class more than ample time to complete the book, the teacher would announce: "Today we are going to discuss the symbolism found in the writing of Jedediah Pratt Russell, a lesser known contemporary of the great John Barton." While the class had its way with me, Rosenbaum's grandson, who had not read a single paragraph of the book, would sit smugly quiet at his desk. The discussion would be nearing its end when the teacher, Miss Jennie James (actually I once had a Miss Jennie James for junior English; she despised me because I was plain lousy at finding the hidden meanings in the great literature of the world), would notice that Young Rosenbaum had once again failed to join the conversation. She would correctly assume, as she had many times before, that he had not done his homework.

Seizing the opportunity to validate her assumptions, Miss James would direct that whiney, condescending voice of hers toward the laconic young Rosenbaum: "Tell us what you think of the book," unwittingly walking headlong into the trap he had carefully laid for her. He would stammer around for a while, letting the angst build in the classroom, before blurting out, "You're all absolutely, absofuckinlutely wrong." All the students would giggle.

"Well," she would say, indignation rising in her quavering voice. "Why don't you share your *specific* thoughts about Mr. Russell's novel."

This would make Young Rosenbaum nervous because, as he would confess, "I don't have any *specific* thoughts about the book—in fact I haven't even read a page—but believe me, you're all wrong. Dead wrong."

Anne Goodson, the star of the class and Young Rosenbaum's girlfriend of the moment, would wave her hand in the air, praying for an opportunity to bail out her dear friend. But Miss James—not to mention Young Rosenbaum—were each, in their own perverse ways, priming for a kill. Taking great care to control her anger, Miss James would say evenly, an unmistakable snide tinge to her voice: "Tell us, Mr. Rosenbaum, how is it that a young man who has not read the book is so certain the conclusions drawn by those who took time to read it are completely off base? Are you given to divine revelations? Have you something original and meaningful to contribute to our discussion?" Smoothing wrinkles from her pegged skirt with the clammy palms of her hands, she would wait patiently, coldly confident that he was about fall flat on his face, again. Humiliated.

"Something meaningful? Nothing about Russell was meaningful," he would say. "He was absolutely crazy."

"Perceptive," Miss James would say dismissively. "Do you have more to add?"

"Well, yes. He was garbanzo beans crazy. So far gone, in fact, that even he didn't know what he was writing, what he was revealing about himself. His shrink had difficulty with Mr. Russell because he was so absolutely out of control when he wrote this novel. He craved approval so much, that anyone who offered it controlled him. Conversely, he assumed that anyone who didn't offer approval—like his first wife—was out to do him in. Russell was mad, mad, mad."

These being his most lucid comments all semester, Miss James would be loathe to rein him in. "I don't recall ever reading that Mr. Russell was in psychoanalysis."

"He was crazy about that too. Swore his shrink to secrecy. The crazy bastard actually hated shrinks," Young Rosenbaum would blurt excitedly.

"That'll be enough of that kind of language," Miss James would say. "Cursing is the sign of an illiterate. English is a very precise language…"

"Right. That's exactly what Russell would say. So to be precise, he was pathologically neurotic, if not paranoid and slightly psychotic. And, depending on whom you believe, he may have even been a bastard as well, at least in the street sense of that word."

"Read the book, then we'll listen to you," she would say.

"I don't need to. I listened to the tapes. My grandfather was his psychoanalyst."

Young Rosenbaum would go on to become a great American academic, another phony pedantic author of ponderous tomes like *Opus Madness: Demons of the literati—the great and the pretenders.* He would dedicate it to Miss Jennie James, who would thereafter boast that she had recognized Young Rosenbaum's blossoming genius when he was in her junior English class. Years later, she would officially change his failing semester grade to an A.

"What's crossing your mind?" Rosenbaum asked.

"Got any grandchildren?"

"One. A junior at Staples. But he's sure no writer. Last time I heard he was failing English. Why?"

"Curious. Writer's curiosity, that's all," I said.

"Fine, now let's move on. What did you want to say?"

"Pardon?"

"What was it you wanted to say."

"Oh that. Nothing really. Your grandson's got it all wrong, that's all."

"What does he have to do with you?"

"Everything. I mean, just tell him that it's wrong to fail English when he has all that talent. Tell him I said so. Tell him it's the most important subject in school…sorry, I got a little carried away."

"No problem, really, I'll tell him." Dr. Rosenbaum sighed; he seemed frustrated, troubled, confused. So was I. "Let me try to focus you a little. I read the book. I'm no literary genius, but from a psychological standpoint it's getting you there. It took us the better part of two years to cover the territory in the first five chapters. You could reduce future bills simply by closing this circle."

"What'd you think about the notes from Sarah's family?"

"What I think is, why'd you show them? What did you hope to accomplish by showing them a partially completed novel?"

"Just as I wrote—accuracy, to balance the historical perspectives on the family, our lives."

"That's all?"

"Sarah's a good critic."

"An artist is capable of criticizing the prose of a professional writer?"

"Actually, she has a pretty good ear for language. And, I've grown accustomed to her reading my stuff. Practically everything. At *Time*, I'd call long distance, read stories to her before I turned them in. She was on target more often than not."

"Why was that? Was she a good writer too?"

"Not at all. But the few times I ignored her advice, my stuff got seriously edited. I can think of only two exceptions—I would have read those to her except she was talking on the blasted telephone to her sister in Cincinnati and I was on deadline."

"So what'd you do?"

"Submitted them. One was on Muhammad Ali, so it had the feel of fiction—I mean he's such a mythical character, he almost begged you to take liberties with story."

"And the other?"

"More technical. On the guy who was building the artificial heart. A damned interesting guy. In fact I won a prize for the story, but it was so technical I thought Sarah would fall asleep."

"So what happened?"

"It was the same both times. When I got home that night—about two in the morning—Sarah was up waiting for me. She accused me of being out with another woman. Even when I produced copies of the stories, she wouldn't back off. 'You always call me when you're doing a story, unless you're feeling guilty,' she snapped. This was true, of course. Instantly, I felt guilty, like I really had been out drinking, like I'd let her down."

"What happened to the stories?"

"Sarah read them. She said they were absolutely the best stories I'd ever written, even though she admitted she didn't know a thing about boxing or mechanical organs."

"What happened at the magazine? What'd the editors say?"

"Same as Sarah. They said they were my best efforts."

"So how did you feel?"

"I was glad Sarah liked them—really happy."

Rosenbaum wrote something on his notepad. "And the editors?"

"I was pleased, smugly pleased. What're you writing there?"

"A note to help the typist who transcribes the tapes," he said.

That beats all, I thought. Probably the transcriber has grandchildren who will use the transcript in their junior English classes too. I'm like a damned open book here. "She have any grandchildren?" I blurted out.

"Who? The typist? How should I know. Why?"

"Just thinking, that's all," I said.

"Jed, she's very confidential. I trust her implicitly, you shouldn't worry."

Easy for you to say, I thought. I should have told him, It's not your brain being spilled out on the carpet, is it? No one's going to write a best-seller about *The Psychoanalysis of Dr. Rosenbaum*, are they? Instead I said, "I hope she isn't a talker."

"Not at all. Now tell me about the notes," he said.

"Did the whole story from memory, didn't need notes," I said.

"What story?"

"The Ali story—I told you."

"Ali? Not Ali. The notes from your wife—Sarah..."

"Ex, former wife," I corrected him. (There was something positively Freudian about his constant referrals to Sarah as 'your wife.' Rosenbaum knew I thought it was Freudian because I had told him so. He insisted it was just a slip of the tongue. 'A revealing slip,' I said.)

"Ah yes, right, former wife. I meant the notes from Sarah and her family. What're you going to do with them?"

"I'm not doing anything with them," I said. "I am withdrawing, hesitating, for the time being."

"That's why you wanted to talk, right? And you probably want me to talk you out of it, right?"

"Wrong," I said. "I only want to know *why*. And spit it out, this is costing me eighty-five bucks an hour and I won't ever realize any of the residuals from your grandson's book."

"What grandson's book?"

"The one he's going to write from your tapes." (Surely Young Rosenbaum would transcribe this portion of the tape so he could read it to the class. "See, I told you. Russell was absostinkinlutely whacko, man. He even knew I'd do this. Miss James, do you think I could be a writer someday?" She would stare at him in utter disbelief, but later would tell a reporter from *People* magazine that she responded unhesitatingly: "You're brilliant beyond your years, so why not the best for you.")

"I see," said Rosenbaum.

"What is it you see?" I challenged. And so it went for another thirty minutes or so. But, the fact is he didn't see as clearly as Rebe...and Rosenbaum and I had been doing weekly sessions, sometimes two, at eighty-five bucks a pop for nearly two years. Not to mention: Rebe was much nicer to look at.

"I see clearer, now. Let's cut this session short. I want to sleep on it before we move on. By the way, Rebe ran across some of your work—she loves it. Would you mind if she read the book...the *drafts*?"

"She gets it...I mean sure. Maybe she'll have grandchildren."

"Safe bet," Rosenbaum said.

The question of the hour was this: Would hers be mine too?

Minding the Tiller

Practically every one of my high school English teachers reinforced the fact that I was no prospective literary luminary. Those who sensed raw talent measured their words carefully: "You may have the mind and the ideas, but you lack discipline and dedication." Teachers like Miss Jennie James—a withered, frustrated woman who wouldn't have recognized a creative idea if it bit her labia majora; who obsessed over sentence structure, noun/verb agreement and split infinitives at the expense of content and expressiveness; whose personal life, or lack thereof, was the only participle she ever left dangling—were harshly unequivocal, as if they were clairvoyants, prophets, seers, or witches.

"Pursue something better suited to your personality—perhaps dentistry or accounting or demolition. Writing requires insight, clarity and precision, not to mention sensitivity and, most of all, subtlety," she sighed. This, of course, only intensified my desire to prove her wrong, show her that I too could write like Sylvia Platt, a classmate and close friend whom Miss James deigned most likely to become the next Jane Austen or Emily Dickinson.

Sylvia could have surpassed Saint Emily, I thought at her funeral a year later. Like many great authors, she departed mortality well before her time, precisely a week before she was to leave for college back east. If suicide was a professional hazard of leading the literary life, then perhaps Miss James had me sized right: I simply lacked the discipline, insight, sensitivity, and subtlety necessary to insert the barrel of a loaded .45 into my mouth, or swallow the entire contents of the nearest medicine cabinet, or, more chicly, fry my synapses with cocaine, booze, barbiturates, and lysergic acid diethylamide.

Later in life it dawned on me that the only place my early critics ever published their ideas and prose was on blackboards of Canyon Mills High School.

I shared this energizing personal discovery with ROT shortly before his daughter and I fled to New York City. We were playing chess; as usual he was a bizarre sight to behold: heeling right in his wheelchair as if he were battling gale force winds, puffing on a recessed filter-tip Parliament, baggy cotton twill pants bunched around his hips as if they had been cinched tight by a drawstring, fly at half-mast. I supposed it was his idea of bravado, letting the world know there was zing left in his mind if nowhere else. Mary Martha Woods Thompson would fuss whenever she saw him so disassembled because she also knew that, as a matter of convenience, he rarely wore underwear. Heaven forbid that he should inadvertently expose himself while the Relief Society sisters from the church were visiting. "Mind the tiller," she would chide, shooting a disgusted look in the general direction of his crotch.

"Jeesh," he would say, feigning embarrassment. "Forgot to batten the hatch." Later he would say to me: "Don't know what the big diff is. She's seen it a million times, and in a lot better condition too."

To be honest, I hoped it would flop out. Once would be enough, and just long enough to resolve, once and for all, whether this particular member, when stripped of its neural connections, adjusts accordingly, like chicken torsos do after they have been separated from their heads—thrashing about like there's no tomorrow before entering into a permanent state of decomposition. My many encounters with ROT engendered a deep respect for paraplegics who choose to go on living. I don't know whether I would make that choice. Who knows? Speculation is one thing. Reality is always quite another. I have never been one to mess much with the course of nature.

ROT caught me eyeballing his crotch. "Jeesh, do I gotta do her up around you too? To hell with it!"

"Right, to hell with it," I said. "Don't bother. It's your move."

"Keep your shirt on, buster. I'm thinking."

"About what?"

"About that Miss James of yours. If she could write, don't you think she'd be out writing, not farting around diagramming sentences on a blackboard? You learn by doing. You've got the brain, now get a tough editor and write your guts out."

So that's all it took—brains, a good editor and guts. Everyone said I had the brains. "Too many for his own good," my aunt once said when my mother told her I was bored and disruptive in school. "He's got to realize that intellect isn't all there is. He may be smart, but he's got to control his impulses. He'll do practically anything—anything that appeals to him at the moment. He doesn't follow well, he's teachable up to a point and then he does what he pleases, dragging the other kids along with him."

I have been doing what I darn well pleased for about as long as my parents can remember, too. They laugh about it now but there was a time—I was barely three—they found me wandering alone through a new neighborhood a half mile away. "It was about then we decided there was nothing we could do," my father often recalled. "You were either going to survive or not. It was that simple."

What they did was impose rules they had no chance of enforcing. What I did was break them. What they did was mete out punishments. What I did was figure out how to lighten them or ignore them altogether. What they did was begin to focus more attention, place more hope in my eight younger siblings. What I did was turn to outsiders, peers and adults, for guidance and approval. This basic pattern was established very early in my life and, thereafter, it varied only in intensity.

At first Rebe was in disbelief, astonished by the story that unfolded.

At four I disappeared into a garage with 11-year-old Elaine George, my next door neighbor and sometimes babysitter, and her friend Sandy Morris. They lifted me onto an empty oil drum and pulled my trousers down around my ankles, taking my white cotton briefs with them. The cool air in the garage aroused Old George, which seemed to delight them. "Pretty big for a four year old," they said approvingly.

Elaine wanted Sandy to touch it. Sandy was nervous but eventually flicked it tentatively with the tip of one finger, then, gaining confidence with each flick and each reaction, she held it with her hand. "It's hard—like there's a bone inside of it. You got a bone inside there?"

For about seven or eight years thereafter, I believed my pelvis housed a retractable bone that would slide into place when the appropriate hydraulics were activated.

"Do ya think he could get it inside us?" Sandy asked.

"Candy bars are bigger and they fit in your mouth," I think I said.

"Not our mouths, dummy. Down there," Sandy said as she pointed to Elaine's midsection. Elaine lifted her dress to reveal her early-pubescent downy hair.

You can imagine the rest…except I had to pee badly, which was only exacerbated by the cool air and the ensuing action.

"You didn't?" Rebe said.

"Hell, I was only four."

"Some wet dream!"

"What was that?" Elaine screamed.

"I didn't mean to, honest," I cried. "I couldn't stop."

"Now I'm going to be pregnant," she wailed.

From that moment on until I was thirteen or so, when I experienced real orgasm for the first time, I thought this was how babies were made: the man sticks it in, cuts loose with a stream of pee that carries little miniature humans into the woman. She would cork up the hole with one of those cotton plugs until the baby was ready. How the poor kid extruded himself from that place remained a mystery to me for about as long as I subscribed to the aforementioned theory of procreation.

"Embellished?" Rebe asked.

"Not a whit!"

"Were you ashamed?"

"About peeing, yes. Otherwise, curious. The guilt came later."

"You're just mature beyond your years about these things," Mr. Jackson, the principal at Canyon Mills Elementary School, told me. The summer before my fourth grade year we moved from the city to the suburbs. It was a mixed blessing. I finally got a room of my own, but I had to prove myself all over again with the kids in the neighborhood and the teachers at school.

I rarely had trouble with the kids my own age. It was always with the guys two or three years older who assumed that I was a threat because I was tall, athletic, and notoriously smart—a deadly combination for any nine-year-old boy.

All summer long, fistfights raged up and down East Cumorah Road. Most involved me. I deliberately provoked very few. I was the new kid, outspoken and arrogant: in short, an irresistible target. Surviving the summer with a few impressive victories of my own, I assumed my enemies would become friends. That was the pattern in the city. As it turned out, suburban feuds were more like those between the Palestinians and the Israelis: the battles I fought that inaugural summer, particularly the ones I won, sowed seeds of hate and resentment that lasted through high school. For all I know, they would have endured a lifetime had I not abandoned Zion for Sodom-on-the-Hudson, and had not the majority of my most persistent antagonists ended up in jail for crimes ranging from car theft to assault and battery. Three were housed in institutions for delinquents before they were out of the eighth grade, one ended up dead, killed in a car wreck—with two state troopers and two other boys—as they were returning to the institution they had escaped a week earlier. My young friend grabbed the steering wheel of the car, which was speeding along the interstate, and abruptly nosed it into a deep barrow pit.

"You recount it so matter-of-factly, almost coldly," Rebe said.

I was neither surprised nor horrified by these misfortunes. At the time, such things seemed quite ordinary. At twelve, I saw a boy knifed in a corridor at school; daily, toughs extorted protection money from less aggressive children; nightly they battled it out with pipes and chains; and on occasion girls would emerge from brawls, their blouses torn to shreds, their skirts in disarray, their budding parts bared for all to see.

"Salt Lake City? C'mon. Hell's Kitchen, Flatbush, the Bronx maybe. This is good stuff. But Salt Lake?" Rebe said.

With the perspective of decades and two thousand miles, these events do seem downright remarkable. Remarkable that they were allowed to occur. Remarkable that I survived. Remarkable that any boy could be exposed to so much so early in the solidly middle class Canyon Mills, an unincorporated village appended to the Mormon Zion.

By the way, you won't see Canyon Mills on any map that I know of. Here's how I'd find it if its precise location hadn't been programmed into my internal homing system: follow the Jordan River north from Utah Lake, west of Provo, toward its outlet in the Dead Sea of Utah, the Great Salt Lake, west of Salt Lake City. As it meanders around the state penitentiary at Point of the Mountain, look east toward the rugged scarp of mountains—the Wasatch Range of the Rockies. Up ahead, locate the tallest peak; that would be Mt. Olympus. When you are more or less directly west and slightly north of its uppermost promontory, you will also be more or less directly west of Canyon Mills. Set the coordinates on your howitzer to reach the first steep ridge of foothills and let your missile fly. With a little luck it will land smack dab in the middle, more or less, of what used to be Old Man Jackson's office. Good luck: I wish someone had used these bearings and a cannon years and years ago.

With the perspective maturity provides, I better understand Old Jackson's observation. However, "informed beyond your years" would have been a more precise choice of words. Mature I was not. Yet.

On the opening day of school I fell instantly in love with a cute, flaxen-haired girl named Jill Stevens. The romance was pretty one-sided, as fourth grade crushes usually are. I thought about her constantly, dreamed about her at night, carved our initials into the underside of my school desk and memorized her telephone number, which I never used. I befriended a boy who lived near her home in the hope that I would just happen to see her when I visited him. She was either oblivious to all of this, or so painfully shy that she didn't know what to do about it. So I wrote a letter to her which, in a way, was returned to sender:

> *Dear Jill,*
>
> *You're over there at your desk doing your work and I am sitting here writing this letter to you because I finished my math already and if I don't do something quiet I'll get in trouble. You are the prettiest girl I have ever met, at least so far, and I think about you a lot. When I see you on the playground I want to run up to you and talk to you or maybe hold your hand or even kiss you if you would let me. I was really angry that you didn't get to be my partner for the dance festival. Someday I would like to come over to your house and talk and play. I'm a real nice guy except my hot temper sometimes gets me in trouble. I could really give you some good help with your math or something. I'm pretty good in school you know even though I get into dutch a lot. This school and Old Lady Jergens are really boring. I mean I don't have anything to do but sit around here dreaming about you, you know what I mean. So call me when you get this letter. I won't tell anyone if you don't.*
>
> *Love,*
>
> *Jeddy Russell*

I put it in an envelope and neatly printed her name and address and, in red ink, "Private." A few days later I was summoned to the principal's office, which is where Old Man Jackson told me I was "mature" beyond my years. "Whatever possessed you to write this?" he asked, waving my epistle in the air.

"I was bored," I said nervously.

"Well her mother didn't know what to make of it either. Jill is still playing with dolls. She doesn't know about boys and love and kissing. Mrs. Stevens was afraid your little letter would frighten Jill half to death. Luckily, Jill never got to read it. I agree with Mrs. Stevens one hundred percent-er-ee. I sure do. How do you feel about that?"

"Dunno. Guilty," I said.

◎ ◎ ◎

The battles that had raged in our neighborhood during the summer had shifted to the school. In short, I had to have been the most fought-over boy in the entire 50-year history of Canyon Mills Elementary. I won more than my share and, as a consequence, spent more than my share of time before the desk of the very intimidating Old Man Jackson.

"You're too smart to get suckered into fights," Mr. Jackson often told me. "Just walk away." He even said that when I laid into a sixth grader who had beat the daylights out of my younger brother. He offered no praise for defending my kin, as guileless a boy as there ever was, the kind who responds to a blow on one cheek by turning the other—good Christian lad that he was—directly toward the bully's incoming fist, which he did just as I arrived on the scene to give the much older boy the licking he deserved.

Unfortunately, Old Man Jackson didn't agree, which finally convinced me that I'd had quite enough of Canyon Mills Elementary, Old Man Jackson, Miss Jergens, the fights, and unlevel surface of this new suburban playing field. Not getting any support at home, I took matters into my own hands, as I often did. An older friend, Steve McCormack, a fifth grader I'd met delivering newspapers, agreed to take me to his school. He wasn't a particularly good student—in fact, I frequently did his math for him before we delivered the *Deseret News*—so he thought it would be great to have his tutor closer at hand.

"This here's Jeddy Russell," Steve said as he introduced me to Mr. Bonner, the principal at Mountainview Elementary. "He goes to Canyon Mills and he hates its guts and wants to go here with me. He wants to be in my class, but he's only a fourth grader, but he does my math real good and reads better'n anyone I know in fifth."

Naturally Mr. Bonner, who seemed like a much nicer man than Old Man Jackson, wanted to have a little private chat. But first, he had to make some phone calls. So I sat in the anteroom for about an hour or so before he motioned for me to join him inside his glassed-in office.

"Let's see, you live in the Canyon Mills district, right?"

"Yes, but I'm only a block away from Mountainview district line. And, Mountainview is as close to my home as Canyon Mills. And I'm bored, real bored. And the kids up there are jerks."

"How do you know you won't be bored here, or that the kids won't be jerks?"

"I just think I won't be bored. And, I know some of the kids in fifth grade already. I mean, you could put me in the fifth grade, couldn't you? I know I can do all the work."

"I'm sorry, but if you come here you'd be in the fourth grade—same as at Canyon Mills. Here's what I suggest. Stay here today. Tomorrow go back to Canyon Mills and talk things over with Mr. Jackson. He's not a bad guy, and he really likes you—he told me so himself. If you decide to leave Canyon Mills, come back here the next day with your records and we'll find a place for you—in the fourth grade."

Old Man Jackson was waiting for me the next morning when I arrived in Miss Jergens' classroom. "I'll see you in my office in three minutes," he said sternly. I put my coat away and sheepishly hung my head before Miss Jergens, who looked at me as though she had been deeply wounded.

"I'm sorry you don't like it here, but I hope you'll stay," she said kindly. "You'd better hurry down to Mr. Jackson's office; we can talk later."

I skulked into Jackson's office, sat in a chair and waited for him to finish a telephone conversation. He glared over the top of his eyeglasses while he talked. Finally, he finished the call and turned toward me.

"You know you really hurt us—Miss Jergens and me. How does that make you feel?"

"Guilty, very guilty," I said.

"We like you, yes we do. Sure we have our moments, but basically you're a nice kid." (Why are people always qualifying their statements about me? Even today people say: "You know, Jed, basically you're a really nice guy, but..." Sometimes I wish I were a real bastard; at least the descriptions would be more precise.) "I've been busting my hump over you all year long and here you go off and try to enroll at another school. By yourself! You don't talk to me, Miss Jergens, your parents... You just go off and do it on your own. How do you think that makes all of us feel?"

"I dunno," I said.

"Well, you may not know it, but I tell you I feel insulted. Personally insulted and hurt. You could have come in here and talked. We could have resolved it. Man to man. I know we could have, I do. In every way you could be the top student in the fourth grade if you want to. I've looked at your achievement test scores and they're all in the high nineties, which is about as good as you can do without being perfect. But to be the top student you've got to do more than just get high marks. You've got to be a good citizen. A leader. So what do you want to do? It's too late to do much this year—you were a new student and all. But next year we can liven things up a bit. I've got some ideas. So, is it go or stay?"

Being mature beyond my years, I recognized immediately that I had made my point. I didn't want to leave only to enter the fourth grade somewhere else. I was fed up being ignored, weary of always being the chief suspect whenever anything went wrong. It bothered the hell out of me that I didn't seem to get along with any of the kids at this new school, and that Mr. Jackson and Mrs. Stevens and probably Jill thought I was strange. Perhaps I was. Who knows? All I wanted to do was fit in. I had the sense that in his own fierce and weird way that was what Old Man Jackson wanted too.

"I'll stay. And I'm real sorry if I hurt your feelings," I said meekly. Whatever Old Man Jackson had in mind would probably be okay. The important thing was he was finally paying attention.

Jeddy Shapes Up

The Canyon Mills Little League summer baseball season that followed my first—but not last—serious encounter with Old Man Jackson was barely underway when I noticed that my left breast was swelling slightly. A mound like a glob of Jell-O seemed to have arisen directly behind the nipple. It was more embarrassing than scary or painful—I hadn't heard of cancer—so I didn't say anything to my parents. I assumed it had resulted from a line drive that had slammed into my chest during tryouts a few weeks earlier. Like sprained ankles always do, I figured the puffiness and tenderness would soon subside.

Instead, by mid-May it was obvious that I had acquired a rather prominent appendage. By July, it had grown to be about the same size and shape as an adolescent girl's breast, as I would discover a few years later. My little secret became public knowledge on the opening day of the swimming pool the following summer, where my friends discovered that Jedediah Pratt Russell was the owner of one rather nicely shaped and very perky wad of firmness that any girl would have been proud of. Thereafter they took to calling me such things as "one-tit" and "homo" and "morpho." As the teasing increased, I secreted my entire upper torso beneath loosely fitting T-shirts, even when swimming ("My skin is extra sensitive to the sun," I sheepishly demurred).

Finally, my father took me to the doctor, who said something vague like, "It's normal, just a natural result of maturation, he'll outgrow it soon enough." I wondered just exactly how many *normal* ten-year-old boys were walking around with one female breast attached to their chests? I told him what my friends were calling me, asked him what morpho meant. He just looked away, embarrassed, and told me to ignore the names, which I thought would be a whole lot easier to do if I understood what they were calling me.

Dave Richards, who lived next door, maintained homo and morpho described confused and conflicted creatures that were half boy and half girl, a horribly confounding condition I was sure God, in all His wisdom, would never let happen, especially to one of His chosen sons.

Getting no cogent explanations from friends, the physician or my father, I took matters into my own hands. Webster's revealed that morpho was synonymous with "form, shape and structure," and homo meant "the same" and was slang for homosexual.

So I turned to Roget's Thesaurus in hopes that I could find a synonym that might be more thoroughly defined in Webster's. And that's when I came across the description "Sexual Abnormality: homosexuality [I already had read that one]; homosexualism [ditto]; intersexuality; intersexualism; epicentism; epicenity; hermaphrodite." Maphro and morpho did sound a lot alike, so I looked it up: "a human being possessing sex organs of both the male and female gender."

God was dead. He may never have existed. Otherwise, there would be no hermaphrodites as defined by Webster's, and there certainly wouldn't be one living on East Cumorah Road in Canyon Mills, right under the noses of His anointed living prophet, seer and revelator and the twelve apostles.

As the left side of my chest expanded, so did the fable about the line drive. It was the only way to salvage what little remained of my honor and self-confidence as my maturing appendage became more and more difficult to conceal, even under loosely fitting shirts.

I stuck to the heroic cover story I'd concocted until Sarah, her feminist consciousness boiling over at our conventional relationship, blindsided me into a backhanded confession midway through our foreshortened marriage. "You need to be kinder, more sensitive and androgynous in your approach to life," she chided, not knowing that I had long ago learned the meaning of androgynous because it followed hermaphrodite in Roget's.

"Androgynous? Androgynous?" I steamed. "The last thing I want to be is *more* androgynous. I've had quite enough of androgyny already."

"I understand," she said sympathetically after I told her the straight story about how the scar under my left nipple came to be. "Now I understand why you try so hard to prove you're a real man." She didn't intend condescension.

Instantly, I regretted letting this little skeleton out of the closet, which is how I felt every time I opened up to her. It seemed she was more comfortable with her image of me—or her ever-changing expectations of what she wanted me to be—than, like the rest of the significants in my life before her, she was with coming to terms with the unvarnished, the honest-to-goodness Jedediah Pratt Russell.

"Follow that thought," Rebe said eagerly. "You may be getting somewhere."

This tenth summer of life was shaping up (forgive the play on words) into one helluvan interesting time. I proved my real manhood by batting .546 against pitchers mostly two years older and getting named as the starting third baseman on the all-star team. I could beat every neighborhood kid in basketball. Despite my tit, I was beginning to fit in; I had even learned to belch rather loudly, a talent that was far more prized on East Cumorah Road than good grades, a strong throwing arm, a big bat and, definitely, a single tit, however perky.

Despite the distraction on my chest, I thought if Old Man Jackson resolved the school issue, my life would finally be in order. I was pretty certain he would put me in Mr. Brown's class because he was said to be adept at handling boys, particularly good students with somewhat less than stellar behavior. Frankly, he seemed like kind of an odd duck to me, but I thought it would be interesting to have a man for a teacher for a change, no matter how weird. The dog days of August were upon us, school was but two weeks away, and I had not yet been summoned to the promised pre-school-year meeting with Old Man Jackson.

We were playing rounders on the ball diamond at the school about a week later. From the row of cars in the parking lot, I could tell that the teachers were already at work inside making last-minute preparations for the new year, raising the windows to rid the classrooms of the pungent odors of cleaning solvents, wax, and fresh paint, and reviewing their new students' records.

Jackson's second-floor office, perched about twenty yards behind the left field fence, gave him a bird's eye view of the ball field and the Oaks, a clump of scrub oak trees where boys often went to settle their differences. As I stood at home plate, I could see the big man lumbering around the room. As if warming up for his role as in loco deity, occasionally he would appear at the open window, scrutinize our ballgame like the Pope surveys the throngs in St. Peter's Square, then disappear.

I was at the plate when I saw him striding along the left field foul line toward us. As he neared third base, kids in the outfield edged in cautiously. During the school year, the sight of Old Man Jackson at the ball field was a sure sign that one or more of us was guilty of something pretty egregious and the rest were guilty by association. Getting too close to the offending party was an open invitation to get trapped in Jackson's dragnet of the schoolyard.

He smiled and waved as he walked directly toward the plate, where I nervously pawed the dirt with a bat. "Mr. Russell, may I have a word with you?" he called out loudly.

We met like players in a pickle between third and home. "It's high time we had our little talk," he said, squinting into the bright sun. "Why don't you drop by my office after the game." The other boys had gathered—near enough to eavesdrop, but far enough away to avoid getting involved.

"Looks like the game's ended," I said.

"Well, then come now," he said as he turned and began retracing his steps back toward the building. I trailed after him—a respectful ten feet or so behind like a well-trained sheepdog or obsequious valet. He was waiting, holding open a side door to the building, when I rounded the corner. "You look healthy—summer's been good to you," he said cheerily, extending his right hand. The slap of his leather soles on the hardwood floor reverberated down the hallways. My sneakers squeaked eerily as they gripped the fresh coat of wax. "I'll bet you hate the thought of school starting."

"Not really," I said. "Nothing much is going on—it's getting pretty boring." This was the truth of course, although it was not what I said to the boys. Through the window in his office, I could see them playing on the diamond below. Occasionally a few cast puzzled stares toward the building, as if they expected me to come hurtling through the panes at any second.

"Ah well, they decided to go on without you—this is more important. Right?" Jackson said.

"Sure."

"So we have some big things in store for you, planned for you." He paused. "Actually, it should be your plan, so let's just say we have some ideas for you to consider. Okay?"

"Okay," I said tentatively.

"Initially, I thought we would put you in Mr. Brown's class—he's pretty good with boys."

I must have sighed audibly.

"So I talked to him," Jackson said, his unblinking eyes fixed on mine. "He looked over your achievement test scores, your work from last year and so on. Well, Mr. Brown had a wonderful suggestion. Frankly, I don't know why I didn't think of it first, it's so obvious."

"What's that?" I said.

"It's simple, really. We think you would thrive in Mr. Woodburn's class."

"Woodburn? Sure," I said. Although I'd heard perfectly awful things about his disciplinary methods, he did have a reputation for turning out good students. I had heard he was one of those teachers who would talk about sex from time to time, which would be good, seeing's how no one else did. I was surprised to learn he had switched from sixth to fifth grade. For a moment, I wondered if the school had ordered the change so he could deal with me and my particular problems.

"You'll have to work extra hard; you'll get lots of homework."

"Okay. Who's teaching sixth in Mr. Woodburn's place?" I asked.

"No one. He's doing it…"

"How's he gonna teach both fifth and sixth?"

"Just sixth." Jackson paused. "You're in his class. You're being promoted to the sixth grade," he said cautiously. "You have the final say, of course."

"Me, in the sixth grade? I don't even know fractions," I said.

"Like I said, you'll have to work extra hard. You can do it if you want to. You'll be learning while the other kids are reviewing last year. You're mature enough and you're smart enough. You can handle it if you want to."

"Mature enough?" What did maturity have to do with it? True, my left breast was probably bigger than any girl's in the sixth grade, maybe even seventh. "So sure, why not," I said, suppressing an urge to pull up my T-shirt and show Jackson just how mature I really was.

"Your parents said you could make the final decision," he said.

"They did? Well then, sure I'm sure." God knows my parents would agree with practically anything recommended by a principal, or a bishop or stake president, or any other authority figure for that matter.

"Then it's set. You've got to promise me you won't say a word to anyone except your parents. On the first day, show up as you normally would. The class sheets will be hung on easels on the front lawn; your name will be on Mr. Woodburn's sheet. Someone is bound to notice it. Just act surprised."

"And if you think a double promotion is strange," I thought I would tell whatever kid excitedly informed me that my name was on Woodburn's roster, "let me show you strange. I'll bet you've never seen a brainy ten-year-old boy with a tit about as large as your big sister's?"

The informer would blush and say something like: "Nah, there ain't nuthin' like it around to see."

"Oh yeh?" I'd say, hiking my shirt up to my armpits. "Whatta you think about that nifty little unit?"

The kid would faint, maybe even have a heart attack, which would earn me a demotion back to fifth grade. In fact, they would probably deem me wholly unfit to attend Canyon Mills and to be a citizen of Zion, let alone to be one of God's chosen sons. I'd be shipped off to the circus, maybe back to the city and my old school.

Of course I did nothing of the kind on the first day of school. Larry Thomas, a sixth grader who played on my ball team, noticed my name right before his on Mr. Woodburn's class sheet. "Hey Jeddy, you're on Woodburn's list," he said, amused but curious.

"Really?" I said, feigning surprise as best I could.

"Big screwup," he said, smiling as if he either knew better or was delighted to have been the first to spot the error of some seemingly infallible authority figure.

"I guess," I said a little sheepishly. "Better find where I'm supposed to go." Larry tagged along as I dutifully played Mickey the Dunce and searched in vain for my name on the fifth grade rosters. Mrs. Ovard, a fifth grade teacher, was taken in by the charade and offered some singularly unhelpful advice: "You won't find your name there," she said, fairly beaming. "Congratulations, you're in Mr. Woodburn's sixth grade class. I was under the understanding Mr. Jackson told you all about it last week?"

Larry looked at me like he had just been hustled. "Wow, so that's what the meeting with Jackson was all about. You must be some brain," he said, before he ran off to tell the others.

Judging from the size of the crowd in front of the door to Mr. Woodburn's class, the sixth grade grapevine had worked rather well. I figured the only thing to do was to focus my eyes on some fixed point in eternity and walk toward the light, which I would have done had not Jill Stevens, still the love of my life, yelled out: "Hey Jeddy, the fifth grade classes are over here."

Blood rushed to my face. "I know," I said. "They've put me in sixth."

"You really are a smarty pants, just like my mother said," she called out, which of course provoked an instantaneous derisive response from my new classmates.

"Smarty pants, smarty pants, Jeddy is a smarty pants," they teased as I walked the gauntlet, searching in vain for a friendly face but getting only aggressive shoves from the boys—the testing had begun—while the girls eyed me as curiously as I did them. It was obvious they had changed dramatically over the summer—a couple of them had boobs almost as big as mine, which in a weird way confirmed Jackson's assertion that I was indeed mature enough to be in sixth grade.

Of Criminals, Queers, and Terrorists

As the newest and oddest member of Mr. Woodburn's sixth grade class, it is understandable that I stood out like a sore thumb, a victim, as it turned out, of a double promotion brought on as much by my streetwise cockiness as my academic promise. Both attributes began taking their leave on the first day of school.

Basic Bastard Woodburn—as the teacher came to be known—didn't help matters much. Minutes after the opening bell, he threatened: "I hope all you young men and women, especially you Mr. Russell, had a refreshing vacation because this is going to be one hell of a school year. If you survive the next nine months with me, you'll have it made for the rest of your lives. Why do I say that? Because I'm going to work your tender little bottoms into the ground."

The Basic Bastard sucked down a gulp of air and then grinned smugly at the new young smartass of the class—that would be me—before continuing.

"I look at teaching this way: Statistics say that about one in five of you will wind up in jail. That means in this class of thirty-eight, we have seven to eight potential felons, not including me, of course." Of course. "My job is to lower the percentages. And if I can't, come hell or high water"—his favorite aphorism—"I damn sure will have identified the seven by the time the year is over." He stared hard at me. It was unsettling, to say the least. I had never considered prison an option, and it disturbed me greatly to think that my newest mentor, Basic Bastard Woodburn, thought otherwise. What chance for the Celestial Kingdom.

History validated the general accuracy of Woodburn's dire forecast. He was not successful in lowering the percentages one whit, however, and at year's end he would not know precisely who would and who would not eventually run afoul of the criminal code of the State of Utah.

Steve Harris and Dan Kelly were both convicted of grand theft auto before they dropped out of high school. Tom White did time for drugs, before he straightened out his life; Craig Standing's frequent convictions were for petty theft and public intoxication (he repented and later became a Mormon bishop); and Denny Harmston and John Liddy chose more respectable routes to jail: they became prison guards (do guards count?). Later, Liddy became my brother-in-law and, like his father and mother before him, an operative for the Central Intelligence Agency.

The girls were a lot more imaginative. One, whose name won't be mentioned because she's now married to a very prominent Salt Lake lawyer (also a bishop in the Mormon Church), acquired an early affinity for the priesthood during her freshman and sophomore college years when she simultaneously *converted* several members of the Westminster College Parsons football team. She magnified her calling a few years later when she made the awful mistake of propositioning an apostle of the Mormon Church, whose name, oddly, was whited-out on the official police report of the incident. Her daring deeds got her excommunicated from the church, which led to her eventual reformation. (That's the desired outcome of an excommunication: first you confess your sins to God, then you seek forgiveness from those you've offended, then the Church disciplines "lovingly.") After her church membership was restored, she enrolled at Brigham Young University, earned a nursing degree with honors, and met and married a fine man from Mormon Pioneer stock, a direct descendant of one of the early apostles of the church. He is now a very big deal in Salt Lake City—member of the Alta Club, Chamber of Commerce, the Country Club, and...you get the picture.

Oh yes, they were married in the Salt Lake Temple, which is directly across the street from the ornate Hotel Utah. In fact the statue of the Angel Moroni atop the center spire of the Temple overlooks the hotel's Main Street entrance, the one my school chum used the night she sidled up to Elder Anonymous and, according to the official police report of the incident, whispered: "I could make you feel simply divine." This was a wholly inadequate come-on. Being one of God's anointed messengers, Elder Anonymous was accustomed to feeling moderately divine seven days a week.

"Whatever do you mean?" he asked. Right then and there, she should have realized this was not your run-of-Zion trick. She should have sprinted out of that hotel as fast as her white, patent leather "come hither" spiked heels would carry her, or said something clever like, "Excuse me, I have to use the facilities." But this girl could be excruciatingly thick at times and this was one of those painful moments. According to the police report, she just edged closer to Elder Anonymous and whispered seductively in his ear, "I'll show you what I mean," and with that she reached down and gave his testicles a very meaningful squeeze, which had to have scared the daylights out of him.

Here's some timely advice. If your lot in life is to go around accosting the private parts of God's anointed messengers, about the last place you'd want to do it is a place like the Hotel Utah, which was then held in trust for God by the Corporation of the President of the Church of Jesus Christ of Latter-day Saints. The Prophet and president of the corporation himself, David O. McKay, lived in an apartment on one of the upper floors. As a result, even back in relatively tranquil 1960-something the place was crawling with city and church detectives. All Elder Anonymous had to do was nod his head and a couple of hundred obsequious private eyes raced up and hauled her off to jail. It's a wonder she ever got bail.

Despite the brazen performance of my classmate, her act was subtler in its symbolism than one hatched by the great brain trust of the class.

Let me make it quite clear that I often wondered whether my friend's reformation and return to respectability was and is a subtle lesson for us all—to me, in particular—regardless of our religious affiliations. Think about it.

Susan Brindle—the Miss Goody Two Shoes and resident intellectual of the class—became the sixth member of the group to get a look at the world through forged-steel bars. It happened in the spring of 1970—about a year or so after the Hotel Utah incident and a week after the student massacre at Kent State University, which set off the most violent anti-war (Vietnam) activity Salt Lake City had ever witnessed. In one day, the front doors to a Utah National Guard armory near the university were blown off their hinges and two commodes at the Mormon Institute of Religion at the university were destroyed by an explosion. A few blocks away, the old College Bookstore, an Army barracks during World War II and recently campus home to the ROTC, was set alight and quickly burned to the ground. A few days later, Susan was arrested and accused of all three.

The evidence tying Susan to the crimes was quite flimsy—shards of Articles of Faith calling cards listing the 13 basic principles that define the similarities and differences between Mormonism and other Christian creeds, with Susan's name printed on front, were found at all three sites. Detectives surmised the cards had been used as packing for the bombs. The district attorney boldly asserted that Susan's beef was with both God and mammon, that it was likely that anyone who would make such inappropriate use of religious materials would likely attack religious institutions (commodes) and their secular affiliates. As the Utah National Guard devolved directly from the Nauvoo Legion in Illinois—led by the Prophet and General Joseph Smith, and its Utah successor, the Mormon Militia—it was, therefore, worthy of "affiliate" status. As was the University of Utah, founded in 1850 as the University of Deseret by Brigham Young and cohorts like my ancestor Orson Pratt. Because her widowed mother couldn't raise the punitively high $50,000 bail, Susan spent several weeks in jail awaiting trial.

Ultimately the jury saw it Susan's way. At trial, her attorney presented a police report of a burglary at her apartment two weeks before the bombings. On the list of reported stolen items were her personalized Articles of Faith cards. Frankly, I thought it quite odd indeed that anyone, even a devout Mormon, would report the theft of such cards. But, there it was, in black and white. Stranger things have happened in Salt Lake City, that's for sure.

Although she was acquitted, the experience seemed to radicalize Susan. Another classmate told me he had run into her a year later in Madison, Wisconsin. She seemed distant, frightened and uncharacteristically fierce. She refused to divulge her phone number and told him he would be killed if he told anyone where she was living.

So, if you're counting, by the early 1980s, when I quit tracking such things because I had troubles of my own to contend with, six of my classmates had spent time behind bars—one or two shy of Old Woodburn's forecast, unless the two prison guards count. However, if one accounts for *every* person in the classroom that September morning, including the teacher himself, Old Woodburn's projection was accurate.

What I didn't know until 1963 or thereabouts was that despite eight children and a wife, and a stellar record as a local church leader, Old Woodburn had an unhealthy sexual appetite for children, especially boys—happily not ones with one tit. When I discovered this, I wanted to barf. My despair quickly turned to disgust at my own naiveté and, as I told Rebe, "I was horrified that none of our parents picked up on it, although most adults of this generation were blind to such aberrations."

But, Lord have mercy, you should have heard the hullabaloo that erupted when Old Woodburn was busted in a public lavatory in Liberty Park for molesting an eight-year-old boy. It was matched only by the stink they raised two years later when Old Morton Kane, my junior high school basketball coach and guidance counselor, was discovered guiding his young charges in ways unbecoming a coach, a counselor, a father of eight. A bishop!

Woodburn's ultimate arrest years later was the coda on my sixth grade year, which was basically awful. If only I knew then what I know now!

Wasn't it enough of a burden for a guy to get a double promotion and a girl's boob, all at the same time? So why was Woodburn implying by his glare that I was destined for jail, and, in doing so, steering even more negative attention my way? I had enough for one day. And here Woodburn was, staring me down, again!

"Well now, Mr. Russell, you've got a mighty big year ahead of you, wouldn't you say?" he said.

"Yes sir, I think so sir," I answered nervously.

"Think? I know so," he sneered. "This old world, which you had by the tail, has gone and done caught up with you, Mr. Russell. If you don't run fast, real fast son, it's going to race by. But, come hell or high water, I'm going to beat you with a stick to make sure you run like you never had to run before. Get my drift, son?"

"What? I mean, yes sir," I said.

"Now class," he said, turning away, "just don't think because I'm leaning on young Mr. Russell here that the heat will be off you. It's just that young Mr. Russell here is, ah, yes, new to this class. But he's been around the block before (wink, wink) and I don't want him or you getting any wise ideas about what you can get away with in Old Man Woodburn's class. You will learn. You will study. Your work will be handed in on time. It will be neat. You will go to the latrine only during recess, except for those little emergencies." He smiled beneficently at Karen Hawkings, both of whose tits were at least as well developed as my left one. "Got that?" Heads nodded.

"Got that, Mr. Russell?" he barked, glaring again. I shrugged compliantly and nodded, annoyed that not only had Old Woodburn embarrassed Karen but he'd singled me out, again. "I'm going to make a little example of you, Mr. Russell—that is if you wouldn't mind?"

As if I had a choice, I thought to myself. I couldn't be any more of an example if you'd hoisted me up the flagpole, stark naked.

I nodded, weakly, submissively.

"I assume you have a voice that works from time to time, at least that's what I've been told," he said, grinning. The kids giggled. "So use it. When you are asked a question, stand up and speak up." I nodded agreeably, again.

"So stand up for heaven's sakes," he commanded. "In fact, stand up and come up here. Obviously you need a little coaching."

As I passed Susan Brindle's desk, the first one in the row, I felt nauseous, on the verge of losing my breakfast all over her. Woodburn grabbed my shoulders and spun me around so I faced the class.

"So, as I was saying, it is customary to use one's voice when responding…and that will require you to move your jaw like so." His meaty paws seized my chin, yanked my mouth open, then slammed it shut, again and again. Ad nauseam. I was too frightened and humiliated to barf. The kids laughed obligingly. "Do you understand now, Mr. Russell?" he asked.

Rebe read intently, silently except for the occasional sniffle.

"Am I stupid?" my mouth gushed before my brain could lock it shut. Woodburn's face reddened, his baseball mitt-sized hands seized the front of my shirt, narrowly missing the tit on my chest. The *educator* pressed me into the air like he was jerking dead weights in the gym, then hurled me the entire length of the room into the coat rack alcove. As this was late August, there weren't any coats hanging around to save me from the wall—just a zillion permanently installed metal hangers, a steel pipe, and thwack! My careening body sent the zillion hangers spinning around the pipe, which created a racket that was positively symphonic compared to the deadly thud my flesh and bones made as they encountered the immovable plaster-sheathed brick wall.

Woodburn hovered over me. "That will be the last time you'll talk like that in this classroom," he frothed, sputtering saliva on my face. He was right about that, of course, although I soon learned that a lot less than the slip of a flip lip could earn one a close encounter with the coat alcove and brick wall.

It was of some solace that before the school year ended practically everyone—save people like Susan Brindle—visited the coat rack involuntarily, or worse. Shy and rail-thin Mary Katherine Blumenstein—another newcomer to the class—was often forced to stand and sing the national anthem solo each morning and was routinely kept in from recess. She became increasingly pudgy and agitated from her daily public humiliations and from God knows whatever else went on when they were alone during recess.

Woodburn's taunting daily lectures about the predictable stirrings of pre-adolescence made everyone squirm self-consciously and no doubt aroused more than a few precocious "homework" sessions.

More overtly, he broke several laminated yardsticks over several healthy young bottoms ("Yes, a clear tell-tale," Rebe offered, shaking her head sadly), slapped a few around for good measure ("another harbinger"), and once came precariously close to pushing me down the school's main staircase ("Again presaging the despoiler of youth and innocence he became, and was, as it turned out," Rebe said, angry, disgusted).

Years later I concluded that Woodburn intended only smug, cruel mockery when he selected Mary Katherine to play the Virgin Mary and me to be one of the Three Wise Men in the Christmas pageant. Later, I learned from Mary Katherine herself that while the other children were at recess, the Basic Bastard had stripped her of her innocence right there in the classroom—months before he asked her to take on the role of the Blessed Virgin.

That I continued to unwittingly provoke terrifying encounters with the teacher was proof positive that I was not at all wise. And the perky little breast erupting on my chest bore sure witness to the fact that neither was I a real man.

On the playground, I was routinely forced to defend myself, like I had when we first moved to Canyon Mills. Soon the word got around that I had inexplicably become a rather reluctant combatant. Even the weaklings seemed to know they could now take a few pops at me without fear of retaliation. I was determined not to return to my old fighting ways—I had enough problems. So like the Chinese hordes, they kept coming at me, even John Liddy, a guy I happened to like a lot.

A gang of kids with Liddy in the center stood around the flagpole when I emerged from the school building late one afternoon in the early fall.

"Liddy wants to see you in the Oaks. Now," Dennis Harmston ordered. I looked at Liddy, shrugged my shoulders and headed for the preferred battleground, even though it was plainly visible to anyone who happened to be looking out of Old Man Jackson's office window.

Reaching the Oaks, Harmston announced: "The rules are: No hitting in the face. Got it Russell?" The mob of boys formed a tight ring around us.

"OK. But if he hits in the face first, I'll return the favor," I countered.

"Don't worry, he won't touch your pretty mug."

To this day, I don't know why I agreed to such a stupid restriction. I was a terrible wrestler and Liddy was large enough to absorb body blows, unless I got lucky and knocked the wind out of him.

We stalked around for a while, both of us reluctant to strike the first blow because neither of us wanted to be accused of starting the fight. Harmston quietly knelt down behind me while another boy gave me a backward shove. Liddy sprang, tearing my shirt, quickly locked his lanky left arm around my head, then bashed me on the side of the head with his right ("It wasn't your face," he would remind me years later, after we had become friends and, eventually, brothers-in-law).

As no one could see the blow except my neighbor Dave Swenson, they all were a little startled when I slugged Liddy squarely on the mouth and nose, which caused blood to spurt all over creation. Harmston stopped the fight immediately, dabbed at Liddy's nose with an old sock, while Swenson tried to convince the angry mob that I had been hit first.

Like a corner man long on enthusiasm but short on judgment, Harmston pushed Liddy back into the ring. He was mad as all hell, blinded by rage, swinging wildly, which surprised me a little. He took a shot at my head. I parried the blow, stepped back, and unleashed a fist that caused his nose to erupt once more.

"You wouldn't have beat him if he hadn't hit you by accident," Harmston said. "He'll get you another time."

There was never to be another time. The next day we bumped into each other before school. "Sorry about your nose," I said.

"Sorry about the shirt," he said. "I wish I hadn't hit you, because I think I could have won if we'd just wrestled, just like Harmston said."

"You're right," I said as it dawned on me that Old Liddy hadn't been mad at me at all. He had something to prove to the others. Perhaps to himself too. Kicking my butt was essential to getting whatever it was that he needed from them. I felt horrible for letting him down. Sometimes it pays to be a loser.

Outside Consultations

Although Rebe had become a regular at the Russell household almost immediately—a thoughtful listener, perceptive commentator—in May she balked when I offered a duplicate set of house and car keys. Frankly, it was a fairly lame symbolic gesture, as I rarely locked the house and the key to the car was always in the ignition.

In October, she cautiously asked to move in a few pieces of her furniture. "I need some familiar objects to hang on to," she explained. But I objected, mildly, because I thought it might upset Janie and Elli. Rebe said she understood. "For now."

While I welcomed her presence, her arrivals and departures were unpredictable, which played havoc with my work rhythms that had become erratic on their own. I'd put the book on hold officially (Wren was concerned, but patient) and had accepted a number of distracting freelance writing and editing assignments from *People.*

Rebe would slip over for lunch, sun herself on the deck, and then depart without so much as a hello, even if she was certain I was at work inside. Invariably, she'd leave something tantalizing behind—pantyhose and bras were her favorites—to tease, to let me know what I had missed…was missing.

Returning home from the city late at night, I'd often find evidence of her everywhere, as if she had sufficient foreknowledge of my erratic work schedule to adjust her comings and goings accordingly. The laundry would be done and folded, fresh sheets on the bed, pasta salads in the refrigerator, plants watered and debrided. Around the first of each month, she'd leave me a stack of checks, needing only a signature, attached to remittance envelopes stamped and ready to mail. For the first time in my life I knew precisely what was in the bank, or, as the case was more often than not, what was not. She also made time to play editor, making typographical and spelling corrections as well as syntax suggestions: "ROS" she noted in margins near one particularly long and winding and horribly overwritten sentence.

"Stylistic. Like JD Salinger," I argued.

"I hated *Catcher*," she said.

"But you have to admit, it was pretty successful," I said, recalling how, as a 15-year-old, *Catcher in the Rye* inspired me. I've read better books since but none moved and shook and influenced me so.

"Success? What's success? Turning yourself into a hermit is success? Success is being part of the world, contributing. Day after day. Success is getting up off the floor after someone has knocked you on your keister," Rebe snorted.

The spring had been unusually warm, which only made it all the more annoying (although I appreciated the income) that I was back to traveling and cranking out celebrity profiles for *People*. Rebe reminded me of what I was missing each time I called home. More often than not she was there, doing what she always did, and increasingly ensuring that the children's visitation schedule was not disrupted, even though it required her to devote precious weekends to the care and feeding of Janie and Elli.

It was a cruel trick of nature that no sooner had I walked in the door after a two-week sojourn in California that one of those dreadful late May nor'easter-type downpours broke out. The wind drove the rain horizontally into the side of the house and kicked up whitecaps on the well-protected lagoon. The sound had to be roiling in six-foot breakers.

Got to tell Elli about this, I was thinking. Warn him to be cautious when out sailing—keep as sharp an eye on the sky as you do on power boats; ply the waters near the Connecticut shoreline...don't drift across the sound to Long Island, where they'd already sighted great whites off Port Jeff...by July they'd be trolling around Bermuda Lagoon.

The doorbell rang. I hadn't even gotten my coat off. No one with any sense would be out on a night like this except, perhaps, those infernally persistent Jehovah's Witnesses. They'd been by several times while I'd been gone, left new tracts, inscribed with urgent, handwritten messages: "The world is careening to its close. Will you be numbered among the elect when Jehovah returns?" I wasn't in the mood for a debate. They'd already recruited way more than the allotted 144,000. I wanted to find Rebe, wherever she was; warn Elli about the whitecaps and sharks; get the lowdown on whatever smarmy pubescent was after my beautiful Janie.

She was so womanly—bright, too—beautiful and wise beyond her sixteen years.

A few weeks earlier Sarah had manipulated the children's activities so Janie and I could spend an entire weekend alone. I had protested at first, but Sarah insisted. "She needs focused time with you…*alone*."

After a meandering and elusive discussion about boys and school—one that more or less convinced me she was more interested in the latter—Janie asked about the novel. "Is it really going to be about the family?"

"Loosely—all fiction is—my way of working things out and making some money too," I said evasively.

"You seem so lonely," she said abruptly. "So isolated. Isn't it time to find someone else? What about Rebe?"

"Rebe? I have you and Elli. There's no rush. No need, yet."

"But we won't be around for long. College is just a few years away and after that, who knows," she said.

"You could always live here while you got started…"

"Dad, did you move in with your parents after college? Heck no. You were married with a couple of kids."

"And that's when the trouble started," I said.

"I knew it. You just wish I weren't here, don't you? You resent the fact that I came along before you and Mom got to know each other. I'm so sorry I caused the divorce, but what could I do? I didn't have any choice about when I came into the world. You guys did." I thought she was about to cry, but she didn't.

"You didn't cause the divorce," I said, taking her in my arms. "If anything, you glued us together. Now, I just feel like you're slipping away before I get a chance to really know you, just like your mother."

"You still love her, even after what she did to you?"

"Once you love someone—once I do—it's hard to stop. You just don't shut it off like you do a water faucet. Bang. Love her? Yes, but it's changed, is changing. But you, you're a different story. Sometimes I feel like you're sand in my hands. No matter how much I try to contain you, grain by grain you trickle out through my fingers."

"That's life," Janie said matter-of-factly. "That's life."

The doorbell rang again. I'd show those fanatics: tonight I'd out-stubborn them. I dialed Sarah's number. Busy. The doorbell rang again. I dialed again. Busy. I checked Penny's number in Cincinnati. Busy. Damn it. Both of them knew the rules. The divorce agreement clearly stated that I was to have free and unhampered phone access to the children at all reasonable hours of the day and night. It was past seven p.m.—the time when I always called the kids—and the phone's busy. You are in contempt of court, damnit. Both of you, Sarah Thompson Russell and Penelope Thompson Packer. I dialed the operator. "I've been trying to dial a Westport number for a couple hours and can't get through. Could you check for trouble on the line?"

"Is this an emergency?" the operator asked.

"No. But they were expecting my call at this hour. Maybe the phone's been knocked out by the storm. Perhaps there's trouble…it's my damned wife and kids, you know?"

"I see, but you don't have to swear about it," she said. She returned less than a minute later. "I'm sorry, but there is conversation on the line."

"Well, tell them to get the hell off," I snapped.

"I can't do that," the operator said.

"Tell them I'll see them in court," I said, banging the phone down.

There was more rapping on the door. And yelling. "Open up the damned door, Jeddy Russell. I know you're in there," a familiar female voice bellowed. Clearly this was no J-Dub proselytizer. I opened the door.

Wet, stringy black hair and darkness obscured her face. Or, perhaps I was distracted by the sight of breasts, plainly visible beneath a drenched, now transparent tan cotton blouse.

Rebe shouted, "Why didn't you open the blanking door? I've been standing out there for a frigging half hour at least."

"Didn't know it was locked. Thought you were the JWs," I said, embarrassed.

"Bet I could convert you tonight," she said, pulling her blouse tight and making plain the effects of the cool rain on her body.

"And, I was talking on the phone."

"To another world, I suppose," she said.

"Actually, to the busy signal."

"Sarah's, right! Why don't you just get a private line for the kids? How many years has it been? Two? Three. Sometimes, Jeddy, you're just way beige."

"Way beige?"

"As in bland, boring, dumb."

"Dumb?"

"Hardly. It's a real bummer…watching you willingly, eagerly drag yourself through the mud day after day. Know what I mean?"

"No. But I'm very sorry I kept you out in the rain."

"Almost excusable compared to the other things you do, like talking to the busy signal, that…forget it. Do you have a warm towel and some dry clothes for this missionary?"

I fetched a clean cotton sweat suit, returned to the bathroom where Rebe had stripped and was toweling off. I couldn't help but notice how the combination of cool air and water and the abrasive terry cloth buffed fresh color and radiance into her skin, the afterglow of something more intimate than rain.

"We have to talk, serious."

"About what?" I said, worried that the somber tone of her voice spelled trouble.

"Life. The book. Old George. And the clap. And closing circles. About knowing when to pull out. When to jump in. All of it. I've been reading the book—the latest chapters. Why didn't you show them to me?" she said, not taking a breath.

Guardedly I answered: "They're only drafts, I wasn't ready…I was away a lot too. I wanted to be around to explain. But hey, I'm here now, an open book: cue me and I'll spill my guts all over the carpet. But do me a favor. When I'm through, please mop up and turn out the lights."

"Give the *poor me* a rest—I've read enough of it. Interesting, surprising—sad up to a point. Now if you'll open a bottle of wine, I'll get dressed and then we can talk…seriously."

I assumed the wine and the preliminary catch-up chit chat—we hadn't seen each other for a couple of weeks—might distract her from the pre-announced mission: talking seriously. I was primed, eager for closeness…perhaps she would stay the night for a change, press her softness against my back, remind me that she was not safely-too-young. ("What's fourteen years in an eternity?" a devout Mormon friend opined after he sensed my concerns about her age. It was just the kind of endorsement I needed to purge guilt from my mind and get on with life and Rebe.)

"I just don't get it. Get you. Get the book. Get anything," she said abruptly, taking a long swallow of wine.

"Not getting it, huh? Well that could be resolved, but I thought you wanted to talk," I joked.

"Cut it out, Jed. No fooling tonight. It's time to be serious for once in your life, which I sense is at a crossroads. You're either going to continue spilling your brains out on the carpet, as you put it, or you're gonna plug the hole."

"You charging for this?"

"Lord willing, I'd prefer to take it out in trade." She smiled.

"Aha, you want me to be your hooker."

"'Lord willing' were the operative words. But why not be my hooker—you've been one for practically everyone else," she said seriously, adding quickly, "I didn't mean it quite that way, Jed. Honest."

"Apt analogy. All my life I've been screwed by everyone," I said.

"Not right. You are not some direct object, or dangling participle," she snapped, her voice rising.

"My, my: a literate nurse."

"You condescending sunnuvabitch. If you want, I'll go now. I'll walk right out of your life. Right out into that awful storm. But before I exit stage left let me tell you this: A hooker doesn't just get screwed. He invites it...for a price. It's only when he doesn't get the customary fee that he feels cheated. All your life you've been asking people—except me—to screw you. And they did and that was fine so long as they paid the price and you maintained control. Then someone came along who eventually freed herself from your obtuse rules, demands and attached strings. She was not your ordinary trick either. She was your sugar mama. She gave so much that you probably didn't need to walk the streets again. In fact she gave so much that her own bank account ran dry...at precisely the time you were substantially overdrawn, counting on her spectacularly large and regular deposits."

"Are you finished?" I said, astonished at the diatribe.

"Oh no...I'm just getting started. Your big trick misjudged you. She assumed that along the way you'd stop charging her. You couldn't because you couldn't...you were addicted...the more you got the more you craved."

"If you're alluding to Sarah, you don't know what the hell you're talking about. I gave and gave," I said. "And what the hell do you know of marriage at the ripe old age of twenty-three?"

"Twenty-four. I'm not talking about love, Jed. Lord knows Sarah loved you mountains. But you didn't want love from her, you wanted approval: approval for what you were, for what you had accomplished. Fair enough. Then you made some very bad decisions. You screwed up. And you wanted her approval for that too. For a while she played along, supportive, loyal, hoping that you'd pull out of it, right things. But you ignored the help that was offered, imagined that nothing was wrong. Finally, she realized she's an accomplice at best, possibly an enabler: your loyalty to her was borne of her long suffering, her patience, her indulgences. But, a sucker she's not…not for long. So for her good…and yours…she throws you out and you feel screwed. And, damnit, you're doing it again…with me… and I'm a bigger sucker than she was. But I can't be a sucker for hookers anymore."

While I sat in stunned silence at Rebe's dramatic, if confusing, outburst, she got up, stripped off the clothes I'd given her and stalked out of the house into the rain. The reverberations of the door slamming brought me to my senses and I dashed after her, out into the storm, which had turned the driveway into a waterway capable of floating a rubber raft. Rebe's car was parked behind mine, keys in the ignition but empty. I called her name as I ran to the road, hoping to catch sight of her in the streetlights. She was nowhere to be found. Or she did not want to be found.

I scoured the neighborhood, and then turned back toward the house, cutting through the yards lining the lagoon that had risen so high the floating docks were nearly level with the lawns. I could hear the halyards slapping the masts of sailboats and, in the distance, I could see Elli's little Sunfish bobbing up and down in the turbulent water, about to break its line. A vertical bolt of lightning in the distance backlit the dock and brought into sharp focus a body, lying face up into the driving warm rain, so starkly visible that I feared surely the neighbors across the lagoon could have seen every single curve and goosebump.

"Lovely night we're having, isn't it Mr. Russell," she said as I stared. "Made me want to rip off my clothes and be pummeled by the elements."

"Terrific idea," I said as I tore off my clothes and lay down beside her.

"Like baptism by immersion. The rain just washes off everything that's gone wrong with you into the lagoon. Ker-plop. Makes you feel squeaky clean, virginal, like you don't know from hooking."

"Right," I said, not at all sure where she was heading, fearful I'd set her off again. I caught my breath. "That was quite the performance in there."

"Performance?" she said. "I meant every word. I just can't stand to see people screwing themselves to death, especially people I care about—okay, love. I've seen it happen too often…not so long ago to me, nearly. Now, I feel like it could be happening again."

"Wait a minute. I don't get it. I'm the one here with the brains gushing out on the deck, the one with the participles dangling, playing the two-bit whore."

"I'm right down there with you Mr. Russell. But you don't see it or admit it because you're so caught up seeking my approval. I know who you are. I know you know who I am."

"Hmm." I didn't know quite what to say.

"So here it is. I confess. I am indeed the daughter of the man who lured your wife away. You think you're still in love with the woman who left you for my father, which destroyed my mother. And, now he's dying. Everything I have loved or do love is dying. Everywhere I look there is carnage; it's all around me. Carnage from Sarah. Can you imagine how much I hate her and I don't even know her?"

Rebe breathed deeply before continuing. I took her hand. She shook it off.

"You don't know hate. When I learned about my father and your wife, I was devastated. I felt guilty, like I'd caused it somehow, like I should do something about it. I mean there I was reading your psychological profile and progress reports, which told me that the woman who screwed you over is also screwing over my very own father?"

"That's how you found out...from reading transcripts of my sessions with Rosenbaum?" She nodded. "How awful," I said.

"Truly...I could see him falling into the same approval bind: craving the adulation he got from Sarah; magnifying her worth, her talents way beyond reality; cowed by her in perverse and destructive ways. You wouldn't have to be an inventive writer to put a clever ending on this story.

"The bastard...the bastard who convinced me, begged me to save myself for my future husband...while he's out making a raving fool of himself and, in the process, destroying everything that is sacred and meaningful—his wife, our family, his lover's family. All the while he's praising me—boasting, really—saying embarrassing things to his friends, like he's the father of the only twenty-two-year-old virgin in Westport, perhaps all of Fairfield County."

"Probably were," I said. "So'd you talk to Quack Quack about it?"

"Yes..."

"Must have been rich," I teased.

"Rich? Embarrassing is more like it. Dr. Rosenbaum caught me reading your files after work one evening. We had a long talk about it...told me to take some time off, and sent me to a medical convention in Boston. I was supposed to take notes on presentations about the psychological problems of cancer patients. Mostly I was supposed to have a good time and get away."

"A kind and generous man, Rosenbaum," I said.

"Exceptional. Very kind. Except, what I wanted most was to lose it. Finally. I was angry. Determined. And, I wanted it to be with someone very experienced, interesting—older, like you: old, but not too old."

"A medical convention was probably the perfect place to find a bunch of not-too-old farts like me."

"Custom made," she said. "There was the doctor—a hotshot from out west, an expert in prostate cancer—who kept staring at me during his presentation. Afterward, he caught up with me at a reception and he invited me out for dinner and drinks. One thing led to another and bang, I'm no longer a virgin. I was so drunk I don't remember much about it except he didn't realize I was a virgin. He saw blood on the sheets the next morning and said, 'Oh, oh. Looks like it's that time of the month again.'"

"Musta been a urologist," I teased, trying to lighten the mood.

Rebe plowed ahead like a woman possessed. "He took me to a party the next night…small party, all docs who got together every year with whatever women were available—mostly locals brought in for the evening, if you get my meaning. Soon a couple of girls were dancing naked around the room. We were all pretty tight. My doc, he just sorta disappeared. Another guy started chatting me up, then pawing at me and pretty soon we were lying on the floor doing it, which would have been embarrassing except everyone else was just as distracted."

I groaned an agonized groan.

"So we're lying there, half crocked and half asleep. He leaves for the bathroom…returns a few minutes later and it starts all over…only this time it feels very different…I realize it's another guy. I'm shocked. But I say to myself, what the hell. You wanted to get experienced and things are off to a flying start."

"Embarrassing, humiliating," I offered lamely.

"Now, yes. Then, not really. It was dark. I was getting what I wanted. I was both the user and the usee. So we did it. A few hours later my doc came back and we did it again…until he asked me to do what I was not ready to do under the circumstances…"

"Let me guess what. Did you see him again?"

"Saw him, but it was like he didn't want to know me. In fact, that's when I began thinking seriously about you…actually I had thought about using you before as a way to get even with my father and Sarah…the doctor got me thinking differently about you," she said.

"How so?"

"Earlier, he had asked me if I had a boyfriend. I didn't want to seem weird, so I said I did. I said he was a writer, but not a very famous one yet. The doctor wanted to know the writer's name…so I used yours."

"Judas Priest," I groaned.

"Well…he said he'd once treated a magazine writer by the name of Russell—a strange guy who thought he could catch gonorrhea from banisters in Grand Central. I didn't think much about it then because I was more intrigued by the fact that I had told him that you and I were lovers," she said. "After I got home I wanted to let you know, but you didn't seem interested…so I sort of stalked you, in my own way. I read all your stuff… from *Time, Life, People,* your short stories in the Westport Library. I'd visit your house when I knew you weren't home; well, I'd walk around the yard, down to the dock, look in your windows wondering all the while what it would be like living with you. I wanted you in the worst way. In every way. For all the wrong reasons. Now, for all the right ones."

"So you know the whole of me," I said. "You've read my short stories, my psychological records, the book, there's nothing else…"

"Reading the book, I began wondering if your Dr. Hartung is the same guy I was with in Boston?"

"What the hell would a urologist be doing at a seminar on the psychological impact of cancer?" I asked.

"Talking about impotence caused by prostate surgery."

"Hartung would remember me. He tried to charge me for the follow-up visits I never made…threatened to sue. But, he's at the Cincinnati Clinic, not at some hospital out west," I said.

"Cincinnati is out west from here," she said.

"So is New Jersey. But they're not 'out west,' which refers to the expanse of America bisected by the Rocky Mountains."

"To a Utahn, perhaps. But not necessarily to a New Yorker. If it was Hartung, I'm lucky I didn't catch something awful from him."

"Or from the other half dozen…"

"For what it's worth, it was a waste."

"It always is," I said.

She eyed me warily.

"Enough true confessions," I said. "Let's go inside. Suddenly I'm very cold."

"I was afraid of that…but not before I finish, and I'm almost there." She hesitated, lifted her face toward the sky, letting rain wash the tears away. And, as if trying to invoke the powers of heaven, she said, "I want to know you like Sarah did, only more. And, I want you to know me like you knew her, only more. I've done all the homework I can do. I'm not safely-too-young any more than you're safely-too-old. I want to know where those daydreams of yours take you...and go with you, if you'll let me. Straight talk, no palaver or angle-playing or word constructs that shade what's in your soul. That's what was wrong with you and Sarah—you kept her on the skin of your soul. You didn't allow her inside until it was way too late. Let me penetrate Jed Russell. Let me love all of him, whatever and wherever he is."

It was a new odd thing for me. This lover knew my mind, but not my body. Usually it worked the other way around like it had—then hadn't—with Sarah. But, now this safely too young Rebe was anything but safely too young. And I had never been safely too old.

The Weight of Being

Within a week, Rebe and I had settled into a very married-like routine: chatting over coffee in the morning, interrupting our work to make plans for the evening, snuggling on the living room sofa while we watched television, dissecting my latest addition to the book well into the night. Apart from my years with Sarah, it was the most intimate I'd ever lived with a woman. It was nice, although I knew if it continued—never mind our separate bedrooms and the fact that Rebe maintained an apartment several miles away—it would kill any chance for a reconciliation with Sarah.

"This is the way we should be living permanently," she said to me one Saturday a few weeks after the dockside encounter.

"It certainly has its advantages," I said, startled that Rebe would press marriage this early, perplexed that the notion of a second marriage could seem so enticing and threatening all at the same time.

"No disadvantages that I can see," she said.

"Just kids," I said.

"You don't want more children? I'm surprised."

"Janie and Elli..."

"That disadvantage is only in your mind," she said.

"Really? Are you really ready to be a part-time mommy to children who are closer to your age than you are to mine?" I worried that as Elli matured, he may begin to fantasize about Rebe like I had about my young high school choir teacher.

"There you go again, shifting your hang-ups onto someone else's shoulders. Living with you, whatever the arrangement, is no problem for me, but is it one for you? Or Sarah?" Rebe searched my face for a reaction. "You're still holding out hope. Unrealistic hope if you ask me. I can deal with it for now. In fact in a perverse way it's almost touching—reassuring to know you won't flee to Tahiti with some nubile young thing when I'm seven months pregnant."

I was thinking mostly about the golf tournament on the television when Rebe yelped: "Jeezuz, Jed, why us?"

"What'd you expect? You've become an integral part of the story," I said.

"Maybe a passing reference or something, but a verbatim report? Did you have a video tape going or something?"

"All from memory," I said.

"Is it photographic or something?" Rebe asked.

"Just well trained. Journalists soon learn that people aren't as concerned about word-for-word accuracy as they were about getting the context, meaning and intent right."

"Same thing, isn't it?"

"Not at all. I interviewed Chris Evert…left the notebooks on a plane… I couldn't call her up and tell her we had to do the interview again, so I quoted her as best as I could remember. After the story was published, she called; said she had never ever been quoted more accurately. I mean how many times have you read quotes that were absolute garbledy-gook, or used out of context to support a flimsy point?"

"Often," she said.

"That's my point. My notes are limited to key words that will trigger my recall of what was said. The rest is from memory…and double-checking facts."

Rebe resumed reading, re-reading, actually. She had finished a third glass of wine before she finally put the manuscript down. "I don't know what to make of it," she said.

"It isn't obvious?" I said.

"So obvious that it's outrageous. Obvious that you've done an excellent job generating a ton of sympathy for Jed Russell, but it's just too unbelievable. It's such fantastic fantasy—way too far beyond the bizarre reality of your life; readers will sense it. Your lapses into fantasy aren't subtle at all—they seem set-up, allegorical," she said.

"Allegorical?" I said.

"Okay, I'll give you a few," she said. "Who would ever think that a young boy in Salt Lake City, of all places, would have intercourse with two neighborhood girls at four, grow a woman's breast at ten, and get a child-beating, pedophile teacher at eleven. Nice Zion allegory. But, really,

Salt Lake City isn't exactly the Southeast Bronx yet," she said. "No one will believe it, me included. I get the allegory...it's interesting, zany, but it goes too far."

"Precisely," I said. "It's outrageous, it's zany, and it goes too far. It's all of those things. It is also very true," I said.

"Don't play me for a sucker," she said. "I know you too well. So okay, maybe the double promotion and screwing the neighbor girls. But the tit thing, the double promotion and the pedophile teacher all at the same time—that's where you cross the line. I mean, where did you ever come up with that tit idea?"

"Where?" I raised the tails of my shirt armpit-high. "You see that quarter-moon-shaped scar under my left breast," I said.

"What scar? There's nothing there at all," she said. "Have you become so delusional that you now expect me to see what you want me to see too?"

"Compare the right side to the left. The left is slightly sunken...tissue and muscle were removed."

"Can't feel much of a difference." Her fingers probed my chest. Her eyes widened, alarmed as her fingers brushed the scar ridge, explored its full semi-circular length. "Holy shit," she gasped.

"Simple mastectomy, snip, snip, slice, slice and my precious old tit was ready for the hospital incinerator," I said.

"Odd that Rosenbaum wouldn't note this in the records."

"Hadn't gotten round to telling him..."

"Two years in analysis and you hadn't...?"

"Wasn't that big a deal," I said.

"Naw, I guess it's not. Your typical pubescent boy grows a girl's breast—an anticipated byproduct of raging testosterone," she said.

"Typical? Anticipated? Not hardly," I said.

"That's the point," she said. "It's an absolutely essential, critical fact. So is the pedophile teacher, which you also kept from Dr. Rosenbaum. It's a small wonder that you're not absolutely crazy."

"That occurred to me after I wrote it down. Until then, I hadn't given it much thought. As I wrote, I began to realize a lot was there that I hadn't acknowledged...hadn't acknowledged for a long, long time. Perhaps denied altogether. A repressed, obliterated history."

"Adding up to what?"

"That I was crazy and weird. Or about to be. A believer, but a phony one; a sinner, defiled, way out of step with Canyon Mills, my parents, friends, siblings," I said. "It was as if I'd stumbled onto the root cause of my inability to fit in."

"Fitting in? Not something I'd say you fret over. *Time* for instance."

"*Time*'s an exception…tolerant place. But look at the rest of the record: no long-term friends, loosely tethered Mormonism, practically zero connection to college and high school classmates, distant with family; I mean there are nine of us and living parents to boot. Have you met them? Do they write? Do I? Do they call? Do I? Rarely."

"Perhaps you're one of those people who were born in the wrong place and knew it right away? Your stuff suggests that…"

"The right place would be…?"

"However, it's demonstrably false that the breast you grew, the early exposure to, frankly, abusive sex, the desire to fit in and please others, and so on evolved into adult instability. You survived, thrived. Those challenges made you stronger, independent, a survivor. If you don't fit in now it's because you will it. Ultimately, becoming like everyone—fitting in—scares the hell out of you because you're afraid of getting lost in the crowd. But it's you, the real you!"

On the one had I want to please people, fit in. On the other, conforming horrifies me. You can't have it both ways. "Well, yes. But…"

"No buts. You can be different and still fit. You seem to think they're mutually exclusive…a girl's breast blooms on your chest and boom, you're ready to join the circus…drift onto the soft shoulder of the straight and narrow way and assume you're in the barrow pit. Consider the possibility that the precise moment you decide to plunge away may also be the moment others are starting to pull you closer and accept and value you for what, and who, you really are. Your quirks have made you an important, contributing friend precisely because you don't fit in, because you don't necessarily go with the flow."

"Interesting perspective," I said.

"Consider it," she said.

"I'm amazed. You really do love me?" I said.

"Heart, mind and soul. Unconditionally."

Burthens from Zion

"So what's engorging your cerebellum today?" Instinctively, Rosenbaum fondled the curved neck of his favorite smokeless pacifier.

What was engorging my cerebellum and other vital organs, addling my equilibrium more than usual, was his assistant, Rebecca Ben-Adams. What I wanted to tell him was this: "She's much better at your job than you are. Give her a raise." I suppressed this impulse, knowing full well it would be hurtful to her career (never mind his kind and generous nature), not to mention our relationship. What I said instead was this: "Conformity."

"Conformist Jed Russell?" he said wryly, as if in coupling the predicate nominative to this noun he had created a world class oxymoron.

"That's the point; that's what's bugging me," I said, uncertain.

"That you don't conform? A professional hazard, I'd say. Does it trouble you?" he asked, tamping down the tobacco in the pipe.

"I mean fitting in, but remaining true to yourself," I said vaguely.

"Are they mutually exclusive?"

"It would seem..."

"Says you," he said.

"And you says?"

"Where it begins...where does it begin for you—the breast *bris*?"

"My androgyny was certainly nonconformist, wasn't it?" I said.

"How so? It had nothing to do with you," he said.

"How so? You ever have a tit? Whether I caused it is beside the point. It made me very, very different. A freak."

"It had to be barely visible," he said.

"Panavision in the theatre of the cerebral cortex of my mind. You begin to wonder: am I a boy, a girl, or a whatchamacallit; will it spurt milk if someone sucks or squeezes hard; am I a more conscientious student because I'm part girl, and on and on?"

"Did you—did you talk it over with a friend?" he said.

"Were you ever eleven?"

"After the surgeon removed it, what then?" Rosenbaum asked.

"I conformed," I said. "I lied."

"Lies often provide broad shoulders for carrying heavy burdens," he said.

"Conforming is more important than honesty?"

"Absolutes are hard to come by."

"Precisely. Should I deny who I am because more forthright disclosures would brand me a nonconformist or cause pain or lead to more problems and questions? Or should I neuter, dilute and homogenize my contrasting pigments—become a splash of beige on the colorful, if well-ordered Mormon mandala?"

By freshman year, I had developed and refined a rather credible piece of macho fiction to explain away the sickle-shaped scar. I'd shrug nonchalantly whenever anyone inquired. I'd retell how I was playing third base when a line drive screamed into my chest; how, grimacing with pain, I miraculously held onto the ball; how my parents worried (when pigs fly) the lump in my chest was cancerous; how the doc said the swelling would dissipate over time, and, when it didn't, how he *lanced and drained* it as if it were nothing more extraordinary than an infected boil.

My father and the doctor dealt with the aberration flat-footedly: "It's a healthy young breast." Thank you very much. "Worse things could happen to you," they said dismissively. Pray tell what? Okay, so a *mohel* with shaky hands would be worse! Besides that?

"It will become less noticeable over time," the doctor said, doubtless cognizant of our family's size and stretched financial resources. "You can live with it," he said cheerily. This was a plainly idiotic notion. I told them straight out what I thought and pleaded that the marvels of medical science be put to good use on my behalf immediately—before I had to confront junior high school and gang showers each and every day.

"You must have been terrified," Rosenbaum said.

"Terrified? Humiliated. I just wanted the damn thing gone. Sooner the better."

After the surgery I was anxious to get a look at the incision, just to make sure he'd gotten every last piece. I talked the nurse into changing the dressing earlier than the doctor ordered. Sure enough, my chest was as flat as any carpenter's dream. A row of black catgut stitches circumambulated my nipple; a small rubber drainage tube, inserted through the incision, remained in place until the stitches were removed two weeks later. They reinforced visibly the major lie I was concocting about a huge subdural hematoma in my chest that had festered for months. "So big, in fact, that it took two weeks to drain fully. That line drive really did a number on me," I told my friends.

And soon I had an urban legend on my hands. The boy who hit the ball apologized every time he heard the story, often recounting, for the benefit of others present, how hard the line shot had been; his astonishment that I'd been able to get a glove on the ball before it fell to the ground and had the presence of mind to step on third, throw to second to end the game: triple play. He and some of my teammates recalled rushing to my assistance, unbuttoning my shirt and watching in utter amazement and horror as my left breast swelled right before their eyes. Even my father abandoned his wont for straight talk. He speculated that the blast from the baseball may have triggered the eruption on my chest like earth tremors provoked Paricutin's rise into the sky over the Mexican landscape in 1943. The legend spilled off my tongue so readily and persuasively that I began to believe it myself!

"What's this?" Emmaline Nebeker asked as her fingers found the cicatrix below my left nipple.

"Old baseball injury…got smacked by a line drive; darn chest puffed up like, well…" My eyes scanned down her face, to her neck and…

"Not that big," she said.

"About as big as this one," I said, cupping hers in my hand. Emmaline was the devoted, card-carrying conformist I dated junior year. At first, she was a very reluctant partner, due largely to wildly exaggerated stories about my less-than-exemplary ways with young women.

But, as she fancied herself an emerging missionary, a prospective savior on Mount Zion, my reputation qualified me as the first lost lamb she could shepherd back to the fold. This was okay by me. Given my strict (in the religious if not the supervisory sense of the word) upbringing, doubtless she figured I'd come easily. I did not disappoint.

At first, she was intrigued and surprised by my gentlemanly behavior. She assumed it was a new and chastened Jed Russell who made no attempts to casually drape an arm around her shoulder or grope for her hand in a darkened theatre, who stiffly shook hands goodnight on the doorstep. For two long months that was all there was…and enough, already. This Lioness of Zion hungered for a taller challenge and, alas, I was but a mere image of my rumored former self. I was like every other Mormon boy, only more so: Daughters of Zion were to be honored and protected, not defiled and debased by holders of the Priesthood of God. Take charge, keep yourself in check; raging testosterone was no bloody excuse.

That we spent countless hours in my father's car parked on the remote mountain roads that overhang the city, talking about things cerebral and spiritual, is a testimony to my intent and ingrained instincts. "Why is it that I have to defend you all the time?" she asked me one night as we gazed at city lights from the highest vantage point in Mt. Olympus Cove. "Everyone says you're such a mover…but with me, nothing. Is there something wrong…with me?"

"Exaggerations. Wild exaggerations. Besides, you're different," I said.

"Different? How am I different?"

"Number one is you don't. Right? Number two, I feel very close to you, closer than I've felt toward any other girl. Number three, I don't. It's fun just being with you…like this."

"No one believes me…they think I'm hiding something," she said. For a split second I thought what I was hearing were the lamentations of someone who really wanted me to try something, be pushy, daring and tempting so she could experience the righteous pleasure that comes from saying "No, please, no, not again."

"Sized about right," Dr. Rosenbaum said.

We became practically inseparable. Together, we skied…attended church meetings often…symphony concerts…movies and homework and family gatherings and did I say church? If there were opportunities to be together, we took them. That's why, early in the relationship, I became decent friends with her father—they called him the Colonel, even though he'd retired from the Marines as a general. He had once been a bit of a rounder himself…long ago, I assumed. As it takes one to know one—or perhaps as a sincere attempt to atone for his errant past—he too had taken a very personal interest in my alleged "reformation," such as it had been explained to him.

"I'm real impressed with the way you've turned your life around this year," he told me one night while I awaited the arrival of his perpetually late daughter. "You'll be the better man for holding true to your upbringing. It's reassuring to know that I can trust you…to honor your priesthood. Emmaline is the most valuable possession I have—I love her in ways that you will only understand when you have children of your own. Every time I turn her over to you, I put my confidence in you—one priesthood holder to another—to return her to me as pure and innocent as she was the moment you left our home. She should do the same for you. It's not easy."

Emmaline was mortified when I told her about our little chat. "He's always saying stuff like that," she said, embarrassed. "Don't pay any attention to the Colonel."

"I was impressed," I protested. "I think more of you…your family. If I had a daughter, that's exactly what I'd say when boys came skulking around."

"Skulking, were you now?" she said, smiling. "What would you do if your daughter wanted to give the skulking boy a kiss?" She didn't wait for an answer; stretched across the seat, put her arms around my neck, and pressed her open mouth to my closed one. Her tongue pried at my lips, which obliged. "Was that so terrible? What on earth have you been waiting for? A voice from the heavens?"

It was no voice from the heavens that commanded me to pull her close—nearer, my God, enough to feel her breasts pressing against my chest. Her thigh innocently grazed temptation as we rearranged ourselves.

As we stayed upright, more or less, temptation was still driving when we abruptly ended our investigation of the sweet mysteries of life two hours later. "Will you still respect me?" she asked.

"More than ever," I said. "I've never…like this before."

"Me neither. So strange—a good strange, but funny, ya know what I mean?"

"Good strange," I said emphatically.

"True. But we've got to be real careful. Keep things in control. You've got to help, cause I can't do this one alone. Okay?" she said sweetly.

"Okay."

"We might need additional help…to avoid temptation…we might want to pray for strength…?"

"Pray? Really? If you want to—sure, go ahead."

And, she did. "Dear Father in Heaven," she began. I didn't have a recorder going at the time, but this is what I remember her praying: "We don't really understand why what happened tonight happened. Jed and I like—maybe even love—each other a lot…someday we may be married in your Temple…give us the strength to control ourselves…be the kind of people we know we ought to be…think holy thoughts when we are tempted…and bless all our loved ones…and Jed that he'll continue to be active in the Church and go on a mission…"

"Amen," I said.

"Next time it's your turn," she said.

"Next time?" I asked.

"No kidding…is this typical for Mormon girls?" Rosenbaum asked.

"I wouldn't know…not Sarah."

Spring skiing in shirtsleeves and light sweaters, catching the intense rays of unfiltered Rocky Mountain sunshine reflected off pristine snow, had browned or singed every square inch of flesh we'd exposed to the elements, even though they'd been slathered in protective ointments. So it was in this somewhat painfully crispy condition that we again found ourselves parked at the top of Mt. Olympus Cove on a mountain road less traveled by, for a new perspective on city lights and the distant illuminated spires of the Temple, obscured this night by increasingly foggier windows.

"They're like beacons along the seacoast, guiding us to safe ground," Emmaline whispered as she snuggled into my chest and kissed my neck.

"Some poor sailor, tempest tossed, still I am?" I said.

"I keep forgetting you know the hymns too… Who woulda thought it a year ago…you've really turned yourself around."

"You have rescued, you have saved," I said obligingly.

"Well, sailor, my lower lights aren't the only things burning right now…how about trimming my face and neck with lotion?" she whispered, biting lightly on my ear. "Don't forget the front…" She guided my hand on an ever-widening circuitous search…until suddenly it touched something it hadn't for years; only this one was different, very different from my own, larger. Our semi-clothed bodies thrust together, again and again, each thrust more reckless than the last. Until it was my turn to pray…and then it was time for instant replay—no stop-action or slow mo!

I placed a hand on her knee. "I don't know if I can stop if you do that," she said, as her girdled loins parted. At various appropriate moments she gurgled these words, parsed herewith as I heard them: "Stop, no, no…more/please again/stop…soon/we need…need/strength…maybe no/should start again/other people/seeing."

"So what'd you do?" asked Rosenbaum.

"We prayed. That's what we did. We prayed," I said. "Although our lower lights burned hot and bright for a few more weeks, before we were snugly in port she threw her Son of Israel overboard for a *sheygets*, a gentile Lutheran buoy."

"*Oy, vits!*"

Shall the Youth of Zion?

Shall the youth of Zion falter in defending truth and right?
While the enemy assaileth, shall we shrink or shun the fight?
While we know the powers of darkness seek to thwart the work of God,
Shall the children of the promise cease to grasp the iron rod?
No! True to the faith that our parents have cherished,
True to the truth for which martyrs have perished,
To God's command, soul, heart and hand,
Faithful and true we will ever stand.

Mormon Hymn

"Admit it, you're so thoroughly brainwashed that you don't know what you believe. Lenin was right about Mormonism: Give me a child until he is five and I'll give you a loyal, ah, whatever. In an odd way, you are living proof!"

Sarah Thompson Russell, July 4, 1980

"I see more believer in you than agnostic. Is there room at the inn for an enigmatic, modified Mormon?"

Rebecca Ben-Adams, Christmas, 1983

"About your, ah, ethnicity. You're not like any Mormon I've known. Not once have you gone into any depth about your theology and doctrines. Most Mormons talk about little else."

Dr. Irving Rosenbaum, April 1, 1984

"You've been so unselfish, considering me and my feelings first, and that's more than I ever did for you. You'll make some 'good' girl a fine husband if you continue to progress. Keep the desire to go on a mission because that's *so* important."

Emmaline Nebeker, May, 1962

"I don't regret a thing. It really doesn't matter whether you're a good Mormon or not. The important thing is to find *you*, be you, one way or the other, whatever *you* may be. Then go for it."

Eleanor Cannon, February, 1963

I had known Eleanor Cannon (Lainey), vaguely, since seventh grade. However, our official coming together as seniors was quite by accident, as these things always are. We both needed debate partners: she was new to the team and my former partner had graduated. I could have selected a more experienced replacement, but, in the end, chose her because she was very bright, exceptionally attractive and disarmingly friendly, a combination I knew would distract and befuddle the legions of smug, smart-ass geeks who over-populated interscholastic forensics meets.

Lainey performed better than expected, adeptly charming our opponents to distraction—male opponents treaded lightly, perhaps fearing overly harsh rebuttals would eliminate any chance they had for more satisfying personal encounters later on. Our only loss was to a team of girls who clearly were not distracted by either of us. I don't know what this says about me.

She was a terrific decoy in other ways, too. I was still reeling from the breakup with say-a-little-prayer Emma. Lainey provided all the consoling I needed. Moreover, I suspected a relationship, albeit a working one, with someone so beautiful and religiously fringy would re-stoke Emma's savior-on-Mount-Zion fires, where flowers, poetry and football had failed.

"Would you say this was the birth of a notion that has plagued you to this day?" said Rosenbaum. "But football? You played football with Emma?"

"Until now it hadn't occurred to me that the pattern of behavior I followed with Sarah was established twenty years earlier with Emma. Interesting," I mused. "As for football: I love the game—but at six foot two, a hundred and fifty-five pounds soaking wet, I was a sack of bones and tenuously strapped joints waiting to be splintered and mashed into the sod. Sophomore year, I incurred so many injuries—from my knees to ankles—that I concluded that basketball, tennis and baseball—sports that rewarded skilled athleticism over brawn—were more appropriate for one so gangling."

Perhaps prompted by her new sheygets significant other, who judged me an athletically talented if recusant iconoclast-without-a-cause who could learn a thing or two about teamwork from lunks like him, Emma encouraged me to give the game another try: "God gave you gifts to magnify..." So I magnified. And it was magnificent until I rolled an ankle in the next-to-last game of the season, which kept me on crutches through the first critical weeks of basketball tryouts.

Like most acts of desperation, this one fell well short of its intended objective. Sheygets was now a college boy, a Sigma Chi no less, which only enhanced his desirability as trophy squeeze, especially when compared to a hobbled, wannabe high school jock on crutches.

Taking the next step with Lainey might give Emma pause, I thought. By Thanksgiving, what had once been just a pretty good debating team had turned into a tantalizing tidbit for the school's hyperactive gossips who routinely magnified their callings.

Although I didn't think so then, with the perspective of two decades it should have been obvious that Lainey was a real find—better suited to me in every way than Emma was or could be. She fit in, although she was hardly a joiner: she had a certain aloofness that seemed to put off football brutes—like Sheygets—stalking trophy game. She was (also) from a historically prominent Mormon family, but her parents had long ago forsaken the church for reasons that were never made clear to me. Nevertheless, they remained loosely tethered to most Mormon values. Ditto, in fact I continued to play pool with her father (another pattern I repeated often: good relationships with the parents) long after Lainey moved on to more promising, attentive and reliable prospects.

I was pretty bitter about Emma—to me she was the poster child for the twisted hypocrisy that permeates the social scene in Salt Lake City. At least I had the fortitude to stow my packaged protest of "I'd rather fight than switch" Tareytons in the breast pocket of my shirt. Emmaline could fake it, put on a holier than thou front provided she and Sheygets took care and prayed often. The Lord would look the other way, or forgive them, never mind that the iron rod she grasped from time to time wasn't exactly the Word of God.

True confession: when I returned home from two years of missionary service, I took perverse delight in rumors that her Kappa sisters and their male consorts had led her down the primrose path to drink and debauchery.

"*Très* vindictive, wouldn't you say?" said Dr. Rosenbaum.

"Yes," I admitted. "Holier-thans put me off, and she fashioned herself into a Holy of Holies."

("Don't let one foolish night ruin your life...don't get to college and play around in the frats 'cause it's just not worth it." Emmaline Nebeker, graduation, 1963)

"You're sure?" said Rosenbaum.

"Not at all," I said. "The rumors turned out to be nothing more than the handiwork from the gossips of Zion, magnifying their callings. But they could have been true."

Determined is how I began senior year—committed to finally living up to the reputation I acquired two years earlier, simply because a couple of Mormon kids turned envious when one of their own had the temerity to actually do what they dreamed of doing. Or so they thought. The abridged story goes like this: A group of musicians, singers and instrumentalists, traveled to Santa Monica, California to perform as members of the All Western States Chorus and Orchestra. We arrived on Sunday and, despite commandments forbidding Sabbath-breaking, joined a free-form welcome reception on the beach. One particularly attractive young woman—a soprano from Pasadena—was winning more than her fair share of attention from my older Utah comrades. It was clear she wanted nothing to do with them. *(SNIP)* After a while she struck up a conversation with me, much to my surprise. We were inseparable for the rest of the week *(SNIP)*. That she was a *shiksa* Californian...an older and wiser senior to boot...had come on to me...and took me to an interesting farewell night party on the beach *(SNIP)* led to several errant and startling calculations *(SNIP)* that were magnified by gossip mongers of Zion *(SNIP)*. Net net: Jedediah Pratt Russell aka Horatio Alger Lothario.

So, from the moment my not-quite-*shiksa* debate partner converted to steady girlfriend, nearly all of the Mormon friends I'd grown closer to junior year began wringing their hands and worrying out loud that without a "like mind" as my guide, I could lose my way again, drift away from our comfortable group. Their concerns were reasonably rational, as I had indeed wandered further and further afield. Friendships reduced to part-time during my epiphanic junior year were resurrected. I found myself stuck in a "neither" world; first as apologist for both sides, then as an intermediary and interlocutor between the powerful Mormon clique that ran the school and a disparate and dissonant group of influential intellectuals, skeptics, cynics, cranks, poets, who liked to raise a ruckus and occasionally talked through their hats.

"Hey Jed-rah-rah, how come only your LDS buds get to do all the prayers at school events—even a Presbyterian like me knows how to pray." Jamie Hogan's point was valid. No Mormon would have mistaken Jamie for a devotee of the sacred: he smoked, drank and golfed, not necessarily in that order. Completely overlooked was his role as the grand Pooh-Bah of DeMolay, the young men's arm of Masonry. He was also a very good putter, so I can only assume God answered his prayers from time to time.

"Your new *friends*"—emphasis Tommy Lundstrom's, my alter ego senior year and throughout college—"undermine school spirit: they smoke in the parking lot, drink on the weekends, and rarely participate in extracurricular activities. At least we care," he said. "And look what they're doing to you."

"Just what are my *friends*"—emphasis mine—"doing to me?" I challenged.

"Maybe you're doing it to yourself. But it's clear you don't belong with them. You're a good member of the church in your heart. A leader, a worthwhile member...at least you were last year," he said.

"I see: 'good Mormon' makes me worthwhile, acceptable, a leader?" I said. "Funny my new *friends* aren't nearly so judgmental about the Mormon in me."

"Didn't mean it to come out that way..."

"But out it came," I said.

Later that year, my *new friends* got graphic evidence of the prejudice, perhaps inadvertent, against them, and my *old friends* got a printed memorial to what too much of a good thing can lead to if left unchecked: the official record of the year, the school yearbook. Not one of the six student body officers was a Gentile; ditto the eight cheerleaders. One held a fairly insignificant class office. More importantly, not one non-Mormon addressed the senior class at graduation, although many of them were ranked in the top three percent of the class and members of the National Honor Society. Of the twenty boys selected to attend Boys State, eighteen were Mormons. The yearbook lays out what I didn't see clearly until years later. I could not be sure whether the prejudice was inadvertent or willful, benign or malevolent (I like to think it was the former). Mormon bigots bother me more than your ordinary bigots because I know they were taught differently. They should be extra sensitive as they have been and will be victims of prejudice themselves.

There is, of course, no way that I can fully understand what it was like to grow up a *Gentile* in Salt Lake City. It is true I expended considerable energy defending my non-Mormon friends, and didn't turn out to be a go-to-meeting kind of guy, myself. However, all I have to do to blend into the Mormon mandala is repent and conform. All a Gentile has to do is convert, which is how brutish Sheygets-the-Lutheran, led by his savioress on Mt. Zion, in-blended to the local scene. It was a politic thing to do, I suppose.

That was Salt Lake City then. I suspect it hasn't changed all that much, which is why I live in Connecticut. As ROT advised, I have not turned my back on the Church. In fact, I like to think that I'm reasonably religious, and certainly loyal, despite a few practices that rub against the gospel's grain.

In high school, my substitute for Connecticut was Lainey Cannon's home, where I could drink as much coffee as I wanted, smoke when it pleased me, have an occasional glass of wine or beer with dinner. It was a place where I found empathy for my struggle, although the elder Cannons were careful not to push me one way or the other.

As the relationship warmed, the elder Cannons did all they could to ensure that whatever unfolded would not be relegated to the rear seat of their '63 Cadillac Eldorado convertible. Once, when she found us partially disrobed, necking on the pool table in the basement, Mrs. Cannon grumped: "There are more private places to be had in this house." A few days later, she straight out told us about the protective measures we could take should the need arise. Thereafter, we retreated to Lainey's bedroom. Ironically, we never went further than Emma and I had on the bench seat of my family's '56 Ford, overlooking city lights.

"Interesting," said Rosenbaum. "What happened to Lainey?"

"After college, she married an Episcopal minister," I said.

"What happened…to your relationship?" Rosenbaum asked.

"A non-starter. I was on the rebound, looking to even the score with Emma. So I didn't recognize the long-term possibilities. Officially it ended before the close of our senior year, although it malingered, on and off, for several months more. I probably will forever regret letting her go."

"It's been twenty years. Your life has changed so much..." said Dr. Rosenbaum.

"I wonder *what if*...it's always basically the same dream. We're driving her father's Eldorado. We stop. I go for food, or off exploring. She drives away, stopping to pick up a hitchhiker down the road. Alternatively, she arrives at my parents' house to pick me up. I'm still in the shower or something. She leaves, after asking my father to have me call her when I'm ready. Dad deliberately forgets. I get dressed, wait for hours, finally call. Her mother's response varies. Lainey:

Alt. 1) entered a convent in Pennsylvania run by radical Marymount sisters and the Berrigan Brothers.

Alt. 2) was crippled in a horrible car accident. ("Why weren't you at the wheel?")

Alt. 3) moved to Colorado City and is about to become a plural wife to a tottering old geezer who looks a lot like several of my more prominent ancestors."

"So you blamed yourself," said Rosenbaum.

"Now, yes. Then, it didn't cross my mind. But recently—since the divorce—I've thought about it a lot. I see the positives I ignored then. I pulled out too soon."

"That's a start," Rosenbaum said.

"A start at what?"

"Accepting responsibility...not blaming others for your condition..."

"I didn't recognize it at the time," I said.

"Like Sarah."

"If I was at fault with Sarah, then yes..."

"What?" said Rosenbaum. "Right, well then resolving church..."

"But, it isn't resolved at all. I'm still out there a zillion miles—one minute defending, the next minute criticizing, or just shrugging."

"It all seems tethered securely, if loosely."

"Opposition in any form implies disloyalty," said no-shades-of-gray Tommy Lundstrom. "Loyal opposition is counter-intuitive...it could just drive you over the edge, out for good. Anyway, how can you oppose what's divinely revealed?"

"Hard to distinguish between the divine and the man-made," I said.

"You'll always find a cause, a rationalization," he said. "Today it may be the Black issue; tomorrow it will be something else. Issues are too easy to find, testimonies are too hard to keep."

"Impossible to have both?"

"Possible? Yes. Probable? No," Tommy said, way too smugly I thought. "Look what's happened to you the last year…little by little, you've turned into a Doubting Thomas."

"So show me the nail holes in your…head," I said, grinning broadly. Tommy was not amused.

Two weeks after high school graduation, I quietly moved out of my parents' house into a small $50-a-month apartment near the University of Utah. My parents had not resisted the move, although my mother wept openly as I loaded my belongings into the back seat of my first car—a battered 1953 Chevy.

"You can live at home until you go on a mission," she said.

"That could take forever," I said, feeling particularly cruel.

"You could save money living at home," she said.

"And so could every other college student in America. Except most go away. Like a fool, I chose a school in my hometown. It doesn't diminish my need to get out. Don't make me feel guilty."

"If you feel guilty, then there must be something wrong with your decision," she said.

Mother's logic always astounded, left me speechless. "Not guilty at all," I lied, "but you're trying awfully hard to make me."

Dad was subtler. While I was at work, he stopped by the apartment house and talked with the landlord, who was also a devoted church member. Dad explained that I was basically a religious boy, but confused. "Keep an eye on him and let me know if there's any trouble," my father confessed, years later. "But don't let him know we've talked."

There wasn't much to call home about. In the six months there, not once did a girl stay overnight, not once did I host a wild party, and not once did I miss church. When I moved out, it was to the interns' dormitories at St. Mark's Hospital, where I was working as a lab technician, running routine tests, electrocardiograms, drawing blood from donors as well as starting intravenous medications on patients with hard-to-hit veins. I was so absorbed by the work that frequently I volunteered to work double shifts, which significantly contributed to my mediocre academic performance, as did the proximity of a hundred or so student nurses who lived in a separate wing of the dorm.

Given my eighteen months experience at St. Mark's, I would

recommend nurses to any young man. They are excellent teachers, straightforward and down-to-earth. Now that I think of it, too many seemed cursed or blessed, depending on your point of view and where you are with your own life, with an almost obsessive need to take on hopeless causes. Naomi Dyson, a recently graduated operating room nurse, was so accursed. God bless her.

"Naomi…Dyson, a Jew?" Rosenbaum asked, his curiosity not all detached and professional.

"Technically, no. Her mother was Mormon."

Rebe had straightened me out on such arcane matters. "I was raised WASP like my father, but technically—and in my soul—I'm Jewish because my mother was and I will it so."

Naomi was engaged to a thrice-divorced man, twice her age, with a history of petty crime. They met as he recovered in the hospital from several deep knife wounds to his belly that were inflicted during a brawl in a cowboy bar in Rock Springs, Wyoming. The romance blossomed despite several official warnings from, among others: the dean of nursing school, various Salt Lake City policemen, and the man's almost-but-not-quite-yet former wife, who claimed there were a few more like her stashed in remote mining towns from Bozeman to Albuquerque. This worked to my advantage, for when it became obvious that we were seeing each other, Naomi's peers and mentors were relieved, encouraging. But to her, I was only deep cover, a serviceable proxy for her miner, thankfully a safe nine hours away. So, she became my *mekhaye* of convenience (by saving a soul, one gives life) too.

As she shaved and prepped me for hernia surgery a month before I entered the mission field, her gentle touch with the somewhat abrasive gauze swabs soaked with green soap produced an altogether natural reaction: "Calm down, my *Fartutster putzelein*," my *mekhaye* sang sweetly and loudly enough for the entire assembled surgical team to hear. "Some missionary you will make, feh!"

True to the Faith

As Rebe settled in, the pace of daily life on Bermuda Lagoon steadied and calmed considerably. Elli and Janie visited more frequently and stayed longer, although they both seemed to spend more time with Rebe than me. Sarah called regularly if only to check on the children, give Rebe suggestions on how to deal with one teenage trauma or another or update our school activities calendar. The relationship between the two main women in my life seemed to be productive—cordial if always focused on the children—even if it was limited to a phone call here, a wave from the window there, a handshake greeting at school events and so on. They seemed to be going out of their way to avoid face time, a heart-to-heart conversation, even though they had much in common to talk about.

By the end of our first year together Rebe supported my decision not to share additions to the manuscript with Dr. Rosenbaum, but she absolutely insisted that I keep seeing him as often as my work schedule would allow. "You're making progress, this is no time to be pulling up short," she said.

"What shall we talk about?" I asked lamely.

"Whatever's on your mind, although I'd appreciate advance warning if you want to talk about me—appearances aside, there's not much to say at this point."

"Appearances bother you?" I teased.

"Sure. Living with a man before marriage was not atop my wish list, however twisted and tortured and pure our living arrangements are. I'm human. I'm also an all-or-nothing girl; I want to be *all* with the man I love. That's you, in case you haven't noticed."

"You want to marry me?" Rebe's eyes rolled. "Okay, when?" I said.

"Today, tomorrow, day after, next week. Sooner is better. How's that for baring the soul? And you?"

"On practically every level, today would be good…but for one unresolved matter…"

"I know, Sarah."

"…and that's nearing an end."

"Really?"

"In a roundabout way, yes…for the first time I can see closure ahead. The fact that I've been able to begin again with you; that despite annoying accommodations I'm feeling profound unconditional love, joy like I've never experienced…I could go on…"

"Really? Please do."

"Would 'I love you' do for now?"

"Yes…" Her eyes blinked.

"Want me to say it again?"

"Yes…" Her face flushed.

"I love you, my *mekhaye*."

"And, I loved you before I knew you in the flesh."

"How biblical," I grinned.

"I mean even before I met you, got to know you…"

"Yes, yes, just teasing. Anything else?"

"Close the circle. Fast."

"You haven't stopped writing, have you?" Rosenbaum asked.

"Every night. But I repent every morning—I've finished several chapters although, as I said, I've got some rewriting to do."

"Look forward to reading it…"

"In due time," I said confidently.

"Hmmm. When we last met, it sounded like we were getting close to seeing you off on the obligatory mission. Want to continue along that line?"

"Why not. Not obligatory at all. Not with me, not with most of my friends. I'd always thought I might go, but it was a slow process. I guess I began to focus because of Greg Hansen," I said.

Rosenbaum's eyebrows raised suspiciously. "Greg Hansen? I don't recall a mention of him before? A high school relationship?" he asked.

"College," I said.

Greg Hansen was born and raised in Provo, and schooled at Brigham Young High School, a private secondary school that passed itself off as a teacher-training school for its namesake university while catering to well-connected Mormons in the Utah Valley. Spurning a scholarship to nearby Brigham Young University, he enrolled in the pre-medicine program at the University of Utah, about an hour's freeway drive north in Salt Lake City. Except when he bedded down on a sofa in my apartment, he made the one hundred mile round trip each day in a beat-up Ford Falcon—usually a six-pack of Olympia Beer kept him company on the return trip.

We met at a rush week party at the Sigma Chi house. Later that same night, we crossed paths at the Pi Kappa Alpha house where a friend of mine from high school took note of the fact that Greg and I looked like twins. "Perhaps the same DNA—you know, polygamy," he chortled. The first day of school we found ourselves in the same Organic Chemistry class.

More importantly, we both fended off bids from the Sigma Chis and the Pi Kaps, opting, instead, to operate outside the extraordinarily powerful Greek system at the university. Such was not expected from children of well-established Mormon families and respected high schools and was tantamount to thumbing our noses at the reasonably well-established, if de facto, Mormon vetting process. One's ticket for life got stamped by attending a good high school (preferably one of the three high schools on Salt Lake's East Bench); the University of Utah (most locals of the day, Mormons included, regarded BYU as second rate, a glorified high school); membership in either Pi Kap or Sigma Chi; missionary service overseas, preferably somewhere in the British Isles or Europe, or, if stateside, in New England; and, after returning home, a stint teaching at the mission home across the street from the temple in Salt Lake City; eternal marriage in the Temple; and lots of kids.

Fraternities and sororities were exceptionally popular on campus, if for no other reason than the simple fact that most of the 14,000 students were commuters, attending classes in the morning, working at part-time jobs in the afternoon, and studying at home in the evening. If you wanted to have anything resembling a "normal" college experience, frats were an easy way to ensure it. And, as I mentioned, it really was a must-do for those with leadership ambitions.

While we were students, the church established its own, more egalitarian fraternity system under the auspices of the Latter-day Saints Student Association. Nevertheless, most well-connected Mormons, student leaders, and wannabe movers and shakers in life joined the regular Greeks. The leftover joiners drank their conformist Kool-Aid at LDSSA.

While I had no desire to join a church-sponsored fraternity, I thought it highly hypocritical (it not fundamentally sinful) for serious Mormons—good Americans too, for that matter—to support clubs whose national charters forbade membership to all Blacks, American Indians and Jews, although most of the Utah chapters bucked their national's bylaws on the issue of Jewish membership.

Yet practically all of my good Mormon friends joined one regular Greek fraternity or another: Pi Kap and Sigma Chi for the boys; Kappa Kappa Gamma and Chi Omega for the girls. It was rumored that girls had to show a recommendation from the bishop of her home ward to win a Chi-O bid. Offspring of apostles and other general authorities of the Church were virtually guaranteed bids from all the "name" fraternities.

In my opinion, Mormons who belong to fraternities and clubs that discriminate against others on the basis of social standing, race, ethnicity, and religion should be prohibited from serving as leaders of the church or entering the temple.

You'd think in 1963, after being discriminated against for 133 years, Mormons would have been highly sensitized to such matters. Institutionally they were—a few years earlier the Church outlawed Greek frats at Brigham Young University because of the caste system it seemed to foster. Unfortunately, this action had absolutely no effect on the "chosen" (children of apostles, stake presidents and bishops) at the University of Utah.

"You're picking at nits," said Eddie Knight, who'd already pledged when I rejected a bid to become his frat brother.

"It seems pretty fundamental to me. How can you be a good Mormon and in good conscience be a Sigma Chi?" I said.

"An irreverent issue for you," he said.

"Irrelevant," I corrected. "How is it irrelevant?"

"You're not a particularly good Mormon, are you?"

"That's irrelevant. Discrimination is a human…American issue too. So even if I buy your assertion that I'm not a good Mormon, which I don't, it's a very relevant issue to anyone with a conscience."

"Let's stick to Mormon, because you are one, good or bad, and I think I'm a good one," he said.

"Okay, how about this: your Sigma Chi membership is not consistent with your religious beliefs. Prejudice—tolerating prejudice—is a far more serious transgression than smoking and drinking."

"Come on, don't stretch the issue," he said.

"I'm not stretching at all. You tell me which is more fundamental to the Gospel—the concept that all of us are equal in the eyes of God, veritable brothers and sisters, or abstinence from tobacco and booze."

"But that doesn't mean that all men have identical intellects, or that their achievement levels are the same," he said. "And the Church teaches that we were born into Mormon families because we fought more valiantly in the war in heaven than did the other spirits."

"Where in the scriptures does it say that?" I said.

"I don't know, but I know that I've heard numerous General Authorities of the Church say that, not to mention my own bishop and father."

"I really don't care what your father, or your bishop, or an apostle says unless he can point to bona fide scriptural evidence or honestly proclaim 'thus sayeth the Lord.' Otherwise, his interpretation is no more valid than mine. What the scriptures say is that we were sent to this world to prove ourselves, that everyone here was valiant in the war in heaven. Beyond that, the scriptures are not explicit at all."

"But doesn't it follow that the more valiant would be rewarded by being born into the more valiant families here on earth?" he said.

"It follows, only if you believe that God stacked the deck and enhanced your chances of returning to Him by putting you with a good Mormon family, which means He all but abandoned the poor slob assigned to the slums of Calcutta. And if that's true, then God's up there manipulating everything that goes on down here, which eliminates free choice, the very issue that triggered the War in Heaven in the first place."

"So how do you explain the scripture: 'Many are called but few are chosen,' which implies that God did some choosing along the way?" he said.

"Simple. We're all *called* by God to do one thing or another, but that doesn't mean we have to *choose* to do it. You become 'chosen' by choosing to answer the call. Because of His intelligence, He may well know what choices you and I will make, but in the final analysis, it's our choice."

"So you think you were just lucky to be born a Mormon?"

"Lucky? I wouldn't say *lucky* exactly!"

"Had nothing to do with your performance in heaven—in the pre-existence?"

"It's more logical to think God would assign a valiant warrior—a guy likely to make the right decisions on his own—to a less stalwart family."

"So you don't buy the idea that good Mormon parents breed good Mormon children?" he said.

"Sure, just like Republican parents are more likely to raise Republican children, Democrats little Jack and Jackie Kennedys. Being born into an ordinary Mormon family doesn't mean I was less worthy than a fellow born into a prominent family. I flatly don't believe that being born a Mormon makes me better than a Catholic or a Baptist. However, I would agree that abiding by the principles and teachings of the gospel will make me a better person than I would have been if I grudgingly lived the principles, or didn't live them at all. Mormonism is like golf—it's just you against the course. If par for the course is 72, and you shot a 73, you were one stroke off your potential."

"If you're a scratch golfer that is," he said.

"Precisely. And if you're not, God is the Great Handicapper. He knows how much training you've had, whether you had enough coaching to get the duck hook out of your drives, or to put more bite or top spin into your approach shots, or the vision to read the greens. That's what the Spirit World [the place Mormons say all go after death to await the resurrection] is all about."

"Where everyone finally gets a look at their handicaps?" he said.

"Sort of. But more importantly, it's where players with handicaps get the training to become scratch golfers, if that is their choice," I said. "And if they take the option, they are no better or worse off in the end than those of us who played to scratch in this life. In fact we scratch golfers have the ominous task of seeking out the duck hookers of life and teaching them to shoot straight. I wonder how many duck hookers Sigma Chi blackballed?"

"We didn't ask for USGA cards."

"Like hell you didn't. What do you call: 'And, where did you go to high school? And, did you know Old So-and-so? And, what does your father do for a living? And, do you have a legacy with good old Sigma Chi?' Not to mention what clothes, accents, haircuts revealed about each prospect. If you get called to serve a mission to the Indians, will you blackball a potential convert because he wears his hair in braids?"

"That's different," he said.

"Is it?" I said. "Pray tell how?"

"It just is, that's all."

"Brilliant," I said.

Three months later, Eddie was called to serve a two-year mission to Argentina where he was instrumental in converting several former Nazis. Lookalikes attract, I thought when I heard what he had done.

◎ ◎ ◎

The golf analogies played especially well with Greg Hansen, a seven handicapper himself. With dumb luck, occasionally I played to a fifteen. Without it, my scores usually edged up into the mid-90s.

"Teach me to shoot straight," I said one day while thrashing around in the deep rough, looking for my ball, fearing that a rattlesnake would strike me at any moment.

"Basically, all you have to do is set up squarely, keep your eye on the ball and follow through. Sort of like the Church: follow-through keeps you straight."

Late in the spring of our freshman year, we were both shooting particularly bad rounds. "We're playing like a couple of hypocrites," Greg said to me as we trudged up the hill to the eighteenth tee. "We should be on the driving range, taking lessons—one wedge after another—until we've grooved our swings."

"So let's hit a bucket of balls after eighteen," I said. "I'll watch you while you hit, then you can coach me," I said.

"God's golf," he yelled as my ball dived into scrub oak clinging to the side of a deep gulch that bisected the fairway near the eighteenth green.

"God's what?" I said, frustrated.

"Golf," he said. His wedge to the green overshot the flagstick by ten feet or so, bit into the grass with backspin that drew it to within a foot of the cup.

"Now that shot was God's golf," I said later as we nursed beers.

"But there's no consistency. We're either going to have to get serious about this and take some lessons or spend the rest of our lives hitting out of the traps."

I scratched my head, confused. "You seem to be driving at something that I'm not getting. Save the analogy crap for English class and tell me what you're talking about."

"Alright. Let's start with the concept of testimony. You say you don't have a testimony of the gospel, right?" he said.

"Not exactly," I said. "What I've said, as you will recall, is if you accept the reality and divinity of God and Jesus, or if you accept the Bible as the Word of God, then Mormonism is as consistent with Judeo-Christian teachings as any religion I know of. As a guide for life, Mormonism is as good as it gets. Trouble is, it's a big pain in the neck to be all that a good Mormon should be. Mormon is not something you'd want to be unless you had been given some divine confirmation that it was true. Intellectual conversion is not a substitute for the spiritual conversion, which can only come after a divine confirmation. That's my problem. So far, I have not made the spiritual connection and I don't see it coming any time soon."

"I could quibble, but I won't," he said. "So okay, so divine confirmation is important to full conversion. Have you attempted to get divine confirmation?" He was baiting and he knew it.

"Not lately, but as you know I've tried before."

"So who's calling the shots here, you or God?"

"If He wants, I suppose God calls the shots. But if He does, He violates some fairly fundamental scriptures like, 'Ask and ye shall receive, knock and it shall be opened unto you.' I've asked, I've knocked. So far the heavens haven't opened."

"How many times?" he said.

"Is it supposed to be an endurance contest? Is there a magic number that indicates 'sincere effort,' 'faith,' 'reasonable perseverance'?"

"Doesn't God say somewhere that a testimony comes line upon line, precept upon precept et cetera, et cetera until you have a full knowledge. Somewhere He suggests the door opens as you bear witness to someone else, become their small *s* savior and in doing so find more of the truth yourself. It says that somewhere, I'm positive."

"In *The Doctrine and Covenants*," I assured him.

"Have you done that? Have you even testified to the truth of the few lines and precepts you buy into?" he said with such fervency that I thought I was talking to Eddie Knight.

"Not overtly," I said, puzzled.

"But, a testimony—even a limited one—is worth sharing, is important to share with others, don't you think?" he said.

"So tomorrow I'll rush up to...pick-a-friend—and tell them that while I'm not at all sure that Joseph Smith ever talked to God, or that there are living prophets who do today, I know for a certainty that the law of tithing is divinely inspired because it teaches giving and social responsibility and discipline; ditto chastity because it imparts lessons of self-control, honor, commitment and discipline; the word of wisdom because it honors the sanctity of the body and spirit and teaches discipline; and whatever. They'd correctly say to me 'If you're so convinced, why aren't you going on a mission for your Church?'"

"So why don't you...?"

"Why don't I what?"

"Serve a mission?" he said matter-of-factly.

"Don't look at me. Why don't you?"

"I am," he said. "Came in the mail yesterday."

"You're putting me on," I said.

He pulled an envelope out of the pocket of his windbreaker and handed it to me. The return address was familiar: 47 East South Temple, Salt Lake City, Utah, worldwide headquarters of the Church of Jesus Christ of Latter-day Saints.

> *Dear Brother Hansen,*
>
> *Greetings. You have been called to serve a mission for the Lord and to administer to the spiritual needs of all God's children who reside within the confines of the Southeast Asia Mission, headquartered at:*
>
> *2 Kowloon Road,*
> *Kowloon Ton, Hong Kong.*
>
> *Your mission president is Elder C. Allan Page. You are requested to report to the mission home in Salt Lake City on June 25th, 1964 for one week of preparatory work prior to departing for your field of labor. Specific instructions for the Southeast Asia Mission, including a complete set of lesson plans, are being forwarded under a separate cover.*
>
> *Remember: "The field is white, already to harvest." In the coming months, prepare yourself spiritually and intellectually for the important calling you have been asked to undertake. Pray diligently and earnestly. Seek counsel from your bishop, your parents, and others who have previously labored in the Lord's vineyard.*
>
> *With you go our faith, love and blessings.*
>
> *With warm regards,*
> *David O. McKay*

"You are like everyone else, only worse," I said. "And, you didn't say a word to me."

"I did, but you weren't listening," Greg said. "I don't have any stronger a testimony today than I did six months ago. But I darn sure will know, one way or the other, when I come home thirty months from now."

"You'll be a Bible banger, just like all the others who repent just in time to answer the call. You'll be so pious, I'll want to barf."

"You don't give me much credit," he said.

"It's not you, really," I said. "It's the system—what it does to people... like you. There's no requirement that you have to come back a smug, holier-than, but you probably will. That's what the system does."

"Maybe I won't," he said.

"I'll be here to bug the bejeezuz out of you if you do."

"Maybe you won't..."

"If you're holier than thou? Believe it—*that* you can know," I said.

"...be here when I get home," he said.

"I'll be here—probably in med school—but I'll be here," I said.

"Who knows? So how about saying the closing prayer at my farewell service?"

"What? Give me a break."

"You're the only one I know who can pray," he said.

"Big compliment, I was hoping it had something to do with friendship."

"That's obvious," he said. "I'm counting on your prayer not to be trite."

"Bank on it," I said. "By the way, Elder Hansen, what's with the beer?"

"The bottle's full," he said. It was.

Missionary farewells (homecomings too) in 1964 had a grand tradition all their own. They were equal parts bar mitzvah, wedding, and funeral, rolled into a two-hour worship service. Often, if one didn't know better one might mistakenly conclude that, but for a few adolescent lapses, the prospective missionary's life to date mirrored the early years of Jesus Christ, Himself. Forgive the blasphemous overstatement: I really meant John the Baptist.

During the Vietnam War years—1967 on—these services were toned down considerably out of respect for the increasing numbers of young men who were called to serve their country before God and church could intervene. It probably goes without saying that farewells are well-attended. If the young elder was once rebellious, it guarantees the hall will be filled to overflowing.

Greg's farewell was nothing but typical. The church was packed with well-wishers, including an astounding array of lovely young women. The speakers recalled his high school years, when he displayed a talent for leadership that frequently was overshadowed by more worldly pursuits. "In a very real way he conformed to whatever he regarded as nonconformist," his father noted from the podium. "His decision to serve a mission is nothing less than a continuation of his nonconformist ways. In the reality of the real world beyond the mountains, volunteering to serve a mission for your church—whether you're a Mormon, Catholic or Jew—is a nonconformist thing to do. Your job, Greg, is to find and teach as many people as you can, people like you who are dedicated nonconformists…"

Greg was terse: "I haven't much to add now. But I hope to have something to say thirty months from now when I return home. Jed Pratt Russell, my best friend and twin in more ways that I can count, is going to give the closing prayer. I encourage you to listen closely to what he says. He's a passionate nonconformist too—he knows the gospel better than anyone I've ever met—and I suspect that it won't be too long before he answers the call himself."

What I prayed was this:

> *We've come to the close of this service honoring a young man who has elected to serve You on a mission. He isn't here because he was coerced or bribed. Like many of us, even some who are already on missions or have served them and returned home, Greg probably isn't even sure that You're there. By accepting this call, he's demonstrating his faith in You. He's depending on You for an answer to his prayers. So please bless him with answers he seeks and the capacity to hear them and distinguish Your truths from man's assumptions. And one last thing Lord, help Greg become a scratch golfer.*

Decisions, Decisions

Wren Hargrave—my long-suffering agent provocateur—was growing restive, possibly because the editors at Americana Books were on his back, rumbling about the rather hefty advance they paid to an unknown author a year or so earlier who, for all they knew, hadn't written a blasted word for them but, in the meantime, had found time to crank out several longish pieces for *People*.

Such grumbling was consistent with recent reports in the *New York Times* that the tweedy publishing industry was forsaking its collegial ways. Acquisition editors with generally irreproachable track records were summarily being dismissed for a single costly handshake deal that failed to pan out. Inspired by threatening missives from some of America's more menacing law firms, authors, who previously had treated advances as if they were unrestricted grants from a family trust fund, suddenly conquered persistent writer's block, healed themselves of chronic lassitude and other nagging forms of self-induced distractions and impotence. It has been correctly said: nothing so inspires as fear.

Even reasonably reliable, well-trusted agents like Wren Hargrave, renowned for nurturing foundering writers through all manner of crises, real and imagined, were often given a Hobson's choice, as stipulated by the stilted legal language in a letter he received about my procrastination:

> *Failure of said writer to deliver a suitable, finished manuscript to said publisher within ninety days from the date of this letter will constitute a material breach of said publisher's contract with Mr. Luminary, requiring him to repay all monies, including expense reimbursements, previously advanced. Please note that the failure of Mr. Luminary to either submit a manuscript or repay monies due said publisher may lead to a*

serious deterioration of the business relationship between said publisher and Larry's Luminaries, Ltd., and all the authors it represents.

It was with some apprehension that I returned his phone call. Most of the advance had been spent or spoken for. I was writing, slowly and unsatisfactorily and, frankly, for reasons that were very personal to me, reasons that I had not shared with him or Old Quack Quack.

"How's the book coming?" Wren asked first thing. I hesitated.

"Fair…slow, but I'm making progress."

"Can I see something soon…anything to help me deal…"

"A half dozen or so new chapters are in rough drafts…would that sate them?"

"Half dozen, more? Good, good…enough. Drop them by sometime," he said nonchalantly. "Gotta dash, but, actually, I called to give you a heads up that Bob Gamma over at the *New Yorker*—know him, right?—lunched him yesterday; he asked after you, said he had the perfect piece…out in Utah…if you were available. I assured him you were, of course. He'll be calling."

"What's the story?"

"He didn't say much, really, mentioned something about a Brother Orson, a religious whack job out in the boondocks—is everyone out there a Jesus freak or what?"

"Not in the sense you mean it," I said.

"Anyway, he'll be calling—sounded like something that might net four, six grand or so, not a penny less…than five."

"Whatever you say's fine…"

"He seems to want to deal direct…old school tie bullshit, you know. No problem…but not a penny less than 5k. Don't go soft for old time's sake…because it's the *New Yorker*, which, by the way, Bob told me was founded by another goddamn Utahn. Di'jou know?"

"A Jew? I don't think so. Harold Ross was Catholic or WASP, I think. Born in Colorado. Reporter for the *Salt Lake Tribune.* Of course I knew."

Rebe undercut what little comfort I had for the new additions to the manuscript. She was totally thrown by, as she put it: "The God's golf bit and Greg Hansen's alleged hold on you. Golf, fine, if you must, but it doesn't jibe that someone as fiercely independent as you…as you have portrayed yourself…would get suckered into spending two prime years banging on doors by someone you hardly knew, a liar at that…I mean, let's face it, you knew each other barely one damn year."

There was more to it, of course, but Rebe wasn't in the mood to talk. The pressing issue of marriage had become even more pressing. Father Vinny was fading faster than expected (don't we all?). "We need to think about a *sooner* date…he may be a sunnuvabitch, but he is my father…he should see me married…even to you."

"Good backhand. Thanks a lot."

"Didn't mean it that way…I mean I know why he's a bigger than your normal sunnuvabitch to you… So, we're even: *très* bitch Sarah looms large to me…sticking it to Dad just when he needed her most."

"Actually, not quite right…she really didn't have much of a choice," I said, nervously.

"Of course she had a choice. She gets him to bail on Mom. He does. A couple of months later…he gets sick…she gives him up for Lent."

"For Elli and Janie…"

"They didn't like him?"

"She could have lost them…unfit to be a mother…was the threat…"

"You? You didn't?"

"He was married to another woman. He lied to her—there was no divorce in process at the time. I checked. It was pretty easy and I was really desperate, furious…put the fear of God in them both."

Greg wrote twice. He extolled the virtues of the Spartan but spiritually rich life he was leading in Hong Kong. I was amazed at his sudden, apparently successful transformation. Perhaps he really had experienced a one-on-one with God. Maybe there was hope for me after all? From friends who were also serving in Hong Kong I learned that his reformation was not quite as complete as he was representing. While he had quickly become fluent in Cantonese and was reputed to be an excellent teacher, he was stretching the basic rules all missionaries agree to follow: remain with your companion at all times; maintain an arm's length between you and any woman; put out of your mind all thoughts of home, friends, girls and other worldly things. In short, become an unnatural man.

Greg was hardly preternatural. He had a habit of sneaking out of the apartment after his companion had gone to bed, roaming the streets of Hong Kong until dawn, doing God knows what but definitely not His work. The two of them, so the report goes, were caught entertaining two women in their apartment. To make matters worse, they were smoking and drinking whiskey when the mission president's assistants knocked on the door. And on and on and on, all while he was simultaneously pressing me to "discover your spiritual bearings," gushing about the "inner peace I've found here in the mission field."

Nurse Naomi's devil-may-care approach to life left me craving every release she offered, never mind that not-so-small matter of her menacing lover in Rock Springs, a bar-room brawler with the wounds, missing teeth and a menacing 8-inch Campobasso switchblade his father had brought home from the war.

There wasn't much peace at the hospital, either.

He was getting intensive care lying face up on a metal treatment table in the emergency room when I walked in to draw his blood. "We need a hematocrit, type and cross match, and two pints," the doctor barked as I stared, stunned, at the battered but vaguely recognizable face attached to the young body on the table. "Stat."

"Blood pressure's dropping," snapped Naomi. "Be quick with this one Jed, or we'll lose him."

"What happened?" I said, cinching the rubber tourniquet around the young man's biceps, tapping the vein in the crotch of his elbow to make it pop up, needle-ready.

A policeman standing in the corner of the ER bay, trying his hardest not to get sick, eyed me warily. "Clipped a telephone pole doing about ninety. If he hadn't been drunk as a skunk, he'd be deader than a doornail already. Course he wouldn't have had the accident in the first place."

"Right," I said as blood spurted into the vacuum tube. "Got an official ID on him yet?"

"Yeh, Fairlawn. Supposed to be the son of a big deal executive at Kennecott," the cop said.

"Fairlawn, Daniel Fairlawn Senior," I mumbled, vacantly. The face was vague in this condition, but Daniel Fairlawn Senior was not, and I knew he had but one son...Danny Junior.

"That's it. You know him?" the cop said.

"Know both of them—the one before you since junior high school," I said.

Fifteen minutes later, I raced back to the emergency room carrying two pints of Fairlawn-compatible blood. "Hematocrit's off the charts, about an eleven," I said. "But the Gods are with us—we had two pints of B-negative in the bank."

"Did Jesus mention anything about resurrection?" the doctor cracked cynically.

"What?" I said.

"He's gone, Jed, bought the farm about five minutes ago and just as well. Look at that crushed skull. Prime candidate for the rutabaga patch."

"Shit," I said. "That poor dumb..."

"Knew him did you?" the doctor said, nodding casually, coolly, clinically toward the tragedy splayed across the table, an arm's length away.

"Knew him well, very well," I said.

"Must be shocked to see him like this," he said.

"Shocked? Hell no," I said as I walked toward the doctor's locker room where I worshipped the always more reliable porcelain God for thirty minutes or so.

Over the eight years or so I knew Danny Fairlawn, I had seen him falling-down drunk on more than one occasion, which should have provided ample warning. He was a good kid, no two ways about it. He was a Catholic trying very hard to fit in. I remember him well because he often saved my pride—he was the only non-Mormon in the group that got sicker than I did on watery 3.2% alcohol Utah beer. I'm pretty sure he didn't like to drink, either. And, it had nothing to do with religion. Obviously.

We got better acquainted after a Halloween night canyon party he missed. Because I looked older than the rest, I had volunteered to purchase the liquor for the night and consequently became the custodian of his pint of Cutty Sark, another no-show's pint of Jim Beam, a cherry vodka and a lime too. I stuffed them inside the lining of a battered parka, which is where they were when my mother, inexplicably, cleaned my room ("I was trying to do you a favor," she explained later) Monday morning and attempted to hang up the coat. They were still there Monday evening when my father confronted me: "Your parka seems to have gained a little weight recently," he said, handing it over.

"Really?" I said.

"Really," he said. "Explain!"

"I was just keeping them for people."

"Really. Like...?"

"Friends."

"For instance?"

"For instance people you don't know, it's none of your business."

"The juvenile authorities might think otherwise."

"They would?" I said.

"I think they just might. And they might also be interested to know how you were able to buy it," he said. "So if you insist on your story, I'll just have to assume that it all belongs to you."

"Well it doesn't," I said. "You'll just have to trust me. I'll give it back to the owners tonight."

"Wonderful idea, we'll do it together: a true father-son bonding opportunity," he said. "Why don't you start by telling me who those people are, and you better do it fast before I put in a call to my friend, Detective Fetzer, down at the juvenile court."

"You wouldn't," I said.

"Trust me, I will," he said.

First I extracted his promise not to turn us in. Then I spilled out the names, adding that they hadn't attended our weekend party. He packed the bottles into a cloth flour sack and we spent the rest of the afternoon and evening delivering the booty to their rightful owners. And their parents.

Frankly, I was surprised that none of the parents seemed particularly upset or concerned, even though I warned Dad that other parents were quite a bit more relaxed about teenage drinking than he was, which was not relaxed at all. I don't think he believed me, really.

As we sat in the Fairlawn living room (it was the last time I saw Danny alive), I thought Dad had finally found a sympathetic, supportive comrade. "I'm just shocked that boys this age would use hard liquor," Mrs. Fairlawn said.

"My sentiments exactly, I don't understand it at all," my father said. His pinched face muscles seemed to relax.

"It's fine if the boys come over here to play a little poker, drink a few beers, in fact I'm happy to give them all the beer they want. But this hard liquor business is just too much—so unnecessary. Thank you for coming by, Mr. Russell, I'll make sure that this issue is dealt with properly," she said.

We walked in silence to the car. Mission accomplished—if nothing else, I'd told the truth, I had forewarned him, drinking was no big deal. My father's head was bowed, resting on the steering wheel as I climbed into the passenger side of the car. Huge tears streamed down his face.

"What's wrong?" I said.

"What's wrong with these parents? You boys are the ones who will pay for their neglect. One day, one of you is going to wind up dead—I just pray it isn't you," he said.

It wasn't.

Visions of Danny lying battered and mangled on the treatment table in the ER, another of him stumbling out the door of a cabin we'd rented for mid-winter ski vacation—finding his body after hours of searching, curled up like a fetus in a ski patrol shack halfway up the mountain—flashed through my mind as if they were part of a highlights film of a young man steadily self-destructing as he tried desperately to fit in.

A ringing phone awakened me from this disturbingly vivid nightmare. "Hematology," I said groggily.

"Is that you Jed?" the voice said.

"Yes it's me alright, who's this?" I said. "What time is it?"

"Your father. It's eight thirty. Are you okay?" he asked.

"Fine. About as good as can be expected after working fifteen straight hours."

"So you haven't heard about Dan, then?"

"Dan who?"

"Dan Fairlawn—he was killed in a car crash."

"*Danny* Fairlawn, yes I know," I said. "They brought him here last night."

"I prayed they'd taken him somewhere else. You okay?" he said.

"I'll recover."

"Don't you think it's about time to come home?"

"I've been thinking about it," I said.

For all practical purposes, I had fully moved out of the dorm room at St. Mark's a week before Christmas, although I continued to sleep there periodically until early January, mainly because the rent was paid up and there was too much going on.

Danny's funeral brought the old crowd back together again for a flurry of introspective partying. Final exams killed another week, and then the usual spate of holiday parties followed. And, through it all, I had to contend with pressure from Naomi, who thought the decision to move home was rash, not to mention inconvenient in many ways.

"You're overreacting to your friend's death," she said. "It's a shame you had to see it in the first place."

"Would that have made it any less real?" I said.

"Less graphic perhaps. Not everybody that drinks ends up dead on an emergency room table."

"That's not why I'm moving home."

"Come on. So why is it a week after your friend dies, out of nowhere you become hell-bent to move home? It's not just a coincidence," she said.

"Actually, it's a coincidence. I've been thinking about it since last summer."

"OK, but did you ever consider how it's going to cramp our style?"

"That may be part of it," I said. "Things aren't as they should be. It's—the sex—is fun enough, but there's no commitment, no nothing. It's all physical."

"Your choice, not mine," she said.

"That's not the 'nothing.' I meant there's lots to be resolved, one way or another…I can't do it here…I'm compromised."

"And you won't be comprised at home? Right!"

Of course Mother was thrilled to pieces when she heard the news. Before I began to move my things in late November, she thoroughly scoured my old room. Each time I arrived to deliver a new box or two of books, clothes and assorted items seemed to coincide with her bread-baking cycles. I thought if for no other reason than her bread, it would be worth living at home again. Randy, my five-year-old brother, was even more delighted. He thought I had left in the first place because he'd squeezed me out.

"I'll stay out of your room, I promise," Randy pledged as I unloaded my clothes from the car.

"You can come into my room anytime," I said. "In fact, you can have it all to yourself when I move out again."

"When you go on a mission. Mom says you're going," Randy said.

"She did?" I said. "When'd she say that?"

"She always says that, but it was last night. She said she thought you'd be going any day now."

"Well don't bet your last marble on it."

"Okay," he said. "But Mom says if you go, I'll go too. So I hope you go because I want to go too."

"It must be in our genes," I said. Randy checked the pockets of his Levi's to see if he could find what I was talking about.

My parents hadn't been so eager to get me home that they caved in totally, but they compromised a little. I promised to abide by the rules—no staying out past one thirty in the morning, no cigarettes or alcohol in the house—if they promised not to bug me about the Church, or a mission. They agreed. I volunteered to pay rent. They declined.

"Save the money for something important, like a mission," Mother offered, earnestly trying to be helpful.

"Don't start, we agreed..."

"Slip of the tongue. I meant, save it for a rainy day. For something important like college...or a mission." She was just incapable of restraining herself.

My first night home, the bishop happened to drop by. Our families were close. Still, I knew the visit wasn't coincidental.

"What a surprise, I didn't know you'd moved home already," he said when I answered the doorbell, belying the fact that he'd probably been tipped off.

"Just today, as a matter of fact," I said, as he opened the screen door and walked into the living room. He pumped my arm ferociously.

"That's good news, Jed, real good news," he said. "It's about time you caught me up on you. You're looking real good, son."

"Well, you probably know I've been working out at St. Mark's Hospital and going to school and so on. I guess that's about it."

"Great," he said. "I'd like to hear all about it, but why don't we do it in private—at the church some night—say this Friday, about seven thirty?"

"No mission talk, right?" I said.

"It might come up, but I just want to get caught up on you."

"Alright I'll come. But no mission business," I said defensively, fully aware of how way leads on to way and that sooner or later all chats between Mormon bishops and 19-year-old young men always get around to the subject of missions.

"Suit yourself," he said.

Between Monday night and Friday night, the Russell house positively bustled with activity. I'd never seen my mother happier. The word that I was seeing the bishop had spread through our massive family like brushfire.

"So I hear the bishop finally got his claws into you," said Ike, my 17-year-old brother. "So where do you think you want to go?"

"To his office. That's it. It's just a friendly little chat, that's all," I said.

"I've got five bucks that says differently."

"Bishop Sanford promised, and bishops never lie," I said.

Many Are Called

Ike read it right. The meeting with the bishop was but a thinly veiled attempt at friendly persuasion. Bishop Sanford didn't come right out and pop the question. If nothing else, he was a man of his word, more interested in finding out what was really in my heart and head than in extracting a lockstep commitment to serve a mission. To him, a missionary experience was no insurance that a man would, thereafter, hold fast to the Church everlastingly.

Ironically, I had once, unknowingly, helped him with his own testimony. He moved into our ecclesiastical precinct—the Canyon Creek First Ward—shortly after I became a deacon upon turning 12. He was asked to serve as the advisor to the Deacon's Quorum. Just before I turned 14 he was called to serve as first counselor in the bishopric, which required him to supervise the Teacher's Quorum of boys, those aged 14–16. As a result, he was in place to ordain me a teacher because my father was unexpectedly out of town on the scheduled day.

As Carl laid his hands on my head, I had the eerie feeling that we had met before, long, long ago. I was moved by what he said; awed, actually because, at the time, he did not know me well at all.

> *Jedediah Pratt Russell...I ordain you a Teacher in the Aaronic Priesthood and seal upon you all the rights, keys and blessings of that office. 'Many are called and few are chosen' is a scripture many assume means that God chooses few... While every man is called to serve, it is unfortunate that many choose not to. As you sit here today, you confirm that you have made that choice. You have chosen to serve God. Just as you did when you were eight, when you chose to be baptized and confirmed. Just as you did again at twelve, when you were ordained to the office of Deacon... And just as you must*

do in the future, when other callings are made—as you are called to be a Priest, then to serve in the higher priesthood and fulfill a full-time mission…if you are to remain in that small group God refers to as "chosen," I perceive the road won't be easy for you. The time is surely coming when the refreshing faith you have shown today will be seriously put to the test. It will take all of your resources—your intellect, your physical stamina, your resilience, your faith, your hard work—to win the battle. I can't say that it will be a battle that you will win, but I can say that God has given you the resources to do it… Now it is up to you. I can tell you that our Father in Heaven has called you to perform great works…He has given you a discerning mind, a tongue as persuasive as any of your ancestors, and, like them, the ability to bear powerful and rational testimony to both Jew and Gentile… But, if used for your own purposes these powers may lead you down a seemingly reasonable path that takes you far from the Gospel's door. Therefore, be wise and prudent. Seek His assistance in all that you do, especially in times of doubt and inner turmoil… As you do, you will become a powerful tool in God's hand in leading many, many of His children to His threshold. I emphasize that this is no mean task you have been called to. I sense there are legions of men waiting anxiously to hear God's word from you, men and women and children who are waiting anxiously for you, specifically, to choose to accept your calling from God. I seal upon you the power to grasp and answer that calling…

Carl's hands were trembling as he extended his right hand to meet mine. Now that I think of it, I may have had a tear or two in my eyes too. What did this man I barely knew know of my family history that I didn't?

("…He has given you a discerning mind, a tongue as persuasive as any of your ancestors, and, like them, the ability to bear powerful and rational testimony to both Jew and Gentile.")

"Which one of the Pratt brothers is your ancestor?" Bishop Carl wanted to know.

"Both, Orson and Parley," I said.

"Both?" The bishop was shocked.

"Both, a fluke of polygamy."

"Both?" He shook his head in disbelief. "I had no idea. Such big shoes."

Whatever prompted him to utter what he had was okay with me for very practical reasons: it singled me out, set me apart, anointed me—before God and man, particularly the annoying boys in my neighborhood—that I was unique, if peculiar in some ways, a prospective influential leader, a good and righteous seed with a mind as discerning as Orson Pratt's and Parley's powers of persuasion.

From that point forward, I often thought Carl paid more attention to me than he did to others in the quorum. Once he had praised me for having a thorough understanding of the gospel—"much deeper than most boys your age," he said—then bitterly groused that it was almost impossible to attend to my questions without losing the other boys in the Quorum. "You must use your knowledge to influence your peers."

Once he revealed to me that he believed he had been given a special calling to look after me: "No matter where you go or what you do, I will always be your counselor," he told me once. Frankly, I was grateful for the extra attention and care. So I was not at all surprised that shortly before I turned sixteen—the age at which I would be ordained a Priest, the third and last step of the Aaronic Priesthood when young men begin to prepare more seriously for missionary service—Carl was called to serve as Bishop of our ward, which also required him to serve as advisor to the Priest's Quorum.

Carl hadn't seemed to notice when I began to slip away, perhaps because I was fairly duplicitous about it. While I experimented with alcohol and tobacco, I had continued to officiate at the sacrament table on Sundays, attended all my meetings, and willingly accepted additional assignments. Underneath the veneer, I was coming apart spiritually. At first it was simple, predictable adolescent rebellion—every boy I knew recklessly sewed a handful of wild oats, and then repented.

But it evolved from rebellion to genuine disaffection for religion generally and Mormonism in particular. I became hypercritical of the hypocrisy of my Mormon neighbors. It was not that they were worse than the average man. The problem was I expected them to be better than average.

And, I was finding glaring inconsistencies to what was then represented as Mormon doctrine—a group of teachings that I labeled the "Better-Than Doctrines."

Chief among them was the doctrine or practice of excluding Blacks from the priesthood. I had listened patiently to all the explanations, theories. None made any sense whatsoever nor were they consistent with the central gospel messages: all human beings are entitled to the fullness of the gospel of Christ. By definition a man and wife and their family could not experience the fullness of Mormonism unless the father held the priesthood.

Carl explained the practice this way: "We don't know why, for sure, but God has His reasons. We know that Negroes will be given the priesthood at some time, and we should be preparing ourselves, and them for that day." While his explanation didn't wash with me, it promised change. It certainly was more reasonable and reassuring than some of the other theories that were often taught as doctrine by respected Church authorities: that Blacks had lost their right to the priesthood by being less than valiant warriors in the preexistence philosophical battle between Christ and Satan; or that Blacks were the descendants of fratricidal Cain; or, both. Each theory ended with the cop-out: "But Blacks will be given the priesthood at some time—probably in the next life."

If I had been a betting man in 1962, I'm absolutely certain that I could have gotten heavy odds—say a million to one or higher—if I had wagered that Blacks would receive the priesthood in my lifetime.

I challenged Carl to show me where in the scriptures—the Bible, the Book of Mormon, or the Doctrine and Covenants or Pearl of Great Price—it said that Blacks were not to hold the priesthood. He was as astonished as I had been to discover there were no supporting passages to be found. He acknowledged that Brigham Young's statements contradicted fairly explicit directives from the Prophet Joseph, the founding prophet of Mormonism, who had himself ordained at least one Negro convert to the office of Seventy in the Melchizedek Priesthood.

"It seems simple enough to me," I had said. "If there's such a policy, it's so fundamentally inconsistent with the basic tenets of the Church that it could only have been instituted by man." I had told Bishop Carl that I believed the policy was a pragmatic way to remove the Mormons from harm's way in Missouri. Mormons were fierce abolitionists and Missouri wanted to enter the union as a slave state.

"Like a family relic, the practice was passed down and institutionalized. Over time it became the propagator of benignly racist assumptions—like Negroes are somehow inferior and other such nonsense. It bothers me that President McKay hasn't recognized this and asked the Lord for guidance. Doesn't he believe in 'ask and ye shall receive?' That's the key to this whole situation," I had argued.

Carl had warned not to get carried away with such logic. He had said the issue wasn't central to a testimony (I wondered about that) and assured me that President McKay was a man of good will who was doubtlessly on his knees every day seeking guidance. "Maybe the time isn't right—the Lord's purposes are not always crystal clear to men," he said.

I had said I wasn't sure that the situation was the Lord's to correct. "If the practice had been instituted by man, it should be withdrawn by man. If the Lord has any concern in this matter, it's not wrapped up in the issue itself; it probably has more to do with how a change will affect the Church membership, possibly even some members of the Quorum of the Twelve. Two of the apostles, at least Joseph Fielding Smith and Ezra Taft Benson for instance, seemed to regard the practice as fundamental doctrine. What chance is there that Elders Benson and Smith are on their knees with President McKay seeking guidance on an issue they consider resolved long ago? Not much of a chance."

Shortly after this discussion—I must have been 17 and a senior in high school at the time—Bishop Carl confronted me about a rumor that I had been seen puffing a cigar downtown, in *front* of the Church office building on East South temple. I laughed loudly because, in truth, the story was absolutely inaccurate. "What an outrageous tale!" I responded. "How do these things get started?"

"It seems to have come from an anonymous, but eyewitness account," Carl said. "Is it true?"

"You shouldn't have to ask," I said. "But since you have, let me tell you if I were seriously disenchanted with the Church, I might do something like that. Only I wouldn't light it—I hate the taste of cigar smoke."

One wonders why Carl didn't follow up by asking how it was that I had acquired a distaste for cigar smoke if I'd never smoked one. I was surprised, but relieved he let the subject drop.

It all came to a head in priesthood meeting one Sunday morning, shortly before graduation from high school. The adult advisor to the quorum—a rather smug, young man, a recently returned missionary—was leading a discussion about the Mormon doctrine of preexistence and the great war of words between God's sons, Christ and Satan, that ensued over how the earth would be governed. Satan proposed mandatory obedience. Christ's plan pivoted around free agency. Fully a third of the spirits sided with Satan's losing plan, and like him, were cast out, never given an opportunity to obtain a physical body. So far, so good.

"Among the remaining two thirds, some were more valiant than others and thus earned commensurate rewards," the teacher said. "The fact that you were born in the covenant, suggests that you were among the most valiant. Negroes can't hold the priesthood because they were less valiant in the war. Any questions?"

Not wanting to transform a church class into a verbal brawl, I bit my lip at the heresy the teacher declared was church doctrine. Doctrine? Bull. I had heard it before. I had asked people a lot smarter than the teacher to prove it and none of them could. Why bother with this ass? The other boys weren't paying attention anyway. What did it matter?

"No questions."

Bishop Carl, who always attended these meetings, was surprised. He stared at me. "Surely, Jed, you have a thought or two?"

"What's the point—it's a Church *doctrine*, right?" I said, plainly irritated.

"That's right," the teacher said emphatically. "However, we do believe that Negroes will be given the priesthood at some time—but not in this life."

"If I say I don't believe it or have doubts, in essence I would be expressing doubt whether the Prophet speaks with God," I said.

"You would," he said, anxious to move along.

"Well then...would you be kind enough to show me—to show us—what scriptures support this?" I said. There was malice in my heart. My intention was to rip the teacher apart, put him in his place, make a fool out of him, get him to confess that he didn't know what the hell he was teaching.

The teacher looked pained as he scanned the lesson plan to see if there were any pertinent scriptures listed. "I don't know what scripture says this, but I can tell you with surety, that the prophets of our Church have said this since the very foundations of the Church back in 1830," he said.

"Wrong, wrong," I said rather defiantly. "Several Black men held the priesthood, performed ordinances."

The teacher said he had never heard of such a thing.

"So how is it that you can be so sure it's doctrine when you don't even know that Joseph Smith ordained Black men to the priesthood? Moreover, time and again, he preached that the fullness of the Gospel of Jesus Christ was for men of all nations, Black and white, bond and free."

"Secondly, I never did say the gospel wasn't for Black men. They can be baptized, they just can't hold the priesthood," the teacher snapped, looking to Bishop Carl for support.

The bishop shrugged his shoulders.

"That contradicts Joseph Smith," I said. "He said the *fullness* of the gospel was for all, regardless of skin color. Isn't it a fact that to experience the fullness of the gospel, one must hold the priesthood...and enter into the new and everlasting covenant of marriage for eternity, which can only take place in the temple, a place Mormon men can visit only if they hold the Melchizedek Priesthood?" I said.

"True. As I said, Black men, at some time, will be given the fullness. But not in this life, period. Let's move on," the teacher said.

"Wait a minute. There are no scriptures anywhere that support your proposition: they simply don't exist. All you can say is: *We don't know why.* Period. Your other suggestion that I was born a Mormon because I was more valiant suggests that my girlfriend Lainey was less valiant because she wasn't born into a good Mormon home. It means the friends I have who were born into really devout Mormon homes—the sons and daughters of apostles and stake presidents and so forth—were more valiant than the rest of us," I said.

"That seems to be the idea," he said.

"If that's true, God must have bought into Satan's plan. He stacked the deck. Not just against some child born in the slums of Calcutta, but against you and me too."

"That child will be given the chance to hear the gospel after we leave this life—in the Spirit World—and choose to accept it or reject it, as though he were in the flesh," he said.

"If we cover ourselves by that way, what's the point of missionary work, especially if the missionary must sell the notion to potential converts that despite their less-than-valiant performance, they may now accept the fullness of the gospel...would you accept a religion that maintained that people like you are inferior, less deserving than those being born under the covenant?"

"If I knew it was true, I would," he said.

"And that's the point. None of what you have said is true. The gospel according to you is just some man's opinion. The real gospel teaches us that, for the most part, God leaves man to his own devices, gives guidance only when He is asked. The problem is, no one seems to be asking about these wacky theories. Then some unwitting soul like you passes them off as doctrine to another generation of gullible Mormons."

"An apostle's teachings are inspired," he said.

"But they are not gospel. Even an apostle is vulnerable to hearsay. As boys, all of them sat in classes just like this one and probably heard the same lines we're hearing now, like: 'Oh, it's been a doctrine since the Church began, or Joseph Smith said it.' But at some point some apostle will come along who'll do some original research. When he does, I can tell you he won't find any scriptural support for these theories, because I have looked and they're not there."

"Are you saying the Prophet and Apostles haven't asked about these questions?" he said.

"Not exactly. I'm saying they haven't asked the right questions...they seem to have blindly accepted the word of others, a forgivable error for mere mortals like us, but unforgivable for 'special witnesses of Christ,' men who claim to be on intimate terms with the Lord. If they're not more careful with their speculations, some of our leaders could find themselves in deep dung with God," I said.

The teacher was furious. His face reddened as he said powerfully: "I can tell you, all of you, that Brother Russell is not in tune with the gospel, and if he pursues this antagonistic course, the Spirit will withdraw from him, and that, my friends, will lead to his own apostasy."

Bishop Carl shifted uncomfortably. Then he spoke. "I think the point Jed is trying to make, is that we should all, individually, come to a knowledgeable and spiritual accord with the doctrines of the gospel."

"Partially," I said, appreciative, but annoyed that the bishop had deemed it necessary to temper my comments rather than the teacher's. "The second part is that no Mormon of sound mind should blindly follow doctrines until he has reason to believe they are correct. The third part is that apostles, though they may be prophets, seers and revelators, are still human and, as such, are subject to temptations, prejudices and intellectual limitations. They are not gods and they would be the first ones to tell you that."

The bishop scowled. The teacher gasped. The other boys whispered to one another. For the simple truth was that many, many Mormons regarded the Apostles—certainly the Prophet—as men who had already earned appointments to the Celestial Kingdom where they would become Gods of worlds yet to come. Their only human characteristic was the mortal condition of their bodies. Apart from that, these men were de facto gods, gods that I had offended by my bold, cynical, heretical challenge.

"Even then you were insufferable," Rebe said. "Honest, now, were you trying to sort out your own doubts...or just being a smart-ass?"

"True confession?" Rebe nodded. "Alright, the smart-ass factor was high on this particular occasion. But, I can be just as gullible as the next guy: so I took apostolic speculation as serious gospel. It was devastating, months or years later, to discover the doctrine was not doctrine at all. It was one man's interpretation of the scriptures. Personal opinion. It made me wonder about everything else that God was supposed to have revealed. Were they of God or man."

"I know all about gullibility...and the bitterness...and how difficult it is to move past it, turn the other cheek," Rebe said.

"Your father, I know that must be tough. But, his faults in one realm don't diminish his successes in the others," I said.

"And you wonder why I find you so attractive? Someone who is so quick to forgive and move on! Someone I could lean on."

"Is marriage the cure?"

"Sure—I officially transfer the burden of the trust thing from his shoulders to yours, but what happened before makes me trust him, everyone, a little less."

"More cautious, you mean."

"No, less trusting, more skeptical, even cynical...guilty until proven innocent."

"You should resolve matters with him while you can," I said. "Before he..."

"It'd take years...we've only got weeks."

It took exactly two days. Vincent Wheeler Adams died just before midnight, a month shy of his fiftieth birthday. Rebe made it to the hospital about thirty minutes before he officially left this world. "In time to say goodbye, to tell him I loved him and forgave him...hoped he would forgive me," she said through tears. "I don't know whether he heard...or understood."

"He understood," I said, holding her tightly.

"How would you know, you were in the cafeteria."

"But you were there...you endured to the end. That picture was worth a thousand words of *mish-mosh*."

The phone awakened us at six the next morning. Hell of a time for Sarah. "Sorry to call so early...how's Rebe's father doing," Sarah wanted to know.

"Much better than he was...he passed away last night," I said.

"I was afraid it was that..."

"What?"

"When they called here for her last night..." Sarah said.

"Really? Odd they would call you..."

"Suppose it's because my phone's still listed in your name..."

"Should be calling numbers for next of kin on the admitting forms," I said. Rebe was awake now, flashing hand signals requesting the identity of the caller. I obsequiously kissed the phone. The code was clear. Rebe's eyes rolled.

"Be kind to her Jeddy...kinder than you were to me."

"How can you say that...I didn't go to ROT's funeral because it was two thousand miles away, the kids were in school, and you wanted to go alone...but I adored that old man of yours."

"Face it, you abhor funerals."

"Someone loves them?" I said.

"Don't let her go alone."

"Like you, she may have different ideas."

"So what? Go with her anyway, insist on it!"

"What are your plans?"

"Tennis in a couple of hours...dinner tonight in Manhattan."

"I meant...not my business."

"So, shit, she knows," Rebe said when I hung up the phone.

"About your father, yes, the hospital called her."

"Shit, shit, shit. My fault. My mother couldn't remember your number, gave Sarah's as the contact for me. She thought it amusing, ironic. I meant to change it..."

"I don't think Sarah would see the irony! It's possible that she has not made the connection."

"Ya think?" Rebe said. "Elli and Janie could have said something."

"Nothing for them to say about that connection...we never discussed it," I said.

Rebe insisted that I forego the funeral, arguing that it would make matters more unsettling for her mother. "It's not you, per se," Rebe said, "it's your connection to Sarah...besides he wanted a small graveside service—family and very close friends only."

"I've been ordered to insist...no matter what you say," I said.

"You abhor funerals...you should write...I insist," she said.

Dear reader, I apologize sincerely for confusing you by presenting a new portrait of myself that, at first glance, seems to contradict the one I drew earlier. Neither is wholly accurate. Weighting both equally won't add clarity. I may have been a victim of well-intentioned religious brainwashing. Perhaps, as Sarah asserted, beguiling temptations of the flesh struck and passed like bouts of the twenty-four-hour flu. They may have loosened my hand-hold on the iron rod, obscured for the moment what I knew in my gut and head.

Or, perhaps over time I have come to recognize intellectually, if not in my gut, that there are as many ways as there are people to approach God, to find goodness and develop spirituality. It's a wholly different matter for me, personally. I was trained to believe that the Church was key to finding and developing a personal relationship with God. Which is why it is nigh unto impossible for me to know whether or not my inability to connect one-on-one has something to do with my less than true-believer relationship with the Church. Some Mormon friends would say I'm a heretic or apostate; others wonder why I even bother to identify myself as a Mormon.

Interestingly many non-Mormons, Jewish friends especially, would insist just the opposite is true. "It's unfortunate there are no Reformed Mormon temples," they might say. I hate labels of this sort because they never accurately reflect reality. Nevertheless, I prefer "reformed" or "modified" to "apostate" or, worst of all, "Jack Mormon," a pejorative often inappropriately applied to all lapsed Mormons when, in fact, it defines hypocrites—those who don't practice what they preach.

I am deeply respectful of values Mormons add to the world; I consider myself an able translator of things Mormon to non-Mormons and vice versa. At times, I admit to being a critic of things the Church and other Mormons do that fall short of the high standards they set for themselves. Frankly, if any one life event propelled me into the middle-man role, it was the two year mission I served to New England.

I had dressed informally for the interview—sport jacket and tie. Nevertheless, my mother, always one to lay it on thick whenever given the chance, said: "You look like a missionary." Normally, I would have responded with something sharp, to put her in her place, to remind her of the promise not to push and badger. But I bit my tongue. She was proud, bursting with joy.

Bishop Carl was more circumspect. "You look pleased with yourself," he said as I shook his hand across the desk.

"Do I? It must be because I did well in school last quarter," I said.

"Excellent," the bishop said. "Bring me up to date."

"I've nearly finished my sophomore year. GPA's around a three-point, but it's been much better than that lately."

"Still in pre-medicine?"

"Alive, if not kicking," I said. "I still have the advanced chemistry sequence ahead—it's usually a real killer."

"Who's your latest…girlfriend."

"No one special."

"That's a change," the bishop said. I shrugged. "How's it at home?"

"Okay—still impossible to study there," I said. The bishop laughed, as if he understood how difficult it must be to memorize bones and muscles while nearly a dozen children roared around the house.

"Your parents must be glad to have you home, but I'll bet they've got the pressure on to serve a mission?"

"The subject's come up, but not very often. They promised to not bug me about the Church."

"So I guess that leaves the bugging to me?"

I laughed. "You made a deal too," I said, surprised at his frontal assault. Usually he was more subtle.

"Mission was the deal. I simply want to hear how you are with the Church. Fair enough?"

"Fair. The Episcopalians at St. Mark's haven't converted me," I said.

"So I've heard."

"You've heard? From whom?" I said. "Then your sources must have told you I was considering a mission."

"They weren't that explicit," the bishop said. "But now that *you've* mentioned it, why don't you fill me in."

"I'm nineteen, nearly twenty, so it's only natural that I'd be thinking about it, just thinking," I said cautiously.

"Just thinking?"

"For the moment. Stay tuned."

"Think you can qualify?"

"Reasonably sure, unless the rules have changed lately."

"Would I violate my pledge if I suggested that we proceed as though we were in a mission interview? Just to give you an idea on what to expect?" the bishop said.

"A clever tactic," I said. "But, what the heck."

"Simple questions first. How are you and the Word of Wisdom doing?"

"Fine," I said. The bishop's eyebrows raised. "Fine, now. Not a problem any longer."

"How long has it been fine?"

"Long enough; it's not a problem," I said sternly, thwarting his attempt to play father confessor.

"Longevity is an indication of commitment," the bishop said.

"Is it? Is that doctrine? Is it specific or does personal judgment play a part here?" I said, somewhat combatively.

"Judgment does play a role..." he said.

"Then, in my judgment it's been long enough—long enough to know I can live it, long enough to know that the change is not just cosmetic. It certainly isn't something I need guidance on," I said.

"Fine," he said. "Tithing—are you a full tither?" he said.

"You have the records—you got the checks each week," I said. Despite my inactivity, I had regularly mailed checks to cover a full ten percent of my earnings. I was surprised he hadn't remembered.

"Why did you continue to tithe even though you weren't attending church?" Rebe asked.

"Habit, I suppose," I said. "I'd been paying tithing since I was five. I guess I thought it would keep my options open. I don't know why, really, I just did. Tithing was a big deal in my family—in the ward. I had seen members sell second cars, take out small loans, and dip into their saving to meet their tithing obligations. My father always said: 'pay the Lord first and the rest will take care of itself.'"

"You're right," Bishop Carl said. "I'd forgotten. Quite a sum, as I recall."

"No more than what was due," I said. Bishop Carl pressed his hands together in front of his mouth, blowing warm air through them as he studied my face. If he was hoping for a tearful confession, he wasn't going to get it from me.

"Why pay tithing at all?" he asked, hoping, I'm sure, that it would elicit a profoundly spiritual response.

"Why not?" I asked, knowing that the bishop would have no ready answer.

"It's unusual that an inactive person would continue to tithe."

"I agree. It would be unusual for an *inactive* person to do that," I said, suppressing a smile.

"I see," said Bishop Carl thoughtfully. "Well, then, have you been morally clean?" He leaned back in his chair, solemnly clasped his hands on the desk between us.

"I'm honest. I treat others with dignity. I try not to take advantage of others."

"Good...that's a good start. How about sexually—are you clean in that area?"

"There have been a few indiscretions that I've repented for," I said. "So yes, I'm square on this issue."

"Would you please be more specific?" Bishop Carl asked.

"I have been specific. There have been indiscretions. I have mended my ways and repented. That's about as specific as I need to be. Those indiscretions would not get in the way of fulfilling an honorable mission."

"I must be specific. Have you ever had illicit sexual relations with a woman?"

"Never anything that I'd be ashamed of. Illicit in my heart, perhaps," I said, offering the explanation I had rehearsed. I hadn't abused or taken advantage of anyone. I exercised self-control. I honored the women in my life, whether they were Mormon or not. On this subject I needed neither an interlocutor nor a personal trainer—I would continue to go direct.

"We've all lusted," the bishop said forgivingly. "So the last question has to do with desire—with testimony. How are you in those areas?"

"Strong on the former, struggling with the latter," I said honestly. "Actually the two are mixed up together. Is my strong desire indicative of an equally strong testimony, or does the former always precede the latter?"

"Both," the bishop said quickly.

"So, to be specific, I'm strong on the fundamentals—or at least what I assume are the fundamentals—if I begin by assuming the existence of God. I'm neither strong nor weak in that category because each side of the God issue is equally troubling. While I can't rationalize God away, I have an equally difficult time rationalizing Him in. Neither is distinguishably more negative or positive; neither has any effect on whether I lead a moral life—in fact I think I would be inclined to live more morally were I a hardened atheist," I said.

"Really? Why?" Bishop Carl asked.

"Simply because there's no pressure. There's no grand reward to forsake. The only reward is that when I croak, or before I croak, I would have the satisfaction of looking back with pride, knowing I had done well: I had helped make the world a better place. In that instance my motives would be more altruistic than if I had been working for pie a la mode in the sky," I said. "I'm like Abou Ben Adhem."

"Abou who?"

"A poem I memorized in sixth grade. Old Abou had been shown a list of men whom the Lord loved best. Abou's name was not among them, so he suggested to the angel that his name be listed with those who loved their fellow men. Naturally, when the angel returned, Ben Adhem's name appeared on the list because the Lord's favorites are all men like Ben Adhem, people who truly care for others. I'm sort of like Abou. As an atheist, I'd get left off a lot of important lists because of one religious arcanity or another, but in the end the Lord, if it turns out He exists, would clearly see that I loved my fellow man and conducted my life accordingly," I said.

The conversation focused on spiritual and intellectual conversion. The latter was the most important "because it will anchor you. All you need is confirmation from that still, small voice," the bishop said.

"Actually, a loud one would work equally as well. But you're right. What I need is the same kind of spiritual confirmation that everyone else in the ward seems to have gotten. I've tried, but nothing. So I can't honestly say I know the Church is true or that Jesus lives. I can say I believe it, but I can't say I know it. I can say it makes sense to me. I think I could tell people how to obtain a spiritual answer, but I couldn't actually testify I had gotten one myself. That's the problem with going on a mission—I'd have to lie," I said.

"As a missionary, you'll covenant to serve as a spiritual guide for others. The Lord's half of the bargain is that He'll provide the answers you're seeking—or at least enough of them so you'll finally know."

"Interesting. Isn't there a danger that I could delude myself into knowing; by doing it, do I indoctrinate myself?"

"You?" he laughed. "You're way too skeptical to let that happen," he said. Even now I'm not sure whether he intended to flatter or needle. Or both. "Do you think that all missionaries know the gospel is true?" Bishop Carl asked.

"Most say they do, although I can think of more whose testimonies were quite suspect, exceedingly shallow," I said.

"Knowing often gets confused for a serious belief," the bishop said. "My hunch is that most of your peers seriously believe when they leave for a mission. A few may *know* it, but they're the exceptions. More of them will come to *know* before their missions are completed, but just as many will return home still seriously believing, somewhat short of full knowledge. In fact, obtaining a full knowledge is the central struggle of life."

"Then, it's not necessary for me to be absolutely certain?"

"No, not absolutely certain, but well on the way, which you have been for quite some time," Bishop Carl said.

"That removes a huge hurdle—one that I thought was insurmountable," I said, relieved. "I thought you had to know before you could go. As long as no one expects that of me, I could serve in good conscience."

"Perhaps you'd come to know along the way."

"It seems logical," I said. "It makes sense that you come to know something by applying it."

"What's left?" he asked.

"Little issues, annoyances, like the Black thing," I said.

"A can of worms," Bishop Carl said.

"I resolved that one a long time ago, as you know. I'm just waiting for the Brethren to ask the right question of God. In the meantime, I think the best thing I can do to help is to baptize a few Black families which will, in turn, pressure the Brethren to research the issue, to ask for specific guidance," I said.

"A revolutionary as a missionary: a time honored tradition," Bishop Carl said—wryly, I thought.

"What you see is what you get," I said.

"Heaven help us all," he laughed.

Over the course of my adult life, I have, on occasion, denied that I was a Mormon, but not because I was ashamed of my background or had apostatized from the faith. I simply did not want to discredit the Church. For similar reasons, at other times I would modify my story slightly: I'd admit that I had been raised a Mormon, but was no longer practicing. These explanations came in handy if I happened to be sipping a cocktail, or smoking a cigarette.

"Did you feel guilt for smoking and drinking?" Dr. Rosenbaum once asked.

"If someone made a big deal of it, yes. In other words, when my parents visited," I said.

"Only then?" Rosenbaum acted as though he thought I had not confessed all, as though my Simon Peter denial betrayed some profound schizophrenia, heretofore undetected.

"For all practical purposes, yes. I mean I'd think about it when I would talk with someone about the Church," I said.

"Not exactly a hot topic in the east," he said.

"You'd be surprised," I said. "I think I have talked more about Mormonism here than I ever did in Utah," I said. I always did my best to avoid bringing up my religion. But with Mormonism, it being as intertwined with Salt Lake City as it is, my efforts often went for naught.

"Have you lived in New York all your life?" the questioner would ask.

"All my adult life," I would say honestly.

"But where were you raised?" he would say.

"In the Rocky Mountains," I would say if I were trying to avoid questions about the Church.

"Where exactly?" he would persist, as if he were preparing a dossier on me for the CIA or a credit reporting agency.

"In Utah—in Salt Lake City," I would finally admit.

"Ah ha," he would say smugly, "I thought you looked like a Mormon."

"I do?" I would say before either denying the faith entirely or offering the caveat that I was raised one; but…I would add that one shouldn't draw the conclusion that all Salt Lakers are Mormons because, in reality, only about half are, and of that half, probably half aren't practicing. No matter what response I offered, the questioner would always want to know more about the Church, a request that I usually complied with unless the inquirer was obviously hostile.

To the people I commuted with each day on the New Haven line, I was known simply as "The Mormon." Whenever one of them would introduce me to a friend, he would always say, "I'd like you to meet Jed Russell, he's a Mormon from Salt Lake City." When I boarded the train in the morning, one of them would usually call out, "Here comes the Mormon," although this practice subsided somewhat after I returned the greeting: "And a good morning to you Jews," which correctly described the religious and ethnic backgrounds of nearly all my friends, and about thirty percent of the commuters on the train. Dr. Rosenbaum had said it was particularly disturbing that Jews, of all people, would take such public note of a person's religion.

"They meant no harm," I assured him. "Besides, I didn't mind the label. In a weird way, I was proud of it. It made me different—intriguing, I thought. Despite appearances, the Church was something I took very seriously. I lacked a testimony, but I knew that there were but two paths for me: Mormonism or atheism. I never could make sense of the idea there was no God, that all the earth and mankind were flukes of nature."

Over the years I had become well informed about Church history and doctrine. This knowledge also gave me greater pragmatism about the Church and its doctrines, not to mention deep respect for the humiliations, murders, and other persecutions that early Mormons suffered for the sake of their religion. I often drew parallels between the persecution of the Mormons and Jews. In principle, if not magnitude and duration, they were very similar indeed.

Like Judaism was for my friends, "Mormon" described both my religious and ethnic background, despite roots on all sides of my family that are embedded in the foundations of the United States—the Pratts from Connecticut, the founders of Hartford; the Hutchinsons of Salem Witch Trials fame, and countless others from the boat that landed at Plymouth, Massachusetts. It was no surprise to me that the descendants of the first American religious zealots and revolutionaries had given rise to the new Christian religion de Tocqueville called the "American Religion." It made sense that the "American" religion would be a curious blend of Christianity and Judaism, autocracy and democracy, pragmatism and idealism, communalism and individualism. I understood my disposition toward dissension and rebellion was genetic. It was the role I had been called to in the preexistence; certainly it was the course that I had chosen for myself. Many are called, few are chosen.

"So if you chose that role for yourself, why did it unsettle you so?" Rosenbaum wanted to know.

"Because I was—I am—never sure it's the right course," I said. "It presents many conflicts, admittedly some of my own making. If I question the direction given by apostles and other Church leaders, am I disloyal? If I turn devil's advocate will I cause someone less able to cope with the complexities and inconsistencies of Mormonism to doubt?"

"Inactivity was your way of dealing with conflicts?" Rosenbaum asked.

"In a way, but that was a conflict too," I said. "If carried too far, it would limit the exposure my own children would have to their heritage; it may have prejudiced their own search for religious bearings. I couldn't persuasively represent to them that something I didn't practice myself was worth exploring seriously: do as I say, not as I do."

Rebe had been gone since early morning. The graveside service was at one o'clock in Madison, fifty miles away, followed by a family gathering at her uncle's home in Olde Lyme. It was nearly six; she'd be home any minute…in need of a drink and talk and affection, not necessarily in that order. I had let her down. I had let her talk me out of attending to the needs of my future family (I do abhor funerals). I would make it up to her this evening: turn off the phones, put on some soothing music—perhaps Glazunov's *Meditation*—encourage her to wander as far afield as she liked. If the weather held, we might take a long swim in the lagoon; perhaps tonight was the night to lower the barriers, loosen the tugs on my wild horses. I headed upstairs to the kitchen where Rebe had been reading the manuscript the night before when *they* called from the hospital.

Sarah glanced up from the manuscript, startled, as I walked into the room. "Oh, sorry, you scared me…I didn't hear you come in the door."

"Been here all afternoon," I said warily. "Car's in the driveway…"

"I thought you went in Rebe's…"

"She went alone…her choice, over my strenuous objections."

Sarah shook her head. I couldn't tell if it was an accusing or agreeing shake. "Mind pouring me a glass of red?" she asked. I obliged.

We clinked glasses: "To Rebe," I proposed.

"And her family," Sarah added. "Jeezuz, Jeddy when were you going to tell me…"

"Tell you what?"

"That Rebe is Vinny's daughter, for Chrissakes. I should have to see her at the funeral to discover this on my own? And, her relatives babbling on about Rebe's new beau: Jed the writer this and Jed the writer that; ogling her goddamn huge sparkling rock. How could you do it?"

"A ring was important, this time. I had no idea you'd be there…were still interested in Vinny."

"After you sabotaged us, why would I tell you anything? Should have kept it going. Kept him well. Wouldn't you have loved having me for a mother-in-law? A new twisted chapter for the book. Which, by the way is pretty good…it's toned down, more restrained than before. It seems like the sessions with Rosenbaum are heading you in the right direction. But God, was I shocked to see Rebe at the funeral…I had no idea Rebe was Vinny's daughter. Vintage JPR vindictiveness: completely over the top."

"We were involved when I figured it out."

"And when were you going to tell me about the marriage: the day before?" Sarah was near tears. I shrugged. "You're making great progress, but I never expected it to turn out this way."

"You turn down an unblazed trail in the woods; the trailhead may be visible for a time, until the path bends, or forks again…there is no clear way back…only a trail that leads ahead, toward whatever the goal is."

"I can guide you back," Sarah said. Tears were flowing. I heard the sliding glass door in my bedroom open and close quietly. "The kids love Rebe, it's like she's their big sister: she's great for them, but this is not the way for you to go…for us. Revenge is not sweet. Revenge is not love. It's no way to build a life…believe me I know…and I'm sorry."

If Rebe had slipped into the house through the slider and was standing anywhere near the hallway door to the master bedroom, I knew she would be able to hear clearly what was being said twenty feet down the hall in the kitchen. Odd, I hadn't heard her car in the driveway. I glanced out the kitchen window—Sarah's car was parked behind mine in front of one of the garage bays. The other lane was free, awaiting Rebe's car.

I'd cautioned Rebe about the possibility of just this kind of scenario and my highly likely, almost predictable response. The book underscored the warning, my premonition that something like this was what I hoped, prayed would happen. And, the sooner the better.

"The issue is not you, or whether I love you, Rebe: I do," I had said. "The issue isn't even about what's best for me, because clearly you are best for me too. It is all about commitment, honor, my obligation to endure to the end. Okay, it's a Mormon thing. For now it's Sarah's choice to live apart, it's not what I willed. If, when she decides to make good on our commitments, I will join her, no matter the pain or personal sacrifice. As I say, it's in my DNA."

Although I thought Rebe was unwise and almost cavalier to dismiss this possibility ("The odds are decidedly in my favor," she said), as we became closer and closer, intimate in ways that Sarah and I never were, I wondered if Rebe's insights into reality and what the future may hold were clearer than mine. But now, standing as she probably was down the hallway, she was overhearing what she never thought she would hear. Doubtless her stomach turned as she processed how I would likely, predictably respond.

"You look troubled, confused," Sarah said, studying my face, which, true to form, probably betrayed what was bubbling around inside my brain, my heart and other vital organs. "Perhaps it might help if we reminded ourselves of what it was like being together…it has been an awfully long time, too long."

My stirrings were predictable and natural. It had been a long time—too long. My body felt it, ached for it; my face revealed it. Sarah moved toward me. I stared, frozen in place—afraid to move forward, or backward.

Where in this hell was Rebe? Was her mind racing in dizzying circles like mine? Was she collapsed in a heap in the hallway? Did she not know that the sound of her footsteps, a door shutting or opening, would be welcome *interruptus*? Sarah's body was closer to mine than it had been for years. When she gently laid her hand on my forearm, I'm sure my body trembled, or was it when her hand slid down my waist, around and behind, pulling, lifting me toward her, pressing? Contact brought a knowing smile to her face. Her free hand aligned my other side to hers… "Yes, yes this would be good," she whispered.

This was all remarkably familiar—my arms wrapped around her shoulders, soft breasts flattened against my ribs, open mouth and tongue poised—yes, this would be quite good. I had written the scene, foreshadowed it well and now fantasy was becoming reality. "Yes, this is quite good," I whispered. "Same old Jed Russell—no matter where he wanders, he remains passionately committed to the woman he married. Jed always comes home."

Sarah's embrace tightened, her upturned face moved toward mine. "That's what I always expected…wanted…what I thought you'd forgotten."

"Rebe, Rebe," I called out. "Where the hell are you?"

Rebe's car pulled into its appointed lane in the driveway several minutes after Sarah's had disappeared down Bermuda Road. I was working my way through a second or third glass of wine when she appeared in the kitchen: radiant, flushed, smiling like she hadn't just come from her own father's funeral.

"Was that Sarah's car in the driveway?" she asked. I nodded. "Long visit? I saw her slip out just before the service started. Figured she might head your way. I'd have given you a heads up, but I figured this is one thing you should deal with on your own, without interference from me."

"The surprise was better, actually," I said.

"She finally get what she needed?"

"Partially, I guess," I said.

"And, you?"

"Not yet. But very soon."

Rebe smiled.

Mission Memoirs

As missionary farewell services go, mine too was typical: the chapel was filled to overflowing with the faithful as well as many who hadn't set foot inside a church in years. Some came because they really didn't believe that I would, in the end, accept the call to serve in the New England Mission, which included all of the obvious states plus the Canadian provinces of New Brunswick, Nova Scotia, Prince Edward Island and Newfoundland and Labrador. They wanted to witness this miracle up close and personal, as they say. More likely than not some of them wanted to make sure I didn't duck out the back door at the last minute, or hire a surrogate to take my place.

At church a week earlier I'd overheard one of the neighbor ladies snip: "How is it possible that Jed Russell is the only boy in the ward his age to qualify for a mission…and he was the most rebellious of the lot?" Although I brushed off such comments, I did wonder whether I was unworthy to serve, whether my sins of commission and omission had exceeded the Lord's munificence. With the perspective that time delivers, my youthful indulgences would have been regarded as pretty predictable and ordinary anywhere else in America but the Mormon Zion.

Unlike Paul on the Road to Damascus, the voice of God had not spoken to me out of the blue. My desire to serve was based on faith and, of course, 19 years of conditioning. I had faith that two years in New England would resolve the testimony issue, one way or the other. The resolution of the testimony thing would determine whether I became what I was raised to be: a devout, participating member and leader of God's one and only true church.

Of the hundred or so missionaries on the platform of the Union Pacific station that cold February morning in 1965, most were young men who looked a lot like me. This probably had as much to do with the fact that most of us had emerged from very common gene pools as it did with the similarity of our garb: dark suits, topcoats, white shirts, conservative ties, and dress hats. Our common heritage, relatively speaking, was confirmed during orientation week in the mission home when an apostle of the Lord asked how many of us were descendants of polygamists. Nearly all raised their hands.

"Although polygamy was ended officially in 1896, the promise that its seeds would deliver righteous, stalwart leaders for generations to come is being fulfilled right before our eyes, right here in this room," the apostle of the Lord proclaimed proudly.

I knew quite a bit about polygamy for, although it was initiated by Joseph Smith, the doctrinal basis for the practice was grudgingly laid out by an apostle and my great-grandfather, Orson Pratt, regarded to this day as the church's leading—arguably only—theologian. Initially he opposed plural marriage, but eventually followed the lead of his prophet's revelation, if not his own mind: "*...God has ordained that the righteous shall have a plurality of wives; for they alone are prepared to beget and bring forth offspring whose bodies and spirits, partaking of the nature of the parents, are pure and lovely...*"

Over here was a *pure* bidding his girlfriend goodbye with a peck on the cheek; over there a *lovely* was already practicing the "keep all women at arm's length" missionary mantra on his mother. However, it was well understood that behaviors at the point of embarkation into the great unknown mission field would not always be *pure* and *lovely,* in the strictest senses of those words.

Like me, many elders had withdrawn from college to answer the call. Others had given up jobs as farmers, auto mechanics, and car salesmen. A few had postponed marriages. For some it was the thing to do if you were a nineteen-year-old Mormon boy; for others it was the culmination of years of study, prayer and anticipation. For a few like me it was a final effort to come to terms with what they had been raised to be. If statistics held, one third or more of our group would fall into inactivity when we returned home two years later; the rest would become part of the bedrock on which the Church organization would rest for the next six or seven decades. In that aspect, missionary service was remarkably similar to the war in heaven, I thought.

There were young women missionaries in the group too—about 15 in all. They were a somewhat different lot *then*. I emphasize "then" because things are quite different *now*. Like other Americans, Mormons are marrying older. *Then*, girls tended to go on missions only if the opportunity to marry had passed them by, which made them a comparatively *ancient* 21, pushing 22. *Then*, women were asked to serve a mere 18 months, which perhaps partially explains why they were not taken very seriously by the men who were required to serve 24 months in English-speaking missions, sometimes more, and 30–36 for foreign-language assignments. At the time, it was widely held that they were considerably more trouble too: there was the problem of security—the worry that young women, living alone, were more vulnerable and therefore in need of protective supervision.

While there was no empirical evidence to support this, women companionships were alleged to be more plagued by emotional strife and petty bickering than their male counterparts. This may have been due partly to different mindsets. Most of the women were, perhaps, somewhat miffed, bitter that eternal marriage had passed them by despite their faithfulness to the gospel. The males, on the other hand, were too young to be married, but were confident that successful service would be a steppingstone to an eternal liaison with a faithful daughter of Zion. That is the way things were then. Today, now that women are more aggressively encouraged to serve missions, some of the archaic assumptions are coming undone, slowly.

Temptation stalked me all the way to New England. It began as the train rolled across the snowbound plains of eastern Wyoming or western Nebraska, I couldn't tell which. George Overton, a farmer from St. George, who had been assigned as my companion for the trip, secured a deck of cards from the porter, and, much to my discomfort, engaged two lady missionaries in a game of hearts.

The fact that we were using playing cards was duly noted by another missionary who sanctimoniously and loudly announced that face cards were tools of the devil. If card-playing was a sin, it was a minor one compared to what the self-righteous traveler couldn't see under the lap table balanced on our four sets of knees. In the process of providing stable footing for the board, Sister Monson's knee had come to rest against my thigh, which aroused certain tensions. When the game ended, I don't know why I didn't insist that we reverse the chairs for the night. Maybe I didn't want to seem an uptight ass. Maybe her leg against mine felt good—harmless, but good.

When I awoke the next morning, I was startled to see Sister Monson's shapely legs resting on the seat next to me, propped at such an immodest angle that I couldn't help but notice the snaps on her garter belt and the lacy edges of her white temple garments. I could have enjoyed the view unmolested, as the other missionaries were sleeping too, but instead, I quickly draped a blanket over her legs and found refuge in the dining car.

In Chicago, we switched trains, which I hoped would provide the opportunity to discreetly move away from the lady missionaries—from temptation. But as they boarded the New York Central, Sister Monson and her companion took the seat in front of ours, and then politely suggested that conversation would be easier if they rearranged the seat back so they could face us again. I was uncomfortable, but couldn't think of a rational reason to refuse. That night, I gave her an extra blanket to cover her legs. After she fell asleep, I headed for the parlor car, where I spent the rest of the night far from Sister Monson, but hardly out of harm's way.

Three college girls, returning to Boston, had asked me about the car full of eager young male missionaries. My answer brought on, quite inadvertently, a deeper discussion of Mormonism. I won't bore you with the details. Suffice it to say it lasted all night; the three agreed to have the missionaries visit them in Boston, and the bra-less one in a miniskirt, Faith ("You can call me Libby") Pratt, eventually converted along with her Catholic fiancé. But that's another story. I was taking down their names and addresses when Faith's unhinged breasts brushed my upper arms. "You wouldn't be one of the missionaries coming to visit?" she asked coyly. A month earlier, I'd have reacted like any other red-blooded American male. But my blood had been sanctified, chastened by the Spirit. I was strong, committed and, in any event, Elder Overton, my companion for the trip, was nearby ready to rescue should the temptation raise more than my eyebrows.

"Not likely—unless I'm assigned to Boston." (Right then, I prayed for a two-year exile to Prince Edward Island.) "But they'll be like me—like them," I said, pointing to several other missionaries who had gathered in the parlor car and were now listening intently to our discussion.

On the way back to our seats, Elder Overton complained that I had violated mission rules. "I woke up this morning and you weren't there. Just what the heck is going on with you?" he said.

"Sorry, I was restless. I wandered around...got dragged into conversation. It was worthwhile. The girl doing all the talking—Faith

Pratt—seemed to be real golden. She's a Pratt, a distant relative I'd guess."

"Golden for a date, or more, maybe," said Elder Overton.

I smiled. "Perhaps, but she'll have to wait two years for one with me," I said. "And it would be helpful if she converts in the meantime."

"Not a chance," Elder Overton said smugly. "She smokes like a chimney."

"So did Brigham Young…so did I," I said.

The president of the New England Mission, G. Buckley Truman, taught me everything I know about humility: "Always give credit to the Lord for your successes." Paradoxically, he was less than tolerant of those inclined to send blame His way: "Well, the Lord just didn't lead us to any golden people this month," they would say, excusing their failures to baptize new converts. Truman's response: "Teach better, work harder, develop a positive attitude: instead of saying I hope and I'll try, make it I will. Those who will it, do it."

Theory was one thing. Practice was another. Just in case the Lord forgot who was responsible for what, the mission office kept exceedingly detailed records (Mormons have a fetish about records, statistics and goals and keeping commitments; folktales assert that the data bank one amasses over a lifetime will serve as evidence for the defense and prosecution come judgment day) and each month published a list of the top baptizers. So giving as much credit to the Lord as is due, with His help I established a "modern era" record for convert baptisms in New England, only surpassed in the entire history of the Church by the inaugural Mormon proselytizers to the region, including, especially, my own great-grandfathers, Orson and Parley Parker Pratt.

Never once did I allow myself to be put in a position that required me to fudge my own far-less-than-perfect conviction. I admit it's quite possible, even probable that people—fellow missionaries and prospective converts alike—thought they heard something I never said. "I *know* if you approach the Lord in prayer, He will provide the answers you seek," I would say, putting emphasis on the word "know." Or: "I *know* you can come to *know* that Joseph Smith was a prophet of God. And, *when* (not if) you do, will you agree to be baptized a member of the Church of Jesus Christ of Latter-day Saints?"

Skeptical, careful listeners often balked at such boldness: "How do you *know* I can *know*? If I answer 'yes' to your challenge, I've effectively conditioned my mind to receive an answer; your promise smacks of a self-fulfilling prophecy," one observed.

So like a debater, I countered: "I *know* because I've seen the empirical evidence—others just as skeptical as you, through study and prayer, have come to *know*. All I'm saying is when the day comes that you *know*—and you control the definition of *know* and the timing—that you act on your knowledge."

This fellow, a history teacher at one of the snottier prep schools in New Hampshire (if not all of America) looked me squarely in the eyes, snugged his bow tie like he was cinching a hangman's noose around his neck, grinned and said: "You've got me—I'd be a damned fool to deny what I *know*, now wouldn't I?"

"Fool, I'll give you," I said. "Can't be sure about damned." He was baptized about six weeks later. Obviously, the Lord was more inclined to answer entreaties from skeptical, stuck-up prep school teachers than He was my own.

Because of my record, I was often called upon to share my teaching techniques with the other missionaries. I tried not to sound too proud; nevertheless, some were resentful, particularly those who knew my personal testimony was quite equivocal. Some groused that I was dismissive of God's role in the conversions. I countered that God's role was a given in all things. I was only teaching human methods, not divine ones. Missionaries should have no doubt about that. Even I, doubter that I was, assumed He was there, even if I had no idea what He was doing. The unanswered question was what could *they* do. What they needed from me was advice about what *they* could do besides asking God to intervene, which, of course, they did regularly. It seemed to me that many missionaries were keener on honing the skill of praying than they were developing effective teaching skills. I swear, some of them wouldn't think of going to the bathroom without first asking the Lord to help them have an edifying evacuation. It wouldn't surprise me if some of them now insist on having a word with the Lord before doing it with their wives. Not a bad idea, I suppose, although it certainly could put the brakes on an exciting evening, like it had with Emma, although, now that I think of it, our prayers often led to even more exciting romps.

What led to a lot of trouble and bother was the conclusion of a speech I gave at a mission-wide conference. Throughout the twenty-minute presentation I'd suggested that empathy and hard work were the keys to success and concluded this way:

"I have heard missionaries bandying about scriptures they obviously don't understand very well. I have seen them silently shake off the dust on the doorsteps of homes of people who rudely rejected them. And I have heard these self-same missionaries profess to be conscientious, faithful servants of God. I say, how can you be devoted if you don't understand the scriptures yourself or the people you are teaching? How can you fulfill your calling if you don't listen with an open mind to the questions that are asked? How can you be conscientious if you don't refine your approach so it reaches and touches more people? I've heard missionaries say: 'But I pray often that I will be led to the righteous in spirit.' I have heard them plead with the Lord to open minds, or to inspire them to say the right things and so forth. To those missionaries who rely solely on the Lord to deliver success, day after day, I say: 'Pray a little less and work a hell of a lot harder. Faith without works is dead.'"

"Excepting your unnecessary use of a mild epithet, I hope your points were not lost on our fellow laborers," G. Buckley said during our regular personal interview later that day. "For you, however, I perceive the advice should be quite opposite: work less, pray harder. You won't be whole until you find an inner conviction that can only come through prayer. Your hard work and your intellect will bring you success here in New England no doubt, but it will mean absolutely nothing if you return home without a testimony burning in your own bosom."

"Can you give me some clues as to what to expect? Maybe I'm missing the answer," I said.

"I can't tell you how it will come. I can only say that it will come—if you are earnest and persevering. But you may be on to something—are you willing to hear the answer when it's given?" G. Buckley said.

"I think so, that's why I'm here."

"In your heart, do you truly believe—have faith—the gospel is true?"

"If I assume Christ was the Savior, it makes sense from then on in, intellectually," I said.

"That wasn't the question. The question was, in your heart do you believe it's true. That's quite apart from your head, although thinking power does play an important role in convincing the heart," he said.

"I have doubts, but doesn't everyone?"

"For a time, yes. I have questions that have yet to be answered by God—profound questions. But I believe, in time, I will get the answers to those questions—answers that will add to my current knowledge and testimony of the gospel. A testimony comes line upon line, precept upon precept. So is there any single gospel principle that you know to be true?"

I thought for quite a while, at least it seemed that way. I worried if I spoke my mind, and the follow-up discussion ran its predictable course, it might result in a dishonorable discharge from the mission field. "Yes, there are two. I know that free agency is God's law, if there is a God," I said. "I know that intellectually and in my heart."

"That's a solid start. Many other key principles flow from that one," he said. "Tackle them, one at a time. Faith precedeth belief and belief precedeth knowledge. What's the other?"

"It's complicated. You have to understand where I've come from. It'd take some time to explain," I said.

President Truman rose, walked to the door, opened it a crack and talked to the missionary waiting outside for his interview. "Elder, you should rejoin the others in the chapel. I'll send Elder Russell for you when we've finished." Instead of returning to the chair behind the desk, G. Buckley sat in one next to mine. "So let's begin. Tell me about the other principle you know to be true. Take all the time you need."

My face burned, my stomach churned. "It's the law against adultery—fornication," I said.

President Truman's eyebrows arched. "That's an odd one, odd that it is one of two principles you know to be true."

"But the two are related principles. Built into the law of free agency is the principle of self-control—with freedom comes responsibility. And fornication seems to have a lot to do with responsibility and self-control. I have to believe that God is not as concerned with the physical act itself as he is about the fact it reveals a lack of self-control, inner discipline. And those two ingredients are so fundamental to keeping one's house in order. Also, he may be more concerned about this sin, because of its compelling, almost addictive nature."

"Is it a compulsion of yours?" he said.

"I struggle with it every day—like a recurring bad dream."

"Is it just fantasy, or is there more to it?"

"There were a few times—in the past—when it was, ah, reality."

"What counsel did your bishop provide on this subject?" President Truman asked.

"None. He asked about it like you do about masturbation: 'Do you have any moral problems?' At the time, I didn't. My life was in control. I had repented for my errors, which I believed were personal matters—between God and me. I didn't need absolution from the bishop."

"You know your doctrine better than that—Christ is your only advocate with the Father. Not a bishop, nor a stake president, nor an apostle. But, as a counselor and friend, he could have helped you come to terms with yourself. Perhaps, you wouldn't be having problems today if you'd sought his guidance."

"Perhaps," I said. "Perhaps I shouldn't even be serving a mission?"

"Do you want to go home?" he said.

"Not on your life," I said emphatically.

"Easy to say. But are you now willing to follow counsel—to the letter and the spirit?" The tone of G. Buckley's voice was stern and righteous if, remarkably, kind. "If it's no, you may as well pack your trunks and ship out. It's better to waffle about at home than here, where you can damage more than your own reputation."

"I will—to the letter," I said.

"We'll see," he said. "First, I want you to contact your bishop. Tell him everything you've told me, including the fact that we've had this conversation. You must follow his counsel precisely and abide by his decisions. I can't promise anything in this regard. He may think it prudent to have you released; if he does, you will be given an honorable release. On the other hand, he may deign it worthwhile for you to remain in New England. Whatever his advice, you must covenant with me, here and now, to follow it."

"I will, only I can't say I'll be happy if he recommends that I return home," I said.

"That's the risk you take, although the other option is to go home right now. So you haven't much to lose," he said. "I give you my word that I too will abide by his counsel for the immediate future, however you must fulfill certain obligations here in order to sustain my confidence in you.

"Here's what I will expect from you: I will want a weekly personal letter from you in which you detail how you are doing with your problems. You should not gloss over struggles; rather you should bare your soul to me each week. Third, should your thoughts become acute or overpowering, I want you to call me. If I am not in the office, the assistants will know where I am. Leave the number where you can be reached and stand by that phone—even if it's on a street corner and a nor'easter is burying you in snow—until I call back. Fourth, in your individual prayers, I want you to specifically ask for help in conquering this problem. And finally, I want you to write to each one of the young women involved—Church member or not—and seek their forgiveness, as they should yours.

"So that I'm not misunderstood, my hunch is that personally you'll stand a better chance of turning things around if you stay. I wouldn't ever recommend doing what you have done. On the other hand, overcoming adversity, conquering compulsions of the flesh, are excellent stepping stones toward acquiring a powerful testimony like your great-grandfathers, Elder *Pratt*-Russell. Like them, your success here has been significant. You have helped many put their houses in order. It is high time you did the same for yourself."

"What year was this, 1965?" Rebe asked.

"1966—March, I'd been out just a year."

"A year before the Summer of Love…and you're out there in a sincere suit preaching the good word, short hair, no drugs, no booze and cigarettes and someone's getting overwrought about a handful of near-misses."

"He may have assumed worse. I didn't provide a lot of detail," I said.

"Still, it was an over-the-top reaction. I can understand a lecture, counseling about honesty and all that. But making you notify your bishop and the girls? I'd be furious if you'd named me."

"No chance of that," I grinned. "No names were mentioned…he agreed to leave it between me and them."

"Incredible. Reveals a lot."

The following Monday, the day missionaries use to relax and prepare for the week ahead, I wrote long, contrite letters to Emmaline, Lainey and Naomi. (Naomi was the only one to write back: "Nice to hear from you after such a long silence. However, I only wish you had done something that was worthy of the apology you offered. If it's okay with you, I will consider it a rain check?") I phoned Bishop Sanford. He was disappointed I hadn't been more forthcoming with him, however he said he was pleased the issue was finally being put to rest. He thought the course President Truman had outlined could lead to greater success. He made one additional request: "I think you should give me the names of the girls involved so I can contact their bishops here."

"Is that necessary?" I asked, pained. "Most of the girls are either inactive or non-members. I have recommended to each one that, on their own, they should seek guidance from their parents and bishops. Shouldn't they be allowed a little free agency here?"

"Good point, however I would prefer to have the information so I can follow-up," he said.

"If I have a choice, I'd rather not. I didn't exactly appreciate it when someone told you I was smoking a cigar in front of the Church office building," I said.

"I thought you told me you didn't do that," he said.

"It was truth. I wasn't smoking a cigar in front of the building. I didn't light up until I got inside," I said.

"You didn't?" he said, knowing full well that I had. "Well, that's all behind you. It's not mandatory that you tell me the girls' names; however, if you conclude it may help them to repent, I'll be here. It's your call. But would you please send me a copy of your weekly letters to President Truman?"

"I will," I said.

"By the way, a family you baptized visited our ward last Sunday—wonderful people."

"Really? Do you remember their names?"

"Jackson, I think. Right it was Jackson—Frank Jackson."

"Jackson? Are you sure? I don't recall baptizing any Jacksons."

"I could be wrong," he said. "How many Black families have you baptized, anyway?"

"You little troublemaker, you," Rebe said. "You snag a few Jews too?"

"Like the Jacksons, I taught a few who eventually converted...but they won't be on my tally sheet come judgment day."

"That I find hard to believe," she said.

Truth was, I didn't baptize the Jacksons. I taught them, and violated a host of mission rules in the process. Perhaps their conversions will provide absolution for my many little sins.

After arriving in New England, my first assignment was to serve in New Haven, where there was a thriving, but small, Mormon congregation, built around a solid contingent of westerners who had migrated east to teach or study at Yale and other colleges in the area.

My companion, Elder Gary Peterson, a profoundly spiritual young man from Mesa, Arizona, cautioned me about the dangers of contacting potential converts by telephone. "You never know who you're talking to. If they're Black, you can usually, but not always, tell by their accent and you can simply invite them to church. If you go door to door, you can pick out good, safe neighborhoods," he said.

Nevertheless the telephone was a handy instrument on inclement days and, frankly, I preferred it to knocking on doors, although the latter had its entertaining moments. Once we had rung the bell for the third floor apartment in one of those classic triple-decker houses found throughout New Haven. The man of the house, being too lazy to walk down three flights of stairs, took to the open porch two floors above us and bellowed: "This is the devil. What the hell do you want?" Without missing a beat and not intending to be ironic, Peterson hollered up: "We have an important message for you from the Lord." The man was so startled—or embarrassed—that he raced down three flights of stairs and invited us in. Four weeks later he and his family were baptized.

The first contact with the Jackson family came at the end of a long and discouraging week. Peterson and I had been on a weeklong fast, in hopes it would move the Lord to open the hearts and minds of a few good people and convince the one family we were teaching to get baptized. By Saturday, I was starving, the family was still stalling, and there were no new prospects to teach. So, once I finished a long telephone conversation with a fresh prospect who seemed particularly interested, I was pleased—the Lord had responded to our fast.

"This one's real hot. He's very familiar with the Church, in fact he wanted us to come over Sunday morning. He's a school teacher and so's his wife," I said, breathless, as I hung up the phone. "They have four children. And this is the clincher: He's read about Joseph Smith. He said, and I quote, 'I believe that prophet of yours was truly a prophet of God.'"

Elder Peterson smiled serenely. "See, the fast worked," he said, reminding me that a day or so earlier I had grumbled about the wisdom of starving ourselves half to death. "If you'd given up, you may never have been led to this family."

"If I'd never dialed the number, we'd have missed them too."

As Elder Peterson steered the rickety Rambler into the driveway alongside the Jacksons' tidy, green-clapboard Cape Cod, my heart was pounding. Judging from the house and the neighborhood, this family was custom-made: they were educated and middle class, the kind of people who always added leadership strength to the Church. I was thinking about this, counting my good fortune, when Mr. Jackson appeared at the door. I was as startled as Elder Peterson was to discover Mr. Jackson was Black. He hadn't sounded *Black* over the telephone, I thought. Peterson handed pamphlets to Mr. Jackson; I heard him issue an invitation to church the following Sunday, all procedures missionaries were instructed to follow on their first encounter with Black families. I interrupted: "But as I said over the phone, we have come prepared to share an important message with you." Peterson shifted uncomfortably, shot me an annoyed glare. Mr. Jackson invited us in.

It was normal to ease into the formal teaching portion of the meeting, so I hadn't been concerned when Elder Peterson talked about the weather and so on. But when he hadn't taken the portable flannel board out of its case, I knew my senior companion was stalling. "Elder Peterson, if you'd set up the flannel board, we can get started," I said, unwilling to follow the brethren on this particular night. Peterson looked pained, annoyed that I refused to follow his lead. But, he followed my instructions as though he were the junior companion.

Although the Jacksons' answers to leading questions we posed in the first lesson virtually replicated the scripted ideal responses—the kind that would have led any missionary in his right mind to conclude that this family would surely be baptized—Peterson tried to abridge and shorten the lesson. I pressed on. As the lesson neared its conclusion, he changed the dialogue again: instead of getting them to commit to baptism "when you know these things are true," Peterson simply told them they could know the truth if they would study and pray.

"Let me ask a question of you, Brother Jackson," I said, taking charge again. "Excuse me, but in the Church we refer to each other as brother and sister."

"No need to apologize. We're very comfortable with the terms," Brother Jackson said.

"The question is this," I said. I paused, trying to remember the exact phraseology of the lesson plan. "If God bore witness to you that what we have told you is true, would you be baptized a member of His Church, the Church of Jesus Christ of Latter-day Saints?"

"It'd be a rather foolish thing not to do," he said emphatically.

I'm sure I smiled. "And you, Sister Jackson?"

"As my husband said, if God bore witness to us, we wouldn't—couldn't deny it," she said. The older children nodded.

"We're having a baptismal service at the Church on"—I glanced at my appointment book, looking for a date three weeks hence—"on the twenty-seventh. Let's use that date as a goal as we continue through the lessons. There are six lessons in all, which means we'd have to meet twice a week to make that goal."

"That's the minimum time required?" Sister Jackson asked. "I mean if we got our prayers answered sooner than that, could we be baptized sooner?"

"Absolutely," I said eagerly. "A baptismal service can be arranged at any time."

The formal part of the lesson was over when Sister Jackson asked the most difficult question of the evening. "Are there Negro members of your church?" she said.

"Yes, but not many. The parish, we call them wards or branches, in Cambridge, Massachusetts has several Black families, although the branch here doesn't have any. You'd be the first," I said.

"We're used to breaking new ground," she said.

"So am I."

"I don't think I've ever seen a family so spiritually in tune," Elder Peterson said, once we were inside the car. "Just the same, we can't go on with this unless they come to church on Sunday. If they come we have to explain, straight out, about the priesthood situation."

"I don't agree with that approach," I said.

"Nevertheless, that's the way it has to be. We've gone too far already. And don't you ever again cross me up like you did tonight," he said indignantly. "I'm the senior companion here; you barely know what you're doing."

"I won't apologize because I'm sure the Lord will forgive me if I erred," I said defiantly. "What if the Jacksons are the ones who get the Prophet to restore the priesthood to Negroes?"

"Not in our lifetimes," Elder Peterson said assuredly.

"Well when it happens, just remember that you heard it here first. Maybe, just maybe, tonight we helped prepare the way."

As luck would have it, on Wednesday the district leader, Elder North, a more experienced missionary, came on tour, which meant that for three days he would work with Elder Peterson while I worked with his junior companion. Effective district leaders, as well as their superiors, the zone leaders, were supposed to act like roving troubleshooters. It was their job to provide at least minimal supervision for the elders in their districts or zones, to sort out any difficulties in the companionships, to aid the various senior companions in prodding investigators toward baptism.

While these visits were normally scheduled well in advance, it was not unusual for the leader to arrive unannounced, striding into the apartment at six thirty in the morning to see if their charges were living the handbook which, among other things, mandated the following daily regimen:

6 a.m.: rise and prepare for the day

6:45–7:45 a.m.: study hour

7:45–8:30: breakfast

8:30: leave the apartment, begin proselyting

12:00–1 p.m.: lunch

1–5 p.m.: proselyting

5–6 p.m.: dinner

7–10 p.m.: meetings with prospective members

10:30 p.m.: in bed, lights out (no exceptions)

These, and other regulations in the handbook, were veritable gospel principles. It was not unusual at all for a district or zone leader or a mission president to ask this shorthand question: "Living the handbook?" This was tantamount to asking about all of the above, plus: Have you put out of your mind and talk all thoughts of home, school, girls and worldly things? Have you transgressed by listening to a radio recently? Or reading a newspaper? By swimming or watching inappropriate movies? Have you addressed any female over the age of eight by her first name rather than "Sister"? And, have you let a female stand nearer to you than a straight arm away?

Without even trying, it was easy to violate the handbook. For instance, what was a missionary to do if an older woman of the Church gave him an affectionate, motherly hug? Or if a young teenage girl cornered him alone in the classroom after Sunday school? Or if an older girl coyly flirted with him on the straight and broad walkway to the church, in plain view of God and everyone?

Who could blame the girls in this remote redoubt of Mormonism, where eligible and worthy young men were few and far between, from taking a shine to a young man who could someday take her to the Temple? Who could fault the missionary, cut off from all contact with the opposite sex at the precise moment testosterone raged through his body, for being unusually vulnerable to flattery, confoundingly aroused by the most innocent *faire les yeux doux*? If nothing else, it proved his current untouchable status hadn't rendered him permanently bowdlerized.

The more difficult problems to resolve were motivational ones. It was not uncommon for older missionaries, ones returning home in a few months, to "ride their suitcases." While it was understandable that a missionary's fervor would ebb toward the end, it could be particularly discouraging to his eager young companion. Therefore great care was taken in selecting senior companions for greenies. Usually the senior was on the rise in the mission hierarchy or had been a consistently productive field laborer. Elder Peterson, a sincere and guileless Christian despite his mindless, rule-bound reaction to the Jacksons, went on to become the mission president's assistant, the top leadership post in the mission. As a senior companion, I only had juniors who were new to the field.

If I do say so, Peterson and I were a class act. His strengths complemented my weaknesses and vice versa. We worked hard, baptized, and we liked each other. Elder North's visit was not to sort out our troubles. If anything he wanted to get to know us better, take a break from his own companion.

Insofar as the Jacksons were concerned, it was good fortune that North returned to his area with Peterson, leaving me in New Haven as the de facto senior to teach and do whatever. By the time Peterson and North returned late Saturday evening, the Jacksons had breezed through the second, third, and fourth lessons, and had promised to attend church on Sunday.

As I had hoped, the Jacksons caused nary a ripple in the congregation when they arrived for church on Sunday morning. Even Elder Peterson seemed pleased, although his pleasure turned to anger when he discovered I had taught them three additional lessons in his absence and had not mentioned a word about it to him. I'm sure he would have made a bigger deal out of it had it not been for two factors: the branch president, Ken Meeks, a Yale physics professor, seemed quite eager to have the Jacksons baptized; and, while at church, the mission president's assistant called us to tell us we were being transferred—Peterson to Nova Scotia, Pratt-Russell to his ancestral territory: Massachusetts. Peterson was being made a district leader and I was being promoted to senior companion. We spent the rest of Sunday cleaning the apartment and making travel plans. Peterson was leaving first thing Monday; I wouldn't depart until Tuesday, after I met the missionaries that were replacing us.

Through tears (surprised the hell out of me) I saw Peterson off, and then returned to the apartment. It had been an intense four months in which I had grown closer to him than any other man, before or since. His spirituality and love had moved me, his kindness and guileless humility had inspired me, his self-discipline and obedience were exemplary. Now he was gone, and I was alone with nothing to do but prepare a briefing sheet for our replacements. I called President Meeks to give him the news. "The Jacksons, have you called them? Please don't drop the ball on that family," he counseled.

"I was about to call—they have two more lessons to go."

"Where are they on the priesthood issue?"

"Haven't discussed it yet," I said, hoping he wouldn't go down that road with me.

"Good, that's something I'd rather handle myself—it's too easy for young missionaries to foul things up."

"Thanks for the vote of confidence."

"Well, you are leaving town aren't you? Who knows what we'll get."

I called the Jacksons. I explained how sorry I was to be leaving, how I had looked forward to teaching them the last lessons and baptizing them and so on.

"Could you come over before you go?" Brother Jackson said.

"I could, but I'm not supposed to go out without a companion," I said, hoping my explanation wouldn't sound too silly.

"Nancy's whipped up some wonderful homemade spaghetti. What if we were to bring it over to your apartment?" he said.

I couldn't think of any rule that applied to this situation, so about an hour later the Jacksons arrived. While they ate, Brother Jackson asked if I could teach them the last lessons on my own, a proposition that was intriguing but very intimidating. I had only recently committed all six discussions to memory and certainly had never taught one singlehandedly. Then reason weighed in: now was as good a time as any to lead, be the senior companion I was about to become.

They sailed through the fifth lesson, the one that covers the points about free agency, eternal progression and the eternal nature of mankind. Sister Jackson cried when I explained eternal families, about the Spirit World where everyone who had ever lived would get a chance to hear and accept the gospel. They flowed freely until I reminded them of the forthcoming baptismal date.

She dried her face, looked me squarely in the eyes and said: "I've been ready since the first lesson." With that encouragement, I filled out the recommend forms necessary for baptism. It was still early—9:30—when I finished. "One more lesson to go—and it's a piece of cake," I said.

"So why not get it over with tonight?" Brother Jackson asked. It was 10:15 p.m.—fifteen minutes before mandatory bedtime—when the sixth lesson was completed; the Jacksons committed to live the law of tithing. With any amount of luck I could be in bed by 10:30. I asked Brother Jackson to close with prayer.

"Before I do, I have a question," he said. "When are you going to tell us why Black men can't hold the priesthood?"

I was startled that he knew about it and hadn't raised the question earlier. In truth, I wondered if I had been set up, if I would now be called a deceiver by the family I had wanted to convert more than any other. "Actually, the branch president wanted to cover that with you himself," I said, wishing I'd asked him to join us.

"I see," he said, miffed. "You're not prepared to discuss it?"

"I am, it's just that President Meeks wanted to."

"If it'd get you into trouble with him, fine. We'll let it pass. But honestly, it'd mean more to us to hear it from you," he said.

President Meeks hadn't really *forbidden* me to discuss the priesthood issue; he was concerned only about our replacements. Surely he wouldn't be offended once he knew the Jacksons had insisted. If I refused, it may look like I was trying to hide something, which I definitely was not.

"Then I will," I said. "But first, let's review where we are: Do you—do you both—know that the Gospel of Jesus Christ has been restored and that Joseph Smith was a prophet of God?"

"With all our hearts," Sister Jackson said.

"How do you know it?" I said, concerned that I sounded like I was questioning the quality of their intellects, their spirituality. In fact, I was a little annoyed that the Lord had been so forthcoming with them, not me.

"We have prayed sincerely and God has answered our prayers," Brother Jackson said.

I suppressed the temptation to blurt out: "Say, what's going on here. I've prayed too and the Lord hasn't answered my prayers and…" What I actually said was this: "What if I told you that Joseph Smith was a heretic, a crazy man; or was simply a good man, but no prophet?" Peterson would be dying on the spot if he'd heard me propose such hypotheticals, no matter the objective.

"I wouldn't believe it," he said.

"Why? What if I showed you evidence from noted psychiatrists that said Joseph Smith was crazy as a loon? What then?"

"Even if he was, it wouldn't mean he wasn't also a prophet," Sister Jackson said. "I simply couldn't deny what God revealed to me as truth." I'm sure her statement must have made me wince in envy.

"What if I were to tell you that Joseph Smith, in his private life, was not unlike many other men of his time—he had some racial prejudices and personal peccadilloes?" I said, leading them to a point where I knew they couldn't back out even if they wanted to, being the honest people they were.

"I'd be very disappointed. Very disappointed," Brother Jackson said. He thought for a long time before speaking again. "But I still couldn't deny that God told me Joseph Smith was a prophet. Was he…a bigot?"

"No he wasn't," I said quickly. "In fact he said several times that the gospel of Jesus Christ was for all men—Black and white, bond and free. However, Mormons had severe troubles in Missouri in the early days because the Missourians feared the Mormons, because of their potential political and economic clout and because they were aggressive abolitionists. Several Black men held the priesthood in those days—Black men had equality with whites in the Mormon Church, something unheard of in the other churches of the day. I'm not sure who it was, but it wasn't Joseph Smith, apparently received guidance that Negroes were not to be given the priesthood at that time. Apparently, Joseph vaguely endorsed the position, perhaps to alleviate some of the persecution. No one has ever provided the reasons for the prohibition, although numerous theories have been put forth, none of which are worth going into because, insofar as I'm concerned, none of them are consistent with the principles of the gospel. Whether God intended this prohibition to be a temporary, expedient way to ensure the greater good—the survival of the Church and to ease persecution of the Saints—we do not know because Joseph Smith was assassinated shortly thereafter. With no one around who understood the genesis and purpose of the policy, and no immediate reason to address it once the Saints reached Utah, the practice became institutionalized over the generations and exists to this day, at least for now."

"Just as I thought, I can't hold the priesthood," Brother Jackson said.

"I'm very sorry to say you're correct," I said. "But I believe that someday, Black men will be given the priesthood and I am absolutely convinced that that day is soon coming. To be totally honest, I can't say that everyone in the Church agrees—in fact they may be holding things up."

"Then there are Mormons who are racist."

"Yes, there are, just as there are in any church. But the doctrine of the Church is not racist. Despite the priesthood prohibition, the current apostles have been adamant about the fact that that policy in no way means that racial prejudice is condoned by God, or that Blacks are in any way inferior. They have warned church members that holding prejudicial views is tantamount to apostasy."

"Why can't your prophet—David McKay—simply ask the Lord and get the answer?" Sister Jackson asked.

"I'm sure President McKay has asked for guidance. But let me suggest this hypothetical. Suppose the prophet poses this question: 'Why can't Negroes hold the priesthood at this time?' What does it mean if the Lord says nothing? Does it mean that He's not ready to provide an answer? Or does it mean that He's already provided the answer? If the latter, if He provided the answer previously, could His silence simply be a way to teach His servants a painful lesson about the importance of reading and understanding His written word?"

Brother Jackson nodded his head.

I continued. "Now let's suppose for a minute that President McKay, or some future prophet, reads God's word and concludes there is no scriptural basis for the practice. The question he puts to God might be quite different: 'I have read the scriptures and found no basis for this practice; I have received no divine guidance that the practice should be continued and, therefore, because the fullness of the Gospel was always intended for all—Black or white—in my heart I am ready to set things aright. Tell me if I'm wrong.' The Lord's options are much clearer. First, He knows the prophet has studied and contemplated His written word; He knows the prophet has lain awake nights wrestling with his conscience; God has not been asked to descend from the heavens in a fiery cloud to teach what He taught us long, long ago. His silence is all the answer the prophet needs. In my opinion, that's the way the change will come. All we need is a prophet willing to ask the question the right way."

"So you think the policy will be changed?" Sister Jackson asked.

"Once the right question is asked, I'm positive the policy will be changed. But, as I said, my views are in the minority in the Church today," I said. I did not want to mislead the Jacksons into believing that all was hunky-dory. I knew they could be an influence for change, but I also knew that their road could be rough.

"If you are so sure, for the time being I can accept this matter on my faith in you, in your faith and testimony." (I must have winced a little.) "Maybe if there are more of us Black folk around, chomping at the bit, we'll inspire the prophet to keep studying and praying," Brother Jackson said.

"Precisely," I said. "But I can't promise it will be easy for you. In fact I can guarantee there will be those moments when you will become so discouraged that you may want to resign your membership."

"I'm sure there will be," Brother Jackson said.

"I don't want to minimize the challenges that lie ahead. They could be arduous and emotionally painful."

Early the next morning I confessed my sins to President Meeks, detail by detail, even the fact that I had stayed up well past the mandated bedtime. "Perfect. I'm impressed. I couldn't have handled it better," he said, obviously delighted. "I'm sorry we're losing you—you should be here to realize the fruits of your labors." He asked me to leave the baptismal recommends with the incoming elders.

"I have a problem with that. First, someone needs to visit them soon—like tonight or tomorrow. The new elders may be too busy getting settled," I said. "And, the real concern of mine is a fear, perhaps unfounded, the new missionaries may not follow up at all once they learn the Jacksons are Negroes. Or, they may represent someone's theory as Church doctrine, which could blow the whole deal. I'd be a whole lot more comfortable if you'd take over from here on in."

"Fine. A good idea. But brief the new elders anyway. Leave the recommends with them and I'll pick them up tonight or tomorrow," he said. "And Godspeed. You're going to be a fine senior companion—I wish they'd leave you here for another season."

"Thanks. I've felt a bit like a heretic these past few days."

A few days after I left New Haven, the new elders visited the Jacksons, laid out their own cockamamie philosophies on why Blacks could not hold the priesthood. Of course, they presented their personal theories as Church doctrine. The Jacksons postponed baptism. It took nearly six more months and several long sessions with President Meeks and other thinking members of the Church before they finally agreed to become members.

That's as close as I came to converting a Black family. However, after I returned home, I did all that I could to encourage a serious rethink of the policy. Some say my activities led to trouble with the church, which friends assumed was apostasy, although I hardly consider myself an apostate.

Nevertheless, as I promised the Jacksons and Elder Peterson, the priesthood was restored to Black members on Friday, June 9, 1978. That evening, I placed a phone call from my office in Manhattan to Mesa, Arizona, to the home of Elder Gary Peterson. When he answered the phone, I said, simply, quietly: "Remember, you heard it here first."

"I remember," Gary Peterson said. "Now it's time for you to restore the priesthood to yourself." "I don't know," I said. "All the cows are out of the barn—it's a little late to be bolting the door."

"It's never too late to herd them in," he said.

"I wonder."

"Only if you haven't the strength to will it."

"That may be the problem," I said. "The road has collected its toll."

HOMECOMING AND FAREWELL

On the morning of the eighth day—the day after the family had finished sitting shiva for Vincent Wheeler Adams—Dr. Rosenbaum summarily sacked Rebe without notice, severance or accrued vacation pay. Various conversations overheard at the funeral and from friends who visited the Adamses' during the traditional seven-day mourning period confirmed what he had long suspected: his chief assistant was consorting with a client of long standing and, in the process, may have, as he self-righteously put it, "not only compromised the integrity of my practice by engaging in unprofessional conduct, but used information contained in confidential files for inappropriate purposes."

I returned the favor. I formally terminated my long-standing, intimate if increasingly intermittent and costly relationship with Dr. Rosenbaum. The certified letter I sent alleged that Rosenbaum, at some cost to me, had utterly failed to produce the deliverables I had gotten for free, along with considerable indescribable side benefits, from his kind, generous and lovely chief assistant. I asserted she had not violated the confidentiality of his files for ulterior purposes, unless there was something ulterior about my wellbeing and hers, her happiness and mine.

The letter declared that his impetuous decision could be construed as a deliberate act of malpractice, as it could unravel the effectiveness of a procedure, however ineffective, that I had bought and paid for. The letter warned that I had consulted with Dr. Irving Tardiff, a celebrated Manhattan malpractice attorney and board certified neurologist (I'd once written a piece on him for *People*) who would be contacting Quack Quack's lawyer, presumably the erstwhile from the estimable firm of Dimes & Nichols, should he, Dr. Rosenbaum, fail to remit immediate full payment for Rebe's accrued vacation time, six weeks of notice, and letter stipulating that her health insurance would be continued until she secured new gainful employment. I offered a reasonable alternative: send a certified check, refunding the professional fees I had remitted over the past two-something years, plus interest and compounding, which I estimated totaled ten thousand and something dollars, not including transportation costs.

A certified check covering Rebe's severance and vacation pay was hand-delivered to Bermuda Road the next afternoon. Refreshed and now well-replenished, Rebe continued roughing out what we would do, must do, once we got to Zion.

The original purpose of the trip was to introduce Rebe to friends and family. Now there was the unexpected assignment from Bob Gamma, my former boss and now an editor at the *New Yorker*, to do a piece on modern polygamy and profile a mysterious *out your way* fellow. "All I know is his first name, Orson, Brother Orson. Is Orson a code word to Mormons like you?" Gamma asked. Orson was said to be a reasonably prominent lawyer from a big family name in Salt Lake City, married to two sisters and about to take a third wife, a teenager young enough to be his daughter. "What's most curious," Gamma said, "he's represented by a pretty heavy DC political firm—Barlow, Adams and Russell. Incidentally, I have agreed that we will protect the identity of the man and the firm."

At a minimum, the assignment would extend our homecoming visit at least three weeks, possibly more, depending on where chasing Brother Orson led.

Homecoming. The prospect of returning to the place and family of one's birth conjures visions of joyous reunions with dear relatives and lifelong friends, people to whom one seems inextricably bound by similar formative experiences, common beliefs, even religions, and wonderful revealing memories, snapshots of events and insights into people that shaped us, touched our lives for better and worse.

It had been more than two decades since I first fled over the Wasatch, that mighty Rocky Mountain fortress that shields Zion from the wiles of New York and Connecticut and New England. I'd acclimated so thoroughly to my new surroundings that Utahns I encountered by chance inferred from the way I spoke, dressed and acted that I was from somewhere else. Had I ever spoken like one of *them*? If so, I did no longer. I could deny it straightaway and get away with it.

Was I ever really one of them? Sure, Salt Lake was home to my parents and their *real* children and their progenitors going back as far as

Anglo-Saxon progenitors go in the Great Basin. Separated now by geography and culture for 20-something years made a recurring fantasy seem even more plausible: if people bothered to look they may have found more than circumstantial evidence to support my suspicions that I may have been separated at birth from my natural parents.

Public records show that on the very day I was born at LDS Hospital, in the high avenues northeast of downtown, Martha Hutchinson Pratt—a young mother originally from West Hartford, Connecticut, but stationed temporarily at nearby Hill Field Air Base with her husband, Captain William Franklin Pratt—delivered a son who died within minutes. Perhaps they were my real parents. Perhaps the couple suffering that day should have been the Parley Pratt Russells of Salt Lake City. Some zealous Mormon medical team took it upon themselves to play God. They determined the surviving "Pratt" boy should be raised up in a righteous, God-loving *Mormon* Pratt family that, otherwise, would have lost its firstborn son. They considered this unusual coincidence a sign from the heavens, a prompting from the Almighty, one that they should not, could not resist.

This selfless, loving act ensured that the surviving "Pratt" boy—that would be *moi*—would be born in the covenant, that he, a child of the promise, would be spared the trauma of being raised up Episcopalian or Congregationalist or, God forbid, an utterly confused Unitarian. In due time, he would be steered toward the first state university God founded a few blocks away from his home, or the second, 50 miles south in Provo. He would never be consigned to those snotty boarding schools that steel young heirs of industrialists for the perils of the world, including Harvard and Yale and their legions of pinko professors, pimps and prostitutes.

As a missionary—first in New Haven, then in Hanover and Cambridge—I assumed my *real* heritage explained why Yale, then Dartmouth and finally Harvard were so personally energizing. I belonged there on the banks of the Charles and the seacoast of New England. Never once in my two-year sojourn there as a religious zealot did I long for Zion and her mountains or suffer the numbing homesickness that routinely affected many others. Whatever eagerness I experienced to return "home" after two years of service had more to do with desire to get on with my life than a craving to be back in the heart of Mormonism. Like several self-assured young men my age in Winthrop House-on-the-Charles River, I too worried that once sequestered behind the Wasatch, I would never manage to leave again.

At my first *homecoming*, my stomach turned—longing for Boston, perhaps—as I stood at the podium ready to speak to people who seemed not to have moved from their pews since wishing me farewell and Godspeed two years earlier. Homecoming services had to be monotonously routine to them, even if they were spiritually uplifting from time to time. Peck's petulant bad boy goes on a mission. He returns home chastened by the Spirit, full of steam ready to slide into the grinding, numbing routine that often bestows the Mormon *look* and *feel*, transforms people into interchangeable parts, riveters on the assembly line, soldiers in God's army, saviors on Mount Zion. Henry Ford's plants never operated so efficiently nor were his laborers so committed.

As a missionary I often approached people on the street who had *that look*: "You *look* like you might know the location of the nearest Mormon Church?" I would say.

"I have no idea…why do I *look* like I might know?" the smart ones asked.

"Well," I would say, "You just have that wholesome, fresh-scrubbed *look* about you, like Mormons do." The objective of this particular flattering gambit was to secure an appointment to teach the contact and his family. Believe it or not, the gambit was reasonably effective.

For two years I had been persuasive. Now I was standing before people who indeed looked like Mormons because they were Mormons. They had that look, the look and life that I was about to be forever consigned to if I tarried long in the land of my birth. I would be a good neighbor, a reliable home teacher, a father of too many children and possessor of too little cash thanks to my big family and the ten percent of my income I would willingly direct to the Church every payday.

To these people of the promise and the look, I was living evidence that the system was quite good at grinding out true believers who would become part of the machinery and produce generation after generation of true believers. Who, but I, doubted that I was substantiation of the Spirit of God moving in man? These people of the *look* hadn't come to church to hear my doubts. They wanted confirmation and reassurance. A thump on the tub here. A bugle call there. A well-timed confessional tear or two. They hungered for a laundry list of stirring or amusing anecdotes, faith-promoting stories, perhaps a joke, a gag, or a play on words, a vague tale about how I became converted, and, finally, my burning testimony of whatever it was I was convinced of. Belief was okay, absolute knowledge was preferred. Whatever I offered they would interpret according to the dictates of their own consciences. They would continue to worship how, where and what they may. If only *I* could…

These people of the *look* and the *promise* were not my people. At least, they weren't people I wanted to be. My people were in New England. I had not wanted to leave them. I had pleaded with G. Buckley to extend my call for another six months. "I am not squared away yet," I'd argued. He'd refused. "It's time to move on. You need to go *home* and get on with your life—put into practice the things you have learned out here," he said. "Find yourself a wife and after you do, make sure she doesn't see her toes for about eight years or so. That'll steady you."

Bishop Carl told me I looked terrified. "I had the sense you were just peaking when you were released," he said. "Of all the people I know, you could have used extra time—maybe some work in the mission office, anything to ease the transition back into the real world." He said there was a parallel relationship between the severity of culture shock and one's missionary performance: the better—I think he meant "more engaged"—the missionary, the more severe the shock, and the longer the decompression. Elders who eased through as though missionary service was a mere rite of passage adjusted quickly, with little pain. A few, for no apparent reason, would drift away from the Church. The majority would slide along for life, passively active, shirking time-consuming, inglorious assignments that didn't come with the trappings of increased authority. These were the young men Bishop Carl and other bishops went after first with assignments and callings that, hopefully, would keep a few of them more than superficially engaged.

The committed, achieving, engaged group posed a different challenge. They were fewer in number. They would need extra time to decompress and think. They wouldn't easily readjust to the laconically comfortable ways of Zion. Their passion, their demand for perfection could lead to radical and abrupt decisions, about-faces. Bishop Carl likened RMs like me to disoriented bull moose in a bog. He laughed, sighed in anticipation of delivering the punch line of the metaphor. "They are strong and powerful enough to butt down sturdy trees at the edge, but skittish enough to plunge deeper into the slough until they are swallowed whole. A doe in heat at the swamp's edge sometimes helps a buck regain his bearings."

All these things, these truths gleaned over the past twenty-one years—for all I knew, they may have been etched in my "Born In the Covenant" DNA—raced through my mind as I stood at the podium, girding to address people who represented everything I hoped I would never be. I was not some veritable returning prodigal ready to confess with chagrin and for their pleasure: "Well Dad, Mom, you were right after all." I had not yearned to be with them. I was not content with their ways. At the first opportunity I knew I would flee the valley of my birth before those mountain barriers became insurmountable, before the powers of Zion remolded me into one of *them*.

The address began slowly, easily, comfortably. I was the "old" Jed: irreverent, blunt, sardonic. "Mothers and fathers, Jed Russell is home. But don't rush to get your daughters off the street just yet. Given the level of female attention I've had these past two years, I'll be content for a while yet with Queenie, the family cat."

Bishop Carl's loud, booming laugh erupted behind me. The warm-up shtick was working. I was just what they expected. Nothing had changed. They were leaning back, relaxing, preparing to enjoy the ride, expecting I would entertain them for the allotted twenty or thirty minutes. They considered me an engaging speaker, one who would surely rev up the younger lads in the audience, get them hepped up to serve and do their parents proud. Perhaps some young woman would hear her prayers being answered. In her heart she would know that Jedediah Pratt Russell, returned missionary and stalwart of Zion, was the man who would take her to the temple of the Lord to be married for time and all eternity. This is the way things are *supposed* to work. This was the way things *did* work. Until they didn't.

"If I speak the truth today, I must confess that I wish I weren't here. If I had my druthers, I'd rather be in that cramped mission office overlooking Harvard Yard, or knocking on ancient doors in Newport and Kennebunkport," I said. My father later said I had pronounced my *a*'s and *r*'s so broadly that "You sounded like you were raised in mainline Boston," not realizing that mainline describes the crusty western suburbs of Philadelphia.

"It's not that I had anything against Salt Lake. Then again maybe I did. I could say this place reminded me too much of what I was; or that the Church, as it lives here, isn't quite the Church I have come to love these past two years." They were beginning to pay attention. They exchanged nervous looks. My father buried his head in his hands, which is what he always did when he expected the worst from me. "But the real reason I have second thoughts about being here is this: there is unfinished business in New England...

"I stand before you to account for myself, to turn the sheets of my missionary journals, page by page, for you to see. I did all the right things. With the Lord's help, I baptized many people, in fact I set a record in that department. You'll see that I was made a senior companion after five months, a district leader at seven, and a zone leader at nine... I taught other missionaries how to teach, gain testimonies, and overcome adversity... The people I baptized have gone on to become branch presidents, Relief Society presidents, Sunday school teachers and full-time missionaries. If such indicates success, you should be eminently pleased with me. If deep affection, love for the region and its people are sure signs of success, then I excelled because I stand before you totally smitten by New England and New Englanders, the home of my ancestors and many of yours. It has become my home."

I paused, eyed the congregation. Smiles, approving nods had replaced frowns and raised eyebrows. This is what they were used to. They were ready to acknowledge the amazing power of the Lord, His skill at transforming scoundrels and reprobates like Jed Russell into productive, if not particularly humble or likeable servants.

"These are but trappings of success...and they have their own rewards," I continued. "For instance, I have now been called to teach new elders at the mission home downtown, where former mission president's assistants, zone leaders and top baptizers are highly valued and sought after... While I am proud of my record, the only thing it should indicate to you is this: in the real world, I would probably be very, very good at selling Tiny Tim Training Toilets door to door.

"My honest, from the heart—from the gut of my soul—report and testimony to you today is quite different than what the written record suggests. My report is as plain as it is brief. I failed."

Pause. People in the congregation averted their eyes as if they expected the worst from me was yet to come.

"In a very real sense, *we* failed.

"Let me tell you why we failed... About 20 percent of New Englanders today sprang from ancestors who came to America stowed like ballast in the treacherous holds of slave ships. The indignities they endured were far more severe and long-lasting than any our ancestors suffered at the hands of the Missourians. Now comes the ultimate, ironic indignity: the fullness of the gospel of Jesus Christ, the gospel of liberation, is not yet for them...

"Across New England, I have seen them hungering for the truth, thirsting for the waters of baptism, longing to be the threads—the earthly catalysts—that unite their families eternally. I have seen their sorrow when we say, 'Not now, Brother. Patience, Sister. Wait a little longer.' And with anxiousness for their families they plead: 'How much longer?'

"For them, and for all of us, I ask you today: 'How much longer?' How long must all of us—Black and white—suffer before we, we who were born in the Covenant, open our hearts and minds so we can hear clearly the answer the Lord has *always* intended us to hear? If you heard His answer today would you be ready to accept it?

"I stand here today to bear witness that the God of Joseph and Brigham and Orson and Parley intends His gospel for all people, whether their skins be black or white. Joseph Smith knew it and said it. I know it as surely as I know that my name is Jedediah Pratt Russell. And I know that each of you can know what I know if you will but hear His answer to your prayers. Never again should a successful returning missionary need stand before you and in good conscience report: I failed miserably. In Christ's name Amen."

It was a confusing, often disappointing time for me. At times, my yearning to return *home* to the mission field was overwhelming. I would find myself parked near the runway at Salt Lake International watching enviously while jets found their wings and then gradually disappeared behind the peaks of the Wasatch Mountains headed for places I longed to be—to the mission fields of the world, to Boston, New York, Washington and beyond. And as I watched I worried that the Harvards of Winthrop House-on-the-Charles River may have been right: once sequestered again behind the Wasatch, in the shadow of the everlasting hills, I might never come their way again.

Although I'd adapted to the changing college scene in Cambridge, New Haven and Hanover, I assumed naively that Zion in her mountain fortress had opted out from the social revolutions sweeping America, that she had been spared the perils of marijuana, lysergic acid diethylamide, speed, indiscriminate sex, anti-Americanism and Communism, not to mention pulsating, hip-grinding rock 'n' roll.

I was wrong, of course. Some of my closest friends had become unrecognizable acolytes of the new sex, drugs, and rock 'n' roll religion that had rumbled through the mountain passes into the Great Basin while I was away in the world preaching the gospel of redemption and deliverance, piety, self-restraint and chastity, a religion led by a living prophet for our times. These messages had resonated with New Englanders, Catholics and followers of Billy Graham particularly, but not exclusively. Even

Episcopalians, Congregationalists and Unitarians thought the world was out of control and that perhaps young missionaries with short hair, in suits, starched white shirts, dress hats and sensible leather shoes had the answer.

Several encounters with a young and skeptical newspaper editor in Hanover, New Hampshire seemed to convince him that we were normal kids, "Sober, serious versions of those Green Meanies up the street," he said, referring to the Dartmouth students a few blocks away. "Missionary service seems to be a Mormon rite of passage, like a prolonged bar mitzvah without the hoopla and money," he observed.

A couple of press releases promoting church events I wrote impressed him enough that he dropped by the events. Later, as I prepared to leave Hanover for my final assignment in Cambridge before returning home, I stopped by his office to say goodbye. As I stood to leave, he took my arm and turned me so I was facing him. "I've been thinking about this for some time and I guess I'd better say it now or it won't mean a damned thing. When you get back in college, think about preparing yourself to become a journalist. You'd do well at it and the profession needs ethical people like you."

It was with his recommendation banging around in my mind that I tracked down the editor of the *Daily Utah Chronicle*, the student newspaper at the University of Utah, an increasingly shrill voice of the emerging interlocked anti-war and pro-drug movements. Most of the editors and writers seemed driven by four objectives: get the United States out of Vietnam; promote the use of marijuana and LSD; get laid; and attack the Mormon Church. Not necessarily in that order.

While I wasn't impressed much by their mindless partisanship, I thought they would be tolerant of, if not in need of, a more reasonable voice: I was politically liberal, critical of the war but supportive of our troops, flatly opposed to mind-altering drugs, and, of course, a straight-arrow, returned missionary who, like them, was searching for his own drummer. Instead of filling out a bunch of applications, I submitted a report on a meeting I'd attended on communism on college campuses, which turned out to be a recruiting meeting run by the John Birch Society.

Some of the speakers were fairly prominent members of Salt Lake society, well connected (in some cases related) to members of the Quorum of Twelve Apostles. They had mangled and twisted various Church doctrines in a transparent effort to link their own arch views of the world to the gospel. In the informal question and answer period that followed, I had sought out one particularly powerful speaker, Reed Benson, the son of a prominent apostle.

I introduced myself as a recently returned missionary, then said: "In your speech, you seemed to imply that the Birch Society shares the same aims as the Church, to the extent that one could not be a good member of one without, in principle at least, being a good member of the other." I asked the question so evenly that I'm sure Benson assumed my views squared with his.

"Not all Birchers are Mormons, but many of them have converted. Conversely, there is every reason why a Mormon should also be a John Bircher—look at the way Communists are attacking the Church these days," he said.

"How is that?" I said, baiting him. The inflections of my voice suggested righteous indignation and surprise rather than doubt. "I've been away for two years."

"Do you think all the trouble about the Negro issue is just happenstance? No, it's the Communists who are telling the Negroes that the Church is racist. And those poor, ignorant colored folks are playing right into the Communists' hands," he said.

"Won't everyone be shocked when Negroes get the priesthood?" I said innocently.

"That's just what they're waiting for—for the Church to rescind God's word," Benson counseled. "Wouldn't that put us in a fine pickle? It would be tantamount to denying we ever had living prophets," he said heatedly, confident that he was speaking to a sympathizer.

"Unless it wasn't God's word in the first place," I said quietly.

"What?" Benson said, astonished.

"Unless the *policy* is man's, not God's," I said.

"But it's not policy—it's doctrine. All the prophets of the Church have taught it as doctrine; and I know in my heart that colored people are not to receive the priesthood because they're children of Cain, descendants of Ham. And, they're not doing much to remove the curse now by cozying up to the Communists."

"What if President McKay said today: the time has come for Negroes to receive the priesthood? What would you do?" I asked.

"That requires me to speculate on an issue I know will never occur. But I tell you if it did, which it won't, there would be many who would say that the Mormons have succumbed to political pressure—and many of those people would be members of the Church."

That night, I wrote out my reactions and impressions and took them to the interview with Steve Taylor, the student editor of the *Chrony*. I told him I'd recently returned from a mission and would like a job as a reporter. He eyed me suspiciously, lit a cigarette, I'm sure to test my tolerance. "Are you sure you could stand being around people like me?" he said, blowing smoke my direction. He asked if I'd ever written anything for publication.

"Press releases in the mission field," I said. He sighed. I told him about the commentary in my pocket about the John Birch meeting. He crushed out his cigarette.

"Could I give it a read?" he asked. I handed him the piece. He read, occasionally saying things like: "Oh wow," "terrific," "what a fucking asshole." When he had finished, he called in a rather ratty looking girl—in time, she would become known to me as Doubting Donna—handed her the piece and asked her if there was room to run it in the next day's newspaper. She read, repeating Taylor's expletives and their modifiers as if it were secret code, a bond between them.

"Far fucking out," she said almost breathlessly.

"Hits fucking hard, way fucking hard," Taylor replied.

When she had finished she eyed me up and down suspiciously, and asked one question: "How'd you get the motherfucker to be so fucking open with you?"

Taylor answered for me: "Let me introduce Jed *Pratt* Russell, an honest-to-God RM, with the name, temple recommend and long underwear to prove it." I shifted uncomfortably, suddenly feeling traitorous—not at all how I had felt writing the piece. It was clear that these people, the ones who had the power to let me share my views with a wider audience, saw me as something of a highly credentialed, unassailable source for information and reports from the enemy camp.

"Are you sure you want us to publish this?" Taylor asked again, as though he hunched I may be having second thoughts.

I had aired similar views from the pulpit and, to my knowledge, no one protested. If they had, I could have always claimed I was misunderstood. Print was prima facie evidence; it would leave little wiggle room. My piece was temperate, loyal. Surely no one would be too upset by thoughtful criticism in an obscure student newspaper—it wasn't exactly the *New York Times*. No need to fear the wrath of the Church. "I don't see the harm in it," I said cautiously.

"You're sure. It could raise the dander of a few people I know," Taylor said.

"I haven't been blasphemous or challenged the power of general authorities or anything," I said.

"No...but some will think you have."

"Only fools."

"So, it will run as a personal opinion column. I'd also like to run an editor's note that would give your background and so forth."

I was excited. I had never seen my name in print before. I arrived early for school the next morning hoping to secure a few extra copies, read the column before my 7:45 a.m. zoology class. The rack in the biology building was empty; so were the racks in the other nearby buildings. I knew the paper had been published because several students in my morning classes said they'd seen it. It wasn't until noon that I finally laid hands on a copy.

I anticipated a lengthy discussion over lunch with the young men who taught with me at the mission home. Most of them were reasonably intelligent and thoughtful, so I anticipated receiving some support—intellectual support if nothing else—from them. As I carried a tray of food toward the table, I could see them talking rapidly, rather animatedly, waving their hands wildly, to emphasize one point or another. Some were hunkered over copies of the newspaper, carefully studying the column, line by line. As I neared the table, all conversation stopped.

"Well, well, Elder Russell. It's nice to know you're still with us," said Greg Hansen, who, as you know, had been a drinking buddy of mine before he'd gone off to Hong Kong on a mission. "I thought you'd gone and traded in your angel chaps [temple garments in local argot] for a pair of Jockey shorts."

I smiled, sat down. Greg stared at the cup of Postum on my tray. I held it to his nose, to reassure him it wasn't coffee. I placed it down on the curved edge of the tray; Postum spilled across the table.

"A little nervous are we?" Greg said. "No one would ever know if that cup were filled with coffee instead, would they?"

"Someone brain-dead, with nothing better to think of might wonder, that's for sure," I said.

"Walking pretty close to the edge these days, aren't you Elder Russell," said Ralph Coltrin, one of the returned missionaries who also wrote for the *Chronicle* occasionally. "You played right into Steve Taylor's hands. He was dying to run a piece like that, he just needed a patsy like you to walk through the door, and he took full advantage…"

"So? Was there something wrong with the piece?" I said.

"Some think so, but I don't," Greg said. "It's the way Taylor handled it—he really used you to stick it to the Church."

"How could he do that, the essay is very cautious," I said.

"Either you are the one brain-dead, or you haven't seen it yet," he said.

"The latter—I just picked up a copy. I couldn't find a *Chrony* anywhere on lower campus."

"You're fortunate to have found one. Most of the racks in Orson Spencer Hall were empty by nine o'clock," Coltrin said. "And Taylor expanded the press run by a couple thousand; he had a reporter hand-carry a couple of hundred copies down to the church office building and the *Deseret News*. A reporter from the *Daily Universe* [the BYU student newspaper] drove all the way from Provo late last night to pick up a bundle for distribution. The *Universe* wants to publish your piece tomorrow if it gets by the censor [it didn't]. Your name is going to be mud before this is over."

I shrugged. Coltrin had always struck me as being a Nervous Nellie type. I opened the newspaper to the opinion section. My piece covered the upper half of the tabloid-sized page, a substantial portion of which had been devoted to a banner headline that looked like this:

Returned Missionary takes Church to task on Negro issue
Jedediah Pratt Russell

Beneath the headline, Taylor had bylined the story with my full name and placed it over the editor's note which read:

> *Ed. Note: Last month Jedediah Pratt Russell returned from the New England Mission of the Mormon Church, where he was the mission's leading baptizer. He is now a sophomore pre-medical student, and is an instructor at the Missionary Training Center in downtown Salt Lake City. A lifelong Mormon, Mr. Russell is the descendant of both Parley Parker Pratt and Orson Pratt, members of the original Quorum of Twelve Apostles under the Prophet Joseph Smith, the Church founder.*

The life struggle of many people in this community and elsewhere is to come to terms with God, whomever He or She or

It may be. For some, the search for enlightenment becomes obsessive and unpredictable; as often leading to the depths of hell as to the glories of heaven (if either place exists). It is not atypical to fruitlessly stalk hither and yon, returning to base camp, head hung low in shame, no truth in hand.

At that point it may occur to the sincere hunter that the evidence (or lack thereof) of God or wisdom or truth (or their opposites) can be found (or not) in people who profess to have it: "If they are good they are true and of Me; if they are not, they are not."

I learned this as a child. I believed it then, I believe it now. I was also taught (and believed) that free agency is God's way, that each man is accountable for his own life, that genetics neither condemn a man to a life of failure nor limit his opportunities to succeed. My life was sweet, tidy. If some idea, principle, doctrine didn't mesh with those two central principles, it was neither truth nor of God.

As I grew older, I realized that life wasn't so neat. By fourteen, a time when I was pretty well converted to my religion, I was confronted with a policy that didn't seem to agree with my neat formula. Not anxious to throw the baby out with the bath water, and fearing I had overlooked important information, I decided to study the issue further.

For four long years I searched the scriptures for clues as to why Negroes are forbidden from holding the priesthood in the Mormon Church. The search was fruitless. There was no convincing evidence to be found.

I was ready to abandon ship then and would have had it not occurred to me that the practice was so obviously flawed and out of synch with the rest of the gospel that it had to have been manmade, an unfortunate byproduct of a perilous time when Mormons were being driven out of their homes in Missouri and Illinois. Surely, I reasoned, if the Prophet searched the scriptures like I had, he would also conclude there was neither a scriptural basis for the policy nor a latter-day revelation. I reasoned, what man had made in error, he could also rend asunder. Be patient, I counseled myself; the time is coming.

During the two years I served as a missionary for the

Mormon Church, I was often asked to justify this practice. I never tried to. Instead, I said it was my opinion that the policy was manmade and would be ended. Some elders thought my position blasphemous, but in my heart and head I knew I was right.

Today—just a month or so back from the mission field—I am willing to admit that I may be wrong. I am not wrong about whether the policy is human artifice, or will be changed soon. My estimate of what it will take to bring about that change may be wrong. To be kind to myself: only partially correct.

A few nights ago I attended a meeting of the John Birch Society. I had no business being there, really. I'm a moderate-to-liberal Democrat—a person with a capitalist's brain and a socialist's heart. But this one was billed as an informational session on Communism, a subject on which I have some academic interest. I listened attentively as a succession of firebrands railed against Communist operatives and fronts in the US—from Nelson Rockefeller and virtually every employee of the State Department to various civil rights and anti-war activists—and clearly implied that my church endorsed the principles of the John Birch Society. After the meeting, I cornered one of the better speakers, Reed Benson, a well-known Utah politician and son of Ezra Taft Benson, a leading apostle of the Church. I asked him directly about his claims that some formal kinship existed between my church and the society. He suggested that his own father was evidence of that. While he and his father are entitled to follow their political consciences wherever they may lead, their choices are no more indicative of what other Mormons should do than is my membership in the Democratic Party.

Feeling rather comfortable about my position, I sought to draw him out. So I asked for an example of compatibility.

"Look at the way the Communists are attacking the Church," he said. Then he expounded for some time on his theory that Communists are using Negroes to get at the Church, to coerce a change in "God's law," which would plainly show to the world that Mormon prophets never talked to God in the first place. (Ipso facto: Mormonism is another opiate of the masses).

His arguments were thin, I thought, especially in light of what I thought would take place any day. If it is not God's law, it could be changed without a revelation, leaving communists with little fuel for their fire.

"It will never happen," he said, because it is God's law—one that had been taught by all the prophets of the Church. Further, he said he had a personal testimony that Negroes were being punished for the sins of Cain, a "doctrine" he said is followed by the majority of faithful Mormons.

While I have utter contempt for Benson's beliefs, his comments did cause me to change my mind. I no longer believe that the policy will be rescinded once the Prophet asks for direction. In point of fact, the prophet may know the answer already. Now it's just a timing issue. It is here that Benson's seat-of-the-pants marketing survey comes into play: the Brethren must weigh the "greater goods."

If they have run their own survey (if they haven't they should) they probably know that there are too many members with beliefs similar to Reed Benson's. They are faithful Latter-day Saints who may be shaken by a sudden change of direction. Like Moses descending from the mount to behold his flock worshipping the Golden Calf, the latter-day prophet may need to postpone delivering the word until such time as he's brought his beloved brethren to heel, gotten them to the point where they can readily accept a dramatic change in a policy that, despite our protestations to the contrary, seems racist to the core.

Many Mormons may not agree, but those of intelligence may admit that it is possible the intransigence of the faithful may be delaying implementation of this important change, a change that will benefit all of us.

For now, Mormons of good would do well to formally reject the racist theories taught by men like Benson, his father and other church leaders that Negroes descended from Cain, or Negroes were less valiant in the War in Heaven. They must fully embrace and assert the only official interim Church explanation: "We don't know why, but we do know that the priesthood will be restored to Negroes, and we are

> preparing and looking forward to that day."
>
> What harm can come from adding this additional thought: "And we hope that day comes soon"?

I was pleased about the piece itself, but horrified at the way Taylor handled it. I had only told him that I was a pre-med student, although the column revealed the fact that I was a recently returned missionary. "I don't know where they got all this stuff," I said, puzzled, concerned, feeling like I'd been taken in.

Ralph Coltrin looked sheepish. "I got suckered too. Taylor asked me if I knew you. I told him you taught with me at the mission home. I asked him why he wanted to know and he said you had applied to be a reporter. He said he thought it would be a good idea to have another good Mormon on staff—to balance things out a little more. He asked if you had been a good missionary. That's when I gave him the details—although I didn't tell him about your ancestry," he said.

"That'd be easy to check. How many people with Pratt in their names aren't related to Parley P. or Orson?" I said.

"Forget Taylor. I'm concerned about you; about your testimony. You seem headed in the wrong direction," Greg interjected.

"Just because I'm an RM doesn't mean I wear blinders."

"You gave aid and comfort to apostates, non-Mormons and Communists," he said.

"The enemy is us—the membership of the Church. We're the ones holding up the change," I said.

"And you know that," Hansen said.

"It's obvious."

"You're closer to the edge than I thought," he said.

"But my balance is deft," I teased.

"Don't be so sure," he said seriously. "I've seen you intellectualize your way out of the Church before."

Letters to the editor poured in. Devout Mormons praised the piece and condemned it in equal numbers. One crank wrote: "It is sorrowful indeed that a missionary so recently returned from the field could be so thoroughly deceived by the Adversary. That he taught his misguided theories while a missionary is nothing but bald-faced treason." My favorite was from Rabbi Aaron Mednick, of Temple B'Nai Israel who wrote: "Jed Russell's example delivers a refreshing reminder to all creeds that subscribe to discriminatory doctrines and practices. He pledges allegiance to his religion's most important tenet—the principle that demands of all men that they think for themselves and act accordingly, which he has in this fine piece of criticism aimed at religionists who willingly distort the gospels to serve their own misbegotten purposes. Other congregations in this city—Jewish, Protestant, Catholic and Latter-day Saint—would benefit from having the likes of Jed Russell in their pews. His lucidity and passion honors the legacies of his esteemed, clear-eyed grandfathers. He has done them quite proud."

I was surprised and, frankly, relieved that the paper received no official rebuttal from the Church, a fact that I used on my friends to prove I had not written heresy.

My contributions to the *Chronicle* increased each week. More often than not, I focused on religious or quasi-religious issues. For better or worse, I tried to take the middle ground. In one column I took note of the changes that had taken place on the campus during my absence: the explosion of drugs.

The column started this way: "Two years ago, when I finally decided to take a heavy dose of LDS, I hoped my actions would lead others to do likewise. Some of my friends got confused and transposed the *S* and the *D*. Instead of going on missions, they went on trips." The column equated drug addiction to "living suicide" and so on. A few Mormon friends said I had subtly suggested religion was a drug too—"Your tone was lighthearted and snide, loaded with negative innuendo," Greg said. "I see you slipping away right before my very eyes."

Perhaps fearing that Greg may be right, I deliberately steered away from church-related news. Toward the end of the term I got trapped into writing a story about a church attendance policy change at Brigham Young University, which had been rolled out quietly after the student newspaper there ceased publication for the year.

Taylor had received confidential minutes of a recent meeting of the academic council at BYU, during which it had voted to expel students who weren't attending church regularly. Personally, I thought the new policy was unreasonable if not unenforceable. Nevertheless, I felt that BYU, a private school supported by the tithes of active Mormons, had every right to do whatever it wanted. It was no consequence to me, but it was to a number of other staff members, the ones who always smelled a rat whenever the Church was involved.

When I volunteered to do the story, other staffers complained that I was obviously compromised. Taylor insisted that my background would enable me to reach sources that no one else could. "They're not going to tell him anything, anyway—we have enough to go on right now," said Doubting Donna, who was quite eager to report this story herself, in fact had already written it in her mind. "How will we know he reports everything he learns?"

"We'll have to trust him," Taylor said, a little grudgingly.

"Frankly, no one's going to have anything to hide here," I said, staring down the rather hostile Doubting Donna. "In fact I'm so sure of that, that I'd welcome a set of itching ears on the line with me."

"Something's wrong with my ears?" Doubting Donna said.

"It's biblical," Taylor said. "Paul, waxing metaphorical about self-indulgent people who manufacture truths that rationalize their bad behaviors, right Jed?"

"Close enough," I said. "An extra note-taker would be helpful."

So, with Doubting Donna and her itching ears on one extension, I called Steven O. Stone, the academic dean at BYU. He was a high-profile guy in important church circles, a frequent speaker—almost a cult figure—on the Mormon lecture circuit. He waxed grandiloquent on inspirational topics like: "Ten Steps to Perfection" and "Success Begins on Your Knees." If a scintilla of the rumors about him were true, he was on a very short list of men being vetted for future general church leadership callings—up to and including apostle. I identified myself as a reporter for the *Chronicle* and revealed the fact that I had received a copy of the minutes taken at the academic council meeting and was now preparing a report for the next day's paper.

"What interest is this to a student newspaper at the University of Utah?" the dean parried condescendingly. "Aren't there stories in your own backyard?"

"BYU is part of the backyard for more than half of our students, Mormon tithe payers who help pay your salary and who are interested in what happens at the Lord's university," I said.

"To the good ones it won't matter. The bad ones will make a big deal out of it," he said. "In which camp are you?"

"Neither. I'm reporting a story," I said.

"Are you LDS?"

"It shouldn't matter."

"But it does…it means I won't have to run through some important background information."

"If it helps, I am," I said, grudgingly.

"For similar reasons, what priesthood do you hold?"

"Oy, Elder," I said evenly.

"A returned missionary?" he persisted, searching for more sure signs of my religious convictions.

"Yes—two months ago—from New England," I said, annoyed and embarrassed by his line of questioning. I should have introduced him to Itching Ears on the extension.

"Then you must have labored under my good friend and colleague."

"If G. Buckley Truman is a friend of yours, then yes."

Itching Ears covered the mouthpiece with her hand, laughed, mouthed: "I told you so!"

"What were you doing when you were released?" the dean asked, obviously still not satisfied with his background check of me.

"I was the mission's leading baptizer, a zone leader," I said angrily, "and now I teach at the mission home in Salt Lake."

"Good, good," the dean fairly sighed. I had measured up. "Then as a priesthood holder you understand the importance of church attendance. That's what this new policy is all about. It's always been an implied policy, we're just formalizing it now."

"Would you explain that, please?" I said, knowing full well what the explanation would be, but figuring it would be better to have it in his own words.

"Well, Elder…what did you say your name is?"

"Russell, Jedediah Pratt Russell," I said slowly, firmly. I knew this guy would be impressed with my name and the genealogy it implied.

"I see," the dean said, obviously rolling these distinguished Mormon names over in his mind. "*The* Pratts. Which one?"

"Both, Parley and Orson, a quirk of polygamy," I said proudly.

"Well, Elder Pratt, as you know, all entering students here sign a pledge that they will abide by Church standards. One of those standards is attendance at church. So if a student fails to attend church, he's violated that covenant."

"Does the policy define regular attendance as seventy-five percent of the time, or sixty-five, or fifty or a hundred?" I asked.

"It's a good faith thing, really, Elder Pratt," the dean said. "The regular attendance requirement is simply a reminder to students that church attendance is important—important to their being and remaining here."

"So, hypothetically, a good student could be expelled simply for not attending his meetings?" I asked.

"Hypothetically, yes. But in reality there are usually other issues associated with an inactive—Word of Wisdom problems, moral errors and so forth. You can pretty well assume it."

"Won't that practice sometimes work against some devout parents, who hope that their son's or daughter's attendance at BYU will eventually lead to sustained activity?"

"The majority will endorse the regulation, but I suppose it will upset a few. But BYU was never intended be a reform school; although, in the past, it has been viewed as that, just as the mission field has. The fact of the matter is, today we have to turn away many, many students because we simply don't have room for all of them. In light of that it would be a shame to reject an active member of the Church in favor of an academically qualified student who doesn't give two hoots about the Church," Stone said.

"Do you see any danger here—a danger of making the student body very one-dimensional; that you may reject many of the most academically gifted students?" I asked.

"You're a priesthood holder so I can tell you that some of the Brethren are very concerned about elitism at BYU. That issue raises its head every time we are forced to tighten admission standards. The problem will become more acute in the years ahead, now that the enrollment has been fixed at 26,000, give or take a few. Some people here are relieved that we're now more academically selective, but I tell you some very powerful apostles are adamantly opposed to the idea that BYU should become the Harvard of the Church, or as secular as Notre Dame. The Brethren will tell you that BYU exists primarily to develop thoughtful, intelligent, active members of the Church. That some of these people will go on to become prominent business leaders and academics is a welcomed incidental, but of little value if the first objective isn't met. Some of the Brethren believe there's a real danger, a liability to the Church in the latter instance."

"Do you mean there's danger in having a cadre of well-educated, but inactive, leaders and academics who take a sympathetic but secular approach to Mormonism?"

"Yes, that's correct," Stone said. "Some apostles see no value whatsoever in having what is referred to as 'the loyal opposition,' a characterization that really is an oxymoron: you can't be loyal to something and oppose it at the same time."

"Interesting. I always thought a man of the loyal opposition was one who objectively evaluated positions, reported history and so on, sublimating his own biases?"

"In secular matters like politics, yes. But it's a different matter in religion. How do you loyally oppose a commandment from God? You can't. That's what the Brethren are against—having people who, in the interest of academics, question God's commandments," he said.

"Loyal opposition has a bearing on policies and procedures, not on commandments, however I can understand that one man's 'policy' may be another's 'commandment,'" I said.

"Yes, well, it's especially challenging when the pronouncements, be they policies or commandments, come from the lips of a living prophet," he said. "Everything that comes from the prophet tends to be regarded as commandments for our times."

"Uh-huh, like the policy you just announced?"

"Some will say so, but no, it's unique to BYU, which is a special place. The bar here is set a little higher than it is for the rest of the Church."

"Or lower, some might argue, depending on their point of view," I said.

"Yes, I suppose so," Stone said slowly, irritated. "No doubt some would, especially the kinds of people who are always finding fault with the Church no matter what it does."

"You said it was a BYU policy. Did I misunderstand?" I goaded.

"Yes, well, you know what I meant."

"Yes, I'm quite sure I do."

The story, which ran across the top of the front page of the newspaper the next day, caused me more lasting trouble, heartache and so on than any one I have written since. I was accused of violating my temple covenants, of abusing a fellow priesthood holder, holding the Church up to ridicule. Some called me a wolf in lamb's clothing, a turncoat, a defiler of all that is sacred. And all I did was publish verbatim what Dean Stone said.

Itching Ears Donna was so impressed, astonished with his candor, with the honesty of everyone I interviewed that she became somewhat sympathetic to the new policy and talked openly of giving the Church a second look.

Dean Stone was furious when I called later in the morning to interview him for a personal profile I was preparing.

"I'm thoroughly ashamed of you. Ashamed because you made a mockery of the priesthood you hold," he seethed.

"Did I misquote you or misinterpret the intent of the policy?" I asked calmly, hoping my own self-control would settle him.

He didn't answer directly. "How do you think the Brethren will react when they see that I said some of them were opposed to BYU becoming the Harvard of the Church?"

"Why would they object? It's the truth and, in my opinion, it's a reasonable position, egalitarian in its own right—even non-members on the *Chrony* staff think it's reasonable."

"I don't give a whit what the staff of the *Chronicle* thinks; I'm concerned about the Brethren. And I tell you they'll think I betrayed their trust."

"But you performed a valuable service. You were open and rational. You made sense of a policy that otherwise would have seemed reactionary, even vindictive."

"The point is, I was beguiled. I trusted you because you claimed to be an Elder, a returned missionary, a Pratt," the dean snapped.

"I didn't volunteer that—you extracted that information."

"Your great-great-grandfather is probably turning in his grave," the dean said. "In fact, if he were alive he'd probably punch you in the nose."

"Grandfathers. Plural. And if you'll recall your church history, loyal and brilliant though they were, the Pratt brothers caused more than a peck of trouble for Joseph and Brigham because they often spoke candidly and honestly."

"Let me tell you, *Mister* Pratt," he said, emphasizing so I wouldn't miss his point that I was no longer a brother or Elder, at least in his mind.

"The name is Russell. Jedediah Pratt Russell. I get your implication."

"Good," snarled the academic dean, famous for counseling young people on how to make their confusing and conflicted young lives more spiritual and successful. "If you haven't already fallen away, you'd better get on your knees tonight and, like your famous ancestors did often, ask the Lord's forgiveness. Then ask Him to teach you loyalty. If I saw you in the celestial room of temple today I wouldn't accept your hand in fellowship of the priesthood. You are on a very short path to apostasy."

"I'm shocked you feel that way, Dean Stone. I gave you credit for having more intelligence than you've demonstrated in this incredibly stupid, self-serving and self-righteous conversation. Read tomorrow's paper and you'll see what I mean."

The next day the lead editorial, "Give the Y a Chance," concluded that the policy was intellectually consistent with BYU's mission, educating future leaders and academics who were, first and foremost, committed to the Church.

> The church continues to thrive because historically it has always equally valued academic achievement and practical accomplishment. Zion was built—and continues to be built—by harnessing the brains and brawn of men and women committed to the gospel. Over time, BYU will likely become the Harvard or Yale of the church. This will occur naturally as competition for admission intensifies and as professorships at the Y are sought out by Mormon academics. To suggest otherwise would endorse the premise that there is something inherently sinful in being too smart. BYU's own motto endorses the contrary: The Glory of God is intelligence.

My bylined column took note of the cooperation and forthrightness of the officials I had contacted, particularly Dean Stone.

> Honesty is always the best policy. It works as well with one's antagonists as with one's protagonists. In this case, Dean Stone's candor made rational sense of a policy that seemed, at first glance, knee-jerk and petty. The Church, as a whole, would do well to follow his stellar example.

Neither piece mollified Stone, who wasn't exactly warm later that afternoon when I visited his office in Provo. "How could you do it? Can you now look me in the eye, clasping my hand in the fellowship of the priesthood, and say you didn't abuse my trust?" he wailed.

"I can," I said, extending my hand. "If my accurate reporting caused you any personal difficulty, I am sorry for that."

Dean Stone pointed to the door. "I'm sorry, but I can't accept the hand of a traitor. Please leave before I say something I will later regret," he fumed.

I was confused, disheartened. I had come to see him, to mend fences, to tell him that my application to transfer to BYU would soon cross his desk. In fact I'd decided to apply because I had been so impressed by him, by his candor and honesty. Fat chance I'd get in now, I thought, as I walked into the office of admissions to retrieve the application I'd dropped off a few minutes earlier.

"Why?" the woman in the office asked, scanning the application.

"If you must know, I've just met with Dean Stone. It became very clear that people like me don't belong here…yet," I said.

"What? You're a member of the Church. A returned missionary. If you don't fit, who does?" she said.

"One wonders," I said.

Officially, instinctively, I started down the steep road to what some may call apostasy that afternoon. As I drove out of Provo in my yellow Volkswagen with a plastic sunflower strapped to its antenna, waving happily in the turbulence, I detoured to a convenience store, where I bought a flip-top box of "I'd rather fight than switch" Tareytons, a six-pack of Coors and continued on down the highway.

Halfway home, rounding Point of the Mountain, I quickly pulled into the breakdown lane, stopped, dashed from the car and spontaneously aborted my protest, and whatever else had been churning my gut, into the barrow pit. Standing upright, I wiped my mouth clean with the back of my hand, shook my fist in defiance at the stark, haunting concrete edifice below me, now bathed in glaring searchlights, centered in on a closed circle of high chainlink fence crowned with razor wire—the final stage for hack actors who follow my script, who smoke and drink and in other ways fail to heed the warnings of my mother's Point of the Mountain doctrine. "Not me, not now, not ever," I screamed, and then drove on down the freeway into Friday night, the Summer of Love, and everything that lay ahead.

Backfilling

Finsterwald stumbled along the street, limping, moaning, groaning, leaving a trail of "Oy vay!" in his wake. A stranger stopped him. "What is the matter?"

"What's the matter? My shoes are absolutely killing me!"

"So why do you wear them?"

"I'll tell you why. My business couldn't be worse. I owe the butcher, the baker, the grocer, the landlord. I have two daughters so ugly who knows if I'll ever be able to get them married. My son is a zhlob and my wife nags, nags, nags until I can go crazy. I come home each night from a fruitless day's work and I look at the bills and at my family, and at that point I could kill myself. So I take off my shoes—and mister, the minute these shoes are off my feet, it's such a mekhaye it's the only thing that makes life worth living."

The Joys of Yiddish
Leo Rosten, 1968

Watching the Xerox crank out ten copies of the finished manuscript produced *mekhaye* like I had never experienced, not altogether unlike what the apocryphal Finsterwald seemed to have sensed upon removing his tight shoes. Depositing a copy at Wren Hargrave's home a few blocks away was particularly satisfying—a deliverable, as promised, never mind the minor fixes that would be suggested by editors and readers: Rebe in Westport, Eddie Knight and the recently divorced Polly Thompson Liddy in Salt Lake City.

On our forthcoming trip *home* I planned to introduce Rebe to Eddie and Polly, true-up her suggestions with theirs and so on. Perhaps she would prove useful in putting together a report on plural marriage in Utah. To be honest, it felt like I had been singled out to report this story. Gamma told me that this mysterious Brother Orson was familiar with some of my work, particularly pieces I had written as a young reporter in Salt Lake City. "He said he knew you to be an even-handed kind of reporter, the type that sees matters from all sides, complexities and all; a bona fide empathizer and I agree with that: you are an empathizer nonpareil," Gamma said. I was dubious. He had blown smoke at me before. If I was an empathizer nonpareil, he was arguably the world's biggest chameleon, by turns a Francophile, Monarchist and IRA sympathizer. Whatever way the wind blew, Gamma made sure it was always at his back. Allegedly, this Brother Orson, pillar of the community that he was, had two wives and was contemplating taking a third, a woman, a girl really, way-way-too-young, young enough to be his daughter.

The manuscript was finished. Done enough. Ready to go to the publisher for final edits, proofing and typesetting. Rebe was out of a job and free to stay in Utah for as long as it took, an extended honeymoon as it were, if only I could persuade her to move up our wedding plans from October to like right now, August.

It occurred to me that even in 1985 we would find Utah much more welcoming if we were newly wed, rather than betrothed. This was a society that, perhaps even today, puts greater stock in written contracts and official ceremonies than it does in a man's word, a woman's intent; as if legal documents and authorization from the state and, perhaps, God Himself were necessary prerequisites to promises made in the head and heart that would be consummated and furbished over the years. Or not, as the case may be.

The furbishing had been underway for months, years. All we needed now was a ceremony and, insofar as I was concerned, an agreement to do it *now* before we returned to Utah and encountered Lord knows what. I secured the appropriate lubrication to celebrate the end of my protracted and interrupted attempts to write a first novel, a sort of memoir, a painful and narcissistic pilgrimage to Canterbury as it were. I also hoped the $100 bottle of vintage 1967 Dom Pérignon might provide all the friendly persuasion needed to convince Rebe that affairs of the heart ought not be delayed. Just in case, I laid in an extra bottle and added a single long-stemmed white rose, an unmistakable token of my unconditional surrender, an eternal pledge to worship at her feet for however long it was possible.

Waving these ensigns of my devotion like a savvy ship's yeoman would semaphores, I signaled to Rebe as she knifed through the glassy-smooth olive drab water of the lagoon toward the dock, then retreated to a chair. I turned to the last page of the manuscript, and lost myself in the uneven, smoky glare of the sun setting behind the lagoon, as I read and re-read the emotional climax:

> Standing upright, I wiped my mouth clean with the back of my hand, shook my fist in defiance at the stark, haunting concrete edifice below me, now bathed in glaring searchlights, centered in on a closed circle of high chainlink fence crowned with razor wire—the final stage for hack actors who follow my script, who smoke and drink and in other ways fail to heed the warnings of my mother's Point of the Mountain doctrine. "Not me, not now, not ever," I screamed, and then drove on down the freeway into Friday night, the Summer of Love, and everything that lay ahead.

If the manuscript didn't fully reveal my mind, it was clear enough. No poor slob high school reader would waste time looking for the hidden meaning in this wrap-up. He couldn't miss the transformation, the mind shift that was underway in the protagonist; he would see clearly its beginning middle and end. The last thing I wanted to write was a story that would require the services of a dim and unimaginative interlocutor, a high school English teacher like Miss James who would turn my novel into something far more ponderous, loaded with double entendres and subconscious revelations of my soul.

Technically, my Freud was the natty Rosenbaum with his dildo pipes. Although I'd fired him, he would also be relieved, pleased that the manuscript was done, done done, even if his lovely way, way too young chief assistant had become my muse and then some. The circle was closed, closed closed. And now, just as Rosenbaum had promised before I sent him packing, I stood on the brink of victory over marriage interruptus.

Came the wet and dripping vision of Rebe floating over me, framed in a vaporous halo created by the burnt red setting sun and the dank seashore air. She appeared as if newborn, still saturated from the fluids of some celestial uterus, dark hair matted in strings to her scalp and face, translucent chalky-pink swimsuit liquidizing into her skin, nipples hardened and erect from cool water…

"What's the occasion?" She stooped to towel moisture from her legs, then thighs and... "The rose is for?"

"You...the end and the beginning," I said a little uncertainly, unnerved by the vision before me.

"Alpha and omega, me?" she teased. Noticing my wandering eyes, she wrapped herself in the towel.

"Not what I meant...but it will do too...the end of the novel," I said, nodding toward the bound manuscript in my hands, "and now to the first chapter of Ben-Adams-Pratt."

She smiled, surprised. "Done already? I got through chapter twenty-two, I didn't see the others on the Mac," she said.

"Twenty-two was it, the end, the circle closed."

"If anything, the circle closed a little on the matter of the church—what an ass, that Dean Stone—but only a little. Besides, the last page said 'End Chapter 22' not 'The End' or 'END BOOK' or '*finito.*'"

"Easy enough to fix," I said. "Now about October..."

"Fix it? You mean end it there? You can't be serious," she said. "What'd Wren say?"

"He's reading now."

"Wonder how he'll see it."

"He was bloody happy to have a *finished* something," I said.

"Sure, but it's not *finished*? It's not to me. You get us powerfully into the Summer of '67, which, while I'm not old enough to recall it first hand, was something of a watershed year for your generation. More to the point, you're about six months shy of marrying Sarah...did you go on vacation for a half year or what? Check in to Holden Caulfield Memorial Hospital?"

"Hmmm *Catcher*." ('*I was trying to feel some kind of a good-by... when I leave a place I like to know I'm leaving it. If you don't, you feel even worse... It's funny. Don't ever tell anybody anything. If you do, you start missing everybody.*') "No visit to the Caulfield Memorial Asylum that summer of '67. It was just off to a hospital in New Haven for the summer to work in the OR School in the fall. Met Sarah in November. Marriage in January. That's it. The important stuff appears early in the novel, have you forgotten?"

"*Carpe veritas*: God answers prayers—the desultory *demimondaine* of Deseret deli descends: a spitting-vision of her spicy and rococo and luscious-lipped sibling. You wangle an intro and, presto, you marry six weeks later. Then we get a caricature of Sarah in the throes of divorce;

characterizations of your divine Mrs. Mulder, that even the diva of diagramming Miss James may rate a tad thin, wanting for flesh, crying out for blood..."

"And what might you say?" I asked, almost irritated.

"Consider me their intercessor and advocate."

"About *October* becoming August," I said.

"*October* will get here in its own due time," she said firmly. "There is absolutely no need to rush it."

Wren arrived with another celebratory offering just as we were uncorking the second bottle, still hashing through what needed to be done and how best, how quickly, *we* could do it.

"Didn't want to miss the festivities," he said, thrusting a magnum of year-old brut my way. "Hell of an effort Jed, really a hell of an effort."

"Thanks." I gave Rebe a smug *I told you so* look. "The ending was okay by you?"

"Whatever ends, ends." Rebe caught his eye. "It was fine, just fine," he said rather weakly.

"Fine, just fine?" I said. "What the hell kind of endorsement is that?"

"Well, a lot better than fine. It works. Now it comes down to this: are you satisfied? You want your salutatory book to be your best effort, to demonstrate the breadth and depth of your craftsmanship. A winner out of the box buys lots of latitude for the second. So it's up to you...is it as good as you've got in you? What are you thinking?"

"I'm thinking...I am very tired, slowly getting drunk and I want to get married again sometime this side of the veil," I said. "And, I'm weaving a story, not Penelope's cloth."

Wren scratched his head. "What?"

"Homeresque metaphor," Rebe interjected helpfully. "Penelope the widow of Odysseus promised to remarry once she finished weaving a tapestry for her dead husband's mother. She would weave by day, undo her handiwork by night. Difference is, Jed's the weaver."

"There's a connection between Jed finishing the novel and that hunk of glitter on your finger?" he asked, nodding Rebe's way.

Lord, was Wren going to negotiate this deal for me too? Make things right with Rebe? Coach us through our honeymoon? Well what the hell, what are friends for?

"Not finishing the book per se," she said, shifting uncomfortably. "Tying issues down is, moving the past fully into the past is," she said. I nodded in endorsement.

"It's fiction, not a bloody autobiography," he said.

"Really?" she said, edgily looking to me for support.

"She's right…there are holes. They can be plugged, easily." By the time the second bottle was drained, we'd (Rebe, Wren and I) mapped out a new close: two chapters at most would do the trick, perhaps one.

"So, now that we've done the outline, how long will it take for the words?" Wren asked.

"Dunno. A week for the roughs; two, three more to polish. Maybe. Depends how it goes…"

"Good enough."

"More time with this *New Yorker* assignment in the middle…and *People* left a message yesterday about doing a profile on some emerging organizational oracle from Utah who's revving up the Fortune 500."

"So a month—say endish of September…I'll buy you more time with Gamma, you handle *People*, okay?"

"Should work," I said.

Now that I think of it—and honestly I really didn't give it much thought until I was forced to—the summer of 1967 was memorable in three distinct, but somewhat commingled ways. In late March, when I secured a position in the operating room at Yale-New Haven Hospital, it was with an eye toward resolving, once and for all, whether my future lay in medicine or journalism, which was just beginning to seriously tempt me. Before I got to New Haven I had: been appointed managing editor of the *Chronicle* for the next school year, signed up for a crash-course media seminar at Yale, and, of course, survived the rather fiery encounter with Dean Stone in Provo.

Arriving in the city of my inaugural missionary experience, where I felt my first profound spiritual connect to the gospel of my blood, I hoped the summer sojourn there, on my own and freed from the restrictions of the mission field, would also steady my foundering, purge dubiety from my mind, staunch my purposeful drift away from the church.

But because of the demanding schedule at the hospital, the more intense than expected requirements of the seminar (perhaps I made them more demanding than they really were—a thinly veiled effort to prove to myself that I was indeed intellectually, if not economically, well-suited to the Ivy League), and the usual weekend distractions—Cape Cod, the Jazz Festival in Newport—I made it to church just twice: The first Sunday after I arrived (I discovered that the Jacksons were now in Cambridge and most of the people I'd connected with two years earlier had moved on as well) and the last before I headed west. I too like to know when I'm leaving a place.

It is not that I had fallen all the way out by mid-August, or had indulged all manner of lewd and lascivious acts. I had my opportunities: like the golden blonde hitchhiker leaning in the window of my car, stuck in Jazz Festival traffic, pleading for a lift to the Cape. This bra-less, semi-stoned vision of what I thought—hoped—the summer would yield offered grass and a place to bed down if I drove her all the way. I damn near took her up on it, although marijuana wasn't my thing then or ever, but decided (I can't imagine why) to drop her at the intersection of two major roads that led off Aquidneck Island toward Fall River, New Bedford, Buzzards Bay and the Cape, because I'd agreed to be on call Sunday at the hospital.

By the time I finally made it back to the pier, the last ferry to Jamestown for the night was about three hundred yards out in Naragansett Bay. I returned—sped, really—to where I had dropped the bronzed blonde chimera, but of course she'd already hooked a ride, probably with some lucky fellow for whom the Summer of '67 was surely turning out just as he willed it.

Unsated, yet frustrated by my lack of personal resolve, disgusted that only a quirk of fate had saved me from willfully (in my dreams) adopting the ways of the world, and now physically alert but mentally weary, I drove on toward morning, taking the circuitous land route around the islands of Patience and Prudence, across the Mount Hope Bridge to Providence and the mainland, and, at last, to the straight and narrow way home to New Haven, arriving just as the eastern sky was reddening ominously.

For me, there was plenty of will, but there was no way. I thought I stood half a chance with this *shikse* Italian Catholic nurse who had an eye for me and smoked a lot (I knew what smoking led to). So we went out. Often. It was more bizarre than working on Eugene McCarthy's grass-roots presidential campaign the following year. She turned out to be about as coy and guilt-ridden as any Mormon girl I'd ever met. And things got goofier after I made the considerable mistake of revealing my religious background. Thereafter, she couldn't shake the idea that I wanted her for a plural wife.

More important was what was happening to America. Ninety miles south, Newark, New Jersey erupted in flames and violence: twenty-something people died. By late July, Detroit was burning too; the National

Guard was called in and before it was over the bodies were stacked like cordwood. Just hours before I departed for home in the wee small hours of a sultry August Saturday morning, New Haven erupted too, forcing me to feel my way through the darkness, around police roadblocks, past burning three-deckers to the treacherous Connecticut Turnpike, south to New York City. Then west to Chicago, and north to University of Wisconsin in Madison for a weeklong student press gathering. I was so determined to catch up on what I had missed in the two years I was a missionary—the growing, interlocked anti-war and drug and free-love revolutions sweeping the country—that when I visited Madison a decade later I was stunned to discover it was virtually surrounded by lakes. The only other memorable event of that week was what became a daily eye-opener: two, sometimes three uninhibited and unashamed nubile young women in the gang shower each morning.

Then it was west across Minnesota, North Dakota, and endless Montana, cutting southwest from Missoula through the smoke-choked Bitterroot Mountains across the panhandle of Idaho to Coeur d'Alene, south through Moscow, Lewiston then Boise and on toward Salt Lake. It seemed like all America—even the mountain forests of Idaho and Montana—was a firestorm and I was in its eye, sensing its searing heat and the changes it was wreaking. Negroes were just becoming Blacks, Puerto Ricans and Mexicans Chicanos, then Hispanics. But Indians were still Indians, Jews were Jews, and Latter-day Saints, of course, would be Mormons forever. The oppressed of the world could learn a thing or two from my clan, which shrugged off the pejorative "Mormon" label enemies and outsiders applied to us and co-opted it into the accepted lexicon of Zion *("If you chance to meet a frown / do not let it stay / simply turn it upside down / and smile that frown away")*.

Bored somewhere near Whitehall, Montana, troubled by visions of the coming Zion and more promising ones of what it would take to put it behind me once and for all, I stoked up with a carton of "I'd rather fight than switch" and real Coors, then drove on—the outward signs of inner turbulence now plain for anyone who cared to see. On this homeward flight, I had no need for a barrow pit at the side of the road. My stomach had toughened and settled. So had my mind, more or less. Just in case, I ditched the "I'd rather fights," cranked open the sunroof and rolled down the windows as my yellow Volkswagen Bug, the sunflower waving gaily in the late summer air, rolled south toward Twin Falls and into what would have been part of The Great State of Deseret had Brother Brigham not been so insistent about, and over-indulgent in, the much-celebrated principle of plural marriage.

By the time I got to Ogden I was aired out, cleansed of the smoke that had trailed me for two thousand, five hundred odd miles. I zigged into the mountains to catch the final leg of the Mormon trail, veered off before Little Mountain and descended through the canyon named after Grandfather Parley. I took the south fork of the interstate that hugged the side-slope of the canyon mouth as it snaked around Suicide Rock, where a spurned Native American maiden was said to have leapt to her death.

There in the shadow of the everlasting hills, spread out below me, literally and perhaps figuratively too, was Zion, once a praiseworthy sparkling tribute to the prudent and orderly urban planning of Grandfather Orson, going steadily wrong. She had sprawled across the flatlands of what was once the bottom of the massive prehistoric inland sea of Lake Bonneville, and now was clambering above its still visible high water scar into the pristine foothills; homes, garages, tennis courts and swimming pools were being lashed to every precarious perch available, ones my ancestors felt better left to eagles, cougars, rattlers and stubborn men with ropes.

But, Zion in all her modern inglory was not burning. Neither was Canyon Mills. Not yet!

The aptly named Jerry Manderill, a *People* senior editor known for rejiggering stories so that they wandered incoherently like Boston's gerrymandered voting districts, was on the phone near noon Monday—first thing by Time Inc. standards. "So you got my message last week," he said.

"I did, a rather cryptic one for you," I said.

"You know him?"

"Know him? Him whom?"

"The make-nicey-nice demagogue that has all the corporate group-gropers agog," he said. "I thought you knew everyone in Utah."

"Be more specific. Utah specializes in growing nicey-nice demagogues," I said sarcastically, reminded of how annoying it was to have practically everyone I worked with assume I would forever have one foot in Gomorrah and the other in Zion. "Does Brother Demagogue have a first and last name?"

"Let's see," he said. I could hear him rustling through papers on his perpetually cluttered desk. "I have a Times *clip* about his *shtick* at IBM, I'll fax it...let's see, uh, his name is, uh, Stone...Steven O. Stone. Know him?"

"Yep."

"Yep? Yep is it? There's nothing more?" he asked.

"Just about. Met him once, a long time ago. Probably you should get someone else to do this…I'm pretty swamped getting the damned book finished."

"You've never turned down a Utah story before [this was true], we could wait a while, there's no big rush. Ideally, what we're looking for is maybe a 300-line profile—that would be enough for this *fonfer*—and a Q and A about how people can apply this shit in their personal lives—he makes a big deal about that."

"Neo-Mormonism for *goyim* masses," I said.

"He's Jewish?"

"No, Mormonish. Non-Mormons are considered gentiles, *goyim*. Nothing's innovative about what he preaches unless you haven't heard it before. Everything he teaches, I learned in Sunday school."

"You're kidding. No one's written that before. Shit, that'd be great stuff—those gullible suits would be horrified to know they're paying megabucks to get sanitized Mormonism fed to them."

"Not sure I can do it…but there's this guy over at the *Times*, well until recently: Mom MacMurrin; I mean Mal MacMurrin. He's from Provo, a BYU grad, probably knows Stone better…might be a better choice, ultimately."

"Not familiar with his stuff," Manderill said.

"Trust me, he's good. But tell you what…I'll check out Stone—couple of phone calls, set up what you want to do and so on—and if I can do the rest, I'll do it. Otherwise, I'll get MacMurrin—I know he could use the work just now. If it's okay by you."

"Okay, I'll take your word on MacMurrin if needs be. You have some big problem with this Stone guy or what?"

"Haven't laid eyes on him in years. I'll check him out and report back. What's the fee?"

"Two grand, maybe five hundred more for the Q and A. I'll send you the *Times* piece and some background from edit ref," Manderill said.

"Don't bother—my file on Stone is thick, goes way back."

Truth was, I'd kept a file on Stone since the painful encounter with him before the fateful Summer of '67. The file was stuffed with clips from newspapers, promotional flyers from BYU, and transcripts of rousing speeches, always modified slightly to fit the audience. Stone drew from a speech he'd delivered in 1967 at a BYU devotional to fashion a rousing pep talk to a leading software development company. "Ten Steps to Perfection," the title he hoped would inspire Mormon college students to take charge of their lives, became "Ten Tactics to Word Perfection."

He preached the importance of humility—"Change Begins on Your Knees"—to senior executives at AT&T, leading the company through the tumultuous aftermath of telephone industry deregulation and the breakup of old Ma Bell. Later he adapted the sermon for its rival IBM: "Real Leadership Comes through Bended Knees." The genesis of and basis for both speeches was a routine little talk he gave to new elders at the Missionary Training Center in Provo: "The Power to Persuade Begins on Your Knees." The adapted speeches were remarkably similar in every other sense—secular terms were substituted for religious ones.

Stone's recent success, phenomenal though it was, only reconfirmed what I suspected of him back in 1967. Like many of us, he too was rather better at preaching good concepts than he was in applying them. His approach to religion and spirituality was quite regimented, mechanical. To him and people like him, the church was just another corporation with its own board of directors and officers to please, and its own arcane corporate politics to be dealt with. Like all organizations, there was a way and way not to play the corporate game, and Steven O. Stone was still playing the game. And playing it well. At one point in his life, he seemed to have roughed out a draft of the guidebook: *Ten Steps to the Quorum of Twelve Apostles*. Perhaps in the aftermath of talking with me in 1967 he'd modified the speech, added two additional steps: "Keep your lip zipped around reporters" and "Keep your ego in check; many people won't be as impressed with you as you are."

Although decades had passed since my first troubling encounter with Steven O., I was surprised at how vivid, frighteningly vivid and fresh it was in my mind. I was quite reluctant to interview him again. It made little difference that this time around the lay of the playing field was tilted toward me. I'd never before turned down an assignment, let alone one *out my way.*

More intimidating was this: when it came right down to it, I had done enough research to know I knew quite a bit less about polygamy than I had assumed initially—presumptuously, as it now seemed. I was writing for the *New Yorker*, not *People;* the piece would run 6,000–10,000 words, not a thousand or two; it demanded substance, depth, perspective and it deserved all of my attention. Do it well and it would establish me as a very savvy expert on plural marriage, a writer who should be paid attention to, especially when he was writing about anything related to Mormonism.

I had enough personal knowledge to do a credible, if once-over-lightly report on polygamy for *People.* I knew I was the great-grandson of two brothers, Orson and Parley Pratt. Both were famous polygamists and foundational leaders of the church—the "brains of the operation," according to a philosophy professor at the University of Utah. I knew my connection to each of them was through one of their add-on wives; that some of their children practiced plural marriage as well; and, when polygamy was outlawed in Utah, the fathers went to prison in Sugarhouse [where another ancestor, Arthur Pratt, Orson's disaffected son from his first marriage, was the warden]; or relocated their families throughout Utah's outback and spent the rest of their lives riding the circuit from bed to bed; or relocated everyone, lock stock and wagon, to the Mormon Colonies established for just this purpose in Alberta, Canada and the Mexican state of Chihuahua. Chihuahua was the birthplace of future serious US presidential candidate George Romney, the former governor of Michigan—and a bunch of my antecedents, too.

If I was to conduct a thorough interview—sympathetic but objective—with a modern-day polygamist like this Brother Orson I'd need to get into his skin, acquire a better sense than I had of what provokes and sustains such fanaticism. The Russells of East Cumorah Road were pretty devout and intense, but not even my mother, who set a place at the dinner table for Jesus, was *that* fanatic. Odd and zany, she was. But fanatical? No way. She wouldn't kill for Jesus, or stand idly by while her husband slept with another woman, no matter who blessed it.

Overpowering sexual cravings could not be the sole driver behind plural marriage. Nor could marital boredom. Who needed to be married to get laid regularly? Not anyone I knew. Lord knows there were plenty of "married" men prowling Manhattan in search of ever more exhilarating sexual encounters, and an equal number of women willing to oblige, even willing to be the "other woman" indefinitely. Some hoped their willingness to hop in the sack with a married man would lead to a permanent relationship. Occasionally it did. But, as often as not the only permanency was a lifetime of playing the other woman. Wink, wink. No one got too upset over permanent extramarital relationships, affairs, flings and one-nighters. This wasn't the case when it came to the latter-day plural marriage practitioners out in Utah and Arizona and Lord knows where else. God would damn—and the law would prosecute—anyone who attempted to take ownership and stand accountable for his sexual adventures, if plural marriage was nothing more than a sexual adventure.

There was zero toleration for the likes of Brother Orson and his lot, people who made no secret of their marital practices. Speaking objectively, Orson's setup had to be a hell of a lot more moral and adult than any number of longstanding extramarital relationships that seemed so much a part of everyday life in New York City, at Time in particular. I had been warned about them, witnessed their sorry outcomes firsthand, ducked more than a few entanglements that could have led to trouble for me, the children and Sarah too.

This Brother Orson was not sneaking around, inventing stories and telling lies to cover his pecker tracks. If he missed the 6:10 express train to Old Greenwich, it wasn't because he forgot the time while diddling his mistress under the table in a bar near Grand Central. Brother Orson wouldn't be raising angry, disgusted children who saw through the lies and who eased their sorrows and tamed demons with other ones, like pot and heroin and cocaine. His wives would not be trapped in a pretty house in some leafy suburb with only a bottle of gin and the neighborhood tool belt to numb her pain and staunch her loneliness.

Brother Orson—could the name be real or was it simply cover, and a fairly transparent clue that he was connected to one of the celebrated first families of Zion too, like the Smiths, (especially the Smiths), but also the Pratts, Youngs, Cannons, Kimballs, Woodruffs, Evanses and Knights, and the rest of those zealots with WASPy-sounding families who got the whole thing going back in the 1830s and used polygamy to jumpstart its growth, its emergence as a force to be reckoned with in the west and, eventually, the entire country?

Mormonism had surely become much more than what was conveyed in Joseph's wildest visions: a fervent and committed community of believers and loyalists with its own unique culture, destiny and identity—the Jews of the latter-days—that overlays state and international borders and binds people together, more powerfully than any single nation with its flag and anthem and laws ever could.

Mormonism may have been borne from visions of visionaries with overactive and very creative imaginations, but it had been built by gritty men and women who were fiercely determined to make something unique of themselves and something wonderful and miraculous of their community. Their loyalty to each other and to their common cause had endured for nearly two centuries. Each successive generation since Joseph's had added its own fresh momentum. The latter-day Zion was indeed something to behold and it was still unfurling.

Such were the conclusions I drew from the research I amassed, information I hoped would help me understand Brother Orson. The turning of my head and heart to my mothers and fathers not only helped me understand Orson better, but it trued-up some of the inferences I had drawn in the consequential aftermath of the Summer of Love: the *Fall of '67* as it came to pass.

I had seen first-hand what inequity had wrought in cities like Detroit, Newark and New Haven: fire, death, hatred, revolution. If you asked me now, perhaps then too as the over-memorialized final half of the 1960s decade unfolded, those years were more about hatred than love. The world had gone mad; responsible people were out of control, good kids from good if permissive homes were doing bad things. Violence and madness and death reigned supreme far away in Vietnam, where a purposeless war was escalating. The carnage was as near as the evening's television news reports. Each week the images were indelibly etched into our minds by moving still photography that seemed so life-or-death-or-dying-like in *Life* magazine. Closer to home, there was the brutality of Harlem, Watts, Selma, Detroit, Newark, New Haven, Buffalo and Muncie, Indiana. Right before our eyes, the goodness, or what I perceived as goodness, was drained out of the world. In its place we got cruelty, hatred, divisiveness, destruction, death and Lyndon Johnson and Richard Nixon and their kind of civil war that turned the hearts of the fathers against their children, and the children against the fathers. Indeed, the whole world seemed stricken by a curse.

The kids camping in the mud of Max Yasgur's farm for the instantly iconic Woodstock Music and Arts Festival were dropping acid, smoking dope and groping each other hoping to find meaning. The death and destruction tarantella continued at Altamont, where Hell's Angels were licensed to mug whomever got in the path of their blackjacks, brass knuckles and hobnail boots. You could walk down a street in any city in America and randomly get gunned down or beaten by a nightstick simply because you were Black, white, brown or yellow; long-haired, short-haired or bald; male, female or other; rich, poor or middle class; Christian, Jew, Muslim, atheist or Mormon. People fried in Detroit and were randomly gunned down in Newark and Los Angeles. Revolution was in the air.

For me, as I arrived home late in August of that hot summer of 1967 when all America seemed to be going up in smoke, the question was plain enough: would Zion rise and shout and burn too? Or would saner heads lead? Would wrongs be righted? Would reason and fairness and kindness overcome all? I was determined to do all that I could to promote a kinder, gentler way to ensure that Zion's flag would remain unfurled and unsullied for all the world to admire.

At the same time, I wanted to test the premise that the church policy prohibiting Blacks from holding the priesthood had little or no impact on racial tolerance in the city—availability of jobs, housing, interracial marriage, and so on.

So, just three weeks into the fall term, the week before Halloween, we produced and published a four-page report in the student newspaper which more or less (this was a student newspaper after all) indicated that Salt Lake wasn't much different from other cities in the United States: families and students of color could not obtain housing in certain sections of the city. This included several apartment buildings owned by and/or with tenants who were prominent leaders of the church, like the Kimball Apartments, located diagonally across the intersection of North Temple and Main Street from the northeast corner of Temple Square.

White landlords in Zion used the same lame excuse used by white landlords everywhere: "Oh it's not me that's prejudiced, oh no; I'm afraid of what the neighbors or other tenants would think," and so on and so forth, ad nauseum. It was a pretty thorough report accompanied by plenty of pictures of student testers who tried to rent apartments throughout the city. One picture was of me and my "fiancée" for two days, a stunning Black woman. The caption read: "Chronicle Managing Editor Jed Pratt and *fiancée* Betsey Craig went searching for an apartment in the exclusive Federal Heights neighborhood near the university and found none that were available to a mixed-race couple." I was proud of the report, pleased with its thoroughness and balance. It was certainly a story the city newspapers wouldn't touch with a ten-foot pole. The report included verbatim reactions from Harold B. Lee, the president of the Quorum of Twelve Apostles, and Hugh B. Brown, a member of the First Presidency of the Church, condemning the obvious de facto segregation in the city; and a lengthy editorial encouraging the city council and state legislature to enact open housing laws.

I braced myself for the anticipated attacks on the accuracy of my report and on my personal character, and accusations that I no longer believed in God or the one true Church and had, in fact, become an enemy of both. I waited. Nothing. Finally, a few days later, a letter arrived from my best fan, Rabbi Aaron Mednick, praising my courage for "telling the kings they're not wearing clothes. Better they hear it from one of their own, one who reasons and writes with the restraint and wisdom inherited from his forefathers, Orson and Parley."

Apart from the rabbi's kind letter, the only reaction I got was from Ernie Ford, the taciturn city editor at the *Tribune*: "Pretty decent piece… teeth must be grinding all over town," he said. I thanked him and assured him they weren't, insofar as I knew. "Hard to tell in this inscrutable city," he said. "Anyway, if you're still interested, that full-time reporting slot, night police, just opened up. It's a start and it should give you plenty of time to do school work…and make a few bucks, eighty of 'em each week. Interested?"

"Very, when can I start?"

"Actually, we're in bit of a bind, could you be here by Monday?"

"I could make it today," I said eagerly.

"Monday will do. But between now and then, come on down and fill out the paperwork. The day reporter will give you the lay of the land at the police station where you will be stationed most of the time—and city hall. He'll walk you through the routine. Hours are five till two a.m.…you come over to the city room at midnight, work the copy desk until quitting time—two or three or whenever the goddamn presses decide to roll. Good training, discipline: editing copy, writing headlines."

Three days later the apartment phone rang with what I supposed was another reaction to the story: "Jed Pratt? This is Emma." Long silence. "You-may-not-remember-me…Emmaline Nebeker," she said softly, nervously, shyly.

"You joke…I remember you by heart, Emmaline." *("I feel that in my own small way I am somehow a part of you and probably always will be no matter what happens. Love ya always, Emmaline." May 1962.)*

"Really?" I could hear confidence building in her voice. "Hey, me too," she said, pleased.

"Long time…I thought I saw you a couple of times up on the hill, but you were always looking the other way, so I wasn't sure," I said.

"Really. Your face must've changed or something. Missions do that. I read your stuff in the paper all the time, and, it's pretty good; but hey, pretty liberal for an RM. And hey, I didn't know you could write either?"

"Don't know that I can…yet…but hey, I'm working at it," I said, mildly mocking her overuse of an interjection that was especially popular on Fraternity Row—a supposed snooty substitute for the hippiesque "like wow" and "like" and "far out" and other variations on theme.

"You can…but hey, I know this is weird, calling like this, after what is it, four years or something…?"

"Five," I said.

"…and me giving you the big lecture on hanging out in the frats, going to the dogs boozing, and you turning into a ferocious GDI and me into a Kappa…"

"A Kappa president, I heard…"

"True—me of all people…but, could we talk sometime? Catch up?"

"We are…talking. I promise I won't hang up," I said.

"In person, I haven't seen you up close for, hey, yeah, you're right it has been about five years and I'd like to…wow…no it's less, I was at your farewell. In the back. Hiding."

"Sure. Where, when?"

"Soon. I graduate at the end of the quarter…and then it's off to California, if all goes according to plan."

"Hey is big in San Francisco."

"Bad habit, sorry. Still on the proper language trip I see," she said.

"Just teasing. Now would be good, if it's not too soon…"

"You haven't got a hot date tonight or anything? It is Friday, you know?"

"You're as hot as it's going to get for me tonight," I said, not intending to say it the way it came out.

"What's that supposed to mean…that I'm pretty boring or what?"

"No…only that my, ah, life is pretty slow just now."

"Sure, now would be really good for me…but hey, sorry, I really wouldn't want to be interrupting or interfering with anything if I came over."

"Just with the cobwebs of my mind," I said. "You want to come here?"

"It'd be best. I'm living between home and the Kappa house. Lack of privacy…girls talk."

"Don't I know it!"

"In case you don't know, I'm very concerned about you," she said earnestly.

"Really? So come on down, tell me all about it and I'll allay whatever concerns you have."

And just like that, it happened. A distant, if still sharply focused memory of a woman who once pledged in writing that she would always be a part of my life—no matter what—but who ran off with a sheygets and ignored the hell out of me like I didn't exist or matter, suddenly re-emerges out of nowhere, five years later, just as I'd finally purged her from my mind.

I had shredded her notes and letters (except for the blasted permanent record in the yearbooks I revisited quickly before she arrived and from which I excerpted pertinent lines for this story: hoping, once again, to be my savior on Mt. Zion, to belay my fall from grace, or prevent it altogether). This time around, who knew why she was worried about me, exactly? The outward signs of my drift had been ditched in a trash can in Idaho, heaved into a barrow pit at Point of the Mountain, and prematurely, if inadvertently, rejected and dispatched where two roads diverged on a mellow summer night in Rhode Island.

Unless you knew me really well and were deft at reading between the lines, my bylined column and reportage in the *Chrony* revealed very little of my growing unease. Regretfully, *Emmaline* hadn't known me in any way for nearly half a decade. And, the *Emmaline* of my memory was never one who was strong on nuances and subtleties, although she was skilled at finding the hidden meanings in literature. Perhaps the new *Emma*—she did introduce herself as Emma, not Emmaline; the more worldly Emma, not the quintessentially Mormon Emmaline—would be savvier and confident.

Emma was even lovelier than the Emmaline I remembered: sun-lightened (I suppose it was from the sun) straight auburn hair cascaded—floated light and free—to the tips of her scapula (the Kappa cool-clip: longishly hip, short and well-kempt enough so as not to be mistaken for the mane of some slackened, snorting, toking Flower Child), not coiled and piled high on her head to resemble the icon of industry on the seal of our beloved Beehive State, as it had been back in our halcyon days together in 1961 and 1962. Somehow this new natural coif made her appear more relaxed and together, never mind that her lightly freckled face belied angst and serious resolve that, frankly, couldn't have had much to do with me, as best I could figure.

She stood in the doorway. I stared. Gaped, I guess. She opened with the trite "Good to see you." My response was a stare, a slight nod, perhaps a deep gasp of satisfaction and astonishment, like I had just performed the ultimate priesthood ordinance: resurrection of the dead. Very much alive, arms around each other, we snugged together, matching body parts from our shoulders to our knees, and just stood there in the doorway enwrapped, soaking in the warmth, the textures, scents and memories of whatever the hell we had been…or were…or could be.

She was flushed as I motioned toward the sofa. I was burning inside out as I filled two tumblers with 7 Up and took a chair at her side, an arm's length away. "You look good, better than ever," I offered, lamely confirming what I'd clearly punctuated with a longing stare and underscored with a full body wrap: rapture.

Emma nodded appreciatively. "Ever the kind, solicitous Jed Russell," she said. *("…no girl could possibly find a boy that would treat her as fine as you have treated me…so unselfish…always putting me and my feelings first…and that's more than I ever did for you. You'll make a fine husband for some 'good' girl in the future…" Emmaline Nebeker, 1962)* "I'm surprised it's taken you so long to find a girl, finally."

"What'd you expect, a boy?" I joked.

"Huh?"

"Kidding. I'm not even back a year yet…it takes longer than that, to adjust to women," I said.

"That Betsey looks like a very sweet girl…"

"Betsey?"

"…Your fiancée in the newspaper. Pretty daring of you, I must say."

"Oh, Betsey, she is rather sweet, stunning actually, quite smart." I was puzzled.

"I don't know if you know, but I have my own fiancé…in San Francisco, in med school…marriage coming up just after Christmas, after I graduate."

"Congratulations," I said, disheartened. "I didn't know. Do I know him?"

"Probably not…a Sigma Chi from Logan, Bill Kimball. He was just returning home from Germany when you left for Boston."

"What ever happened to Sheygets…I mean whatshisname Barry, er, Vicars who cut in on me?" I did my best to smile nonchalantly, pleasantly, brotherly.

"Barrett…Barry Vicars." She blushed deeply, hesitated, sucked in a deep breath. "This'll probably sound pretty crummy to you, but Barry—you know he converted to the Church and went on a mission?" I nodded affirmatively. "Bill was his first companion. Bill looked me up when he got home…and…"

"Soon Old Barry gets a 'Dear John…'" I snickered.

"Pretty crummy, huh?"

"No, just typical, predictable."

"You mean me doing something like that...?"

"Not what I intended: standard operating procedure."

"For what it's worth, Barry's gonna be best man at the wedding."

"Now there's another testimony to the brotherhood of the priesthood for you," I grinned. "But if you asked me, it's cruel and unusual punishment. Even I wouldn't wish such a thing on Old Barry."

The brotherhood of the priesthood thing had taken advantage of my own g-g-grandfather Orson, a devoted husband, profound thinker and self-taught physicist who almost single-handedly shaped early Mormon theology. While he served his first mission in Great Britain, at least one—possibly two, if rumors and later public allegations are accurate—leaders of the Church *courted* (and Lord knows what else) his wife Sarah with the goal of making her one of their concubines either here on earth or in the great hereafter. Who knows?

Distraught at this crass betrayal from his beloved brethren while he was off serving the Lord, Orson contemplated suicide on his return home, distanced himself from Church leadership and was eventually excommunicated, albeit temporarily. His brief absence from the quorum cost him seniority and any chance he had of succeeding Brigham Young as prophet, seer, revelator and President of the Church.

I was also very familiar—firsthand, more or less—with the history of my great uncle Samuel's own "Dear Sam," received while preaching the gospel in Scotland. He returned home just months before the victor in the love triangle was nominated to serve as a general leader of the Church. When the Prophet called for a sustaining vote of the eight thousand or so Saints assembled in the Tabernacle on Temple Square for semi-annual general conference, the expected sea of upraised hands seemed to indicate another unanimous sustaining vote, as these things almost always are.

As a formality, the Prophet asked if there were any objections. Young Sam not only raised his hand in protest, but stood tall in the pew to signal before God and his fellow Mormons his righteous opposition to the man who had dishonored his priesthood, at least in Sam's eyes. The next morning's then anti-Mormon *Salt Lake Tribune* carried a banner headline reading: "Young Russell Bucks Church Authorities" and a detailed report of scorned Sam's accusations.

Although he went on to become a respected attorney and founding partner of a high-powered law firm in Washington, DC, Sam never recovered fully from the crushing blow to his heart and soul. I was a teenager when he died a bachelor—a fairly wealthy but embittered hermit—surrounded at his passing by his beloved and trustworthy books, ceiling-high stacks of yellowing newspapers, and the few indulgent family members who saw the goodness and decency in their embittered old bachelor uncle, who like his Uncle Orson was betrayed by men he would trust with his life, fellow holders of the priesthood of God.

"Actually, my relationship with Barry was pretty well over before he left for Germany; he figured it was you..." Emma said, sheepishly.

"Really? Guilty conscience, I suppose. Had I known, I may have stayed home myself." I grinned insincerely.

"He worried constantly that you'd reappear at some point. I didn't actually say anything to disabuse him of that possibility...in fact, I sort of suggested that I couldn't shake the thought that you were my first...and all...and I almost called you then, but didn't because I didn't know how you'd take it, whether you'd tell me to go to hell, and I couldn't deal with the possibility of rejection...but I've grown up and that's why I wanted to see you." She caught her breath. She placed her hand on my arm.

"Why, so I could reject you finally or cleanse your conscience so you can run off guilt-free to the temple and time and eternity with what's his name, Bro. Bill...Kimball?"

"No, be kind and listen. I've been having the same kinds of thoughts—dreams all over again lately—since last spring when I saw your first column in the *Chrony*. I can't shake the dreams and I don't know what to make of them. You know anything about dreams?"

"Yes, but not the kind you're having or would want to hear about. Seriously, no. Absolutely nothing. But sounds like they're nothing more than romanticized rehashes of first love..."

"It's not just first love...it's first *everything*." Emma's voice cracked.

"First *everything*?" I scratched my head. "Well, we had a lot of firsts... but not a first *everything*, although *everything* crossed my mind from time to time."

Emma smiled. "Well, I'm still waiting for my first *everything*, how about you?"

"You've only got a month to wait. Wish I could say the same," I said.

"When's the date for you and Betsey...I hope you have time to think things through carefully…the temple?" she asked, nervously.

"Betsey?" Now I got it. Emma was still playing the savior on Mt. Zion. She figured I was marrying my *pretend* fiancée. She was worried to death because she knew the marriage couldn't take place in the temple because Betsey was Black; probably she had a heap of other condescending racist worries as well. I was tempted to string her along…

"Haven't even talked about a date, yet," I offered, then I quit. "Actually, Emma, Betsey and I are not an item…she was just my fiancée for the day, while I reported the story. We wanted reactions, and brother did we get them. People seemed relieved when I said I was from Connecticut—new to Salt Lake."

"Really. Well, whew! Big whew. I'll bet you did get a big reaction… so there's no one in your life right now." It was a stammering statement of fact, relief and satisfaction. She smiled. I smiled. And so we talked until well past two…about firsts (and almosts) and lasts, and fears and hopes for the future until we both fell asleep on the sofa. We awakened at four and moved to the bed where we prayed together. (Was this the subtext to Dean Stone's lecture to young marrieds at BYU: "Celestial Soaring on Wings of a Prayer"? How would he adapt it for this opportunity?)

When we awoke, it was Saturday morning; we continued on for most of Saturday, awakening Sunday morning in time for worship services, and continuing as the Spirit prompted for what was left of November and into December, and this was the morning and evening of our first day, and we saw what we had created, and it was good, even as Bill and, in due time, Sarah, and Christmas bore down and in on us.

Righteous Seeds

Outcomes of all important matters, especially affairs of the heart, have everything to do with good timing or the lack of it. Our timing—Emma's in particular—was just plain awful: there was a diamond ring on her finger, engraved invitations were ready to be mailed, in her purse was a written recommend from her bishop that would admit her to the temple (unless she confessed her recent dalliances with me) when it came time to marry for time and all eternity...to Bill Kimball—or practically anyone she chose.

Anyone with a lick of common sense knows that spontaneous flings on the eves of marriages are highly inadvisable and shamefully inappropriate. Generally, rational thinking has very little to do with it, which is why such momentary lapses of trust and commitment are not particularly uncommon anywhere in America, everywhere in the world, even in Zion amongst a people who presume they are especially called and chosen.

This sudden reconnection, resurrection of old love, was no narcissistic indulgence, no tempting appetizer before the banquet. Nor was it driven by last-minute jitters, per se. Our *call it what you will* (I summarily reject "fling") was intense, profound and deeply seeded. Therefore, it was also considerably more dangerous because there was a certain symmetry to it. This *call it what you will* was the resumption of an eternal journey commenced a half decade earlier on a winding mountain road, overlooking city lights and focused on the illuminated spires of the most famous Mormon temple of them all.

True, it detoured abruptly because it could go no further at the time without provoking dire personal and spiritual consequences. As a result, it had lost momentum, been fraught with the usual stops and restarts, reconciliations and betrayals, mindless silences and snubbings that often plague intense late adolescent entanglements, disentanglements in particular.

Despite these many setbacks—and, for a long time, a dearth of anything concrete to go on—raw, completely unwarranted hope thrived. What reason had I to hope that Emma would suddenly reinsert herself into my life? None! What reason had she to think I would risk seeing her, opening myself wide and vulnerable once again? None, but she dared make the phone call anyway.

When Emma wrote she would always be a part of me no matter what, I believed it even though I told friends her words were the kind of presumptuous and patently self-centered stuff you'd expect from a bona fide narcissist. Truth was, the old Emmaline had it right: she had indeed become an unbidden and unmasked nocturnal intruder, who frequently hacked into the unencrypted galleys of my mind. Night after night. Year after year.

Now, as fleeting night visions transformed themselves into a reality that was as heady as it was physically fulfilling, our relationship that "Fall of Love" nevertheless seemed just as vague and ephemeral and confused and dangerous as it had back in the spring of '62 when we had nowhere to go but *trouble* and *serious trouble* and *virtually unforgivable and irresponsible trouble.*

I would return home from work to find her sleeping soundly, awaken early to emptiness—she'd already fled under the camouflage of predawn darkness. That would endure for two or three frustrating days. It was encouraging that she always returned, homing like a pigeon to the nest we were weaving, validating what we had begun a quarter of our young lives earlier; confirming that this chosen son was worthy to be her eternal companion. He *should* have wavered with Lainey; he could have veered sharply off course with Naomi, but her menacing knife fighter fiancé in Wyoming soberly reminded that the wages of sin could indeed be death. He had been vetted by the mission field, which revealed him to be an unusually capable spiritual leader of others (if not yet himself). He had abandoned other momentary temptations and distractions along various roadsides from Newport, Rhode Island to Madison, Wisconsin. As the hymn encouraged, for one reason or another he kept the lighthouse burning even if Emma and I had made a mockery of the old hymn:

Brightly beams our Father's mercy from His lighthouse evermore,
But to us He gives the keeping of the lights along the shore...

Dark the night of sin has settled, loud the angry billows roar;
Eager eyes are watching, longing, for the lights along the shore.
Trim your feeble lamp, my brother, some poor sailor, tempest tossed,
Trying now to make the harbor, in the darkness may be lost.
Let the lower lights be burning! Send a gleam across the wave!
Some poor failing struggling seaman you may rescue, you may save.

As I recalled these events a few decades after the fact, this fresh and compelling insight flashed through my mind (Rebe got me thinking about it): My lifelong method for dealing with rejection and loss has never been to return the favor in kind, or to organize some kind of penultimate act of revenge. Instead, in bizarre, sometimes self-destructive ways I turn the other cheek, like the good Christian boy I was trained to be. I campaign resolutely to prove I was sized wrong. I pursue whatever standard my detractors set for me with a zealous, almost angry energy that is hard to describe, like when the editor at a new Time publication didn't want me from the moment corporate policy forced him to take me on. I was there for nearly a year until I found refuge down the hall on the start-up staff of another embryonic magazine called *People Weekly.* A few months later, I freelanced a piece for my former boss that he published virtually as written.

"I think I underestimated you. I wish you hadn't left us," he said.

"Thank you—I worked very hard on this," I said. "Saying goodbye means more if both people feel the loss."

"Salinger?" he said.

"Holden Russell," I countered. He smiled.

Frankly, that is how I intended matters to end—or continue—with Dean Stone. I'd written the second-day column and editorial, commending his candor and integrity. I had considered transferring to BYU to prove to myself and others that I could report accurately and thoroughly and still be loyal, honor my priesthood, keep the trust of the brotherhood.

Now, many years later, as I prepared myself for a trip west, I wondered whether it would be wise to revisit the scene of a *crime* that had left me so shaken, one that was permanently etched in my mind. Who was I kidding? I was still having trouble saying goodbye to the likes of Stone. He wasn't the only one of the brotherhood who felt empowered to judge me harshly; to warn that I was edging closer and closer to apostasy. People like Stone operated from the assumption that only I would feel the loss, that my loss would matter very little to them or the church, that the decision to stay or go was not influenced by them, that it boiled down to personal decision and testimony. It was implied that if one lacked a testimony—a spiritual witness from God—that you just hadn't tried hard enough, or that you weren't worthy, for some reason or another, to receive the more sure witness from Christ.

Stone hadn't felt the loss like I had. He had to deal with the fact that he was never asked to serve as an apostle. However, he became filthy rich peddling sanitized Mormonism—how to succeed in the castrating corporate world without sacrificing your testicles—but I knew that business success, fame and a disgustingly large bank account do not begin to compensate someone like Stone, who smugly thought he had a better-than-even chance of being called to serve as an apostle.

Naturally Stone's handlers were quite pleased that *People* was interested in doing a profile. I sketched out the usual requests: candid pictures at home with family, with staff, around town; periodic access for several days and a couple of formal interviews and so on. "No prob, we're excited," the handler said. "What else?"

"I did a piece on your boss several years ago."

"Really, where?" the handler asked, probably embarrassed that he hadn't done his homework as thoroughly as he thought he had.

"Believe it or not, in the *Chrony*, at the U," I said cautiously.

"Oh, well, then you must be a local boy," the handler said. I could hear the relief in his voice, like I'd heard it in Stone's voice as he became aware that I was a returned missionary who had served under his friend, G. Buckley Truman. Local boys weren't as demanding as outsiders. They were more easily intimidated. There would be extra buttons to press, especially if you thought of yourself as called, chosen, entitled—"*apostle without the calling*" is the way his handler put it after he knew that I knew a thing or two about the Mormon organization and his boss.

"Obviously, then, I was," I said.

"LDS?" he asked in a way that presumed he knew the answer would be yes.

"Look, just let him know. Frankly, I've got a lot on my plate, so I'm not sure I want to bother with this…"

"I'll get right back to you," he said eagerly. Which he did about an hour later. "The man says 'no prob.' Pretty flattering piece you wrote on *the man*, if I do say so," he slurped. "I can't tell you what a piece in *People* will mean for us—especially written by someone who is sensitive to the spiritual genesis of our important work. *The man* asks if you will have time to participate in a temple session with him."

"Tell *the man* I'll have to get back to him on that…as I was saying, my schedule is really quite jammed and it's getting tighter by the minute."

A day after Emma flew into temporary isolation, the afternoon after I'd written my first story for the *Tribune*, Sarah Brooke Thompson descended the stairs to the Crimson Commons, a small wannabe delicatessen in the basement of the student union, where I was lunching with her brother-in-law, John Liddy. True to the advance billing, she was the spitting image of Liddy's wife Polly. "Look, babe," Polly had promised at a Halloween party a few weeks earlier, "if you liked kissing these lips, you're gonna love my little sister." She was right on all counts.

Because Emma reappeared shortly before Polly made the official introductions, I didn't get around to actually calling Sarah for a first date until early the following week, and then only because Emma insisted. Telling Emma about Sarah and what I expected and why I expected what I did, without divulging any of the intimate details of the Halloween party encounter, gave me a sense of what it must have been like when Orson or Parley sought approval from their first wives to take a second, then a third and so on. I wondered if the current-day Brother Orson got as edgy as I did breaking similar news to the women in his life. Surely the Dean Stone of Orson Pratt's generation had a canned inspirational speech for such occasions: "Seven Sure Steps to Seventh Heaven and a More Sure Celestial Marriage."

"The interest in meeting her pre-dates your, your re-emergence," I told Emma. "Now that you're here, I'd just as soon let it go, except if I back out now Polly and John will wonder why, and you know John's a Sigma Chi and he probably knows Bill Kimball, and I mentioned in passing that we had chatted recently. John knows our history…he's just the kind of suspicious fellow who would put two and two together."

"No need to rationalize. Better that *you* be certain than wonder," she said as if she had her mind made up about me; as if my attraction to Polly's sister Sarah was the only unsettled matter between us and an eternity together, never mind the diamond on her finger and the promises she had made to Bill Kimball to get it.

"I was beginning to think you'd never call, that there was something wrong with me," Sarah said. "John mentioned you might be a little distracted by the new job and other things. I just assumed it was another girl." And, so we went out to dinner the following Friday night.

Emma was sleeping when I returned home. As promised, early the next morning I helped her move out of her room at the Kappa house. "If my sorority sisters get nosy, just tell them you're an old friend from high school…and be sure to act like an old *pal*," she cautioned on the short drive up South Temple to the sorority house on Wolcott, adjacent to the campus.

We quietly loaded my car and were in Canyon Mills by eight thirty, stacking the boxes in the basement of the Nebekers' new home, higher up the steep sides of Mt. Olympus. The Colonel was plainly delighted, if surprised, to see me. He pumped my arm up and down, then, dispensing with formalities, hugged me almost as tightly as Emma ever had. "I thought you'd fallen off planet until Emmaline told me you were Jimmy Olsen for that *damned heathen rag* downtown. Always figured you to be a Clark Kent type, if you get my meaning." He grinned broadly. "Stay for breakfast," he ordered.

"I'd love to, sir [truth], but I'm due at the *damned heathen rag* at eleven [also truth]." At eight that evening I met Sarah for dinner and dancing. Emma was sleeping when I arrived home at one. She dragged me out for church the next morning—sort of church: the regular half-hour broadcast of the Mormon Tabernacle Choir from historic Tabernacle on Temple Square. Then I was off to Sarah's for Sunday dinner with her family, and on to the *Trib* for regular night police duty. Happily this Sunday before Thanksgiving was so quiet that the only thing that woke me was the periodic ringing of the interoffice phone tied directly to the city editor.

"If nothing happens soon in this goddamned city, we're gonna be running a hell of a lot of white space tomorrow morning," Ford bellowed.

"Should I invent something?" I joked.

"Yeh, go rob a bank."

"I'm no Sabbath breaker."

Once the jet reached cruising altitude, Rebe laid a three-inch-thick folder on the seatback tray table between us. "Perhaps you should finally read this background, before you sally forth to interview your Brother Orson," she said. As usual, but this time for completely understandable reasons, I'd left the research until the last minute. Happily Rebe had assembled a reasonably thorough set of documents chronicling my own family's history with plural marriage, which I knew, by and large, paralleled other original Latter-day Saint families.

By virtue of the complicated, twisting, looping genealogical trees wrought by plural marriage arrangements, not to mention the sheer volume of its human yield, I have often thought a little persistent research would reveal that I am related to practically everyone living along the Wasatch Front, if not all the towns that often seem to appear out of the sage brush every thirty miles or so, according to the plan laid out by the most famous, imperious and didactic Mormon leader of them all, the rugged capitalist and strategic kingdom-builder Brigham Young.

It was the visionary Brigham who figured putting down small towns—re-supply centers—every thirty miles or so along the routes heading southwest to Los Angeles, West to San Francisco, northwest to Oregon and Southeast to Sante Fe and Mexico would be a shrewd way to separate itinerant Gentiles from their cash. Moreover, it was also a savvy if ambitious political maneuver, for it staked out the territory for the Nation of Deseret with a sea outlet in San Diego, should the government of the United States of America once again turn its back on the Mormons, as it had done in Missouri and Illinois.

I finished reading just as the plane burst over the mountain fortress that encircles the home of my youth. There beneath the wings of the jet was the Valley of the Great Salt Lake, adorned in orderly grids from mountain range to mountain range: from Canyon Mills abutting Wasatch Range on the east, to the world's largest open pit copper mine in the Oquirrh Range at the west rim of the valley; from the bookend of Ensign Peak just north of Temple Square, to its opposite in every way, the state penitentiary at the base of the sandy foothills at Point of the Mountain in the south. "Behold the glory of Zion," I whispered to Rebe. "While reading these past five hours, it occurred to me that this city and its people might not have survived if they hadn't agreed to abandon plural marriage."

Rebe was surprised that I knew so little about polygamy, and what little I knew was decidedly one-sided. For instance, I was quite well aware that plural marriage had delivered on the promise of raising up a more than ample supply of missionaries and church leaders. By contrast, I didn't know much about the people it disenfranchised, like Orson Pratt's first wife, Sarah, and a number of her children, including Orson's namesake son.

Nor did I know much about how a man went about breaking the news that he was interested in taking another wife. I knew the current wives had to consent, but how exactly that was accomplished was a mystery to me. Although Sarah, as his first wife, had special privileges, I knew that Grandfather Orson's plan to equitably divvy up his limited time drove Sarah away and provoked him to write this epitaph on their failed marriage:

> *You once professedly believed in the sealing ordinances, according to the revelation on marriage... You at several times did put the hands of others into my hand, and did give them to me as wives...after several years had elapsed I proposed to you to commence living upon the principles of greater equality...this proposition you positively rejected... You doubtless looked upon this trial as one too great to bear for you...*

The potential for abuse and betrayal was huge. Imagine if some *worthy leader* of the Church dropped by the house. On one level you might welcome this emissary of God, embrace him warmly in the full fellowship of the priesthood and all that. On another, you could never be certain that his visit was so divinely altruistic: he may have come to feast his ravenous eyes on your fourteen-year-old daughter innocently rolling barrel hoops in the yard.

"No different than the rest of the world," Rebe suggested.

"True, except in the real world you wouldn't hesitate to toss the greasy sunnuvabitch out on his ass," I said. "Bouncing one of the Lord's anointed messengers would be an entirely different proposition to a Mormon, a citizen of Zion, especially if the anointed of the Lord laid it on thick: "It has been revealed to me that yonder virgin daughter, fruit of your loins, was called, chosen and anointed from the foundations of the universe to bring forth my good and righteous seed."

"It didn't work that way," Rebe said.

"Not always, but you can bet that more than one of the Lord's anointed messengers manipulated matters to fulfill his own selfish ends...they may have called themselves Saints, but they were very human," I said. "Imagine how furious, bitter you'd be if, to honor your priesthood and keep yourself in good standing with the higher-ups, you had to pull in your horns, back off—follow the brethren, submit to authority, even unrighteous dominion—and allow one of your leaders to walk off, uncontested, into eternity with the woman of your dreams, or your daughter."

"I can't imagine you allowing it."

"The uncontested authority thing across the board, the way it influences practically every aspect of living in Zion—the directive to *follow the brethren* is what got me thinking years ago," I said softly, fearing I might be overheard by one of the brethren on this inbound flight to Zion. "Failure to follow, to subordinate professional goals to the needs of the Church, to Church authority figures, is what Stone was talking about years ago when he accused me of violating my covenants. In his mind, I was subordinate to him. I violated his trust. Once you've crossed the line, you can go back...but it is really never quite the same."

For very personal and obvious reasons, I am grateful for polygamy, particularly that Orson took Margaret Graham as his tenth and last wife—he was fifty-seven and she was just sixteen—because the union eventually led to my birth. My mother was his granddaughter.

On Parley's branch, my father's line, I descend from his fourth or fifth wife. Two of their daughters married my great-grandfather and, well, you see how complicated things can get, fast! Now you understand why practically every Mormon who has been around for more than a generation or two is connected by blood to every other Mormon. This is not necessarily bad news: should my organs ever fail, there are probably several thousand donors out there with very, very similar DNA, and most of them live in the cities and towns lining the overland trade routes in the intermountain west.

As I said, I'm here because of polygamy. Not for a minute can I fathom why the US government chose to exacerbate matters by incarcerating more than a thousand polygamous fathers and forcing others into exile in Mexico and Canada. What good came of that? Did the government also crack down on businessmen and philanthropists who kept mistresses stashed in safe houses? Or sailors who had a girl in every port? I think not. The hypocrisy is quite outrageous. My conclusions are not particularly dissimilar from those drawn by the philosopher John Stuart Mill: *"It is difficult to see on what principles but those of tyranny they [The Mormons] can be prevented from living under what laws they please."*

Seems to me the federal government made its tyrannical intentions about the Mormons clear enough long before plural marriage became an issue. The government failed to intervene when the Missouri governor issued an order calling for the extermination or expulsion of Mormons. It failed again when it refused to prevent the Mormons from being driven from their homes in Illinois and Missouri. More remarkably, after the Saints made the barren and uninhabitable Valley of the Great Salt Lake bloom, and transformed it into a robust economic center, the government and its armies again attempted, quite unsuccessfully, to invade and either lay waste to Zion or bring it yelping to heel.

The question wasn't *if*, but *when* and *how* the government would attempt to rend Brigham's and Grandfather Orson's kingdom asunder. Which is why I think all but the most fanatical of my ancestors heaved a huge, if bitter, sigh of relief when the ever-pragmatic church blinked. It decreed by way of the celebrated manifesto of 1890 that plural marriages were forbidden henceforth in this life, although some fudging continued, apparently, through the early decades of the twentieth century.

Read a story about Utah and the Mormons today and, invariably, plural marriage will be mentioned for historical reasons and because so many people—sincere and presumably ex-communicated Mormons like this Brother Orson I'd be interviewing and other opportunists, rogues and scoundrels—continue to find the concept of multiple wives an altogether appealing concept. This should not surprise anyone familiar with practices common in the "outside world," where men and women everywhere have long been applying this concept serially, aided by liberalized divorce and cohabitation laws, or under the guise of longstanding illicit love affairs. Do it for sexual gratification and the government looks the other way. Do it for religious reasons and you could end up in the slammer, in Utah especially.

If he were living, Grandfather Orson would doubtless warn contemporary adventurers to look beyond the transitory, prurient titillations of the bedroom to the daunting responsibilities of plural marriage: heavier workloads, economics, personal anguish and lifelong conflicts between the wives. He would likely dish consonant admonitions to the more conventional libertines of our day.

The Colonel commanded my presence on Thanksgiving Day. "Yes, yes, I know you've got other commitments. So, come early, eat a little, burn it off with some football, then head off to meet your new girl's parents," he insisted.

"Aye, aye, sir!"

Trouble was the Colonel had consulted neither his bosom mate nor mine. According to Emma, neither thought it was a particularly brilliant idea, "although I certainly know how pushy Dad can be…he always thought he'd connected with you, like you were the son he never had. Different with all the others. Anyway, the big problem is Bill's flying in for a couple of days."

"Didn't know. So what do you want me to do?" I asked.

"Get sick. Get called into work at the last minute. Anything," she pleaded. "This wouldn't be a good time to, you know, and I've never been a particularly good actor."

So I called Thanksgiving eve, explained that my work schedule had changed at the last minute.

"Sorry you can't make it, I think you'd enjoy meeting Bill," he said. "What time are you due at work?"

I hesitated, stammered. I hadn't thought through the details of the lie. Hadn't anticipated a challenge from the Colonel. "One," I lied. This was the telephone. He couldn't see the lies in my eyes, as my own father often had.

"Well, heck, come by in the morning, for breakfast. We can do the football then. If you can still throw like you used to, you may stand half a chance at beating the extended Nebeker team—you'll have a pretty good receiver in Bill."

The Colonel was right, Bill was an able split-end and, so far as I could tell, solid in practically every way: top of his medical school class at Stanford (so Mrs. Nebeker boasted), first counselor in the bishopric of his student ward. And, it was quite obvious that he was deeply in love with the lovely Emmaline. Moreover, and much to my surprise, he seemed quite pleased to meet me.

"Finally, I formally meet the legend in his own time," he kidded as he grasped my hand.

"Formally? Legend?"

"We met briefly, in passing. I was rush chairman at Sigma Chi… when you turned us down for good reasons that I'd never considered. It got me thinking, and I resigned before spring quarter," he said.

"Really, so how come the hots for a Kappa chick then?" I teased back.

He cocked an eye at me. Smiled. "You, of all people, should know. Need I say you shouldn't have been quite so candid with the likes of Eddie Knight and John Liddy."

"When I see Liddy later today, I'll be sure to tell him you ratted him out."

"Really? How's he doing…marriage wise…that wife of his is some piece…"

"Be careful where you go with that, I'm dating her younger sister," I said.

"…of work. That's a relief…I thought you might be trying to cut my grass."

"Lawnmower's in the shop," I demurred.

We laughed loudly. The Colonel arrived at our side. "Comparing notes are we? So have you told Jed you're a Pratt descendant too?" he said.

"One of the thundering herd from Parley," Bill said. "And you?"

"From both Parley and Orson; a quirk of polygamy," I said.

"That explains your antipathy for frats," he grinned. "Bold, forthright, egalitarian and pig-headed."

"You forgot loyal."

"That's a given."

"So, you *will* stay for dinner, then," said the Colonel.

"Tempted, but I think it's time I was leaving."

Thanksgiving afternoon with Sarah's family—my first encounter with the entire sisterhood of Thompsons and their husbands (one of whom was my longtime friend John Liddy, who would eventually become a CIA agent; another was obstetrics and gynecology resident Dr. Reese Packer; and the patriarchal Old ROT, who had been an OSS operative behind enemy lines in France and Germany and God knows where else during the big WWII)—went well, remarkably well.

The reception was extraordinarily cordial, especially from Old ROT, who seemed to sense that Sarah and I were engaged in something serious. Truth is, had I not been compromised, conflicted, and preoccupied with Emma, I'm sure things would have been a lot further along with Sarah than they were. Polly's forecast was absolutely on the mark.

Sarah and I departed the happy gathering for time alone, eventually arriving at my apartment around six thirty for what turned into our first sustained close encounter, one that could have turned more intimate and prolonged had I not been concerned that Emma would walk through the door at any second, and had we not promised to return to the Thompsons' by nine. We made it, barely, disheveled and frustrated, no doubt looking like the half-spent foxes in the alliterative forest fire analogy.

The following afternoon, having completed a piece for Sunday's paper on sons—those who arrived home safely from Vietnam in time for Thanksgiving as well as those about to depart—I was about to head up to the Thompsons' when the Colonel strode into the cramped newsroom at the police station.

"Always wanted to see the fourth estate in action," he said cheerily. "Truth, we just dropped Bill at the airport and I had to kill some time while Emma and her mother do some shopping, so…let's share a soda."

"Your command is my wish sir," I said. "But, I've got an appointment in about an hour." We headed for the lunchroom down the hall. I snagged the drinks while he secured a table in the corner, far from klatches of convivial police going off shift.

The Colonel seemed to be intently studying my face as I neared the table. "Something on my chin?" I asked.

"No, no, sorry to gawk. I guess I was trying to read your eyes, sense how you're doing, how you're taking all this."

The Colonel was always one to cut straight to the issue. "I assume you mean the forthcoming marriage?"

"Heckuva swell fellow, Bill Kimball. I knew you'd like him, a god-send, if you asked me," he said. He exhaled as if releasing carbon dioxide he'd stored up for a year or two. "Still, seeing Emma and you…I have to wonder about you…what you had going was no passing romance, if you asked me."

"It wasn't, but it was over five years ago."

"That long? Did I ever tell you the holy hell I caught for that little chat with you, about trusting you, man to man, to honor your priesthood with Emma. I couldn't convince Emma and her mother that you'd appreciated it. You did, didn't you?"

"I did, I really did," I said.

"Never had such a talk like that with anyone…not because I'd catch holy hell again, but because I've never felt the need to."

"Thanks for the vote of confidence…"

"Not that. Sometimes I get a sense of things that others don't. Emma's mother was pretty horrified. 'They're barely sixteen—give them space, Colonel,' like there was no way a couple of teenagers could be profoundly in love. But I saw it in Emma's eyes, so when I saw it in yours too, I had to say something, anything to help you keep things in check until the time was right."

"You were right…and it worked," I said, assuming he was looking for confirmation that his intervention was well-timed and that I had honored my pledge.

"So is the time right?" he asked bluntly, fixing his eyes on mine.

"Oh yes, I think she needs Bill in the worst way."

"Not what I had in mind, but I'm somewhat relieved to hear you say that." He leaned back in the chair, stared at the acoustical ceiling tile, an activity that seemed to drain his face of color. He propped an elbow on the table, rested his head on the heel of his hand, and leaned toward me.

"Well, it's been some helluva ride, I can tell you that, Jed. And, in the pit of my stomach, I have this feeling it ain't over yet. Just when you think things are settling down, Emma surprises."

I laughed. "She was always been very good at keeping everyone back on their heels," I said, grinning.

"Just the half of it," he sighed. "Never was keen on the way she let you go…in essence running off with a new guy, before she'd closed, delayed or whatever with you."

"I got over it."

"Perhaps, but she never did. The pattern repeated itself with whatshisname, Bill's companion, the Lutheran kid she converted. She gets him baptized and within a year—a couple of months before he departs on a mission—she's got something new going on. And you probably have heard all the rest."

"I heard a lot that I don't necessarily believe."

"Well believe it…it was the damned sorority, booze and some frat boy and booze and you know where that leads…"

"Eventually to Point of the Mountain," I said, smiling a little.

"Same parable, different kind of prison, if you get what I mean…the guy was almost predatory."

"He may well have been that," I said. "But you have your daughter sized wrong."

"I don't think so…"

"I know so." Now why did you say that, I asked myself. Watch yourself.

"You weren't around, how would you know?"

"I'm a very good reporter…I do my homework," I said firmly.

"This came from her?"

"Good reporters always protect their sources."

"Like our bishop." I could tell the Colonel was relieved a little by what I said, but still frustrated. "So, good. Whatever! Now the problem is front and center. It's here and now. There's a stack of invitations at the printer's, dresses, the cake, relatives flying in, you name it and it's all done. Here's the rub: all the signs are there that she's getting ready to bolt again…from another heckuva nice fellow, don't you think, who turned her away from that hot pants predator. And I don't know what I can do about it…"

"You sure?" I was instantly hopeful for personal reasons, even if I was troubled deeply by the Colonel's obvious distress.

"Not positive…but she's been gone a lot, for days at a time and she's been acting confused, conflicted, almost frightened."

"I can understand," I soothed, attempting to put his worries to rest. "I'd imagine there's a lot of pressure on her right now."

"She always had a lot of confidence in you, trusts your judgment, especially lately. This reassures me," he said, re-establishing eye contact. "This reassures me because the Jed Russell I know would do everything in his power to encourage her to do the right thing, wouldn't he?"

Flattered in a sense, humiliated in a way, I nodded.

"Then I will count on you," he said firmly.

Because he was leaving town the evening after our arrival in Salt Lake, we had agreed to meet Eddie Knight for breakfast at our hotel. "I'm not going to have a lot of criticism to offer—except what you'd expect to get from a bishop," he'd said when I called to set the appointment. "But I do want to meet your Rebe…a patient daughter of Job if there ever was one."

Except for a few extra pounds around the middle, Eddie hadn't changed much: the slightly updated version of the horn-rim glasses he wore throughout high school and college made his baby face look like it still belonged to a sixteen-year-old, straining to pass the ID check at the state liquor store. Yet he was now a successful real estate developer, the father of six children all from the same woman, a former bishop and current stake president, a decent man, if a little on the narrow and judgmental side.

As he sat down at the table, he cast a disapproving glance at the brimming cups of coffee in front of us. "None for me," he said as the waitress aimed the pot toward his cup. "Water will be just fine." Clearly intrigued by Rebe, he grilled her about the facts of my life, ones that the distance between New York and Salt Lake had obscured. "So," he said, hesitating, "what has become of my old friend Jed? What do you think about him writing a novel, a thinly-veiled tell-all memoir of our youth?"

Rebe blushed, then regained her composure. "It's like practically every story in the book, you really can't tell exactly where reality leaves off and fantasy begins."

"I agree," he chortled. "Given what I saw as a bishop, it is always the straight arrows, the serious kids around here who blow out all four tires at the same time. They're the hardest of all to get back on the straight and narrow way. Like Jed."

I winced. "Don't think we have enough time left in our lives to debate that one," I said. "So, does the book have the ring of authenticity to it?"

"Apart from the fact I couldn't tell where the fiction began?" he said, chortling again, pleased that he'd gotten a good one off. "Actually, it was a little too detailed for my tastes; even though you've changed the names to protect the innocent—hah, hah, hah—people who know you are gonna be able to identify who's who..."

"I've worried about that," Rebe said.

"Out of the mouth of babes comes wisdom," he said. "Heed Rebe's advice."

"Were you uncomfortable with what I wrote about you?" I asked.

"Uncomfortable? Yes. Was I really that smug, self-righteous?"

"Were you? Past tense?" I teased. Eddie winced.

"Okay, the truth. I got real concerned about the sections on Emmaline. They're pretty rough and, frankly, she hasn't turned out to be the self-centered hypocrite you make her out to be...she'll be completely embarrassed, floored, devastated."

"Embarrassed, I don't think. Last time I looked in, Bill had already gotten the whole low-down on Emmaline and me from his loyal, trustworthy if indiscreet frat brother. That would be you," I said.

"That's the problem, Jed, Bill Kimball is no more. He passed on, cancer, about three months ago."

"What? He was one helluva good man," I said. "What happened?"

"Yes, he was a very good man. Even very good men die." Eddie's eyes fixed on mine, then he quickly looked away. "I don't know all the details. But it was very fast, cancer of the liver, I believe. As I understand it, it's quite a mess—their daughter is reeling—sounds like four of her wheels came off the track and then some. It's not going to help to read this stuff about her mother."

"Judas Priest!" I was stunned. "This is a real problem..."

"Just forget it, Jeddy," Rebe said.

"I'll figure out a solution...I do hear what you're saying, Eddie."

Eddie looked at Rebe. Solemnly, Rebe drew her index finger across her throat, from left ear to right. It was a sure sign to Eddie that he had gotten his way, a sign to him that she would give her life rather than renege on the covenant she had just made.

"Thank you, Rebe," Eddie said. He paused, puzzled. "I thought you were Jewish."

"I am. What's that supposed to mean?"

Now it was the indiscreet Eddie's turn to be embarrassed. "No offense meant. Just the opposite. Perhaps Jed will explain sometime," he said. His eyes whispered apologies, confessed his foolish presumptuousness, his betrayal of pledges he'd not kept.

"How about sometime like right now," she demanded.

I shrugged. "Your hand gesture inadvertently suggested that you might be a very worthy Mormon, a temple-worthy Mormon, especially to an old-school Mormon fixated on such things," I said.

"Perhaps Elder Russell will explain more…when you're in the temple," Eddie said.

Emma returned to the apartment late Sunday—even later than I had, so it must have been at least midnight. I was entrapped by her arms and legs when I awoke at seven with barely enough time to make it to class. We reversed the arrival and departure schedule Monday night because Sarah met me for breakfast at 2 a.m., after I finished my night duty at the newspaper. (Things went swimmingly; in fact, I needed every excuse in the book to dissuade Sarah from returning to my apartment for what little remained of the night…) And Tuesday night, Wednesday morning Emma was just plain gone, which was small relief because Sarah wasn't; I met her there for dinner at 9:30 p.m. and she was asleep in my bed when I returned home around 2:30 a.m.

If Emma's absences were subconscious or conscious byproducts of emerging erotodromomania—no better short-term way to deal with compulsive, confusing, mind-warping behaviors than to steer wide of them—you couldn't have proved it by the way she greeted me late Wednesday evening, my day off. Dinner was on the candlelit table; from the portable stereo Johnny Mathis crooned "*Chances are 'cause you wear a silly grin / the moment that I come into view*" as I stepped through the door into an incredibly warm embrace, which turned much warmer as I realized Emma was wearing only a robe. "Not a word about anything. Just dinner, wine and me," she said softly, biting my ear.

"Wine?" I said.

"Wine not?" she teased. "You do drink it from time to time, I believe."

"Well fine, me, but you?"

"Would you rather I wouldn't?"

I hesitated. "Your choice, but it's not something you need to do to please me."

"Hate to see you drink alone," she said.

We did not add liquid fuel to the fire, but the outcome of the evening-cum-night-cum-morning was as anyone with a lick of common sense would imagine, which only reinforced my belief that long ago Shakespeare got it right: *Refrain tonight and that shall lend a kind of easiness / To the next abstinence: the next more easy; For use almost can change the stamp of nature.*

I had intended to talk seriously, bring this increasingly delicate situation to its obvious conclusion as swiftly and painlessly (for Bill) as possible. Given the Colonel's limited perspective on the matter, I knew the solution at hand may not square with his preferences, initially. But, if he knew what I knew, I would be honoring my pledge to him. I would have done all in my power to see to it that Emma (and I) did the right thing. Then Emma greeted me at the door…waltzed me around the room, her light bathrobe slipping, clinging, gaping…plied me with wonderful food (I can't even begin to recall what, exactly) and 7 Up (that I do remember, explicitly)…and for many other reasons that had everything to do with human regenerancy, I willfully became undone. Anon. Anon!

In the few hours of darkness remaining, clammy and spent, we became one flesh, coiled and wound and knotted as tightly as braids in a ballerina's bun. Replaying the videotape of these events, recorded deeply in my organic data bank, using sensors that have been adjusted and updated and refined over the decades as circumstances and fresh perspectives warranted, leaves me at a complete loss to pinpoint what provoked me, us, to finally address what the future had in store for us: possible disasters, certain disappointments and shocks, inevitably church "discipline" and the humiliation that comes with it.

Perhaps I was provoked and troubled by Emma's fickle, superficial approach to relationships, life and keeping up appearances? Perhaps my growing interest, on every conceivable level, in Sarah moved me to act? Or, perhaps my lifelong penchant for measuring up, pleasing others—in this case the Colonel—spurred me on? More likely, I was brought to my senses by the resplendent refractions of the sun through the sparkling prism on Emma's left ring finger as we ate breakfast that December morning in 1967.

"What are we gonna do about that?" I said, glancing at her left hand.

"Oh, sorry," she said as she reached to lower the window blind behind her. "Better now?"

"Yes, thank you, but not exactly what I meant. What I meant was…"

"Yes, yes, I know I'm procrastinating…it just makes my stomach turn to think about it. I just wish we could run off to Idaho, just get it done. End of story."

"We?"

"Me, we," she said.

"I agree, *we* need to get it done very soon; Idaho or here…so what about Bill?"

"I dunno…I dunno, something."

"Okay, I'll butt out—your problem to resolve. So us: the timing, the place?"

"This could take a while…and I've got a 7:45 class."

"Skip it—this is very important."

"So's class—it's a review for the final exam."

"I give…here I am damn near flunking every class because…of everything *we've* been doing; give me a little hint as to what you're thinking."

"So, okay but then I do have to go to class. When: June. Where: the temple." My jaw must have dropped. Maybe I gasped. Probably all the blood in my head plummeted to my toes. I could feel water beading on and in my nose, of all places. "What's wrong? You look positively sick?"

"I'm fine, surprised a little." I smiled. "You're right, this will take time…so, go to your class, we'll talk later. But start to think this through: Just what in the hell are we going to do about *us*, if you get my meaning, between now and June? And, the temple, even if I was willing, just how would we go about doing that?" She started to say something. "Sssh," I said, kissing her on the lips. "Not now. Go to school. Think about it. Everything. You can trust me."

Saving Graces

The editors suggested that I take note that this book was written in three, more or less, "sittings." Some were rather more like periods of indentured servitude if you asked me. Had the publisher not provided a considerable advance, and had I not spent every cent of it and then some, I would have permanently stored this manuscript in the file drawer alongside the earlier misbegotten attempt at writing a memoir.

In compliance with the publisher's directive—yes, it was a directive not a suggestion—here's my explanation, the exculpatory statement as it were:

> *Dear Reader:*
>
> *The lion's share of the story you are reading was prepared from 1983 to 1987. In 1993, to further protect innocents, some minor mechanical and structural changes were made: fictional names were created for some locations, institutions and real people, particularly those I thought might be offended or embarrassed for one reason or another. As these changes rippled throughout the manuscript, they created, as they say, "collateral damage," which required additional mending and restructuring. Which led to more adjustments and so on and so forth.*
>
> *Which gets us well into the New Millennium; I have not yet had a "Road To Damascus" vision or anything remotely close to one; we are still awaiting the second coming of The Messiah, or the first, depending on your point of view; we have survived the greed of the nineties, a time when fiction created vast overnight wealth for the inventive, and comparative poverty for those who failed to find the hidden meanings in fairly novel business plans.*

I am getting ahead of myself. Shortly after everyone thought the Y2K computer issues would turn the world into chaos and anarchy, my nurturing and exceedingly patient publisher got swallowed up in a hostile takeover by one of those sprawling entertainment conglomerates with legions of overpaid attorneys and bean counters who had nothing better to do with their days than make trouble for struggling, persevering word merchants like me who were having a tough time closing circles.

To make matters worse, I had no one to run interference: Wren had retired to Marco Island and wanted nothing more to do with "Cabalbatrossinc" (his combination, not mine) although he reminded me that the publisher and its predecessors had more than recouped its investment in me in the early 90s, when with my blessing, it sold movie rights to a section of the book, which was then in outline, that some B- or C-grade producer transformed into the script for a soft-core porn hit film called Delilah of Deseret.

"If anything, with or without a finished manuscript, they owe you big time. Only your guilt, okay integrity—misplaced integrity, if you asked me—prevents you from collecting," Wren said.

I responded to the first demand letter from Cabalbatrossinc by telephone and was immediately transferred to the person who signed the letter, who transferred me to the suit actually handling the matter, who bounced me to a skirt who refused to give me her name and said she was "pursuing the matter" for Cabalbatrossinc. Ms. Suit was not at all pleasant.

"Oh yes, Mr. Russell, I'm quite familiar with situations like yours—no prob if you finish the manuscript, finally."

"I'm getting there," I said. "And..." I rambled on for a while, explaining in detail why I had been unable to release the manuscript before now.

"Whatever," Ms. Suit snapped dimissively. "Getting there is no longer good enough, kind sir. This is a goddamn business, sir. Run the numbers and, with interest and compounding, you'll see that, in essence, Cabalbatrossinc has advanced a pretty hefty chunk of change for absofuckinlutely nothing."

"Nothing, in this case, suggests the probability of something..."

"And, that's gonna change. For good and sound marketing reasons. Because of the Winter Olympics in Salt Lake next year, Mormons are gonna be hot, hot, hot for a while, which may actually help us rationalize in cold, hard business terms why we've been so goddamned patient with you. Windows of opportunity shut fast. So we must have a finished manuscript by February or we're calling in the howitzers."

"End of the month or beginning?" I said.

"Don't press your luck," Suit snapped.

"I'll email my map coordinates...we'll see if you're as good at shooting azimuths as you are shooting off your mouth."

"This conversation will end..."

"Look, mizz, I fully understand that this is a most unusual circumstance. But, I was quite clear, in writing—"

"Screw your lame CYA letters; they have no standing with Cabalbatrossinc."

"—as to why I was temporarily withholding the book, and when it would likely be ready for release—I think the outside date was in time for the fall list of 2003—and I assure you, the timing had nothing whatsoever to do with the blasted Olympic Games, or open windows and—"

"Now it does," Suit interjected rudely.

"—in the files, you'll find correspondence from your antecedant..."

"Aunt who?"

"...confirming its acceptance of my proposal, which included my permission for it to recoup some of its investment in me by licensing the worldwide motion picture rights to a section of the book that was then in detailed outline form..."

"That and four-fifty will get you a double latte grande at Starbucks."

"...which became the basis for Delilah of Deseret." Finally there was blessed silence at the other end of the line. But only for a moment.

"No way," she gasped. She gurgled as she spoke like she was drowning on her own saliva. "Très hot, bawled my brown eyes blue, and hunky Trevor Hardwick."

"A distorted and pretty gawdawful adaptation of the story that made somebody a pile of money, which has not yet been

shared with me, as per the agreement with your Auntie Cedant. However, my counsel advises that when I submit the completed book manuscript, you will owe me a small bundle plus royalties, plus, what was that you laid on me, right: compounding and interest."

"This is news to me, Mr. Russell." Suit now sounded almost human. Respectful even. "Honestly, I had no idea…but I'll look into it right away and get back to you."

"Whatever," I said. "I have picked up right where I left off. No surprises. Everything will be as outlined." In truth, I had written the detailed outline for Delilah of Deseret from the finished manuscript, more or less, which was then locked away in my study, awaiting the passage of time, a few polishing edits and minor adjustments, and, most importantly, a final blessing from Rebe—my counsel, my lover and, eventually, my wife (not always in that order).

And, so we continue.

Emma took most of the weekend to think about *when* and *where*. By the time she showed up Sunday afternoon, I'd had three more days of Sarah and was therefore beginning to think *who* should be added to the short list of critical issues needing resolution. Emma was not in the mood to talk, exactly.

"Look, if we get serious now, it could affect the rest of the day and night…so let's reverse the order; do the easy part first, save the difficult stuff for last. Who knows, what we do first *could* have bearing on the outcome," she said.

"No doubt about it. For instance, keep this up and December 30 will be upon us…and we will have but one choice…"

"Coeur d'Alene!" she giggled mischievously.

"Sun Valley is closer. Idaho would be a choice now or later…but I'd imagine the Colonel and his mate are planning a pretty huge party, and Bill's taking time out of med school and…" I was saying as Emma pressed against me, massaging my neck with her lips.

"Later, please, now I just need you…"

And, as we had previously cast all restraint to the wind, gorged like inchoate ravenous parolees, anon and anon, it had become our nature to behave naturally, we were once again undone, suggesting that the answer to *when* should be *now*, immediately, ASAP; and the where, for now, was a block away in a small office in city hall.

The *who* was above me, flushed, released, glassy-eyed, staring down into my fogged pupils, which seemed coated with a translucent membrane of Vaseline. Her breasts shimmered invitingly, like an oasis of palms in a desert mirage. "Do you aspire to the spires of my temple?" she teased.

"Yes, although it's clear my aspirations may not be yours exactly."

"Not now, Jed…you don't mean that, I know."

"But I do…city hall would be best…"

"You would *never* take me to the temple…?"

"Never is a long time. Let's stick to *now*. Now, I couldn't, not *now*! And you couldn't, shouldn't go even if I suggested it."

She buried her head in my chest. "There's only been you…and who would ask anyway? I have my recommend and you have yours…"

"That's another problem too…mine lapsed when I was in New England and I haven't renewed it," I lied. The fog was lifting slowly. "But that's beside the point. There's a principle involved here."

"How could you let it lapse?" she said, petulantly sitting down on the mattress between my thighs as if she intended the physical discomfort from being bent backwards to punish me for letting my temple recommend expire and being unwilling to do whatever it took to secure a new one.

"Beside the point. The point is the principle: how could *you*, *we*, go there now in good conscience unless we *both* believe what we've just done is no one's business but ours and God's?"

"That's why June makes more sense…maybe later, what's the rule?"

"And, in the meantime…I mean do we just abstain? Not very realistic…I couldn't, I wouldn't want to."

"So, what are you saying?"

"As I see it, the timing is now—as soon as possible. The place—any place but the temple. City hall, as I was saying."

"You would do the temple eventually, as soon as possible. You—"

"For you, yes…"

"—won't ever reach your potential—bishop, stake president, who knows—if you don't marry in the temple. I want you to be all that you were called to be; I want to be proud of you…"

"Would a great journalist do?"

"Well that too…of course…you know what I mean."

Trouble was, I knew exactly what she meant. Trouble was, I was seriously compromised. Emma was sitting astride my hips, leaning back as far as she dared, creating an exquisite pain that seemed to arouse the *natural*, the *enemy of God* in us, provoking me to once again recklessly abandon reason for another exhilarating flight. And, the *natural* woman creating all the exquisite tension, the savioress on Mt. Zion above me, seemed eager to follow the priesthood on another astral mission. Onward and upward we zoooomed!

Rebe and I argued on the drive out to Polly's house, near the mouth of Little Cottonwood Canyon on property that had once been part of a 2,000-acre ranch that my ornery, embittered and reclusive great uncle Sam—the obstreperous founder of Barlow, Adams and Russell—bought up and let lie fallow for as long as he lived, which thereafter was sold, tract by tract, to absorb the homes of Zion's upwardly mobile baby boomers. In deference to Emmaline's recent problems, Rebe demanded that all references to her be deleted. Period. End of story.

"I don't see how I could do that without basically redoing the entire book," I said.

"Perhaps then it's time to start writing *real* fiction instead of stuff that is, at most, a half step removed from reality. You simply can not invade the privacy of *this* woman at *this* time. She must be at wits end," she said.

"I need to finish, for us…the book would be done, the journey over… Cabalbatross would be off my back, and, more importantly, we could marry…"

"Oh right, that. Honestly, Jed, there is no linkage between Emma, finishing the book and our wedding. My decision to marry you was made long, long ago—way before you got around to giving me a ring. My mind couldn't be changed even if you copulated with a ewe in the middle of Main Street while the six o'clock news crew was videotaping…"

Cattle and sheep and various assorted wild critters had once roamed the foothills and glens of the Wasatch, as had I. As a youngster, I'd hike south from Canyon Mills to Union, then work my way up the rocky bottom of Little Cottonwood Creek—a raging torrent in the spring that virtually ran dry by August—to my Uncle Sam's lone bungalow, once the site of a grist mill, sequestered in a creekside grove of towering cottonwoods. Now his land was a patchwork of neatly laid out streets and relatively expensive homes that, though one was somewhat different from the next, exuded the look and feel of products that had been extruded from the same assembly line. Here was a Lincoln, over there was a Mercury

Cougar, across the street sat a Pinto and all of them would be Edsels in no time.

Polly Liddy's house was the racy, irreverent Mustang of rough-hewn logs and soaring roofs she and John had designed and built on Twin Peaks Drive, a grand name for a 400-yard-long cul-de-sac whose upward progress was blocked by the Liddy aerie. Their driveway snaked around the first sharp perpendicular thrust of the Wasatch, up to a house, perched on a natural outcropping of rock and earth, overlooking a hillside of scrub oak, the street, and, on a clear day, the lights of the city, lying 14 miles to the north and west.

In the rear, a sheer face of a granite cliff formed a formidable barrier around the yard, pool and adjacent stone lagoon, which ducked under a natural rock overhang, over which a sheet of recirculating warm water plunged. (On more than one occasion, Sarah and I had sequestered ourselves in the warm cavern under the rock, made private and warm by the wall of cascading water, spray and rising steam.)

Most breathtaking of all was the view straight up the face of the mountain from the backyard into the clouds. From this vantage point, one could not make the hidden valleys and gorges with year-round fields of snow and ice and pristine springs that oozed right out of the rock, then gathered in brooks and pools. I had often drunk from them simply by sticking my face full into quality water that sells for five bucks a bottle or more in fashionable Manhattan watering holes.

I was amazed that John had given all this up without much of a fight when he and Polly divorced. I'd heard that he was allowed to visit, from time to time, and partake in the beauty of the house he had helped design and build and pay for.

Two cars were parked in the open garage, but no one answered when we rang the bell: once, twice, thrice. "She couldn't have forgotten we were coming—we talked to her two hours ago," I said.

"Probably out buying an emergency supply of oxygen for us," Rebe said.

So we strolled around the yard, taking in the views below and above us; around to the back and the shimmering pool and waterfall. When we had completed our brief walkabout, we laid down on a chaise lounge, our eyes up the mountain, which created the illusion that the granite cliffs were growing out of our chests and were about to topple over and bury us.

I was drifting off to sleep in the warm sun when my reverie was interrupted by laughter—giggling really—coming from behind the falls. There was splashing, and then two bodies emerged as one from the shallow depths of the spa. They separated as Polly spied us on the lounge: "Oh, sorry, is it *that* late already?" she said as she strode up the stone steps of the spa toward us, just as uninhibited as I remembered her. I looked for a towel to throw her way; she seemed unconcerned as she sat down on the edge of the chaise lounge next to Rebe, legs splayed invitingly, I thought.

"You must be de-famous and de-licious Rebe," Polly grinned, wiping excess water from her eyes with the back of her hands. Rebe smiled, laughed.

"You're just as Jed described," Rebe said.

"And what would that romantic old fool know about me?" Polly winked my direction. "Well now that you've already seen all there is to see, the water's great…as you've noticed you don't need *no* suits. That's my *good friend*"—Polly gave a knowing wiggle to her eyebrows just in case I missed the emphasis she put on *good friend*—"Lainey Robinson over there," she said, waving an arm toward the flushed face framed by a head of dark hair that bobbed above the lip of the lagoon. "She knows all about you two, too." *Good friend* Eleanor Robinson waved, signaling her acquiescence.

Never before—perhaps in a forgotten dream—had I sat in broad daylight (or dark of night, for that matter) in a pool of warm, bubbling water with three attractive women. Three attractive, naked women. Grandfather Orson would be proud or disgusted or empathetic (I couldn't be sure). Even though he crafted the theological basis for plural marriage, he didn't engage in it himself until prodded and, ultimately, commanded to do so. He, too, seemed to recognize what I was now feeling: it was sensory and emotional overload that most men could not long endure without burning out. Everywhere I looked (except toward the heavens) were bare breasts, tanned slender legs and thighs and more; some of the scenery was recently familiar, some not—but for this moment of profligacy, the unknown was just as thrilling as the known.

"I guess it goes without saying that you like what you see," Polly said, motioning toward what I could sense was my very natural reaction to the visuals. The women (Rebe too) laughed loudly. "I thought your book was much, much improved over the parts Sarah read to me. Pretty spot on, to tell the truth. Especially about my dad."

"Glad you liked it," I said. "Always happy to have another set of eyes.

What were your impressions, Eleanor, or should I call you Lainey?"

She shifted a little, folded her arms across her breasts. "Lainey would be fine. I liked it, I really did. Your protagonist, however, was hard to figure: unnecessarily tough on himself; belying…almost…serious ego, inferiority problems. Was this just a literary device, or is that the way it really was…for you?"

"Hard on himself? Inferiority problems? I don't recall more than a little useful self-deprecation," I said. "You recall the sections?"

"It was more than self-deprecation. Well, actually, you're pretty tough on yourself throughout the story; it's like you really believe that all the bad things were payback for some previous error. Like the commuter train. I dunno, but I got the sense that *you*, well the *main character*, really began to believe *he/you* caused it to run late, or persuaded the stripper to peel off her clothes. Or that he/you shouldn't have been there in the first place to witness it…like he/you knew or thought he/you belonged home in Zion. Go figure."

"Huh," I said. Such thoughts had never before occurred to me. But, as Eleanor—Eleanor fit her more than Lainey—rambled on, I sensed that relief/satisfied/confident feeling I often got when I've unwittingly assembled an anchoring section of a jigsaw puzzle. Truth is, I had indeed felt guilty, ashamed and uneasy when the stripper bolted through the 6:05 to New Haven. Was it guilt, paranoia? Rebe might say such feelings were narcissistic: "Believe it or not, Jed, not everything that happens in the world has something to do with what you did."

Eleanor seemed to agree. "But chronologically it begins before that… it's a life pattern. The garage sex when he was a little boy was clearly not his doing. It is equally clear the girls are in charge, yet it seems to bring him pain and guilt, well embarrassment. And, then he grows the girl's breast—wow, big-time guilt even though there's nothing he could do about that. Then comes the biggest head trip in the wake of Emma. Rebounding, he hooks up with a girl, uses her a little, then regrets it years later. God, I'll bet she'll read this and, after she cries a river, she'll say, 'He wasn't that calculating, he was kind and hey, I had a sense of what was going on too.'"

I looked at Rebe, Polly. Polly shrugged. "Some perceptive chick I've got there, don'tcha think, huh?"

"Some," I said. "Truth is, there was remorse about the *rebound girl*; I could have handled the situation a lot better, been a lot more honest. I *really* missed a golden opportunity." Eleanor's unblinking eyes fixed on mine. Rebe coughed. Polly finally broke the silence.

"Rebe, what you say we dip under the falls and let them hash this out?" Polly said.

Rebe laughed, confused. "What he probably needs to do is visit her and sort things out...but you're absolutely on the right track, Eleanor," Rebe said. "He shoulders blame whenever there is blame to be shouldered. That's his way still. It's almost perverse how he creates the crisis, presses the limits so he can feel the guilt, rejection or whatever. He is always first in line to take the beating for what he failed to do exactly right. Frankly, from what I can tell, the woman doesn't seem to have been made worse for the wear...what—she finishes college, marries a minister."

"The *Right* Reverend Robert Robinson, rector to the high WASPs at St. Mark's downtown," Polly said sarcastically.

"Probably has kids in college by now," said Rebe.

"Pomona and Williams," Eleanor said.

"See—successful, happy as hell," Rebe offered.

"For the most part. But divorced; messy, still messy," Eleanor said.

"So, you know her, then?" I said.

"Know her?" Eleanor was pleasantly annoyed. "Good Lord, Jed, have I changed that much? Lainey Cannon, remember me?"

We had been in Salt Lake nearly a week and, frankly, were comfortably settled into the large guest bedroom and attached den at Polly and, uh, Lainey's house. When they learned I was still awaiting the summons from Brother Orson, who was not adhering to the schedule he'd laid out through the intermediary, they encouraged us to stay on and cranked up so many ominous and bizarre "people are watching you" Salt Lake stories that I thought it best to take them up on the offer. Rebe eagerly agreed.

As neither Brother Orson nor his agents were calling, I tried tracking him down through various old contacts I had in Utah law enforcement, friends I'd made long ago when I was a cub police reporter and they were young city cops. Now they were detectives: some worked undercover for the attorney general, another had landed a position with the FBI, which was then just beginning to pay serious attention to the new cults in Utah practicing plural marriage. None had ever heard anything about someone named *Brother Orson*. Like me, they doubted he would turn out to be reasonably well known in the community, as the intermediary had alleged. Just in case, Parry Farnsworth, a city detective now working for the AG, provided me a long list of men and women who were "alleged to be cohabiting unlawfully right here in the valley" as he put it, "not hidden away on a ranch sequestered in the mountains."

"It's a touchy subject around here given the fact we do zilch about unwedded people who live together or people who screw around," Farnsworth said sympathetically. "Regular cohabitating is a technical violation of Utah law too. So while we don't exactly ignore plural marriage—we have a reasonable sense of the *who* and *where*—we keep the guns in the holsters unless there's some kind of child or spousal abuse going on… or unless the people rub our faces in it, embarrass us in the media like that damned egomaniac Brother Joseph did in *People* magazine. Incidentally, did you have anything to do with that story?"

"I was outta there by then," I said.

"Well, if your Brother Orson is wise he won't go shooting off his mouth, or making it too obvious who he is and where he lives and what he does for a living. I hope he knows that. Does he know you're from Utah?"

"It's not something I volunteered, although it wouldn't be hard to figure out and he seems to have done his homework on me," I said. "Why?"

"Well, he may be a little more forthcoming if he knows you have some familiarity, sympathy for polygamy…"

"Perhaps empathy, in a very abstract way, but familiarity? Not until recently," I said.

"Did you grow up with blinders on?"

"I didn't think so…I'm a Pratt, so I knew that I hailed from polygamous roots and all that. Like about eighty percent of the Mormons in Salt Lake. I've heard stories about Davis County…and there was the huge family compound out on Dimple Dell Road between Big Cottonwood and Little Cottonwood canyons…but that's about it. Nothing firsthand, familiar. Just rumor and tall tales."

"That's just the tip of the iceberg; there are thousands of 'em, and thanks to our generation, it's growing, not shrinking," he said. "Drives the brethren downtown crazy. The Church comes down hard on polygamists. Get caught and excommunication is an absolute certainty. But the clever ones don't get caught by the Church; they lie about their worthiness to go to the temple. So many have current recommends, and, as I say, we're reluctant to get involved for a lot of reasons."

"Like what?" I said.

"For starters: suppose we bring someone to trial, and they get help from some smartass lawyer at the ACLU who argues that because polygamy is a religious practice it is protected by the constitution—that was the compelling argument the Church made way back a hundred years ago. And it was a good one…"

"But the prohibition of plural marriage was found to be legal," I said.

"Legal as legal was defined then under bigamy statutes. But, the constitutionality of prohibiting the *religious* practice of plural marriage never has been addressed by the high court. Never needed to be. Recall that to gain statehood, Utah was required to incorporate language in its constitution forbidding polygamy; it's the only state constitution with such language. And, this section of the Utah Constitution has never been tested in the federal courts either. We prosecute polygamists today using Utah law."

"So, are you saying…"

"What I'm saying is with all the screwing around that's going on in the country, no one really wants to see the federal courts or the US Supreme Court weigh in on the plural marriage matter. Given the court's more liberal interpretation of civil liberties, not to mention the prevailing tolerance for various forms of technically illegal living arrangements and kinky sex, the court could rule that polygamy is protected. God bless our founding fathers. Point is, no one really wants that to happen either. Not at this late date. Imagine the chaos here if the right to practice polygamy was upheld? Imagine the pressure it would put on the Church?"

"Pressure on the Church? How so?" I asked, although I knew the answer.

"The Church was under pressure from the federal government when it 'suspended' polygamy. Surely, you know that 'polygamy' is still a doctrine of the Church, albeit a suspended one. A Supreme Court decision permitting it put pressure on the Church to lift the suspension. It's a lose-lose proposition. The Church would either have to rescind the manifesto and control polygamy, or it would have to come up with an explanation that, essentially, debunked what had been taught as doctrine for more than a century."

"In the face of a hypothetical court ruling favorable to plural marriage, couldn't the Church nip any controversy in the bud by stating that monogamy remains the policy of the Church; that while plural marriage remains an eternal principle, it was a temporary temporal policy instituted to build up the ranks of Zion?"

"Ever the pragmatist," he said. "You should work in Church PR."

⊙ ⊙ ⊙

As the first full week of December 1967 neared its end I was feeling anything but pragmatic, and I was beginning to sense what it must have been like for my polygamist forefathers Orson and Parley. No resolution was in sight to the not-so-incidental matter of Emma. My interest in Sarah was growing by leaps, if bounded for obvious reasons.

I was even getting a taste of what Grandfather Orson must have endured as he tried to keep some separation between the women he loved, especially between the others and his first wife, Sarah. At least his Sarah knew about the other women in his life and vice versa. Emma knew about my Sarah, but my Sarah did not know that Emma and I were *cohabitating* for all practical and spiritual purposes. This kind of secrecy caused Joseph Smith no end of trouble with his own beloved Emma. He didn't exactly confess straight out that he had been commanded by way of a revelation to institute the practice of plural marriage so as to raise up a good and righteous seed, swell Zion's ranks so it would become a political force to be reckoned with in Missouri, Illinois. He hadn't shared with her his vision that Zion, wherever it was, may one day be its own country, or an especially blessed state of the United States, a land choice above all other lands. Joseph's Emma was none too happy when she discovered that he had taken up with the housekeeper, the comely 16-year-old Fanny Alger. And, on it went.

Ever sensitive to my criticisms and peculiar situation, my Emma kept herself out of sight for most of the week using the lame excuse of studying for final exams. This provided more opportunities to be with Sarah as well as time to face up to the cold, hard academic facts of life: given all that had gone on this term, I was ill-prepared for test week myself and was in danger of getting Ds or worse in a couple of classes.

I started negotiating on Monday and by Friday, after literally begging and pleading and revealing more than I cared to about what had gotten in the way of my studies, I managed to wangle an *Incomplete* for every problem class excepting "The History of Religious Philosophy," taught by a preeminent Mormon antagonist, Professor Waldemar P. Read. He listened patiently to my tale of woe, asked a few pointed questions, and then requested that I return the next day for his decision, which I did.

"Young man, I've looked over your grades for the term. For the most part, they are quite respectable. The mildly overly enthusiastic arguments you presented in your term paper, "The Pragmatic Rationalism of America's Religion: Mormonism," were, nonetheless, quite compelling. I awarded it an A because some of your ideas were fresh, if a little underdeveloped; and, because of all the thousands of Mormon students I've taught and challenged over the years, you are the first to take issue—in writing—with the eminent Dr. Harold W. Schneider's rather didactic dismissal of Mormonism ("*...a classic illustration of how preposterous nonsense can be sanctified and hallowed by the sufferings and labors of an heroic people.*") in his excellent *A History of American Philosophy,* a text I've used in this class for nearly two decades. Your alliterative rejection—"abstruse academic absolutism" was as exacting as it was pithy. Given the challenges you are facing now, and with not a little empathy for one who strives to work and study and love full-time, simultaneously (let me tell you son, you cannot do it all, well), I will award you an A grade for the term provided that you give me your word that you will continue to develop the proposals in your term paper and prepare a memorable honors thesis before you graduate. Meantime, if you have the time between what's none of my business and then, you may want to read up on Orson Pratt, you should be familiar with his name."

"I should be—he's my great-grandfather."

"Really? Why am I not surprised? He was the brains of the whole operation, if you asked me. Smith delivered the raw concept, Pratt added the substance. If Brigham had listened to Orson, Mormons would have had a theology to crow about, one that would have merited quite a bit more than that patronizing line in Schneider's text."

Awash in pragmatic joy, I returned to the apartment and to Emma, who had just completed her last exam and was awash in her own excitement over the formal end to her undergraduate years. Her desire to celebrate, and mine to make some decisions, were on a collision course. Nevertheless, I was prompted—by who or what, I am not sure—to call in sick. This was the only time, ever, that I feigned sickness to avoid work. Forgive me.

And so we began our celebration at two in the afternoon in the usual way, which was supposed to be followed by dinner and dancing, then more of the usual. Trouble was we were both so exhausted that we fell asleep by five, awoke briefly at nine for more celebration, then fully collapsed until eight the next morning.

Over Cheerios and milk on whatever day it was, Emma, unprovoked, jarred my eyes open with this question: "So how's it going with Sarah?"

"Quite well, given the distractions," I said honestly.

"Are you in love with her?" There was only kindness and empathy in Emma's voice.

"As I say, hard to tell with the distractions. Could I be? Exclusively, except for the reality of you. You must have similar conflicts about Bill and me."

"I guess…I was thinking about him last night when we were, you know, and I was wondering what he would be like, would it be the same or different?"

"Probably different, not necessarily better…or worse," I said, cautiously. This was no time to bring up the size thing and what the hell would she know of that anyway. What did I, for that matter?

"Not necessarily worse…but better because of the temple issue," she said, hesitating.

"Temple…eventually, you mean."

"Or worse, or the same with him if I didn't do the temple now, to begin with."

"Then worse or the same, Emma, because honestly it wouldn't be a particularly brilliant move to do the temple now with anyone…him or me…you've got to face up to that. Soon."

"It could be a big problem—how would I tell him the temple is off without risking the marriage?" she said.

"I assume you mean Bill? You wouldn't have to tell me," I said.

"Yes, Bill; it could blow the whole thing. It'd be a whole lot easier to do Idaho with you right now and be done with it."

"*Easier* should have no bearing on a decision this important…you're talking about a lifelong or longer commitment."

"Why can't women do polygamy too?" she said, seriously enough that I provided an equally serious answer.

"Hah, I feel your pain," I said. "But it's polyandry when one woman has two husbands, not polygamy. And, there's no history of polyandry in our backgrounds. And it means you'd have to have two willing consorts and I'm definitely not a candidate."

"You wouldn't share…with your cousin…" she teased.

"Not in the sense you mean it. So your choice is Bill, then?"

"I don't know how I'm gonna tell him…"

"So Bill is your choice," I said, more emphatically.

"It'd kill him…I'd be humiliated…Idaho with you is very tempting, convenient."

"I'm not a 7-11," I said sharply, worried that she was about to unravel emotionally. "I happen to think—know—Bill's deeply in love with you; he's strong, he's loyal [I knew nothing of the kind, of course] and he's a

Pratt for Heaven's sake. What the hell more do you want?"

"You don't have to talk like that…let's just go to Idaho…"

"Stop. We can't do that…for a lot of reasons." I paused, searching for good and logical reasons why *we* couldn't *run off to Idaho*. "Truth is, I'm much further along with Sarah than I represented [lie one]…I'm not ready to make a marriage commitment now [lie two] and if I have to make a decision now, it would be to hang in there, wait to see how things turn out [lie three]." In truth, I was more inclined to *run off to Idaho*. The rest would take care of itself. Hah!

"So I could be out there all alone three months from now: no you, no Bill, no nothing," she said, verging on tears.

"Look, Emma, I love you…so it's with love that I tell you, that I know you really do love Bill, and by God, he loves you too…I saw it in his eyes, I heard it in his voice. You want unequivocal love? Bill's more than my equal, he's as good as it's gonna get. You've made some mistakes? Hasn't everyone. My gut tells me Bill would understand."

"Perhaps. But he won't understand not going to the temple…he's in a bishopric…I can't surprise him like this at this late hour. He'd be humiliated. He'd just walk out on me."

And so the conversation went, for hours. Finally, shortly before I was due to leave for work, I found myself agreeing with—offering, actually—to broach the subject with Bill in my own oblique way when he returned from California. If I judged him the type to fly off the handle, I'd so advise Emma. Thereafter, I agreed to stand by her decision, whatever it was, even if it was to enter the Temple of God under false pretenses (but to save face) with him or *run off to Idaho*, with him or me.

Before I shoved off for the newspaper that afternoon, we celebrated this important decision in the usual way. It was the beginning of evening of our last day, which extended well into the next week. Of course it was satisfying to the natural, carnal man I had become. And, on Wednesday, the day of Bill's return, I cried, then called to arrange a meeting with him the next evening.

"It's a fairly pressing personal matter, I could use some Pratt advice," I said cheerily.

"Everything's fine with Emma, right?" he said, nervously, I thought.

"Radiant and healthy as a horse last time I saw her," I said, honestly. And so he agreed to meet late Thursday at Lamb's Grille, a newspaper hangout I knew would be pretty empty by nine or so.

He was waiting in a high-backed booth in the rear of the restaurant when I arrived at 8:45, edging my way toward him past a contingent of chain-smoking reporters and editors overstaying the evening dinner break. It was Christmas. "How do you stand working with them…all the smoke," Bill said as he stood to greet me.

"You get used to it…you know, when in Rome…"

We sat quietly for a moment, eyed each other across the table, cautiously. Ordered sandwiches and sodas. I could tell he was nervous, too. "Look, this is only about me," I said.

"I guess my face betrayed my concern, huh," he said. "This wedding stuff absolutely has me tied up in knots. All I needed was for something else to go wrong. I'll offer a free piece of Pratt advice: when you do this, just do it: *run off to Idaho*."

"Thought about it, actually," I said.

"Idaho?"

"That too. Getting married. So I'll cut to the chase: although we barely know each other, I trust you. And if you betray my confidence, I can deny I ever said anything of the kind." He grinned.

"So, what's weighing you down besides genetic Pratt melancholia and paranoia, which I fully understand?"

"As I said, marriage. Things with Sarah—she's John Liddy's sister-in-law, remember—are, ah, heating up."

His laugh was so loud, newsmen at the counter turned our way. "This should surprise? Her sister is some…"

"Yeh, yeh, I know. And, so is Sarah."

"How long's it been?"

"A month or so," I lied. "A little too early, I know…"

"No, no, I knew for sure after a week with Emma…it's been a while since then, but honestly, we're no better off getting married today than we would have been eighteen months ago…worse off, actually, in some respects."

"Right. Well…here's the rub," I said, eager to get this over with as quickly as possible. "It's our parents. Mine will want the marriage to take place in the temple. Her mother seems inclined that way too. She's saying things like 'The only daughter of mine eligible and with an RM' and all that stuff. Her dad says he doesn't care, but, hell, his dad was in the First Presidency, a protégé of Orson Pratt's as a matter of fact. So, even though he's inactive, he may still prefer the temple too. Sarah could go either way."

"So do the temple then."

"Well, that's the problem. I'm in a bit of a pickle and she may be too, for all I know. Who knows? So about two weeks ago I'm at a newspaper party and this girl, a society reporter, and I start talking, hitting it off… and, well, she needs a ride home. I provide it and one thing leads to another, and…we make a weekend of it plus a few more days."

"Really, I wouldn't have expected that from you," he said.

"Should I be flattered? Of course I feel guilty and embarrassed, stupid really…"

"It's not like you're the first…or the last guy who ever got carried away with himself," Bill said, sympathetically.

"…so now I'm faced with having to tell Sarah, to explain why the temple is out of the question; or fudge and go through with a temple ceremony, if that's what she wants. So you're in a bishopric, what would you advise?"

"I'm not the bishop, keep that in mind. I take it your recommend is current." I nodded. "So then, you could fudge it if that's your choice. As for beginning your life together with a lie, well, it's not the most advisable thing to do, and it would be kinda awkward, but…does she love you…?"

"Of course, but…"

"If she loves you, she'll understand; however, if she's having normal second thoughts, she might not understand at all…especially an event so recent."

"So what would you do?"

"Hey, this is about you, not me," he said sharply, defensively, I thought.

"Sorry, I meant what would you do in the unlikely event you were in my situation?"

"Yeh, I know what you meant…it would come down to how much I was in love. This is a pretty dicey time anyway. Which is why if I were in your situation and had the option—like you do apparently, to get married outside the temple say, so her parents can witness the ceremony—I'd jump at it…and I wouldn't say a damn thing until I was at least a year or so into the marriage, if at all. I think I'd have to be very certain that my wife-to-be could handle it, before I fessed up." He seemed to be drifting off, like he had other things on his mind.

"If you were in my situation, right?"

"Oh yeh, right, if I were in *your* situation."

"Flip it on its head—what should I do if I discover she's slept with a man besides me."

"Not the situation, so why go there."

"I don't know it's *not* the situation…but it's quite possible and you never know. You know her sister."

He smiled. "From what you've told me about you, you'd be hard pressed to hold similar behavior against her, wouldn't you say?"

"Sometimes it's harder to forgive someone else than yourself," I said.

"More often it is just the reverse," he said seriously. "The one thing I wouldn't do is wait—it will drive you crazy and probably ruin the relationship. You reach a point, like Emma and I did in September, where you've got to take it to the next level or be prepared for it to fall apart. Thank goodness I was in school in California…" his voice trailed off. "You probably understand…"

We talked on and on. Our sandwiches had long since been consumed plus three sodas and several waters. The waiters were setting the tables for the next morning as I stood to leave, exhausted. "Sit for another minute or two, please," he said quietly. I followed his order.

"I've got to tell you, I'm relieved. I was really worried in November when Emma told me she'd finally reconnected with you—I'd seen it coming way last spring when your first column appeared in the *Chrony*. It was worrisome because as far as I was concerned you were the competition even though you may not have known it then or even now."

"So far as I know, I was never competing against anyone. If anything, I was just competing for Emma, I'm sure you understand why…but it ended, really, a long time ago."

"From your point of view, but not from Emma's. The reconnect in October was deliberate, necessary; I'm relieved to have survived it so far…"

"Headed down the home stretch."

"…and, now, I can say it's good she did it. She has a lot of trust for you, in case you haven't noticed."

"No one's more surprised…"

"Trust is the evidence of profound love," he said.

"Never thought of it that way, but you could be right."

"Anyway, you asked for help, now it's my turn: how about sharing a few insights into the girl, the family you seem to know so well and who trusts you so much?" he asked.

"Shoot…but I think you may overrate her estimation of me—the result of Pratt paranoia, no doubt," I said. "Remember, she's the one who walked away from me."

"So what? Trust me, she trusts you. She feels like she let you down and, worse, that letting you go let the Colonel down too."

"Oy, if I'd only known, I could have saved her from you," I grinned. "So what's up?"

"Got your word: this is between us?"

"Scout's honor," I said, holding three fingers aloft.

"Suppose you were in the same dilemma with Emma that you are with Sarah?"

Did he know that Emma was my dilemma, that Emma was the recent lapse I would have to explain to Sarah if explanations were necessary? Perhaps there was a simple way to make sense of this mess: introduce Bill to Sarah, then stand back and let nature take its course. He admitted his attraction—was it lust?—for Sarah's sister. And, I knew firsthand that Sarah too was a more than adequate proxy. That's not what he wanted. What he wanted to know was how would I handle a similar hypothetical situation with Emma, if I were the one marrying her, not him. How would I explain to Emma, the Colonel and his mate, and her sisters that I was the one to blame, the sinner who could not qualify for a temple recommend for at least a year because I'd had a momentary lapse, a one night stand, with another woman. "It'd be tough, very tough to tell the *old* Emmaline, the one who abandoned me for Sheygets back in high school."

"Sheygets?" Bill asked.

"Barry, your missionary companion, a Gentile, a sheygets before he converted."

"My take too—she wouldn't understand at all. Double it for the Colonel."

"Hold on. I was talking about the *Old Emmaline*. I think Emma's different: broader perspective on things, a little more experienced, older, wiser."

"I wonder," he said.

"Wonder on. You asked my opinion. I gave it. As for the Colonel: well, my sense is that he's been down the winding path a few times himself, so at least in the abstract he'd understand. He's very protective of his daughters, so he may have a harsh thing or two to say; it would be worse if you were boinking his daughter. I don't have much of a sense of Emma's mother, except she's always been very down to earth, like the Colonel. They'll be terrific in-laws," I said.

"True. So you think Emma could handle news like that from you…"

"From me? Now? I'm pretty sure she could," I said confidently.

"...that it wouldn't blow the marriage..."

"I'm not the one marrying Emma, but if I were, I think she'd get over it."

"...in the temple?"

"Whoa...you just gave me the opposite advice. So no, I don't think the temple arrangement would hold for all the hypotheticals you laid out, although it's conceivable Emma would insist on the temple, for *appearances'* sake. She's into *appearances*, in case you haven't noticed. It's her Achilles heel, in some respects. But, like you said: dishonesty is a hell of an unstable foundation for a new marriage. Is this a philosophical discussion or do you have a *specific* concern about Emma?" I was getting worried that somehow I'd revealed the real reason for our man-to-man chat.

"Emma? Heavens no. Me. Very similar to your situation, different circumstances; a little more premeditated, retaliatory, overreaction to Emma and...and...well, you, frankly; what I feared you could mean to Emma and me. And there was a party, an attractive med student who'd been eyeing me, who didn't care that I was engaged; she just wanted to do it; and you and Emma had just connected and I was feeling pretty down and worried..."

"Lord have mercy," I said.

"So you think I should tell Emma..."

"Actually, I'd let it slide for now...just deal with the temple issue for now."

"But that would be tantamount, at this point, to a confession of sin."

"Why? Just because you're in a bishopric doesn't mean you no longer have significant doubts about the Church; and principles and integrity—ta da, ta da, ta da—that are at least as important as sexual fidelity."

"She'd never buy it."

"Oh, I think she might...she's been hanging around me for a long time...she's heard similar philosophical arguments before: they'll resonate."

"You'd back me up, then?" Bill asked, surprised, pleased.

"Absolutely. As I said, I'm not competing."

"Don't suppose you'd consider being my *John the Baptist*...smooth the way with her?"

I scratched my head. What kind of a box was I putting myself in? Was I ready to take myself out of the running? If not, if people knew what I knew—if Bill knew what I knew—would I now betray Bill's trust if Emma and I *ran off to Idaho*? Would smoothing things for Bill be tantamount to betraying Emma and myself? Was this a double-edged sucker punch or what?

"I'll do it, carefully," I said cautiously, "but only on two conditions: after I've been your *John the Baptist* and prepared the way, you, Emma and I must meet and talk matters through, thoroughly; and, no matter the outcome of those discussions or pressure from her, you will not agree to go to the temple until the two of you are right with each other and your consciences. Deal?"

Bill looked me squarely in the eyes and thrust his hand toward mine. "Deal. You should reconsider your feelings about the gospel: the Church needs bishops like you," Bill said. Yeh, right! If he only knew.

Nearly all the waiters had gone home when we finally rose to leave. "You boys solve all the world's problems tonight?" the cashier said as we paid the bill.

"No," I said cheerily, "but I think we may have at least defined a few new ones. Sorry, we did lose track of the time, didn't we?"

"No matter. From where I stood, it looked serious, important," he said.

On the street, right under the towering blue spruce Christmas tree in front of the Tribune Building, Bill veered toward his car at the curb, then turned back to face me. "Look, I know this hasn't turned out exactly the way you envisioned things," he said softly, sincerely.

"Life rarely does, it seems," I said.

He embraced me and hung on like he might not let go. "If it matters, I do love Emma in ways I have only begun to fathom." His eyes were tearing.

"I can only imagine; I know the feeling is mutual, even if she might seem like a deer in the headlights at times. Truth: I do think you're the kind of husband she needs, deserves; it wouldn't have worked with me. I would have transformed her into something she's not. Or, vice versa."

He drew back, studied my face intently. "So you'll be in touch soon… we've only got a couple of weeks…"

"Tomorrow, absolutely tomorrow," I said firmly.

"I hope I get the chance to repay this huge favor someday," he said, his voice choked.

"What goes round tends to come round; in some way, I'm sure you will. Like keeping Emma happy for an eternity," I said as we shook hands in the warm fellowship and trust of the Pratthood we'd established.

Exhilarated from the exchange, feeling more honest and trustworthy than I had in many, many months, years even, I headed true north up Main Street toward the illuminated spires in Temple Square, turned east to the mountains and home, where a chastened and worried Emma awaited word that I hadn't inadvertently, stupidly, selfishly thwarted her chances for eternal progression and happiness with Bill as goddess and god, co-creators of new worlds in a celestial kingdom to come. For all she knew, she and I would be making a fast getaway to Idaho.

The Closing Circle

The splendid log and glass cathedral with the majestic views at the end of Twin Peaks Drive shimmered in the glow of the purple-red sunset as I headed the car up the driveway, returning to home base after another futile daylong effort to track down Brother Orson and his consorts. I'd talked with Bob Gamma who said Orson's "people" had been trying to get in touch; and still no call summoning to me to his boudoir, wherever it was in the 82,000 square miles of desert, mountains and salt water that constitute Utah.

"Southern part, I think," said Gamma, a wholly unreliable source for accurate geographical facts. For all I knew, Brother Orson might be living in Arizona, or St. George, or Cedar City. Or, hell, he could be in the shadow of the everlasting Wasatch in southern sections of Salt Lake City and County, one being virtually indistinguishable from the other. Wherever Brother Orson was, Gamma was certain I would find him. If Orson's lawyer didn't call, then I'd locate him using divining rods and frequent prayers.

Laughter echoed off the granite cliffs behind the house as I headed up the stairs and around the garage toward the voices. There they were, the three of them, clustered around and on the double chaise lounge near the pool. Rebe lay face up, bare breasts into the warm evening canyon breezes, her head rested in the wedge framed by kneeling Polly's thighs; Rebe's legs formed the equal sides of an isosceles triangle, which was closed by Lainey's hips and pelvis. At the moment I arrived, a set of hands was massaging Rebe's shoulders, while another set kneaded a calf, then swept over a thigh.

Polly called out nonchalantly as I neared the giggling ménage. "An important call came in again today from that same pushy attorney in Washington who called yesterday. Quite peeved that I'd forgotten to tell you he'd phoned, but as you can see I've been more than a little distracted. Now wipe that suspicious scowl from your face and go call that ornery old bastard back...we're just having some good, clean fun, aren't we Rebe?"

Rebe gurgled. "These two are something...this is sooooo relaxing."

"His home phone number's right there on the pad by the portable," she said pointing toward the outdoor table. "He said it was important you call tonight." I found the phone. Who the hell did this Wendall Haig of Barlow, Adams and Russell think he was anyway, getting rude with the grandnephew of Samuel Isaac Russell of Salt Lake City and Washington? Although Sam was regarded as wise, even a brilliant counselor on constitutional law, particularly First Amendment issues, he was ordered to take his abrasive, cantankerous ways and small fortune home to Utah where he offered his counsel by way of letter and, eventually, telephone while transforming himself into a moldering recluse and chronic crank.

Rebe's thighs were being softly stroked as the attorney came on the line. "Haig here," he said forcefully as if he was accustomed to being in charge...of everything.

"Wendall Haig of Barlow, Adams and *Russell*?" I said.

"The same."

"Jed *Russell* here, returning your call, how may I help you," I said.

"You're helping by returning the call finally...I was beginning to think you'd inherited some of your legendary uncle's elusive qualities... I've left messages for you all over bloody hell—Connecticut, New York, your hotel in Salt Lake, your parents, who by the way didn't know you were in the valley. They do now."

"Why the manhunt? What's up?"

"You desire to visit with Brother Orson, or so I'm told; he's willing. I assume you are still interested in talking with him as well?"

The hands were taking in ever wider swaths of Rebe's inner thighs. Her eyes were closed. "Yes, still interested, but I'm killing a lot of time here waiting for him to call..." Polly worked Rebe's shoulders and neck and...

"There are a few formalities that you must agree to for this to go forward."

Hey, despite Uncle Sam's reputation, I'm a pretty informal guy, usually, like right now I'm talking to you while... "What formalities?"

"I'll fax out a document that will spell it all out..."

"Just talk it; I'm about a million miles from the nearest fax." Without breaking rhythm or unhanding herself, Polly shook her head vigorously to get my attention, and then gestured toward the second floor of the house.

"So I'll talk it...but you'll need to sign the document before we can proceed," Haig said.

"Christ, that wasn't part of the deal."

"There was no prior deal, this is the only deal," Haig said firmly in that smug, lawyerly I-have-a-firm-grasp-on-your-tender-parts-and-now-if-your-heart-and-mind-will-kindly-follow tone.

The deal was this: Polly was stroking Rebe's upper half and Lainey had worked all the way up to...well the sun wasn't shining so how the hell would I know, exactly. "What's the deal, then?" I said, trying desperately to focus on the stupid phone conversation.

"You will use a pseudonym—Brother Orson will suffice, however, you may, at your discretion, select another pseudonym that suits your literary needs. You will neither name his employer nor describe in specific terms his profession nor clients, nor make any other disclosures that may identify said Brother Orson, which will include the locations or identifying descriptions of his home and/or homes and/or other domiciles, past or present, current and past names of spouses, children, schools, places of worship et cetera et cetera et cetera. And, of course, you warrant to protect your sources, notes, and other research materials even if they are requested by your employer, said *New Yorker* magazine, or subpoenaed by any court of competent jurisdiction."

"Were you reading from a legal brief or is that the way you normally talk? Did anyone bother to preview this horseshit with Bob Gamma?"

"Who's Bob Gamma?"

"He's in charge at the *New Yorker*."

"I'm in charge here," Haig said. "Frankly, I wouldn't know Gamma from Harold Ross or that Steven Stone fellow. Of course, you are aware that both are Utah boys too?"

"Yes, yes, though they're hardly in the same league, if you asked me. Anyway, you'd think someone would have bothered to lay this on Gamma, before he went to the expense of sending me out here. I'm supposed to be preparing a goddamn piece of journalism, not some sizzling piece of fiction."

"I made it clear to whatshisname, the publisher. I have no idea what he said to Gamma. In any event, Mr. Russell, there will be no additional contact from Brother Orson until you sign the document."

"Hmmm. You wouldn't take my word that I'll protect my sources—it'll take a while to track down Gamma; he'll have to get the document reviewed by his lawyers and that could take days..."

"Normally, we require a signed document. Hmm. But perhaps your reputation, your connections here and there would allow us to proceed on your word...could I get back to you later...?"

"We're going out shortly." Rebe shook her head, vigorously disagreeing. Polly smiled, then continued kneading the taught skin over Rebe's ribs. "Morning would be better...although you could leave a message with contact numbers and so on."

"Orson will contact you, not the other way around."

"Am I going to be blindfolded and handcuffed too...I mean I do know this place like the back of my hand. At some point, he's going to have to trust me," I said.

"We'll be back to you. Have a pleasant evening, now."

"Already am," I said.

"Do you need a little help unwinding, honey?" Rebe teased.

I did.

On my homeward trek up East South Temple, snow began falling as I passed in front of the hulking granite edifice of the Alta Club, where the brokers of power in Zion—Mormons, gentiles and Jews; politicians, businessmen and religious leaders—gathered over breakfast or lunch to sort out the past, present and future of the city. A block later, as I crossed the street to my building, I could see Emma standing, waving in the bay window of my third floor apartment, backlit by the lamps in the living room. She greeted me in the lobby as I brushed snow from my coat. She was anxious, naturally; surprised, dumbfounded actually, that things had gone so well with Bill. I edited the report of the evening's conversation, but it included this important strategy: "If needs be, explain to curious parents and relatives that both of you have decided that there are some unresolved matters of principle: important questions, doubts, that would, until they are resolved, make a mockery of a temple ceremony."

"I can't believe he bought it."

"What's to buy...there are issues that need a resolution. It's pretty straightforward, honest. He's got issues, you've got issues; you wouldn't want him doing something against his better judgment and vice versa."

"He has issues too? What kinds of issues?" she asked.

"Everyone has issues, that's my point: there are plenty of potential reasons why a marriage should not be made in the temple. Your particular issues are your business and no one else's. Ditto Bill's, whatever they could be."

"Hmmm, well we've got more immediate *issues* upstairs." Emma said. "Sarah's here, sleeping, if I didn't wake her when I left. You weren't out the door but ten minutes when she called—seems the two of you had made plans for this evening."

"Shit, she got off work at nine thirty, I was going to meet her at the store…and I got talking with Bill and…shit." We boarded the elevator.

"She got off earlier. She called. I explained you were with your cousin, my fiancé, who'd just flown in from California, and probably had lost track of the time, but would probably be home soon, within the hour… so she walked here and waited. We had quite the nice chat…you're right about her…then she fell asleep on the sofa, which is where she is now."

While Sarah slept, Emma and I sat at the small kitchen table, where we could keep an eye on the sofa. "So the three of us will have a chat, ah"—my watch revealed it was past midnight—"tonight at—" The phone rang.

"Jed, this is Bill…you sound out of breath."

"Bill?"

"Bill Kimball…"

"That Bill Kimball. Ha, ha. Long time no see. Ha, ha. Surprises galore tonight. Just walked through the door to an apartment full of sleeping people when the phone started ringing." Sarah stirred on the sofa. Emma was at the kitchen table rolling her eyes. "Emma's here and so is Sarah; they've been talking for hours, laying me bare, no doubt."

"Good. I called the Kappa house and the girl there said Emma might be headed your way…that's why I called. Mind if I join the party—I'm at U, so it'd take me about ten minutes, max."

"Hey, c'mon down. The night's still young."

"God, it's past midnight," Sarah said, rubbing sleep from her eyes. "I'm due home by one."

"The roads are getting pretty bad…you could stay here, I could call your mother and tell her you fell asleep on the sofa," I said.

"Yeh, right; she'd have the whole sheriff's department down here faster than you can say Miranda Warning…"

"Or you could bunk with me up at the Kappa House," Emma volunteered. Wink, wink.

And so Sarah did the responsible thing: she called home. "You'll never believe this. When I told Mom where I was and the plan for the night, she told me stay put—the roads up in Oak Hills are buried in about a foot of snow."

When he arrived a few minutes later, Bill confirmed that even the byways at lower elevations in the city were slick and treacherous, "and it's just starting to come down hard."

Lots of good reasons to stay put. On the other hand, and definitely from my perspective, there were plenty of objective motives to break up this little carousal before it stumbled across a touchy subject or slid into a ditch we couldn't back out of. But Mother Nature was having her way with us: no one seemed inclined to brave her wrath or, as I had suggested, make use of the sleeping bags and extra bedding I'd fetched from the closet, which gave me the opportunity to stash any incriminating remnants from Emma's many recent sleepovers.

Bill was telling Sarah about his encounters with her sister—how John would try to sneak her out of the Sigma Chi house early in the morning and, when caught, would pretend that she'd just dropped by for breakfast; how all conversation would stop when she'd show up. "Frankly, it's probably a darn good thing John married her when he did: she could have had her choice of practically anyone in the house; I don't think I've ever met a more disarming girl—straightforward, fun, friendly, not a phony bone in her body and my goodness she was attractive, almost as attractive as you."

It was pretty clear that Bill was quite smitten too, first by Polly and now by Sarah. Perhaps this would ease the pain should Emma and I *run off to Idaho.* Emma shot me one of those *So what am I, chopped liver?* looks, just as Sarah brought him up to heel: "So I understand you and Emma are to be married soon if everything gets sorted out."

Bill looked at me. I shrugged. "What I said was there were some general last minute issues, premarital jitters stuff that we were talking through..." I explained.

"So everything's okay then," Bill said, looking at Emma. "So you're set then?"

"Set? Well we haven't talked yet—you, Jed and me—that's tonight, but that should be easy if we're both okay about not getting married in the temple just now; if that doesn't affect things..."

"It gives me some pause because of our parents...but it's not something we should do given my situation, I hope you understand," Bill said.

Sarah was looking downright uncomfortable and confused, which was completely understandable. While it was obvious to me that she and

Emma had indulged in more than idle chatter while they awaited my return, Sarah was only generally aware of what was going on, not specifically up to speed on Emma's parcel of "issues." Of course both she and Emma were completely unaware that Bill's oblique reference was to his own burden, not Emma's. "Maybe I should go home…or go to bed, so you can talk," Sarah said.

"No, no, stay put," smitten Bill said. "You're almost like part of the family, anyway." Sarah looked really confused. "I mean, I knew your sister," he added quickly, fearing he was about to betray me and my acknowledgement that matters were heating up with Polly Thompson's little sister.

"So, as I was going to say tonight, your situations present some challenges: what to say to parents, to friends, making alternative arrangements," I said, edgily.

"The invitations to the reception are already in the mail…so no matter what we do now, everyone that comes is gonna think we got married in the temple," Emma said.

"Brilliant," Sarah said passionately. "What you do is no one's business but yours. When I get married it's gonna be a civil ceremony first—so my parents and all my friends can all come. Then the temple, if I feel like it."

"Take that opening quick, Jed…ha, ha, ha," Bill said. Sarah was even more confused, as she should well have been. I ignored Bill's comment, treated it like I would meddling from any pushy relative.

"The problem is our parents…and the other people invited to the temple ceremony," Emma said.

"So one solution—and, personally, I think it has theological merit—would be to tell your parents that you have thought long and hard about the matter; have reached the decision that eternal marriage is such an extraordinarily sacred and personal matter between the bride and the groom that…"

"It is," Bill and Emma said in unison, emphatically together.

"I think I know where you're going, and I like it," Sarah said conspiratorially.

"Yes, yes…and therefore it's something you believe you should do on your own, so you can focus on each other at this special moment, as you embark on your journey through life together."

"Oooh, I love it, it sounds so romantic and spiritual," Sarah giggled. Bill and Emma were still confused.

"So the morning of the big day, you go off to the appropriate spot, get yourselves married. The rest of the day remains just as you've planned it.

A year or so from now, you deal with the matter of sealing the marriage, perhaps in the Oakland Temple. No fuss, no bother, and no dishonesty if you choose your words carefully. Mind you, I don't intend to suggest deception. Sarah's got it absolutely right: it's no one's business but yours. You owe no one an explanation. Let your parents provide their own explanations to the few relatives invited to the actual ceremony. I'm positive the Colonel won't blink an eye; how about your parents, Bill?"

"There's just my mother," he said. "She won't like it, but she knows I'm headstrong about things like this...and if the Colonel's leading, she'll follow. But you forget one thing: they could check up on us."

"Would your mother even think to? I'm sure the Colonel wouldn't. Frankly, I don't know how they'd go about it in the first place. There's no point to it; however, be sure to cancel your reservation for the sealing room."

"It all seems so manipulative," Emma said.

"Acting ethically is manipulative? Getting you to absolutely, positively believe that the only *real, first class* marriage is a temple marriage, now that's manipulative," Sarah said indignantly. "Brainwashing that makes good people like you feel guilty because of 'issues' on what should be the happiest day of their lives, now that's brutal manipulation."

Emma smiled. "See, I was right about you Sarah: you and Jed were made for each other." I grimaced, more busybody relatives. "You two should join us on the 30th."

"Two weeks? Some things would have to happen pretty darn fast," Sarah said, giving me one of those *That's your cue, buster* looks, obviously not embarrassed, like I was, by Emma's pushiness. All eyes turned toward me.

"So, then, have we devised a reasonable outline for a plan?" I said.

Emma and Bill started to speak at the same time. "Where?"

"City hall opens at eight."

"City hall? Now that's a big downer. Another church maybe, a home. Anything but city hall," Emma said.

"We can figure this out on our own, Emma," Bill interjected. "But an idea: Jed, you came home from your mission this year, right?" I nodded. "So, if I'm not mistaken, your minister's certificate is valid through the end of the year..."

"Don't even think it: I'd need special permission to perform weddings and..."

"Would you try to get permission...for us, all of us, it would make the event even more special," Emma said.

"This is getting good. If you can do it, Jed, you really should," Sarah said confidently. "You work for a newspaper, reporters have influence..."

And, as the sun rose over Mt. Olympus, it dawned on me that Sarah had become part of my intimate family, some of whom she now slept with on the floor of my living room.

Mary Martha Woods Thompson, who probably hadn't gotten a minute's sleep, called at quarter to nine. I grabbed the phone before it could ring a second time. "Good morning, Jed. The snow has stopped, the sun is out and I'm ready to make breakfast."

"I'm the only one moving at the moment...we were up talking until sun-up—everyone's still asleep...on the floor," I said.

"We? The royal we?"

"Emma—the Kappa girl—and her fiancé stayed the night too." I was doing the very best I could to assure Mrs. Thompson that everything was on the up and up. I was surprised she had encouraged Sarah to stay. It was so nonchalant for a mother who had once locked out Polly because she showed up five minutes past curfew. "I'll get everyone moving. Would, say ten be okay, although Emma and Bill have wedding things to do."

And so, at about ten minutes to ten Sarah and I arrived at the Thompson home in Oak Hills. No sooner had we sat down at the dining room table than Old ROT came rolling down the hall in his wheelchair, ever-present Parliament dangling from his lips. "Just thought I'd check to see if you two looked any worse for the wear," he said, grinning thinly.

"Up the whole night talking," I offered a little too eagerly.

"Sheesh, and here I thought you had a clever scam going on. Imagine my disappointment," he said.

I grinned. "I'd imagine the only truly terrific scam is one the other guy never figures out."

"Heh, heh. So I hear tell you're a son of Orson too," he said.

"Too?"

"That's where the middle of my handle comes from; not a descendant, but better: he was my own father's mentor; Dad absolutely idolized, deeply respected the man—his brain, stubbornness, his innate goodness. Not a pretentious bone in the man's body, according to my father. I heard all the stories from the time I was yea high."

"Great-grandson, actually, of Orson's; double great of Parley's," I said.

"Hah, another kink of polygamy: a double Pratt...'course both of us would still be spirits drifting about in heaven without polygamy. Given the condition of my rotting old corpus, I'd prefer being a free spirit."

"From what I've heard, your rotting old corpus is but a corporeal extension of your life as an embodied free spirit," I said. Sarah looked alarmed. This was only our second or third meeting, our first real conversation.

"Hah, hah, I see my darling youngest daughter has already let all the family skeletons out of the closet."

"Not all, I guess. Yet."

"Yes, yes, but I suppose she'll expose all of them, sooner or later. You'll need little spicy gossip to liven things up, especially if you intend to make it through a whole GD eternity together."

Mary Martha was horrified. Sarah was mortified. "Don't mind him, he can get awfully presumptuous sometimes," Mrs. Thompson apologized.

"Presumptuous am I?" he said. I could tell he was baiting. "Hell, M&M, you told me yourself that you sensed Jed was the real deal from the moment you laid eyes on him. I'm merely adding my assent to your inscrutable clairvoyance." He grinned at me. "So, what are you waiting for, the Second Coming?"

"This isn't China," Sarah interrupted. "I think I have something to say about the matter."

"That you do," said Old ROT condescendingly. "So?"

"And, Jed has something to say about it too."

Old ROT pulled in his taunting horns, sort of. "Well then, just be quick about it…you never know when this old bag of bones will be hauled off to the dog food factory."

Inadvertently, I stayed on at the Thompsons' for the day. Inadvertently because after getting thoroughly skunked by Old ROT at chess, I fell asleep sitting up on the living room sofa and didn't awaken until the five o'clock news was on the boob tube. Secretary of State Robert McNamara and General William Westmoreland were blathering about the progress—the lack of progress—of the war in Vietnam.

"Lying dirty kikes," ROT sneered at the screen. Then he saw me, awake, conscious, startled.

"Kikes, what's a kike?" I asked, for I had never before heard the pejorative.

"A lying, cheating, treacherous bastard—like those two. It's a slur, a Jewish slur, but not something you'd ever want to call a Jew unless he was also a lying, cheating, treacherous bastard too."

"Yiddish or Hebrew?" I said.

"I don't think either. More like Ellis-Islandish. You speak Hebrew and Yiddish too?"

"Too?"

"Like Orson and my father," ROT said.

"Right. No Hebrew, but a little Yiddish I learned from my grandmother. You?"

"Yiddish better than Hebrew because I used it more," he said.

"Really? Where?"

"In the war, but an eternity it would take to tell, so perhaps in the next life or never, whatever the case may be. Chess?"

My three women—Rebe, Polly and Lainey—had a plan, which they laid on me as September turned into October and still no word from Brother Orson or definitive guidance from his esteemed legal counsel in the nation's capital. On the Saturday or Sunday before Thanksgiving, Rebe and I would stand on the flat rock path that separated the spa from the pool, humbled beneath the majestic sheer granite cliff, and before the gods and the wannabes, water cascading from the overhang over the stone spa, assorted friends, relatives and undecideds assembled on the deck and lawn—Rebe and I would, finally, become of one flesh officially and legally. Hallelujah, amen and amen.

"There's one problem: the expense of flying back out here," I said.

"It's what, October 5 and you're still waiting to hear from the mysterious polygamist and you've got plenty of writing to do otherwise, so that gets you, at least, to the end of the month, comfortably. What's another week or two?" Rebe argued. "And, I forgot, there's still Stone to do, if you ever get around to it."

"It's already been a hell of an imposition on Polly and..."

"Imposition on us? Pffft!" Polly snorted. "I should be so imposed upon for the rest of my life. Rebe's an absolute delight, which makes you almost bearable. Don't you go relying on me to excuse your perpetually itching feet: 'got to run now; wish we could spend more time to get to know you better; just about revealed something about me I shouldn't have, so I'll be begging your leave, *running off to Idaho...*'"

"Hey, I know it's Utah—the mountains must be toppling in on top of you about now," Lainey said. At least Lainey sensed my practice of getting in and out of town as quickly as possible; how the place, as beautiful as it was, made me edgy—fearful that those mountain walls would block me out of the world forever. "But, hey we're up here in the clouds—what's beneath us is beneath us. For as far as the eye can see, it is *beneath* us, if you get my meaning. From up here it may be just a mirage. Don't be misled by what *seems* to be the case, Jed."

"Besides, I figure the earliest you can flee is Halloween," Polly said. "Hey, that could be the day: what a rich opportunity to invite a few more hobgoblins into your life. We matrons of honor could descend the Wasatch on brooms—how fitting—to attend to the aching-to-be-ravaged virgin and her betrothed, the perplexed and pietistic Petra-Pratt: upon this rock I will build my crutch. Perhaps Sarah should be there to give you away, or turn you loose. Finally!"

And, so the happy date was cast in stone, in granite. Halloween!

Test week was over at the university, and for all anyone at the *Tribune* knew it had been an especially grueling one for their youngest reporter and full-time student. No doubt my bleary eyes and wan complexion conveyed the predictable tell-tales of sleep depravation; my shaky hands and leaden feet witnessed visibly to caffeine withdrawal. For the most part, my colleagues' assumptions were correct, never mind that my bone-numbing weariness had quite a bit more to do with too much Emma than desperate, last-minute cramming.

No matter. My reward was general assignment over the last pre-Christmas weekend, one everyone presumed would be deadly slow. It would likely provide ample opportunities to rest, or demonstrate personal enterprise: nose around for interviews with interesting people in town for the holidays; gather seasonally appropriate human interest and "sights and sounds" of the city stories. It would be a rare opportunity to do whatever I wanted, provided my personal assignment folder was empty and that breaking news didn't get in the way.

A note from the city editor, Ernie Ford, was in my folder when I arrived for work Saturday morning:

> *Jed: See me, per Rabbi Mednick, who called. Said he'd been trying to reach you since November...which reminded me: we haven't done a Chanukah piece. So return Father Mednick's call finally and throw together a 20-incher with art for Sunday's split page [the front page of the local section].*

I tracked down Ford. "Look, it's Saturday. I'm not gonna be able to get to Mednick until late today—it's his Sabbath. Probably he'd take my call, but it would be quite insensitive to interrupt, don't you think?"

"Never thought about it. So later then—I still need the piece for Sunday's split, which means I gotta have it, by seven-thirty, latest eight, but I'd have to chase it in then," Ford said firmly. "Okay?"

"I'll do my best, but if I don't start talking to him until sunset, it'll be pretty tight. You could give me a couple extra hours if you'd break it in city edition Sunday and carry it over into the Idaho and state editions Monday."

"Nice try. Jews live in Idaho too, believe it or not…and I need the story for all editions Sunday. I'll be the editor here with the fucking brains, you just be the goddamned reporter with good legs and nimble fingers," he snapped. "Okay?"

"You'd think an editor with all the *fucking* brains would know a little something about Sabbaths," I said, teasing. To his credit, Ford was the kind of grump who invited wisecracks and was as good at absorbing them as he was at dishing.

"Whaddaya expect from a goddamned lapsed Catholic? Stations of the Menorah," Ford snorted, very sarcastically.

"So I have the day to get the story done…the whole day…?"

"No, it's not the goddamned Sabbath for the sinners of Zion…unholy shit could happen…so let me know where you're gonna be."

"At synagogue, holy father!!"

In keeping with the tradition of the Sabbath, more or less, I walked the four blocks to Temple B'Nai Israel, where services for Reformed Jews were conducted at sundown Friday (this I learned after I got there). However, Mednick was presiding at Temple Montefiore, a few blocks away, where conservative Jews were convening for Saturday morning services. I was ushered into the rabbi's office, which had the intimate feeling of a study carrel buried deep in the stacks at the old university library.

While I waited, I perused the stacks, selected several appropriate books, and strapped together, in longhand, a feature that included the story of Judith, prayers and traditions of the season. All my story lacked was a few quotes and a description of this year's commemoration, which Mednick happily supplied when he joined me a couple of hours later.

Shortly before four, I called city desk and told Ford the story was finished, that the copy boy should stop by the synagogue on his regular run to the police station. That settled, plus the fact that I would not be returning to the office for the final hour or so, but would be available at the synagogue should anything unholy be visited upon Zion, I joined the rabbi in his small office, right-sized for the diminutive Mednick (no more than five foot five and a hundred and forty soaking wet). Adrift in the massive leather chair behind the desk—he had to stretch to keep both feet planted on the floor—Rabbi Mednick looked rather like a schoolboy testing out his father's office, not the spiritual chief and interlocutor for the city's two Jewish congregations that were on similar if somewhat tangential paths to God.

Mednick thanked me for the story, which he said was not what he had come to expect from either of the Christian newspapers in Salt Lake City. "Usually they do a feature on us once a year at Yom Kippur, not Chanukah, a minor holiday that's becoming major simply to give our youth something to get them through the very distracting Christmas season."

"I hadn't thought about it until you mentioned it, but it must be especially difficult at Christmas for Jews—the minority of all the minority religions in Salt Lake."

"Teaches you how to bend without compromising important principles. Mormons are rather good at bending too: just look at how your people go overboard at Christmas even though they believe it's not Christ's real birthday and is more of a pagan holiday than a Christian one."

"Merry Chanukah," I offered.

"Happy Christmas," he replied.

"If only it were," I said, not meaning to sound as forlorn as I apparently did.

He told me he had called to praise my piece, months earlier, on open housing. "But tracking you down this past month or so has not been particularly easy—then I saw your byline in the *Tribune*...so I take it you've launched your professional career a little early. Will you stick with the *Trib* after you graduate in June?"

"Still have a couple of years of school left—if I don't crash and burn in the meantime," I said.

"Really, I pegged you for older, although I should have figured it out—you got back from your mission about a year ago...good, that gives us a couple of years to get better acquainted," he said, slapping his thighs enthusiastically. "So what troubles you in this joyous season?" he asked, genuinely concerned, a kind offer to help lighten my load if I so chose to unburden myself on this man I barely knew, but who seemed to have respect for me (despite my youth) and a solid sense of my history and traditions.

"It's a *meshugene* situation," I said.

"Yiddish, you know?" Mednick asked, surprised.

"My grandmother taught me. It's a family thing—passed down from Orson and Parley Pratt."

"I'm familiar with the story, Orson's success at mastering Hebrew. I didn't know he conquered Yiddish too."

Sparing him the gory details of her recent past with me, I sketched Bill's and Emma's backgrounds, explained their predicament and their desire, their reluctant decision to act conscientiously, their desire not to hurt or embarrass themselves, their parents and other loved ones and so on and so forth. I made it clear that both could, despite their personal misgivings, simply bite the bullet and proceed as expected. In reality, no one but them would know they had entered the temple under false pretenses.

Then I laid out their plan and the logic behind it. Because invitations were already in the mail and, given the nature of Mormon temple marriage ceremonies—small and intimate, usually attended only by close relatives and very dear friends who were also temple-worthy, followed by much larger receptions at the couple's local meetinghouse—a last-minute change of venue for the ceremony itself would be known only to a few. And if they decided to act on their belief that it made spiritual sense to go alone to the marriage ceremony—their first sacred act as husband and wife—people would be left to their imaginations to draw whatever assumptions they would about something that was none of their business anyway. Most would assume the ceremony had taken place in the temple of the Lord.

"There is a Yiddish proverb that precisely addresses this situation: *A halber e'mes iz ganster lig'en* [a half truth is a whole lie]," Mednick said, smiling wryly if kindly. "I trust that you are schooled well enough in the Bible to be familiar with the prophet Jeremiah?" He took my nodding head as a yes. "Then, you and your cousin and his fiancée should consider the seventeenth chapter, the middle of the chapter." He retrieved a King James version of the Bible and handed it to me. "I believe the verse begins with 'heart...'"

"I think I know it from memory—scriptural support for the fact that the Lord values good works as well as belief," I said, flipping quickly to Jeremiah and reading the verses aloud.

"9: The heart is deceitful above all things, and desperately wicked: who can know it? 10: I the Lord search the heart, I try the reins, even to give every man according to his ways and according to the fruit of his doings."

"Between now and their wedding, they, you, should become convinced in their hearts that they are square with the Lord in whatever choice they make. I understand that certain behaviors preclude entry into Mormon temples, unless one chooses to be dishonest. Seems to me the Lord is only interested in what's really in your heart. He seems to think that outward signs of piety are good only if they are connected, anchored to sincere belief, intent, personal honesty."

"I will pass along your sound counsel," I said.

"And, if I can be of further help to the young couple—I do so hate to see young people in turmoil at such an important time—please don't hesitate to call on me," he said.

"Actually, there is one more thing. They are quite adamant about having a ceremony in some kind of religious setting. City hall won't do. Would you have any suggestions? It would be a very small group: just the couple and the witnesses, for legal purposes," I said.

"Have they selected someone to perform the ceremony?" Rabbi Mednick asked.

"Not yet. Actually, they asked me to do it, but that would require..."

"What a wonderful gift and what a *mentsch* it would make you...a true act of brotherhood," Rabbi Mednick said, enthused and suddenly animated. "I tell you what—and I wouldn't suggest such a thing normally, but you and I have this *simpatico*—you get whatever authorization you need to conduct the service (that shouldn't be difficult for a smart reporter, an ordained minister who reports on city hall in this city of all cities) and the three of you can make use of my study. It can be dressed up a little to suit the occasion. We could even arrange for a few of our staff to serve as witnesses. It'd have to be very early in the morning...and very low-key and discreet."

Emma and Bill were anything but low-key about the rabbi's proposal. They were doubly pleased when I told them I'd obtained appropriate authorization to conduct the ceremony. (I won't explain exactly how I did it, but it didn't hurt that ministerial credentials I'd been given as missionary were technically valid through the end of the year; and that I had new friends in high places in city government; and that I would be supervised, more or less, by Rabbi Mednick.) Sarah was the most delighted of all: "This is so wonderfully romantic and so perfect: you performing the ceremony for the girl who was once the love of your life, sort of like you're giving her your blessing, your approval to move on."

I shot Emma a disapproving look, which Sarah picked up on. "Hey, Emma didn't spill the beans—Polly and John blabbed way, way back," Sarah said.

"Cuts right to the heart of the matter, just like her sister," said Bill, grinning broadly. "I'd say, John and Polly got the story about the two of you dead straight, but that was a long, long time ago, wasn't it!" He winked at me. "It is true; I will feel a whole lot more secure when my cousin is tied down himself. How are things going in that area, Sarah?"

"My parents are pressuring…but so far, there's no ring on my finger; perhaps Jed has one in his pocket…"

All eyes turned toward me. "Heck of an opening," Bill said.

"No ring's in my pocket…but…" I stepped into the kitchen as I spoke, opened the junk drawer and retrieved a roll of gold twine I'd used to secure Christmas presents. On my knees, I tied a piece around Sarah's left index finger, knotted it snugly, then frayed the ends so that at first glance it more or less resembled a ring. "I promise to replace this symbol of my love as soon as possible if you will pledge before God, Bill and Emma that you will marry me just as soon as possible."

"Now this is romantic." Sarah kissed me like she never had before, as if for the particular benefit of those assembled she was staking her claim. Emma cheered. Bill mopped his brow in mock relief.

The phone message from Wendall Haig of Barlow, Adams and Russell confirmed that Brother Orson would take my word that I would protect him, should push come to shove. As a precaution, I had checked in with Gamma who, frankly, was uneasy with the arrangement but, considering the time it would take for legal beagles to approve a detailed written agreement, told me to proceed. "There are plenty of precedents for protecting your sources, the thing is I don't know Utah law, but you're not going to move there permanently, are you," he said. It was a statement of fact.

The message directed me to join Brother Orson for breakfast at the most conspicuous meeting place in town, the Alta Club, smack dab in the heart of Zion, at the corner of State Street and South Temple; a soft wedge shot from the Greco-Roman granite building that housed the president and apostles of the church; kitty corner from the Lion House, the manse where Brigham Young kept several of his 20-something wives. I last passed by the club on my way home from a memorable late-night discussion with Bill Kimball. "He will meet you in the lobby, between seven thirty and eight; he'll find you and from there everything's up to the two of you."

Because we were meeting where we were meeting—the Alta Club—I didn't exactly expect him to show up in a pair of bib overalls and rubber irrigation boots. However, I was a little startled to be greeted by a man who dressed like he was indeed a captain of industry, a sincere suit that was no off-the-rack model either. From the way the jacket gently hugged the contours of his body, you could tell it had been handcrafted from scratch. Ditto the white, textured shirt, its Eton collar starched stiff; plain sliver links that were designed to be etched with his initials, but weren't, joined the generous French cuffs, which extended a tasteful and proper full inch beyond the sleeves of the suit jacket; and well buffed moc-toe English oxfords—probably from Church's.

And, there I was in my usual attire: tweed sport jacket, gray flannel slacks, tie and penny loafers that had last been shined before we departed New York. Orson's sartorial package put me way, way back on my heels from the start, not just because I'm intimated by stylish attire, but because I just didn't expect it.

"I would suspect you're Brother Russell," he said, after checking his topcoat whilst surveying me discreetly from a distance. I'm sure my eyes betrayed my astonishment. "Not what you envisioned. Fair enough. You're much better dressed than what I would expect from a descendant of the perpetually shabby Orson Pratt." He grinned broadly, shook my hand. "I've arranged a private room—we can talk freely and take as much time as you'd like."

Over breakfast he sketched out the basics: he had two wives, sisters, both of whom lived in the Great Salt Lake Valley. He was a partner in a very well known law firm in the city that had affiliations in Washington, New York City, and Los Angeles; and, was a very active board member of several well-established and influential organizations, the kind that care about personal legacies and connections. "I try to stay busy in public ways, to avoid being called to Church assignments that might eventually prove embarrassing to the Church or me. Of course I'm not likely to be called to any important leadership position because I've been divorced, officially."

"Divorced, so you've been married three times?" I said.

"No, twice, both legally. I'm divorced from my first wife, however we remain bound spiritually and economically—not much difference from what you might see in an amicable divorce." I was scribbling furiously. "That's rather distracting, and how can I be sure you'll be able to read your handwriting?" he said.

"They're but major concept reminders—the rest comes from memory," I said.

"So I've heard, but if it's just the same to you, I'd like to record this and future interviews. Of course I'll provide you with a transcript, which I'm certain you'll find to be verbatim." He placed the tape recorder on the table, hit the play/record button. "Now where were we, yes, my arrangement is rather like an amicable divorce—we have an understanding that overrides the court order: we remain bound as husband and wife even if I've moved on to another marriage, in the legal sense."

"Your wives, they agree with this procedure? Are they free to opt out at any time?"

"Actually, they proposed it. But, yes, they agreed at the outset, before we married; and, of course, they're free to go their own way any time, but that has never been an issue."

"Would they agree with you?" I said.

"Ask them yourself…if they'll talk to you. One of them is a little gun-shy of publicity—for the children's sake—but I'll see what I can do."

"Children? How many children do you have all totaled?"

"Not as many as you'd expect. Nine: one from my first wife, eight from my second, ranging in age from twenty-seven to five."

"The children are aware of the situation."

"They're aware they have other brothers and sisters because they see them every day, but no, the rest is kept from them—they've got to live in the community and they've got to be free to make choices of their own. Frankly, I'm not sure I would encourage them to do as I have done."

"Why?"

"It's an expensive proposition for starters; as any divorced person will tell you, it's difficult to maintain separate households, meet each child's needs in terms of cash outlays as well as personal time; there just isn't a lot left over of either at the end of the day."

The interview wound on for more than three hours—the early lunch crowd was arriving, but I had many more questions, basic ones. He agreed to introduce me to his wives and children, let me see how they lived and so on.

"I have a few more questions, if it's all right."

"We're good in this room for another 30 minutes," he said.

"Good: you seem like a very typical, successful civic leader in Salt Lake, an active member of the Mormon Church; what got you interested in polygamy in the first place?"

"Like you, I suppose it's genetic." He grinned at me. "But, a favorite uncle was married several times. Even though he tried to make the divorces amicable, he failed miserably. As a result, my cousins grew up without a father. They would have been better off if he'd been a real polygamist, as opposed to a serial one. Does it not strike you as odd that society tolerates, condones—some would say 'provokes'—serial polygamy, while it condemns and prosecutes the more socially responsible alternative?"

"You make a rather old argument, don't you think?"

"Old? Yes. But still valid. We don't hunt down men who are out there sleeping around. You live in New York, so you know it's pretty common. All I've done is adapt my situation to conform with existing state and Church law."

"Subjugation of women is another objection to—"

"Subjugation, baloney," he snorted indignantly. "Talk with my wives… they are free to do as they please with their personal lives as well as regards their relationships with me—I have no hold over them. The support I provide now would continue should they ever disavow the commitments we made to each other. Both are well educated—the first is a professor of chemistry at the U; the second is a registered nurse practitioner specializing in midwifery."

"Impressive, however it hardly puts them above the law," I said.

"We operate within the law, technically. For argument's sake, the constitutional question has never been fully resolved. If your Uncle Sam were alive, I am certain he would agree with me. When does the government have the right to intervene? I believe the government has the obligation to intervene when it can be shown that certain religious practices endanger innocents; it is less clear that it has the right to interfere with the decisions of consenting adults. People who subjugate, defraud or coerce others ought to be hunted down and prosecuted, but it is a serious mistake, a very slippery slope, to single out a group simply because they don't conform to some convenient, ephemeral societal model."

"Ephemeral?" I said.

"Yes, laws, attitudes change constantly. Laws forbidding adultery and fornication are on the books in many states. Ditto ones restricting various homosexual and heterosexual relationships. They get raised these days only in very nasty divorce and child custody litigation; no man is ever sent to jail for fornicating with a woman or another man. That is as it should be. The irony here is that the very people who argue that governments should not get involved in 'bedroom' matters, are usually the same *liberal*—I employ that term advisedly—zealots pressing governments to do something about polygamy. Eventually, the laws on plural marriage will change. Plural marriage won't work for most people, but it does work in situations like mine."

"Is there not a certain amount of fraud, manipulation or coercion involved when you decide you're interested in another woman…and how do you go about it, exactly?" I asked.

"There could be if I took the initiative. As I mentioned, my wife, or current wives, do the choosing. They decide when it's time; they select the woman; they ensure she's interested and then they point me. I suppose I have the option of rejecting their choices, but so far it hasn't happened. When we learned my first wife could not have more children, she suggested her younger sister, who was recovering from a pretty awful experience with her fiancé: he left her waiting at the altar, so to speak, and then some. The two of them are taking the lead in choosing the third, should there be a third. I'm not so sure…"

"This would be the teenager…the 17-year-old?"

"It would be, but please understand that nothing will happen until she's at least 18, or older," he said, hesitantly. "And, it's just a concept on the table… I'm not sure about it at all."

"So you are not, ah, courting her just yet?"

"Not officially…she's a school chum of one of my daughters. She had problems with her own parents, so she's been living with us for several months. My first responsibility is to help her sort out her relationship at home. So, in a vague sense, we're courting—we're getting to know each other more, slowly. It's very similar to the others: we talk, do family things, until we are all comfortable taking the next steps. If we become comfortable, the next step would include a legal, technical divorce from the current spouse, followed by a marriage to the new spouse. All of them attend and participate in the marriage ceremony, in the temple."

"Do they remain in contact after the marriage?"

"Hard not to—they live side by side. Separate houses, same piece of property."

"Do the women get along?"

"Well, yes, generally, but they do have their ups and downs, occasional bouts of envy and jealousy, even though they are sisters."

"And the children?"

"They're all of different ages…but they get along fine—as well or better most siblings. Each one was born when I was legally wedded to his or her mother," he said.

"So you cease sexual activity after the divorce?" I asked nervously, fearing I was ferreting for interesting specifics that might add some prurient titillation to the story, never mind that it really was none of my business. Or anyone else's for that matter.

"Intimate relationships are built on quite a bit more than sex. Each child was born of a legal marital union and I'll let it go at that," he said firmly.

"I assume the children take your name…what about the wives after the divorce and new marriages?"

"There's only one, for now. And, she has continued to use her married name, like many divorced women do."

"And that name would be?"

He shot me a puzzled, concerned looked. "Our agreement says you can't publish or divulge my name, right?" I nodded in agreement. "The transcript should note that Mr. Russell reconfirmed his acceptance of this agreement by nodding his head. Is that correct Mr. Russell?"

"Yes," I said, loudly enough for it to be heard by people dining in adjacent rooms as well as Brother Orson's tape recorder.

"Actually, I thought you'd been told my real name by now, by Mr. Haig or the PR guy," he said. A waiter appeared at the door and informed us that that our private room was reserved for lunch, but that we could continue our conversation in a nearby reading room.

We slipped unnoticed through the lobby, now bustling with men in sincere suits and insincere smiles. I sensed I knew many of them, but it had been so many years I couldn't be sure. Just as well: I'd have had to introduce them to someone I didn't know. Brother Orson wouldn't work with this lot.

As we headed toward two overstuffed leather chairs in a far corner of the room, I caught sight of a man I instantly recognized, headed my direction, his luncheon companion close behind. "Could you be that big shot New York journalist Jed Russell that shook his dust off on Zion?" the little man boomed, sticking out his hand as he strode toward me.

It was Aaron Taylor, father of a lifelong friend, former communications director for the Mormon Church and now publisher of the *Deseret News*, the Church-owned daily newspaper in town. I blushed, smiled.

"Well, Brother Taylor, what are you doing in a seedy joint like this," I joked.

His luncheon companion obviously knew Brother Orson because they shook hands warmly before Taylor extended his own hand toward Brother Orson: "Always good to see you, Brother Stone," he said, before turning to me. "I assume you remember his brother, Steven. As I recall, you wrote about him a number of years ago, when you were a student at the U. A memorable piece, as I recall."

"And, he will be writing about me again, shortly," said Steven Stone, who wrapped his right hand around mine, stretching his thumb until it made firm contact with the knob on my wrist bone. "Have you decided whether you will be joining me for a temple session?"

"Still working on the schedule," I demurred.

"Perhaps Dill will want to join us," Steven said. The other Brother Stone nodded his head approvingly.

Although Sarah and I hadn't officially announced our intentions, we'd settled into a routine that, from all appearances, must have looked very committed. Because her mother didn't drive and her father couldn't, I picked her up for work each day. When I didn't need the car, I loaned it to her so she could run errands and so on for the family. Each day I was becoming as indispensable to the Thompsons as they were to me.

By pre-arrangement, Sarah and her mother had gone off in my car to do some Christmas shopping, more or less leaving me in charge of Old ROT for the afternoon. Because he was occupied in his shop—recording messages to his tape pals, CIA operatives no doubt, around the world—I shoveled snow from walks and driveway, washed the lunch dishes, neatened the kitchen, and made a pot of coffee.

"If that's fresh coffee brewing Mary Martha, I'd love a cup in the living room, please," Old ROT called out. I could hear the wheelchair creaking its way across the hardwood floor in the workroom.

"It's fresh coffee, but it's not Mary Martha doing the brewing," I called out. "Just the same, I'll pour you a cup and meet you in the living room."

The wheelchair was parked under a wooden card table when I arrived with the coffee and a tray of English butter biscuits. "Wouldn't have thought a returned missionary would know how to make coffee," he teased.

"Wouldn't have thought a son of an apostle would drink it," I responded.

"When I was a lad, coffee wasn't the big deal it is now," he said lamely.

"Cigarettes too, I suppose?" I grinned.

He winced. "I must remind myself not to give you openings. Have you got time for a quick game of chess?"

"Now there's an oxymoron if there ever was one: a quick game of chess. But seeing's how your wife and my... Sarah are out shopping in my car..."

"Sarah doesn't need a ring or a string on her finger or yours; she's got one in your nose, hah, hah, hah," he said.

"Then I should return the one in my pocket?" I said, setting up the pieces on both sides of the board. He seemed not to have heard me. Just as well.

"I wouldn't let it burn a hole in my pocket if I were you," he said, studying the board, arranging an opening gambit in his mind.

"Wasn't planning to...is that your approval?"

"Were you asking me to approve something?"

"No," I said.

"Surely you weren't asking my permission to propose to my daughter?"

"No, not permission to propose," I said, flustered by his aggressive tone.

"Good thing. She'd likely want to know how in Sam Hill I was in any position to be handing her over..."

"That much I know. However, it would be reassuring to know we had your support and blessing to proceed..."

"Seems to me you've been proceeding pretty well without it up till now, what's the big diff whether you have my blessing or not?"

"Wouldn't make a difference...it's just I'd like to give her the ring tonight and I didn't want to surprise you or her mother."

"Surprise, hell, she came home the other night flashing the GD string you tied around her finger. M&M thought it was sweet. All I could think was, for a Pratt you really lay on the shtick." He was grinning now. "Support? You've got my support. Approval? Well, you've got it tentatively: I'll approve of the marriage when you make it last. Until then, every time you get into a touch-up with my baby girl, which you no doubt will, remind yourself: I only get the old bastard's approval if I make this work. So, I give you my support and tentative approval on one condition..."

"Condition? What, I've got to mow your lawn and shovel your walks?"

"Better you than the GD block teachers," he grinned. "Here's the condition, it's just between us: you give me your word that you will never, ever walk away or give up on my daughter and the family you create together."

His steel gray eyes were unblinking, penetrating. He extended his hand to seal the agreement. I took his in mine. "You have my word."

The column of ash attached to his smoldering Parliament dropped onto our clasped hands, sealing the pledge: ashes to ashes, dust to dust.

Later that evening, over dinner in my apartment, I told Sarah about the covenant I made with her father. She was mortified, of course: "I can't believe you actually asked for my hand…"

"Well I didn't ask for your hand…I asked for his support, approval. He seemed pleased that I'd asked."

"Probably was…the other two certainly didn't say two hoots to him."

"So, once we do this, there's no getting rid of me: I've given my word." As I was leaning over to kiss her, the phone rang. With one hand she pulled my head toward her breasts while she snagged the phone with the other: "Hello, Jed and Sarah Russell residence." She hugged my face to her body. "Well, yes, Mr. Russell is a little indisposed at the moment; Colonel Who is calling?" I slid a hand under her skirt, played itsy-bitsy spider on her thighs. "Colonel Nebeker…" She pointed at the headset, mouthed "Do you want to talk?" I nodded affirmatively. "He'll take the call, Colonel Nebeker, just hold on…ah yes, well thank you very much, we're both quite thrilled, but no, we haven't set a date yet…in fact, how did you know? Ah, I see, Emma of course, I should've known you were *that* Colonel."

"Lovely, lovely," the Colonel said over and over again when I came on the line. "Emma told me all about her…and I can't wait to meet your Sarah. I trust you will be bringing her to the reception?"

"I suppose she will be going to the reception." Sarah nodded affirmatively, eagerly.

"Well, I know you're *indisposed*…so I won't hold you long. But, do you have any idea what's going on with Emma and Bill?"

"I do: that is, they're getting married on the 30th, as scheduled."

"I know, I mean this business about going to the marriage ceremony alone, on their own, no parents, just them?"

"Whatever they're doing, I know they're doing the right thing."

"You sure about that?" he asked.

"A month ago you were worried they might not get married at all…"

"That I was..."

"I gave you my word I'd do all within my power to persuade Emma to do the right thing...I kept my word...they are doing the *right thing*."

"Anything else you can tell me? Her mother's worried, heartbroken. She really wanted to be there for the marriage ceremony. For all we know, Bill and Emma could be *running off to Idaho* in the morning and returning home in time for the reception that evening."

"That could happen, I suppose. But, that's silly. I can tell you that they're not *running off to Idaho*. Tell her I said she'll make a wonderful mother-in-law and not to worry. Sarah and Bill are doing the right thing, their way," I said.

"Wonderful that Bill's asked you to be best man—you two really hit it off better than even I expected." Seemed to me the Colonel's statement was as inquisitive as it was joyful: coating the inquisition with honey, as he was, he hoped I would be flattered into revealing more of what I knew.

"We've done rather well by each other," I said, eager to get off the phone and resume with Sarah.

"Tell me," Sarah said when I hung up, "do you go out of your way to form close relationships with the fathers of the women in your life?"

"Go out of my way? No. It seems to happen naturally with the fathers of the women who count."

"So Emma counts..."

"She did...a long, long time ago...almost as much as you count now—witness my promise to your father today," I said.

"What does it say if the daughter has a mind of her own?" she said, leaning back on the sofa, parting her legs to provide more room for my hand.

"What, are you planning to bolt already? Usually it takes a couple of months," I said, smiling. "I promised the Colonel I would do everything in my power to see that Emma did the right thing." Sarah's eyes closed as my hand slipped inside.

"You did a lot more than that, I'd say, and I only know the half of it..."

"And, I promised your dad that I would never walk away from you or our family. And that's a promise you can take to the bank."

"Slowly," she whispered.

"Your first?" Sarah nodded affirmatively. "You guide me; I'll follow wherever it leads us," I said. A hand grasped me firmly and deliberately pulled me toward her, held on like she, too, would never let go.

Trapped in the Mormon Moment

There are appropriate times and places for self-analysis. It is better indulged *before* proposing a completely wacky bit of subterfuge, a well-intentioned if half-baked gambit. Chances are *someone, somewhere* will take your mad scheme seriously. Once they do—as they surely will—you can never be certain how the lunacy will play itself out.

Never in an eternity did I expect Bill and Emma to endorse fully the deceptively clever if loopy workaround to their marriage dilemma. "Brilliant," is how they in unison responded to what I imagined was, at best, a pretty flimsy straw man, a corny inside joke that would be lost on practically everyone. *Question: In the heat of passion, to get his way what did the Jewish boy promise his Mormon sweetheart? Answer: Temple schmemple. So who's to quibble at a time like this? You want a temple, you get a temple. Now, please?* Worse, Rabbi Mednick's Yiddish cautionary—*a half truth is a whole lie*—stuck with me like a bad dream. It troubled me that neither Bill nor Emma saw the plan for the whole lie it was.

I pressed on only because I assumed that they would amend the plan ad nauseum until, in the end, they would come to their senses and revert to Mormon Standard Operating Procedure. A tearful and earnest confession would follow, and a civil ceremony would be hastily strapped together involving family and close friends. However embarrassed, they would not have been the first couple to have been so compromised at the last moment, nor would they be the last—no, not by a long shot.

But, as they say, my zany straw man had *legs*. It was a plan they deemed "brilliant" fergawdsakes, and if that weren't enough, "stunningly brilliant." And, this is about when the matter took on a life of its own and, in a blink of an eye, raced out of control.

I was caught off guard when they asked me to perform the ceremony, which is why I foolishly acquiesced initially and agreed to go out of my way, really, to get permission from various legal entities. Right then, I could have—should have—ducked. It would have been easy, smooth and very wise. The plan was preposterous. But my ego had been fogged by their praise and adulation, my id had been lubricated and massaged, my superego stoked. It hungered to be what they wanted me to be: *brilliant, cleverly brilliant*. So I bought into their outrageous suggestion, lock, stock and ego.

Of course, I was quite certain the civil authorities would have better sense; they would say no and I would be off the hook. And they would have, I am positive about that, if I hadn't mentioned that the ceremony itself would take place in Rabbi Mednick's study, that the esteemed rabbi himself had proposed that I conduct the service, and that he would be signing the legal documents as would I.

And so we plowed ahead with the *brilliant, cleverly brilliant* plan, as designated by drivers who were stone-cold sober. Frighteningly sober. Distressingly untroubled, guilt free for now. I knew it couldn't, wouldn't last.

Given what Emma and I had routinely enjoyed in the month leading up to her marriage, it was quite perverse of me to agree to preside at her wedding ceremony. When Bill found out, as he surely would (I could see that far down the road), he would understandably come to view my role in all this as the ultimate humiliating act of betrayal, gross hypocrisy, manipulation, sneering mockery.

It would make little difference that I had not *betrayed* his trust *per se*: Emma and I engaged long before Bill was a known entity to me. And, frankly, with similar sins of his own weighing him down like concrete boots and ripping at his bishopric conscience, he too was standing on moral low ground. At least Emma's lapse was with someone who counted quite a bit more than his retaliatory one-night stand with *Old Whatshername*:

Your name please?
You told me once I'm sure
As we embraced at bedroom's door
Your name please?
You said it when another was in mind
Further distracted by mouths entwined

Your name please?
You said it anon and again
as we pressed close, skin to skin
Your name please?
A reminder before we have to go
Your name please?
Each other we ought to get to know
Pray write it down, for like as not
In an hour or so, I'll have forgot

However, should Emma confess the real purpose of my heart-to-heart with Bill at Lamb's Grille he could charge manipulation. Her admission would doubtlessly provoke Bill's acknowledgement that he too had persuaded me to be his interlocutor. "Double agent" they might cry, and there I would be, estranged and reviled by both of them, the spy who came in from the cold, the sucker caught between the rock and a very hard spot. For Emma and Bill, the playing field had become remarkably level. The truly great deceiver in this scam, that proverbial lamb in wolf's clothing, the willful half-truth-whole-lie teller was me. Were my intentions good, my motives pure? Who knows?

Opportunistic might be added to my lengthening rap sheet were it not plain that the ultimate opportunistic, malicious and self-serving act would have been to turn Emma against Bill or vice versa. It would have been oh so easy, and completely transparent to both of them. Tempting too, I must admit. Did I love her, did I not? Was Bill simply a convenient and guilt-free way to rid myself once and for all of Emma, her pretensions and hypocrisies? About such complex matters, this much I *know*: it is quite possible to know absolutely nothing

And *mockery*? Mocking whom, precisely? Me? How about *torture* and *envy*? Torture it was: I should not have longed to be in Bill's shoes. More than anyone, I knew how good and bad it could be. Yet, in my heart, I coveted the role and woman I helped him acquire.

Admittedly, I was not in my right mind. My right mind knew that life with Emma would result in serial acts of fraud, each one intended to please her and measure up to the limiting standards established and enforced—kindly, for the most part, I should add—by the various judges of Zion. If I practiced my part over and over again, getting the mechanics down pat like I once mastered the fingerings of treacherous segments of Rachmaninoff's Third Piano Concerto, I could divine the religion score as well. In truth, I was never really ever sure where *doing the Word* left off and *believing the Word* began. The *Word* says as a man *thinketh* so is he. How about *doing*? Is *doing* a more overt sign of belief, perhaps a belief longed for but not yet found? Would anyone give a damn what I *believed* so long as I *did* what believers did and then some? Were most true believers just ordinary skeptics like me doing good for goodness sake, deliberately allowing their do-gooding to be mistaken for true belief? Does it matter?

In my right mind—those rare moments when it was unshackled from the enslaver in my trousers (this had to be what my mother was warning me about obliquely when she fretted about the dangers of tight Levi's)—there was absolutely no *regret* that I'd let Emma slip away. Absolutely None. My right mind had taken Thoreau's counsel to heart: *Live each season as it passes; breathe the air, drink the drink, taste the fruit, and resign yourself to the influences of each.*

By contrast to every player in this astonishingly conflicted love quadrangle, Sarah was the innocent. Had she been aware of all the details, she would not have derived pure joy from abetting and participating in the artful scheme that, in her mind, mocked self-righteousness and one-upped the "keeping up appearances" busybodies of Zion. With mischief twinkling in her eyes, she raved "*scathingly brilliant*" as if she was Hayley Mills plotting against the nuns of St. Francis school for irascible girls.

Had Sarah known that I had let my *trousers* do my thinking for me—that Emma and I were still intimately engaged—she would have told me what to do with the diamond ring intended for her left ring finger. She never would have supported this subterfuge we were creating together. Nor, surely, would she give comfort to the liar she intended to marry, if for no other reason than what it foreshadowed for her and yet-unborn children. She never would have become Emma's kindred spirit, trusted soul mate, and co-conspirator. Most of all, on the heels of such an outrageous betrayal, Sarah and I would not be careening toward the altar like there was no tomorrow: first our wedding date was set for June, then March something, then mid-January.

I know not what Sarah was thinking (it's not like we ever talked openly about this subject, ever, although in retrospect it is indeed a wonder Emma and I weren't found out) but it seemed she was fiercely determined to get married, no matter what, like marriage to me was the key to her eternal life and, more immediately, her temporal salvation. Perhaps it also offered release from an inner torment known only to her.

To tell the truth for a change, it was not unlike the feeling I had for her and the marriage. In due time, I suppose I hoped she would elevate the natural man in me and turn me toward my spiritual destiny, whatever that destiny was and even if it wasn't the destiny Emma seemed to have in mind. Sarah and I held on tightly like we instinctively knew that any slackening or loss of momentum would lead to the collapse of our very compatible physical relationship. Perhaps we both hoped it would lead to something quite a bit more.

Sarah was proofing a draft of the script for Emma's and Bill's ceremony. "Oh, I do love this a lot: '*The sum which two married people owe to one another defies calculation. It is an infinite debt which can only be discharged throughout eternity.*' You write so beautifully."

"Thank you," I grinned. "When I see Mr. Goethe, I will let him know you approve."

"Really, Goethe. It sounds soooo Mormon," she said.

"Very appropriate for the occasion, don't you think?"

"I do…in fact, could we use it too? For our *occasion*?"

"We could! Interested in discharging some of the eternal debt?" I teased, aroused by the resonance of her alluring *occasion.*

"Interested, but not now, I want to finish reading…and then, I've got to run and do some family things. Could I borrow *the car* [not *your car,* but *the car,* as if she already owned title to at least half of it] until tomorrow morning? And, oooh, before I forget, Emma called; said she may drop by to read, make suggestions."

"Emma and Bill here? When?"

"No, *she* not *they*. She's coming alone—Bill's in Logan. She may get here soon, before I leave. It is okay…the two of you alone…isn't it?"

"Yeh, it's okay…but…" This was no time to put on a worried man face, one that might belie the lies we were all perpetuating, some more willfully and comprehensively than others. My willfulness now included the certain knowledge that perusing the script for her marriage ceremony to Bill was not *all* Emma had on her agenda. For instance, she needed to retrieve personal items she had stowed in the apartment over the past month. Emma may have said she might arrive before Sarah departed, but I was quite certain she would show up safely *after*. This was pragmatic. This was no time to risk what an overly familiar look or hug might expose.

As forecast, so it was. And just as well. Emma was lovely. She noticed that I noticed—it was impossible to miss it given I was wearing tight

Levi's like the ones my mother had objected to. She moved toward me, so, naturally, I moved toward her. She thought it was funny that I was nervous, trembling as I held her in my arms. "I never used to make you all shaky," she said. "Funny, I went all wobbly when I read your words, like they were meant for you and me. Were they? Don't answer that. I've memorized them all, phrase by phrase. Each time I recite them in my mind, my knees grow weaker." Tears rolled down her cheeks. I fetched tissues. More tears arrived. "Am I doing the right thing?" she sobbed. Honestly, I couldn't tell if the tears came from deep within her soul or the special effects side of her brain.

"Yes, yes, Bill's precisely the kind of man you *need*," I soothed, knowing full well that this was absolutely true, insofar as her needs went, never mind that it did not take into account my crushing sadness over the painful realization that I was not the right one for her needs and vice versa, despite our amazing and satisfying compatibility in bed. I was slowly coming to believe there really was more to a good relationship than great sex even if I was not exactly sure what the *more* was.

Would anyone ever be as good? I pulled her close; her breasts were soft, her body warm. She was not interested in honor-bound brotherly affection—not with Bill ninety miles away in Logan, and Sarah off with her relatives for the evening and my words racing through her mind bringing tears to her eyes, and making her knees weak, her heels round. Even at this late hour, I was flat out incapable of brotherly hugs. My unaroused self knew she was not the right one for me. But exactly who was right? Was Emma as good as it was going to get? Mind you, she was pretty good.

She commented on the fresh, unfamiliar scent on the pillowcases; proposed, insisted on a visit to the laundry room in the morning before Sarah returned. I observed that, for the first time ever, she was bare under her sweatshirt and blue jeans—"This I could have done with in high school," I teased.

We were face to face on the bed; she above, confident and superior, arched backward to optimize the angle and pressure. She leaned forward to fiddle with the silver buttons on my Levi's…pop…pop…room for one hand…pop… "Whoooooooah shit, I'm gonna be sick," she moaned, which she promptly was: on my chest and neck, on and in the fibers of the orange shag carpet as she ran for the bathroom, where she knelt humbly before the Great Porcelain God, Himself, for the next half hour. I washed off as best I could in the kitchen sink, dressed, then waited while she showered.

"Don't even think about it," she said as she emerged, flushed, drawn, a damp towel clinging tantalizingly to her breasts.

"Saved from sin by the flu…good thing my mouth wasn't open," I laughed.

"Felt unsteady and feverish all day…pre-wedding nerves, I guess. I mean it happened so suddenly, and all over you, I'm so humiliated, so sorry."

"Crime and punishment. Served me right for being where I shouldn't have been."

"My guilt too," she said.

"Always takes two…"

The Colonel called the evening before the wedding and commanded: "If it would not be a terrible inconvenience to Rabbi Mednick or you, Emma's mother and I, and Bill's mother, will be attending the ceremony in the morning. I'm not sure what's behind this—nor am I sure I want to know—but, as Emma and Bill have made their decision, we want to support it by being there for them."

"Yes sir. I understand, sir."

"Just how much do you understand?" he barked.

"I understand that they are doing the right thing and that it's a mutual decision," I said as boldly as I could. "I understand why you want to be there. Beyond that, I will only encourage you to not leap to conclusions: they could be flat wrong. At best they would only be partially correct. What Emma and Bill really need from you right now is unequivocal support, love…"

"They have that, I'm hurt if they supposed it was contingent on doing things my way," he said quietly, as if his lungs had abruptly luffed.

"If you've been conditioned all your life to please others, to accept their standards and set your sights on goals that were established for you, your efforts to measure up may lead to unsatisfying ends. You may sublimate or compromise or deny who you really are, what you believe or what you really want from life. As half-honest way leads on to way…well you know—*the half truth becomes a whole lie.*"

"Good line, mind if I use it?"

"It's not mine, it's Yiddish. I'd say Emma and Bill are done with the half lies. They've returned to 'Go' and are beginning on a much firmer, more honest basis that will likely enable them to keep their marriage together over the long haul."

"I could quibble, but I think I get your point, a thick between the ears, half-assed jarhead though I am," the Colonel said. "Under the circumstances, it is hard for me to say thank you for what will transpire tomorrow because it isn't the *right thing* I had in mind. I don't know all the details, nor do I want to. So thank you anyway for keeping her, them together. There were times when I thought you might claim her for your own. I wouldn't have objected to that, not at all. In case you don't know, I would have welcomed it."

"I'm flattered and surprised, thank you."

"There you have it. You will not know how this tears at a father until you have a daughter of your own who is about to make what you deem a serious mistake and you come to the realization that there's not one damn thing you can do about it except depend on the kindness and goodness of other people. Thank you for your goodness and kindness. As for what's to come, I hope you've dead reckoned it."

Rabbi Mednick was pleased, relieved actually, that the parents of the bride and groom would be attending. Overnight he had the office cleared out. A few folding chairs encircled a small padded platform on which Bill and Emma knelt. With the rabbi standing at my side, I began:

"We gather here today to witness as William Parley Kimball and Emmaline Marian Nebeker voluntarily set aside their individual *lives,* ones they have heretofore pursued on their own in favor of *one* that they will live united as one flesh, husband and wife, inseparably bound, conjoined for as long as they both shall live. It is a virtuous yet daunting commitment they undertake joyfully, agreeing to be equal partners—leading when appropriate but always supportive of each other under every circumstance. Coleridge wrote: '*Sympathy constitutes friendship; but in love there is a sort of antipathy, or opposing passion. Each strives to be other, and both together make up one whole.*' Shakespeare put it more poetically: '*Let me not to the marriage of true minds / admit impediments. Love is not love / which alters when alteration finds.*' You two imperfect people, laden with your own unique burden of successes, failures and personal histories and intrigues unite today, agreeing, eager to shoulder the other's burdens, to make the other strong at weak places; to be each other; to learn to love unequivocally, forgive willingly and seek forgiveness unhesitatingly. Another prophet laid out a viable philosophical guide for marriage: '*No power or influence can or ought to be maintained…only by persuasion, by long-suffering, by gentleness and meekness and by love unfeigned; by kindness and pure knowledge, which shall greatly enlarge the soul without hypocrisy...*' William Parley Kimball, do you covenant before God and these witnesses that you will always love, honor, cherish and forgive Emmaline Marian Nebeker, and that you will continue to do so, through sickness and health, through exhilaration and tedium, through righteousness and transgression, for as long as you both shall live?"

"I do," Bill said, whispering an aside to me that only he and Emma could hear: "Tough words, cousin." I nodded.

"Emmaline Marian Nebeker..." I repeated the pledge. "Now if you will both say these words after me: 'With all that makes me who I am now and tomorrow, I covenant to you Emmaline/Bill, and to God, that I love you today and will tomorrow and forever; that I will honor and treasure you no matter how daunting the obstacles; that however rocky the path we walk becomes, we will walk it together, side by side.

"'I will praise your goodness, willingly forgive your errors and shortcomings, and I will endeavor to help you become all that you are capable of being. I will always be your trusted and loyal friend, your passionate lover and your eternally committed partner.' Having heard your vows to each other and to God, I ask anyone here who objects to this union to speak now [pause: I held my breath and bit my tongue] or join me in supporting Bill and Emma. I pronounce them one flesh, husband and wife. Mazel tov!"

Tears flowed. I couldn't be sure if mine were tears of joy or agony or relief. It didn't matter.

At the evening reception Eddie Knight cornered us at the refreshment table. "Surprised you're the best man at this shindig...that's mighty big of you, pal."

"Bill's a cousin," I demurred.

"Oh, really? And, this lovely *thing* would be?"

"*Thing*? Oh, you mean Sarah... Sarah Thompson meet the erstwhile and inanimate Eddie Knight, the self-appointed still small voice for all who know him too well; Eddie, Sarah, my fiancée."

"Fiancée, really? Sister, have you got your hands full," he grinned. "When's the unhappy day?"

"March...but we may move it up," Sarah said matter-of-factly. "He is quite the handful and then some, isn't he?" Her eyes twinkled mischievously, but her double-entendre was lost on Eddie because he was on the hunt, trying to get at what was none of his business, as always.

"I guess you were with them in the temple this morning for the ceremony?" It was a prying question, aimed at uncovering whether I was still in the fold. Eddie had his doubts, significant doubts.

"I was there for the ceremony. As you might expect, it was quite lovely and special and private."

When he had finally drifted off into the crowd, Sarah turned to me. "What a mega-huge asshole."

"He's really not that bad..."

"No, I know an asshole when I see one and he's as oversized as they come. Dumb too: he didn't even get your sarcasm or my obviously lurid reference. I was prepared to play the dumb innocent. But, he was more interested in zooming in on whether you'd gone to the temple. I can't believe you tolerate people like that."

"I have been training for people like him for two-plus decades," I grinned.

Later that evening, Sarah and I drove Bill and Emma to the airport with as many suitcases as we could fit in and on my tiny yellow Volkswagen. While Bill and I chatted at the gate for the departing flight to San Francisco, Emma and Sarah disappeared into the ladies restroom for what seemed an interminably long visit.

"Everything okay?" Bill asked when they reappeared. Looking rather peaked, Emma nodded.

Sarah rolled her eyes. "I think the excitement of the day just extracted its toll from Emma's tummy...you may want to get her a ginger ale as soon as you're on board. Uh, but before you go, a request: would you mind if Jed and I borrowed from your script for our wedding?"

Emma looked at Bill. They both looked at me. "It's okay by us, Jed wrote it. I guess it's up to him."

"We'd love it if you both come back for it...in March," I said.

"In January," Sarah said.

"January?" Emma gasped.

"Seems to me, when you know, you should just get it done before anything happens."

"Couldn't agree more, in fact that's what I told Jed a few weeks ago," Bill said. "But we can't afford to return so soon...not that our absence should slow you down. Get it done. Our thoughts and love will be with you." He took Emma's hand and steered her toward the boarding door, then turned to face me. We embraced like close brothers, a short goodbye for what turned out to be a long, long time.

A few weeks later, we borrowed liberally from the script I'd prepared for their ceremony. Old ROT, who turned out to be something of a Goethe devotee too, heartily approved: "Don't you forget a damned word of what you promised today," he said to me, privately. "I'm counting on you."

Just in time for Valentine's, a package arrived from Bill and Emma bearing a bottle of champagne and two long-stemmed glasses. The note inside read:

> *A toast from us to you on this day of love. Raise these glasses high to all of us and to the next generation, which is on its way here. There too, in a little while, perhaps? We can only hope.*

In August, Sarah was in her seventh month when we got another card from California, this one with photographs and a handwritten note from Bill:

> *Dear Jed and Sarah: Please welcome Marian Sarah Kimball to the world—a spitting image of a Pratt if there ever was one and named in Sarah's honor.*

In October, Sarah mailed a corresponding birth announcement to them:

> *Dear Em and Bill: Returning the compliment, meet Jane Emmaline Russell, and if she isn't a veritable twin of her new little cousin, she's as good as it gets. Keep in touch. Often.*

Though it was a heartfelt pledge, for reasons that had everything to do with timing, geography—they remained in California and within a year we were in New York—and the demands of life, common inertia and other unrecognized circumstances, we failed miserably to uphold our end of the covenant, as did they. The occasional garden-variety Christmas card—"Love Emma, Bill and Marian"—allowed us to track them from California to Chicago for his residency and on to Massachusetts General Hospital in Boston for a year or two, then home to Utah for his career, at which point the cards ceased arriving.

"Before you leave town, Jed, let's get together for lunch," Taylor said, as he and Steve Stone headed toward their table.

I turned to my luncheon companion: "So it's Dill Stone, is it? Would Dill be short for Dilworth?"

"It would…and, may I remind you, the confidentiality agreement is still binding," he said.

"I don't know about that," I needled. "I've known Taylor all of my life, and your brother since college. You didn't exactly *reveal* that your brother was a superstar motivational speaker and author who has corporate America eating from his hand. The confidentiality agreement, such as it is, applies only to information you divulge to me, not stuff I dig up on my own. And, that was an example of digging up stuff on my own. But I'll think about it. Whew, who knew?"

"You may feel more honor-bound once you've met the families and had an opportunity to fully assess the situation," he said, irritated even though I was teasing.

And so a meeting was hastily arranged for that very afternoon at the Stone compound, located at the mouth of Little Cottonwood Canyon, along the banks of Little Cottonwood Creek I used to explore as a boy, property once owned by my Uncle Samuel Russell of Barlow, Adams and Russell. In fact, the Stone compound was very near where the grist mill and Sam's cabin had been located, a few miles down the foothills from Polly and Lainey's granite hideaway.

As I interviewed Brother Stone's family, one by one the young children disappeared outside to the large playground, the older ones helping the younger with their jackets. "This scene is quite idyllic," I said, observing the tenderness between the children.

"Be patient, it's likely to change at any second," Stone counseled with a chuckle.

"Ralph, you're the oldest…so you've seen all this unfold. How would you say your father's marriage to two sisters has affected you, personally?" I asked cautiously.

Ralph thought for a moment, glanced nervously at his father. "Honestly, it's not really a traditional plural marriage if you asked me. But whatever *it* is, *it* wasn't difficult at all at first because I really wanted a younger brother and my mother couldn't have more children. But her sister could, and along came Richard." He put his arm around his brother's shoulders. "A spitting image of me, wouldn't you say?" I nodded in agreement. "And, then the girls: great we finally had a real family; and pretty soon it was all you could do to get five minutes alone with Dad. Actually, the divorce was pretty tough on me—just the idea of it, even though I knew Mom and Dad were close, that Dad's new wife was her sister and they loved each other and all that!"

"It was probably easier for the middle and younger kids," Liza interjected. "We knew that Dad loved our mom and her sister, Ralph's mom. It all seemed quite normal. Relatives are supposed to love each other, aren't they?"

"Will that change now? I understand there's some talk of a third marriage, a young woman who is younger than most of you..." Lots of nervous giggling. "How are you approaching that?" I asked.

"We do know her pretty well, so if it happens we won't have to get used to her," Jenny offered.

"Right, I forgot she's living here. How does she feel about the prospect of, ah, becoming a stepmother to people her same age or older?"

"You could ask her yourself, Mr. Russell."

"I will when I meet her..."

"But, you have, she's sitting there right in front of you." The blushing young—way, way, *way* too young if you asked me—Marian, nearly 18, was barely an arm's length away. My own Janie had just turned 17 and she seemed a hell of a lot worldlier, savvier and more mature than this girl, presumably raised and sheltered in the shadow of the everlasting hills. Yet, in my mind at least, Janie was no more ready for marriage than she was prepared to fly to the moon unassisted. And, marriage to a polygamist? She'd be laughed out of school. The thought of it made my heart skip a beat.

Marian blushed again, smiled shyly. "To tell the truth, Mr. Russell, this all must seem kinda weird to an outsider like you," she said very directly. "But then, consider the fact that this family is my family; they took me in when I couldn't make it work with my mother, after I discovered, after living with my dad for 16 years, that he wasn't my real dad because my mom fooled around with another guy—the sperm donor."

"You mean your mom deliberately went out and got herself pregnant by another man?" I asked.

"Not exactly, well, I don't know. Who knows? I wasn't exactly there now, you know? I don't even know the sperm donor—my real father—because it is all pretty hush-hush. So, if you asked me, irresponsible fornication is much worse than polygamy; it's like polygamy without accountability. Irresponsible polygamy. For all my special sperm donor cares, I could be out on the streets doing drugs."

"Were you doing drugs before you came here?" I asked.

"No, of course not...but, hey, I could have been; you never know what *could* happen out there when you have no one to trust and rely on. Have you been downtown recently, seen the zombies hanging out in the malls? Hey, it's a real scene."

"Really? I don't make it a practice to hang out in malls."

"Well you should," she said emphatically. (Marian was obviously not the shy, demure girl she appeared to be at first glance.) "You might learn a thing or two. Salt Lake City—it's not as isolated from the outside world as outsiders like you suppose."

"Outsiders like me?" I said.

"People from, you know, New York City, the media. Living with this huge family is a much better alternative than the streets. Than drugs. Than sleeping around."

"Partly guilty as charged: I'm from New York City and the media. But, for the record, I was raised here...my parents and all eight siblings live here."

"Really? Cool. I didn't know. Where."

"Canyon Mills and thereabouts...none of my brothers or sisters would be thrilled if one of their daughters or sons was considering a plural marriage."

"I haven't decided yet either; I was just considering it for now. Intellectually, it makes sense in this instance. Brother Stone is a very good man, a superb father. The family has been very kind to me. Him too."

"Your parents...they're okay with you being here?"

"Okay? I wouldn't say okay exactly. My mother knows where I am. She's not exactly happy about it, but there's not a whole lot she can do, that's for sure. She's got her own problems, like finding a new husband..."

"Parents are divorced?"

"No. My dad passed away last spring, just before I left home. We were all very close then."

"You and your dad?"

"Me and my dad...and my mom. Very tight. We're still close, but it's different."

"Does she know you're thinking about becoming a plural wife to a man old enough to be your own father?"

"She may have an idea, but hey we haven't talked about it specifically, yet...because Brother Stone hasn't decided whether he wants to take another wife. And, hey I'm still 17. So, I'll go to college for a while before anything happens. And, then I'll make a decision."

"College. Local?"

"Perhaps the U, but, who knows. I mean, hey, until I left home I was thinking of Wellesley, and I've applied to Smith."

"Janie, my daughter, has applied to Wellesley too. I assume you've got the grades to get in?"

"I got into Wellesley last year—technically, I'd completed all my high school graduation requirements last spring. I applied to Smith after my father died."

"The prospective picture is almost surreal. Let me get this straight: you'd really go off to Wellesley or Smith, and then return to Utah to become a plural wife?"

"Pretty weird, right? But, hey, why not? Other classmates will go off to New York and become the mistress of some publishing magnate. At least my relationship would be on the up-and-up and have real commitment behind it."

"Your classmates at Smith or Wellesley may see a big difference; you'd be unique," I said.

"So I've heard. They're into that militant feminism and the lesbian crap. Big deal. Why should feminists and lesbians object to plural marriage? They should be my allies. Aren't some of them walking evidence that good, decent, honorable men are hard to find?"

"A reasonable point," I said, unwilling to engage in a debate.

"Is it true the lesbian influence is pretty strong there?" she asked.

"The rumors are probably exaggerated. I know plenty of straight girls who've done well, who haven't felt overwhelmed by the pressure, such as it is or may be. And, as I say, my daughter is applying—she's very straight. Are you LDS by birth?" I asked.

"By birth and by choice. Our family is very devout. Before he died, Dad was our stake president, bishop before that."

"About your mother: would it be possible to ask her a few questions?"

Marian thought for a moment. "Well, Mom really doesn't know *all* the details—so you wouldn't bring them up unless she asks? All she knows is that I'm living with a classmate, the daughter of a woman who *may* be a plural wife and that I think highly of Brother Stone. So does my mom, as a matter of fact. They've known each other for a while."

"Years, back to when Marian was born," Stone interjected.

"That's about as far as it's gotten," Marian continued. "Except some very general discussions about how plural marriages work."

"I won't bring it up unless she does; I'll leave it to you to tell her the rest. Brother Stone, any problem with this?" I asked.

"Keep in mind that my relationship with Marian is purely speculative at the moment; she has a lot to sort out, after all. My wives broached the subject with her sort of indirectly and, as I was led to believe, I think it would be fair to say, Marian, that you were *curious*."

Marian blushed again. "Brother Stone is one of the gentlest men I know—like my own father. Why wouldn't I be curious? A 40-year difference isn't much in an eternity and I certainly would rather have a third share of a good man than a hundred percent stake in a total loser like the sperm donor, who didn't have the guts to take responsibility for his actions and connect with his daughter. He probably doesn't even know or care that I exist. He just got his rocks off good with my mom, then skedaddled."

Stone's eyes rolled in their sockets. "Pretty harsh talk under the worst of circumstances. It could be he doesn't even know you exist. I'd say there's a better than even chance he's a half-decent person. You never know. Keep your mind open."

"So, when might we be able to meet your mother?" I asked.

I could tell the question made Stone uncomfortable. "Well, hey, she's expecting a visit from me this evening. Would that be soon enough? I should call ahead to warn her," Marian offered.

"Problem?" I said, to Stone.

"No, none, really. I just thought it might be a little premature, but what the heck. Perhaps you would be kind enough to deliver a package—some legal documents to her, pertaining to the estate of her late husband."

My eyebrows raised.

"Our firm has handled most of her late husband's estate planning work for nearly 20 years. Most of the routine work was done by one of my junior associates; I personally took care of a couple of sensitive, confidential family matters," he said.

"This predates his death—Marian moving in with you and all that?"

"Oh yes, by several years. Her father would not be pleased at all that things have turned out as they have. He was fully aware of my situation and thought it a responsible and pragmatic solution to the issues my wife and I faced. But his own daughter? I am sure that would have troubled him deeply."

Within an hour Marian and I were in my car, alone, on our way to visit her widowed mother. As we drove, I wondered if I was about to become the Geraldo Rivera of magazine journalists, a sensationalist who descends on a family to deliver a particularly disturbing piece of news while the cameras are rolling. I saw myself asking the loaded question: "Tell me, Marian's Widowed Mother, how you feel about your daughter considering marriage to a man nearly three times her age, a polygamist? Is it a father-fixation thing? And, is it true this daughter was conceived out of wedlock by someone she refers to as the sperm donor, a man who was not your husband? In her subconscious mind, does this wild-eyed, angry young daughter of yours really want to blow your lover's brains out, one way or another, to teach him and you a lesson or two?"

"You know how to get to the Cove?" Marian asked as we headed down Wasatch Boulevard toward the city.

"Like the back of my hand—the old stomping ground, as it were," I said. "Where in the Cove?"

"Top, as high as you can go," she said.

"Really. By Neff's Canyon?"

"Right at the entrance."

"Know it well. If you'll forgive a confession, in high school my girlfriend and I used to park there on the natural road—Lakeshore Loop was our code name—carved out of the mountainside by the waters of prehistoric Lake Bonneville. Fantastic view of the city if you bothered to look."

"The road you probably parked on has a few houses now—but it's still a favorite *parking* spot. My mom said it was pretty weird living in the house overlooking where she used to go to make out as a teenager...honestly, I can't imagine my mother doing stuff like that...but she's human. I'm living proof!"

"Normal," I said. "So, what is it that interests you in becoming Brother Stone's latest wife? You're attractive; you seem bright and well educated."

"Hold on. I'm not actually doing anything yet. I know he's a good man. That's a start. He isn't going to get me pregnant then disappear, like my own bio-dad did. I'm just considering it and I wouldn't even be thinking about it if Jenny's mom and her sister hadn't brought it up."

"Really. How did that happen?" I asked, curious as to how two devoted wives would go about procuring a new young lovely for their husband.

"I don't recall it all, exactly. I think I was talking about how much I enjoyed being part of the family; one of them added that there was a way I could become a permanent member of the family and she laid it out, real casually, like it was a joke. At least I took it for a joke, at first. I went along with it and pretty soon, I was asked to join in family gatherings with the older married children."

"Seems to me they could have offered to hook you up to one of the Stone sons. That would have made you part of their family. And neither one of them are married," I said.

"Actually, the boys got pretty angry when Brother Stone asked for their opinions. They were polite at first, but Ralph, he's an attorney too, told his dad it was risky business, something that would probably get the attention of the police and, in any event, would violate his pledge as an attorney to uphold the laws of the land and the state of Utah. And, then he asked me, right in front of everyone, why I would be interested in an old fart like his father."

"I like this Ralph, he doesn't pull punches. So why would you be interested in such an old fart?"

"Oh, I don't know…it's an intriguing idea, not something that any of my classmates would ever think of doing," she said.

"That's it: you'd do it for the shock of it, just to be different?"

"Ultimately, no. But right now, it certainly is getting attention. I mean Jenny—that's Brother Stone's daughter who goes to school with me—is especially uncomfortable with it. And, well Ralph got my back up good… and, as I said, Brother Stone is attractive…I find older men very interesting, deeper, more approachable…"

"Even ones old enough to be your father?"

"Sure, absolutely, why not? You're probably old enough to be my father, and I wouldn't say you are unattractive, in fact," she said. Her face reddened only slightly as her voice trailed off. Truth was, even though she was about the age of my Janie, I found her attractive and exceedingly engaging: tanned, slender long legs, long straight brown hair pulled back and woven into a tight braid that reached down to the small of her back. I could understand Stone's interests—prurient and intellectual.

"He has always been very kind to me. I have this feeling that most men, perhaps not you," she said, eyeing me questioningly and fiddling nervously with a blouse button, "become very different people once you start having sex with them and it's obvious that this isn't the case with Brother Stone. He's as kind and loyal to both his wives as he is to me. Oops, you should have turned right there…no problem, it's just about as fast to turn down by the shopping center. Remember it?"

"I do. You loop around the stores and eventually hit Mt. Olympus Way, turn right and drive all the way up to the end; left, right, wind around some more and there you are in nosebleed territory. A number of my old friends lived in the Cove…"

"So you went to Canyon Mills High, then?"

"Uh-huh," I said as we headed up Mt. Olympus Drive toward the water tower near the widow's home.

"Hmmm," Marian said. "My mother was at Canyon Mills. Maybe you knew her then?"

"She have a name?"

"Emma Kimball."

"Now there's a first-rate Mormon name for you. I knew only a few Emmas, but I don't think I knew any Emma Kimball."

Marion seemed relieved. Her nervous fiddling had succeeded in undoing a couple of buttons on her blouse, and now she was thoughtfully massaging her throat as she talked.

"That was dumb of me. Kimball's her married name," she said suddenly. "Her maiden name was Nebeker."

If I didn't react visibly or audibly, it's not because her answer hadn't knocked the gas out of my gut and injected a megadose of emotional digitalis straight into my heart. Perhaps I was overreaching, connecting way too many dots. "Emma Nebeker. Strawberry blonde hair."

"Sort of, I guess, hard to remember the natural color," she said bitingly.

"Your dad's Bill Kimball from Logan, a doctor?" I asked cautiously.

"The same. You knew him?"

"Great guy. I met him during rush week at the U. He's a distant cousin."

"Who isn't out here?" she cracked.

"My first wife knew him too, ditto her sister," I said evenly, almost casually. "And, yes, I knew your mother in high school. I was at their wedding. Mind if we drive around the Cove a bit more, before heading up to your mom's place?"

"Not at all." She was eager to talk more. "That must have been something: my straight Mormon mother and father married in a Jewish synagogue by the sperm donor she was sleeping with right up to the time she gets married," Marian said, rolling her eyes.

"Your parents told you all that?"

"Not immediately. Not until Dad got real sick."

"I'll say this much: the wedding was something, they looked pretty happy and in love to me. And your grandparents were there too," I ventured, trying to regain my internal composure and get a good grip on where this conversation was headed.

"My mother promised Dad she'd tell me after he was gone; he wanted to be sure I knew I wasn't genetically predisposed to getting hemochromatosis, the liver disease that killed him…because he wasn't my biological father."

"Good Lord," I said. "Hemochromatosis? He was about the right age. But probably didn't kill him if they got to it early enough [fatigue, diabetes and impotence are side effects of the disease], but if left undiagnosed too long, it can lead to congestive heart failure."

"That's way more than he told me, and he was a doctor. But we already know that he and my mom weren't into telling me *ev-er-y-thing*. Apparently my dad had great respect for the old sperm donor—he must have been some kind of smoothy as my mother claims—even if he was some kind of gender freak of nature."

"A what?"

"Freak of nature," she blushed. "Hermaphrodite, half man, half woman. You know after Hermaphroditos, the son of the Greek gods Hermes and Aphrodite, whose form was merged with that of the Naiad Salmakis to form a creature that was half male and half female."

"You do know your mythology, don't you?"

"Read up on it. One thing led to another, really," she said.

"So the *freak of nature* had the organs of both sexes?"

"Don't know about that, for sure. All Mom told me is that he had a real girl's breast until the doctors removed it when he was a teenager. Told Mom the scar on his chest was from a baseball injury. Our hero. After Dad was diagnosed with hemochromatosis, he tracked down the medical records for the *freak of nature sperm donor* just to see if the genes I inherited made me susceptible to any other genetic diseases. Heaven knows why my dad would respect someone so weird and disloyal—a relative, for heaven's sake. It's safe to assume *freak of nature's* male organs were functioning properly because he slept with my mom right up to the week before he performed the marriage ceremony—can you believe it?—that united my mom and dad. And the organs worked as they should have: I'm living proof."

"Is that what your mom told you?"

"Are you kidding? My *speak-no-evil* mom tell me something like that? Hah! About three years ago I did math as part of an assignment for a junior high health class. Nägele's Rule sets the gestation period for the normal human embryo at 266 days from conception, or 280 days from the mother's last period. Right?"

"Roughly, not taking into account a woman's size or irregular periods," I added calmly.

"Right, pretty good for a guy. You do know your stuff. You could have passed my junior high school health class with flying colors. So, counting back 266 days, that would be something like 38 weeks before my birthday, July 31, 1968, about November 10, 1967, give or take. While artificial insemination was possible then, the donor and recipient were usually required to be in the same location, hospital, clinic et cetera, right?"

"Right. More or less."

"In any event it's pretty unlikely that a Mormon girl engaged to be married in the temple would be inspired to make that night in November, 1967 different from all other nights and have a close encounter of the most intimate kind with a turkey baster…"

Of course I laughed loudly. Marian Kimball was a Pratt alright.

"In any event, Dad was away in med school at Stanford at the time. While it is true that sperm from med students was often used for AI then, Dad's wouldn't have survived a flight home to Utah. Just kidding. Let's get real. So that means that Mom was spreading her legs for the *freak of nature* on November 10, give or take. A month and a couple of weeks later the *sperm donor,* now posing as a make-believe rabbi, performs the ceremony that links his cousin, my dad, to my mom and me. Come to think about, what were you doing, Mr. Russell, on or about the evening of Friday, November 10, 1967?" she teased.

"What else? I was in my apartment on East South Temple in downtown Salt Lake City practicing my turkey basting skills."

"I deserved that," she laughed. "But, *seriously*, that's why I left home. Mom didn't think it was right, no matter the circumstances, to impose on him after all these years. He has a family and kids and *other* obligations. I say I'm still one of his *other* obligations too and so what if he's inconvenienced? What about me? The jerk should have thought about that possibility before he started basting."

"Normally, men aren't exactly clear-headed when they are about to make like a turkey baster," I added.

"I mean I'm not mad at him, really, or bitter, honest, I'd just like to meet the *freak of nature* and his kids—they're the only real family I've got left, besides my mom."

"What about your brothers and sisters?" I said.

"There are none. I'm an original, one of a kind, singleton. Another *freak of nature.* Apparently, Daddy was sterile. More bad genes."

"So, from the moment they knew he was sterile—what, at most a few years after you were born, your dad must have known you weren't his biological child and your mom must have been found out," I said.

"It was such a disgusting, a last-minute, disloyal, dishonest, carnal *slam bam thank you ma'am* event instead of one filled with passion and true love..."

"Look at it another way: that *freak of nature* gave your mom and dad a child they never would have had on their own, did he not?"

"True, true, true," she said.

"And, they were loving and kind; they raised you and looked after your every need, did they not; and you've turned out rather well, until now?" I lectured.

"True again, but you'd think that sunnuvabitch *freak of nature* would be interested in me, but there was no love to this act; it was just raw lust..."

"As one who has been a sunnuvabitch and deposited his share of sperm irresponsibly, I suppose, I can assure you that real passion and profound love provoked your creation. If there was anything intentionally carnal and craven about the act committed the evening of November 10, 1967—actually it was the morning of our first day, November 11, 1967, the *Autumn of Love*—it was lost on me; it seemed so right, so spiritually and breathtakingly *right.* So long overdue. Recalling it now, stirs me. You should be so lucky."

From the car, I phoned Dill Stone and left voicemail letting him know Marian would be returning to her mother's home permanently. I informed him that some recent developments presented ethical dilemmas for me, ones that needed to be resolved before I could continue reporting the story on his modified, pragmatic, even admirable approach to plural marriage. Likewise, the current dilemmas and my previous contacts with his brother Steven may have compromised my ability to report objectively on him and his motivational programs for corporate America. I left a similar message with Steven Stone's handler, who pressed for a detailed explanation. I declined. "If Steven wants to pursue this, he knows my car phone number."

The next call was to Rebe. "It's gonna be about another hour at least...I'm at Emma's house...Emma Nebeker Kimball...the Emma from the novel."

"Oh really? Well, I'm not surprised. Do come home and tell all. Are you okay?" she asked, concerned.

"More or less, okay. Feeling a little betrayed, perhaps deservedly so. In any event, I'll be home the moment I hear from Brother Orson, I mean Stone. I will," I said.

"Wait, you meant Orson, not Stone, right?"

"They're the same Stones," I said, wearily.

"Now I know you've lost it. You can't mean that Brother Orson, the polygamist, is a pseudonym for Steven Stone?"

"No. Brother Orson is Dilworth Stone, Steven Stone's brother."

"You're not kidding," she said.

"I am not."

"Mormons are just too weird," she said. "But I love *you*, just the same. And, I hunched most of the rest a long time ago."

"What rest?" I said defensively, indulging half-truths, full lies again.

"Come home and we'll talk about it."

"Ask Polly if we could have Emma Nebeker over for dinner tomorrow night."

Rebe repeated my request out loud. "Of course, I wouldn't want to miss this one for the world," Polly answered, loudly enough for the whole world to hear.

"So she knows?" I said.

"I hunched what she knows. They've known for some time."

"They?"

"Polly and Lainey. Sarah clued them in months ago. By the way, Sarah's flying in tonight, if she can get in with this snowstorm."

"Sarah? Really! Why? What snowstorm?"

"I invited her, that's why. Look outside your window, sweetheart. The white you see is not a mirage."

On the drive to Polly's, Dill Stone reached me on the car phone, said he understood completely the dilemma I was in, wanted to make sure I'd remembered to deliver the packet of legal documents to Emma. It was still lying there on the back seat of the car.

"No problem," Dill Stone said. "When you get to where you're going, open the packet. One of the letters inside is for you. It's from Bill Kimball; he wrote it several years ago. It should explain most everything."

"Will it explain why you wanted to tell your story to the *New Yorker*?" I asked, trying to stay focused on my driving in near whiteout conditions.

"Partly. It will explain why I knew you would empathize with my situation," he said. "Now hang up and drive. This would be a terrible time to end up in a ditch or worse."

I stumbled into Polly's shortly before eleven and immediately called Emma to make sure her conversation with Marian had gone as well as could be expected. It had gone better than well; at one point Marian said she understood how her mother could be interested in a "turkey baster like Jed Russell." While we were laughing about that, the front door opened and in trudged Sarah, dragging a heavy suitcase and a trail of freshly fallen snow behind her.

"Thank God full instrument landings are possible in Salt Lake. Wish taxis used them. We couldn't see a foot in front of us all the way here. Where the hell is *everyone*, anyway?" she asked, annoyed.

"I'm an *everyman*, does that count? Hello, nice to see you too," I said, covering the phone's mouthpiece with my other hand.

"Sorry, well hello *daddy*," she snickered. "I meant Polly and Lainey… and the stunningly classy Rebe, of course."

"In the spa, I think…"

"So, while we're alone, just answer me one bloody question that's been bugging me for a hell of a long time: when we got married, were you *as* in love with me as you were with Emma? I mean, my God, what deception and manipulation?"

I waved the phone, pointed at it. She was oblivious. "You know I was madly in love…" I said.

"That was later; I'm talking about when we married. Were you in love with me or just the idea of being married? And, if it couldn't be with Emma, you'd make do with me? Is someone on the other end of that phone or are you just waving it around to get me out of your hair?"

"It's Emma—Emma Nebeker Kimball," I said softly.

"Beautiful, why didn't you say so?"

"Sarah just walked in. She says hello," I said into the phone.

"Yes, yes, hello Emma. When will I see you?"

"Tomorrow. Here. Emma's joining us for dinner," I answered for her.

"This is gonna be rich—all the women that Jed Russell ever loved in one place at the same time; lies, truth and consequences with no place to run or room to hide." She disappeared into a bedroom, then reappeared a few minutes later wearing only a terrycloth robe, just as I was wrapping up the conversation with Emma.

"I hear there may be a marriage in the offing, is it still good to go?" Sarah asked snidely, leaning over, baring most of a breast as she angled to get a better look at Bill's letter lying unfolded on the table.

"In a fortnight, if Rebe can survive all this," I said.

"If she has any brains, she would have abandoned ship long ago. But, like the rest of us, I suspect she's a lot tougher than she appears at first glance."

"She is…but this is very, very different from what she bargained for. It's a lot to ask of anyone, let alone someone so young," I said.

"Don't impose your concerns on her. By the way, speaking of Rebe, I had dinner with Doctor Rosenbaum before I left Connecticut. He said to give the both of you his best. He was shocked when I told him what might soon unfold—I mean Emma, not the marriage—and insisted that I tell you that he thinks you are unusually good at surviving and thriving amidst chaos. It never occurred to me before he said it, but I think the good doctor is absolutely dead right," she laughed.

Sarah disappeared into the storm, leaving me at the kitchen table to ponder how predictably natural I had become over the years, still shamefully half aroused by her. The letter and packet from Stone, Worthen, Ashton & Kanaday kicked the carnal out of me.

Dear Jed:

Writing this letter is one of the more challenging experiences of my life. I think you will understand why. If you don't, I'll explain more when I see you next, which probably won't be for some time, unless you are as unlucky as I am.

As promised, long ago, shortly after our daughter Marian was born in summer of 1968, Emma and I discussed our separate premarital dalliances. When Emma went into labor six weeks before her due date, I was needlessly worried because, as it turned out, she gave birth to a full-term, eight pound, ten ounce daughter.

Emma confirmed that I was not the biological father of Marian, but that you were. Despite my own premarital transgressions in this area, you can imagine my shock, and the sense of betrayal I felt—not just by Emma, but, illogical though it may be (I mean, you didn't know me, really, when you and Emma reconnected) by you as well. Had not my covenant with Emma and you mandated that our "true confessions" lead to deeper understanding and forgiveness, not divisiveness and marital discord, the revelation about how Marian was conceived would surely have destroyed our marriage.

A few years later when I discovered that I was sterile—we think from my exposure as a young man to insecticides on the farm—I began to view Marian's conception and birth as a fortuitous, if inadvertent, blessing that gave me a wonderful daughter, a child I never would have had without your intervention.

I began to regard Marian as your gift—yours and Emma's gift—to me, not unlike the gift you gave by insisting that Emma was better suited to me than she was you. I will thank you eternally for the blessings that are Emma and Marian: they have given purpose to my brief mortal sojourn and inspired me to hold on to life by my fingernails for as long as I can, never mind the excruciating pain and the resources I have at my disposal to end my life quickly and ethically.

I have been told that if doctors do not find a compatible liver for me, that I will die prematurely—probably within five years. In that event, I have one last favor to ask of you, in the spirit of the Pratthood we formed long ago: please take care of Marian and Emma in whatever way you deem appropriate to your particular circumstances at the time of my death.

Their financial needs are secure. What they'll need most is guidance and assurance from a man who loves them both unequivocally, which I know you do.

I understand that you and Sarah are contemplating divorce at this time: I hope you both come to your senses. However, should your marriage be beyond rescue, Emma will shortly be wanting for a husband, and Marian a father.

In any event, given the closeness between Emma and Sarah, the fact they have similar occupations, and that Marian is the same age as her half-sister Jane, it would be truly wonderful if you could at least arrange to have everyone live in closer proximity to one another.

In whatever ways you deem possible, I know you will deliver.

Your brother forever,
William Parley Kimball, M.D.

◉ ◉ ◉

When I finally joined the women under the steaming waterfall, I was within an arm's length or leg length of every woman—excepting Emma—who had ever meant anything to me. It was a good-looking lot to say the least. They represented the real substance of my *twinkling* in this sphere: they were my history and legacy. Surely grandfathers Orson and Parley would empathize with the practical dilemmas brought on by multiple, concurrent or serial, romantic entanglements. Surely my grandfathers also understood the nuances and textures of such relationships, how one can simultaneously adore and abhor the same woman, or several women. Old ROT would add his share of empathetic aching too. However, I am quite sure the Colonel would order me drawn and quartered and, well, you get the picture.

Fifteen minutes of visual and mental overload, not to mention the lurid banter, was more than I could bear. "You all seem to know as well as I do how my story turns out, so there's really not much point in discussing it." I took Rebe by the hand and said quietly: "It's late, I'm exhausted, and we need to be alone. You know, the traditional way: *just* one man and *just* one woman."

We were shivering as we snugged together under the billowy duvet, face to face. She hugged me tightly, draped a bare leg around mine and ratcheted me closer.

"Whatever you must do, you must do and everything will be fine," she said confidently, quietly.

"Turns out, it's not quite that simple…"

"*It* is, *it* is quite that simple. Trust me. I may be young. I may even be naïve in some respects. But trust me, I understand *all* the issues and options. What I am telling you is this: I made my decision about you long, long ago. Nothing will change that. Whatever you decide to do now, however odd or unconventional, is totally up to you. I am with you *whatever comes*."

"*Whatever*?" I asked, surprised. "Just like that? No equivocation?"

"Just like that. What-ever! *What-ever comes*!" Rebe said firmly. "Janie, Elli, and Marian; and Emma, Polly and Lainey. Sarah too, I suppose. *Whatever comes, comes*. They are my children, my sisters, my family as presently constituted. All of them should be there to place my hand in yours, Jed-love, as we are officially and legally transformed into one mind, one body and one spirit: unconditional lovers, *whatever comes*, from now to Everlasting."

The Everlasting

What came most immediately was an alleged literary evaluation from the same "Mormon intellectual and critic" who had reviewed the first four chapters of the manuscript years earlier. This time around he summarized the finished—well, not quite finished—version for a prospective publisher this way:

> *The language in Closing Circles is fresh, its humor sharp, its dialogue edgy and well written. Yet, it has to be the most self-obsessed work on the planet. Is any man that obsessed with his schlong? But, take note of this: Jed Russell has got me schlinging Yiddish too.*
>
> *Apart from that, the novel's most striking feature is its precarious tautology, one that someone like Yeats would surely describe as "self devouring (Things fall apart; the center cannot hold...)." It is a structure that I have never before encountered: a book written in the first person about an author writing the very book you are reading. Interesting, challenging, if risky.*
>
> *Worse, he seems to willfully sneer in the faces of generations of literati, whom he admittedly distrusts and detests, by violating the first rule of good literature: create a definable conflict capable of resolution.*
>
> *As the story wraps up, Jed is tantalized by a young woman who turns out to be a daughter he didn't realize he'd fathered; a few hours later he slithers off to a steaming mountainside spa with all the women he ever banged (in his mind if nowhere else), each one eyeing the other with one carnal thought after the other. Grab your chair, clutch your heart: instead*

> *of reaching a satisfying dénouement the book abruptly ends because—it is now clear—Jed Russell (and the reader too, I should add) never really understood what he was looking for in the first place and so, of course, he never finds it.*

Voilà: A hidden meaning is discovered. Whatever *it* was that I wasn't looking for, I found. Life works that way, does it not? It surprises, astonishes and stuns so routinely that one can only conclude that in the illusive reality we live in, only the unpredictable is predictable.

If Rebe were listening as attentively as she once had back when those holier-than-holy-grail-like dot-coms ruled Wall Street and the rest of the world, I would ask her who would have dared forecast that bribery and graft would become hallmarks of the Winter Olympic Games in the Mormon Zion. Or, that two jetliners from Boston commandeered by radical Muslims, trained by remnants of the Mujahideen the US once backed with guns and money in Afghanistan, would rend asunder the twin towers of the World Trade Center in the Mecca of global capitalism?

Las Vegas gives odds on practically everything. No doubt the odds on World War III are not favorable to we denizens of Planet Earth. But, would the actuaries of the Strip make book on a sequence of frightening endgame scenarios that would provoke long shot players at Aqueduct and Pimlico to take a flyer on a global Armageddon as laid out in the Book of Revelation?

Or, for another $2, the Daily Double: the Four Horsemen are propelled out of the starting gates by a successful suicide nuclear bombing of Manhattan or DC. Or, the Trifecta: all of the above coupled to a scenario in which the USA retaliates by bombing the usual suspects to kingdoms coming, or somewhere out that way.

Yes, I know: should anything of the kind occur, no one would be around to collect. On the off chance someone survives, the electronic banking system would have melted down, rendering winning ticket stubs worthless as the dust from whence they came. The only beneficiaries would be the actuaries and their backers who lived well in the here and now.

Keep this in mind. Way back in early 1996 you could have gotten enticing odds on this absurd Trifecta: a bribery scandal that would nearly scuttle the 2002 Winter Olympics in Salt Lake City would be resolved by my upbeat Pratt cousin, W. Mitt Romney—a reasonably liberal Republican, but Republican nonetheless. He would use the Games as leverage to get elected governor of the Commonwealth of Massachusetts, the most Democratic state in the union, which he would use as a steppingstone to the White House in Washington, DC? Or, the quadrifecta: his chief rival in the Republican presidential primaries of 2012 would be another Mormon "cousin," Jon Huntsman. Who but the prophet Isaiah or, possibly, Joseph Smith, would dare forecast such unlikely stuff?

Now, for all we know, Cousin Mitt and Cousin Jon could become Presidents of the United States of America, the major-domos of what's left of Mother Earth once revolutions subside in Egypt, Libya, Syria, Nigeria and all those other Middle Eastern and African places we never paid much attention to, but should have, had we known what was good for us.

For that matter, what auger was there that the flip-talking attorney from Cabalbatross Publishing House—*Ms. Suit* as I had come to call her because I could not remember her name from one disheartening encounter to the next—and her turbocharged platinum American Express card would still be on the hunt in 2012, nearly a full decade after she had glibly proclaimed that the whole world was caught up in *The Mormon Moment,* a twinkling she supposed was as fleeting and unsustainable as bouffant hairdos, Hula-Hoops and hardons. "I know that you must absolutely, positively have to know that wholesomely hunky former Massachusetts governor, Mitt Romney, and his five unbearably buff and gorgeous sons," she gushed breathlessly after I took her call.

Like many before her, Ms. Suit had come to assume I had the drop on everyone who had ever lived or touched down overnight on that hundred-mile stretch of arid flatland and sagebrush between Brigham City and Provo, the heart of the Mormon Corridor, the promised land Joseph foresaw, the desolate valley no one wanted in the shadow of the everlasting hills, somewhere in that expansively vague territory Bob Gamma always referred to as "out your way."

"Cousins. Jon Huntsman too. Mormon cousins. Same great-something-grandfather, different great-something-grandmothers," I deadpanned, like I was auditioning for a stand-up gig at the Comedy Club.

"Reeee-ahhh-ly," she would purr. "Then we should do lunch very soon. On my plastic, please. Somewhere out your way."

And, so we would, trapped, as we were, in this everlasting Mormon moment.

◎ ◎ ◎

ACKNOWLEDGEMENTS

As this novel was aborning for more than a decade, the list of people who helped along the way is reasonably long. I will name only a few.

I am in deep debt to my wife, Diana, for abiding one painful rewrite after another; restructure after restructure, all of which required that she alternately be my mother confessor, shrink, and incisive and uncompromising if patient critic.

Our dear friend's, Michael Appleman, dedication to the cause bordered on fanatical at times. He discovered many hidden meanings in this story, ones that I hadn't noticed until he pointed them out. He made me feel really smart and subtly clever.

Brian Hall, author of *The Saskiad* and *I Should Be Very Happy In Your Company*, the historical novel based on the Lewis and Clark expedition, read and offered pertinent suggestions and counsel. In particular, he commiserated, which made the prolonged and often discouraging search for an agent and publisher more bearable.

Gloria Gardener not only copy-edited the final manuscript, but suggested many important changes that improved the story itself and eliminated gratuitous scenes that may have offended religious readers. Gloria also reintroduced me to Mrs. Helen Mulder, an English professor at the University of Utah whose tears over a simple essay of mine long, long ago provoked me to consider life as a writer. In tribute to her, she is mentioned by name in the novel. I'm still not certain whether to bless or curse her. She probably feels the same way about me.

Along the way, a version was submitted to my brother-in-law, Ryan Englund, another voracious reader despite the fact that he makes a living as a management consultant. He offered solid advice and I listened.

Before she was officially my mother-in-law, Hildegard Ames, an inveterate reader, perused some very early rough drafts. I'm grateful that, despite what she read, she still showed up for our wedding.

Her granddaughter—my youngest daughter Bailey, a fine writer herself—became the first family member to read the current edition from front to back. "You write long sentences," she observed. Then she texted this cryptic review: "Done with the book!" Later came the earful of advice, most of which I took.

Way, way back, when the book before you was still a very, very rough concept, Robert A. Franklin—then a senior executive at Madison Square Garden—gave it a careful read, offered solid suggestions, and cheered me on in ways that only a true friend would. The novel and I are much the better for his many insights and kindnesses.

Along the way many other friends chipped in with suggestions and criticisms. "So when is this going to be out there, already?" Richard Russell, a friend and distant relative in Salt Lake City chided, time and again. Susan Stevenson, read and wondered if the events from our shared childhood were the genesis for the book. Ed Andrus, another lifetime friend, read and asked "who knew?"

Shortly after the manuscript was accepted by Gray Dog Press, Ernie Ford—Ernest James Ford, Jr. officially—a dear friend, mentor and unintended and affordable shrink, passed away unexpectedly. He was the model for the *Salt Lake Tribune* city editor described on page 264, a character that now bears his name. He was an extraordinary, if under-recognized, journalist, editor and human being. He is missed.

In retrospect, authors too often minimize the serious help they received from their editors and publishers. The fact is this: had not Andrew Marcus Corder, my editor, convinced Gray Dog's founder and chief executive, Russ Davis, to take a chance on a book that was out of their Pacific Northwest comfort zone, *Closing Circles* might still be a manuscript searching for the light of day. I will forever be in their debt. Corder's edits were sensitive and deft. Davis' enthusiastic collaboration would be welcomed and appreciated by any author.

Finally, while he had little to do with the novel itself, Jack Connors, a very serious but engaging mover and shaker in Boston, once offered prescient, inspirational advice about life: "it's only a movie," he observed. He should have added that while you cannot rewind the tape, you can always repent. Which I do! Often.

RB Scott
Dover, Massachusetts
December 22, 2011